SOUTHGATE VETERANS
MEMORIAL LIBRARY
14680 DIX-TOLEDO ROAD
SOUTHGATE, MI 48195

D0769922

PRAISE FOR
D

"A terrific science fiction mystery. Ryan provides a fabulous treasure that will have his appreciative audience anxiously awaiting his next entry in this wonderful universe."—*Readers Guild*

"Scandalously fun and lusty and complicated."
—*San Diego Union Tribune*

PRAISE FOR
GLORIOUS TREASON

"Four stars...An entertaining romp, this book is more than a satisfying second entry in what has so far been an interesting and exciting satirical pulp SF series."
—*Romantic Times*

"Quirky, offbeat and delightful... The must-plot of action and political intrigue in this en thriller. C. J. Ryan creates a wo that readers can actually im —Harriet Kla

"*Glorious Treason* is very much fiction of yesteryear with cur Considering the kinds of miss given, there is always something corner. Bureaucracy in th definitely a game for swinger

PRAISE F
THE FIFTH Q

"C. J. Ryan has done a really cl characters and reality to life... keep surprises happenin
—SFcrowsnest.com

DUE	
MAY 0 7 2008	
AUG 2 3 2008	
JAN 0 9 2009	
MAR 0 2 2009	

Also by C. J. Ryan

DEXTA

GLORIOUS TREASON

THE FIFTH QUADRANT

BURDENS OF EMPIRE

C. J. RYAN

BANTAM BOOKS

3 9082 10822 0560

SOUTHGATE VETERANS
MEMORIAL LIBRARY
14680 DIX-TOLEDO ROAD
SOUTHGATE, MI 48195

BURDENS OF EMPIRE
A Bantam Spectra Book / September 2007

Published by
Bantam Dell
A Division of Random House, Inc.
New York, New York

All rights reserved
Copyright © 2007 by C. J. Ryan
Cover art by Paul Youll
Cover design by Jamie S. Warren Youll ©

If you purchased this book without a cover, you should be aware
that this book is stolen property. It was reported as "unsold and
destroyed" to the publisher, and neither the author nor the publisher has received any payment for this "stripped book."

Bantam Books, the rooster colophon, Spectra, and the portrayal of a
boxed "s" are trademarks of Random House, Inc.

ISBN 978-0-553-58903-0

Printed in the United States of America
Published simultaneously in Canada

www.bantamdell.com

OPM   10   9   8   7   6   5   4   3   2   1

BURDENS OF EMPIRE

· 1 ·

Lord Kenarbin cut a splendid figure as he stepped out onto the dock, and knew it. He was tall and trim, strikingly handsome, with medium-length silver hair curling over the tops of his ears and piercing blue eyes that commanded the attention of all who fell under their gaze. His strong, slightly bony nose suggested Hazar blood, while his smooth, swarthy complexion implied a complex genetic heritage. In his ninety-seventh year, he looked as virile and vigorous as a man half his chronological age.

Kenarbin carried himself with a diplomat's aplomb and a drill sergeant's precision. His shiny black knee boots, formfitting white breeches, and gold-trimmed deep blue tunic were accented by the diagonal red sash draped across his torso, signifying his Imperial mandate. His features automatically assumed a familiar, well-practiced mien of amiable determination and boundless self-confidence. He paused and stared into the mid distance for a few moments in order to let the swarm of media imagers record his arrival.

Aside from the gaggle of media reps and the cluster

of official greeters, both human and native, there was not a lot to see. His Cruiser had splashed down in a broad, sluggish river, brown and oily—the local Mississippi or Amazon, he supposed. The dun-colored landscape offered little in the way of vegetation or relief, and the chill, steady wind sweeping in from the river felt unfriendly and forbidding. The sky was cloudless but yellowed from its cargo of dust and debris, and the single cold star provided a weak, unflattering orange radiance.

In the distance, the dark towers and crenellated walls of the city looked medieval, and the smaller structures dappling the plain could have been the huts and hovels of serfs. A patina of age clung to the place—a reminder of the weary millennia of experience boasted by this civilization, which had achieved star travel when humans were still scrimmaging with Neanderthals and mammoths. Yet it was this world that had been conquered and occupied by the upstart humans and their burgeoning Empire—an outcome emphasized by the sheltering canopy of military vehicles that patrolled the ugly sky above.

Denastri, he thought. Well, he'd seen worse.

Kenarbin took it all in, then turned to face his welcoming committee and offered them a hearty smile. It was met by unsteady grins from the humans and the blank, impassive gaze of the indigs—Empire slang for indigenous species. The Denastri, he had been told, were not a demonstrative race, and the expressions on their alien faces might have meant anything at all, or nothing.

We are not welcome here.

The unavoidable thought did not trouble Kenarbin unduly. Humans weren't really welcome in most places they went. It didn't matter. The Empire was here, and it was here to stay. It was Kenarbin's job to get the locals to accept that immutable fact. *They don't have to like us,* he reminded himself, *and we don't have to like them.*

Lord Kenarbin had been coming to places like this

for more than half a century, representing the Empire with skill and imagination. In the process, he had become something of a legend, having pulled Imperial fat from fires that might have consumed lesser negotiators. His reputation was well and justly earned, and if the job had become familiar from repetition, it remained a point of pride with him to do it to the best of his considerable ability. These days, Emperors used him sparingly, recognizing that his very presence magnified the significance of any mission on which he embarked: Kenarbin was here because Denastri was important, and Denastri was important because Kenarbin was here.

Three years earlier, in a swift and relatively bloodless little war, the Imperial Navy had smashed the small, antique Denastri fleet, putting an abrupt end to thirty thousand years of conflict within the minor grouping of stars known to Terrans as the McGowan Cluster. While the local tides swept endlessly back and forth between the Denastri and their neighbors, a millennium of relentless human expansion had finally brought the Terran Empire to the doorstep of the McGowan Cluster, 1053 light-years from Earth, and henceforth the locals would have to behave themselves. The backwater world of Denastri, and everything on it or under it—particularly the latter—now belonged to the Empire. His Imperial Highness Charles V had decreed peace, and peace there would be.

Some of the locals had refused to believe or accept this turn of events, and even the presence of a division of Imperial Marines had failed to convince the holdouts. If anything, the sputtering insurgency had picked up steam in the preceding year, making life uncomfortable and dangerous for the Terrans who had come here for the sake of Imperial power and corporate profits.

The indigs, in any case, were a fractious lot, split three ways and as eager to slaughter each other as they were their human overlords. Instead of meekly bowing before the overwhelming might of an Empire that spanned two thousand light-years and encompassed 2673 worlds with a population exceeding 3 trillion, some of them remained determined to fight on, heedless of the consequences for themselves or their lackluster little world. Kenarbin had come to reason with them.

Sanjit Blagodarski, the Imperial Governor, stepped forward and extended his right hand. Kenarbin clasped it in both of his.

"Welcome to Denastri, Lord Kenarbin," said the Governor.

"Thank you, Governor. Good to see you again, Sandy. You're looking well."

His first lie, less than a minute after setting foot on the planet. In fact, Blagodarski looked awful. Drawn and frazzled, he seemed to have aged twenty years during the ten since they had last met. The Governor shrugged off the obvious falsehood with a weak smile and introduced his Imperial Secretary, a Level XII Dexta functionary named Freya Benitez, and the commanding officer of the Occupation Task Force, General Steven Ohashi. The general gave Kenarbin a crisp, military nod along with a firm handshake. "Glad you're here, milord," said Ohashi. That, in itself, struck Kenarbin as an ominous note; Marines were seldom happy to see diplomats on their turf.

"And now," said Blagodarski, "it is my privilege to present the Premier of Denastri. Honored Premier, may I present Lord Kenarbin?"

The alien stepped forward and extended a four-fingered hand, which Kenarbin took in his. Its flesh felt cold.

"Vilcome to our furled," said the Premier, with obvious effort.

"Thank you, Honored Premier," Kenarbin replied as he stared into the dark, vertical slits of the alien's eyes. The creature was vaguely humanoid—two arms, two legs, nearly as tall as Kenarbin. But its face was narrow and noseless, with large, drooping, triangular ears, sallow skin, a sharp, pointed chin, and a mouth that would have looked at home on a rainbow trout. The vertical almond-shaped eyes seemed to be all pupil, and looked like the entrances to shadowy, unexplored caverns. From a narrow bony crest at the top of its head sprouted a long shank of blue-black hair, braided and bound with thin colored threads. The Premier's clothing consisted of a belted saffron-colored robe that fell nearly to the ground.

Kenarbin released the Premier's hand and touched a stud on his tunic, activating the translation software on the computer pad in his pocket. "Honored Premier," he said, "I bring sincere and heartfelt greetings from His Imperial Highness, Emperor Charles V." He paused to let the Premier's own pad translate his words into the fluid tonal language of the Denastri, then continued. "The Emperor has asked me to convey his deep personal gratitude for your service to the Empire, and to your world. He expresses his confidence that, working together, we shall restore peace and prosperity to his loyal subjects on the rich and beautiful world of Denastri."

He paused again as the Premier absorbed the translation. Kenarbin studied the Premier's face carefully but could detect no identifiable reaction. After a moment, nictitating membranes closed in from the sides of the Premier's eyes in an approximation of a blink. Then the Premier spoke in a flowing, almost musical passage that was pleasant but incomprehensible to human ears.

The computer rendered the translation in a soft, precise, androgynous voice. "You are mostly kind to be here, generous lord," it said. "The words of Imperial Highness Fifthborn Charles are registered in deep appreciation by this humble Thirdborn. Peace and prosperity inspire all to high wishfulness. It is a goodness."

Kenarbin frowned and furrowed his brow. He had

been warned that the translation software was still a work-in-progress, but he had hoped for something better than this.

"A goodness, indeed, Honored Premier," Kenarbin said. "I look forward to working with you to make it so."

"Yes," the Premier responded. "Work will make good. We will build again that which has fallen and return—*unknown word*—to Denastri and the felicitations of Fifthborn Charles and his grasping Empire. Yes."

Kenarbin glanced at the Governor, who tilted his head a little and offered a wan smile. "You'll get used to it, milord," he said.

"I think I know what he's saying," Kenarbin said. "I just wish I could be sure that he knows what *I'm* saying."

Blagodarski shrugged. "We manage," he said. "For the most part. We should be on our way now, milord. We'll have you safely into the Compound in a few minutes. It's not wise to linger too long in an exposed position like this."

"It isn't? Why not?"

"Because we make too good a target, milord," General Ohashi explained.

"It's not as bad as it sounds," Blagodarski added hastily.

"The hell it isn't," Ohashi mumbled under his breath. The Governor gave him a sharp, reproving glance, but Ohashi looked away, focusing his gaze on the far side of the river, as if searching for snipers.

Kenarbin nodded. "I see," he said. "In that case, gentlemen, ladies, Honored Premier, perhaps we should continue our discussion in the Compound. I look forward to seeing your capital city, Honored Premier. I understand that it is older than any on Earth."

"Earth is young," the Premier agreed. "Denastri is blessed with the continuing wisdom of all our time. Perhaps you will learn—*unknown word*—from us, Lord Kenarbin. A goodness."

"Undoubtedly," said Kenarbin. "A goodness."

The party began moving along the dock. Kenarbin noticed that the dock was flanked by squads of armed, helmeted Marines, who snapped to attention as he passed. Ahead, surrounding a small fleet of limo skimmers, the Marines were accompanied by what appeared to be native Denastri troops, hefting Terran plasma rifles. They were noticeably taller than the Premier and their skins were more orange than yellow.

"Fourth- and Fifthborns," Blagodarski said as they walked. "Warrior caste."

Kenarbin nodded. "Fine-looking troops," he said to the Premier, who seemed momentarily confused by the comment and didn't respond immediately.

After a few moments, the Premier said something that the computer rendered as "Beauty is in the eye of the beholder."

Kenarbin, surprised, looked at Blagodarski. "The software has trouble with clichés," the Governor explained. "Garbage in, garbage out, I suppose. Not that what you said was garbage, milord."

"Perish the thought," Kenarbin replied with a chuckle.

At that instant, a dazzling burst of intense white light blinded him. A split second later, he was deafened by the thunderous crack of a concussion device. Stunned and all but senseless, Kenarbin felt hands grabbing at him, clutching his arms, and dragging him, then lifting him. He flailed out uselessly and shouted something equally useless, then felt himself being thrown bodily into what must have been the backseat of one of the limo skimmers. Someone shoved him down onto the floor of the vehicle, and he felt it lifting and moving.

Security, he thought. *They're getting me out of here.*

Sound and sight gradually returned. He tried to turn over and push himself up, but found himself being pushed back down against the floor. "What's happening?"

he demanded, his own words sounding faint and distant. He could hear no response, and saw nothing but a blurred smudge of maroon carpeting, an inch from his nose.

Kenarbin calmed himself. There had been other attempts on other worlds, and he knew the routine. Security people would treat him like a sack of highly valuable potatoes until they were certain that the threat had passed. Annoying but necessary. He could hear the high-pitched whine of the skimmer now, competing with the ringing in his ears. He wondered if the Governor and the Premier were safe.

Minutes went by, and he felt the lurching, darting progress of the skimmer. It seemed to him that they ought to have reached the Compound by then. He managed to twist around a little and turned his head to look up. He expected to see burly Marines on the seat above him. Instead, he found himself looking into the narrow orange-tinted face of one of the Denastri warriors.

"What's happening?" he asked again. "Where are you taking me?" The Denastri offered no response. Possibly, he had no translation device and didn't understand.

Kenarbin again tried to push himself up from the floor, but the warrior rudely shoved him back down. The first tickle of fear and suspicion began to dance at the edges of his mind.

"Dammit, what the hell is going on here?"

The Denastri leaned forward a little and stared down at him. The alien eyes looked placid and unsympathetic. "You is ours," it said in Empire English.

"What? What do you mean by that?"

"Vord is 'hostage,' yes?" the warrior asked.

Comprehension flooded into Lord Kenarbin in a cold, unwelcome wave.

"Yes," he said at last, "that's the word."

· 2 ·

The sun glared in Norman Mingus's face, bright enough to be annoying, even through the polarized panoramic dome. Poised just above the irregular peaks on the rim of Shackleton Crater, its unrelenting radiance was an imposition on an old man's eyes and gave Mingus yet another reason to resent the necessity of these semiannual excursions to the South Pole of Luna. He envied Charles, sitting opposite him, twenty meters away, on the far side of the three-tiered circular amphitheater where the Imperial Oversight Committee was pleased to hold court. The solar inferno was comfortably positioned behind the young Emperor's right shoulder, and he had to face only the less constant, if much closer, fires of angry Parliamentarians.

Ninety degrees to Mingus's right, Lord Nepali looked characteristically haughty, as befitted the Chairman of the Council of Lords; and ninety degrees to his left, Prime Minister Edith Singh looked typically harried, as befitted the leader of a popular assembly facing elections in four months. Arrayed to her left, curving around the table until they collided with the Imperial retinue flanking Charles, various Government ministers were busy consulting with their aides, camped in the second and third tiers behind the main table. Seated to Singh's immediate right, Minority Leader Jimmy Karno, florid-faced and combustible, had been coming to these meetings for almost as long as Mingus, and deftly rode herd on the squabbling minority MPs strung out to his right.

Mingus's own retinue was small; he preferred to travel light. Loyal, steadfast, encyclopedic Hiroshi Kapok, his Executive Assistant Secretary, sat on his right, and on his left, his Assistant Secretary for Administration, fussy, grandmotherly Theodora Quisp. Behind them sat a handful of superfluous aides, ready and excessively eager to provide assistance in the unlikely event that Mingus should require any. He had been attending these meetings for forty-four years, ever since he became Secretary of the Department of Extraterrestrial Affairs back in 3176, and he knew the drill. He was here to serve as a target, nothing more; a dartboard at which angry and ambitious MPs could fling their missiles. Mingus accepted the necessity but didn't enjoy it. The only good thing about the Imperial Oversight Committee meetings was that they gave him the opportunity to spend a day in the buoyant ease of one-sixth gravity. It was a minor perk, true, but at 133 years of age, Mingus appreciated it.

As Secretary of Dexta, Mingus was responsible for running the Terran Empire. Parliament passed laws and raised taxes, while the Emperor and the Household handled military and diplomatic matters, official appointments, and other Imperial concerns, great and small; but it was Dexta that actually made the whole thing function. The vast bureaucracy oversaw the day-to-day affairs of the Imperial Government, rode herd on the profusion of local planetary governments, and tied everything together through the provisions of the all-encompassing *Dexta Code*. In some respects, Mingus reflected, he was the most powerful human being who had ever lived. But he still had to answer to Parliament.

Prime Minister Singh called the meeting to order and formally, graciously, tediously thanked His Imperial Highness and the Dexta Secretary for deigning to attend this meeting of the elected representatives of the 3 trillion people they ruled. She made a few opening remarks for the sake of the media, then turned the floor over to Lord Nepali, who made some more unnecessary remarks. Then Jimmy Karno was permitted to put in his two crowns' worth of polite invective. It was all as stylized and predictable as a Kabuki performance but—in Mingus's view—much less interesting. That thought spawned another, and he wondered if there would be any sushi available at the postmeeting buffet.

Singh launched into the formal agenda, which leaned heavily on matters involving revenues and expenditures, giving the MPs the opportunity to howl about taxes and government waste. Since Parliament was responsible for all of the taxes and much of the waste, Mingus didn't pay close attention to what was said. When a question was directed toward him, he deflected it and let Kapok deal with the inquiry in stupefying detail. Charles employed the same tactic, giving members of the Household Cabinet an opportunity to show off their obfuscatory talents. No one learned much of anything that they didn't already know, and if something new or surprising was said by anyone, it somehow escaped Mingus's notice. The meeting droned onward with the dramatic speed and force of an oncoming glacier.

If Mingus disdained the politics and posturing inherent in these meetings, he nevertheless respected their underlying gravity, which was much more portentous than a mere sixth of a gee. The Imperial Oversight Committee represented not a glacier, but an iceberg—or at least the visible part of one. Here, the underlying discontents of Empire broke the surface and offered themselves for formal inspection and comment. The vapid ditherings of the media could be ignored, mostly, and the strident plaints of pressure groups and corporate interests could be swept aside, suppressed, or bought off, as the occasion required. But Parliament held the Imperial purse strings, and nothing Mingus or Charles wanted to do would ever come to pass without the support of at least some of the people in this room.

Mingus reflected that a representative democracy was not the ideal form of government for an expanding empire. The Romans had understood that, long ago, and replaced their republic with a more effective Imperial system. The Americans, on the other hand, had never quite come to terms with the contradictions of empire, and had paid the price. The old republican Terrestrial Union had dissolved in chaos that endured until Hazar finally consolidated power and proclaimed the Empire, 698 years ago. But the yearnings and aspirations of the people—human and otherwise—could not forever be suppressed or ignored, and over the centuries Parliament had chipped away at Imperial prerogatives until now, in 3220, the balance of power teetered precariously atop a pyramid of competing interests.

The Empire was in trouble. Mingus had known it for decades, but had hoped—naïvely, perhaps—that the inevitable reckoning could be postponed beyond his time. Let the next generation deal with it. His own generation had seen enough sorrow and tumult and, Mingus believed, deserved a respite. He had labored to see that they got it, and his efforts had resulted in a half century of relative peace and prosperity.

But the Terran Empire, like others before it, was a victim of its own success. With the conquest of the Ch'gnth Confederacy in 3174, the last remaining external threat to the Empire had been removed from the board. For a thousand light-years beyond Imperial space, in every direction, no existing power was capable of thwarting the continued expansion of the Terrans. There were, to be sure, a few minor impediments, like the fledgling Zukkani Hegemony, waiting a couple of hundred light-years beyond the Frontier in Sector 4. The Zukkani, a race of vast pretensions and minimal subtlety, had carved out a miniempire of forty or so worlds, but they posed no immediate threat. The Empire would have to fight them someday, Mingus presumed, but probably not on his watch. The outcome, in any case, would be a foregone conclusion. The same applied to the handful of other races that might object to the onward march of *Homo sapiens.*

Paradoxically, it was the very absence of an external threat that now imperiled the Empire. Many historians, Mingus knew, held that it had been the rise of Islam in the seventh century that had forced the consolidation and forged the power of modern Europe. It was not until after the temporary decline of Islam that the Europeans, deprived of a strong external enemy, fell upon each other in two centuries of fratricidal insanity, polluting the historical record with names like Napoleon and Hitler, Verdun and Auschwitz. The later fall of the Soviet Union had much the same effect on the Americans, who built their doomed empire without ever admitting to themselves what they were doing. The Terran Empire, at least, harbored no illusions about what it was and what it meant to achieve.

But without the balance and focus provided by external powers, the whirling centrifugal forces inherent in so vast an empire were bound to tear it apart someday. Mingus, a lifelong student of history, knew that the larger an empire grew, the harder it was to govern. He also understood mathematics; the old Earthly empires only had to deal with two dimensions, but the Terran Empire was condemned to grapple with three. Thus, the Empire,

2000 light-years in diameter, comprised some 4.2 *billion* cubic light-years of space, with a surface area on the Frontier of 12 million square light-years—all of which had to be patrolled and policed. If the task was not inherently impossible, it was certainly daunting.

Mingus accepted the implications of the unforgiving math; but Charles, alas, did not—or at least, he refused to face them. Charles was the third Emperor he'd had to deal with during his time in office, and, by far, the most difficult. Bumbling old Darius had paid little attention to the niggling little details of his realm, which was probably just as well. Gregory hadn't been around long enough to make any difference. But Charles, now in his seventh year as Emperor, was young, arrogant, and ambitious. At thirty, he was finally showing some signs of maturity; perhaps the recent birth of Henry, his son and heir, had something to do with that. Yet his essential character was unlikely to change, and Mingus knew that at his core, Charles was a cold, ruthless son of a bitch. *Takes one to know one,* Mingus wryly conceded. Age might mellow Charles, but it was not likely to improve him.

Charles wanted to continue—and accelerate—the Empire's headlong expansion, regardless of the cost. Edith Singh's ruling Imperial Solidarity Party supported him in that ambition. Singh was smart, if not necessarily wise, and understood the mathematics as well as Mingus. But she and her party believed that the only way to overcome the forces pulling the Empire apart was to outrace them. "The only way to ride a tiger," she had once said to Mingus, "is with spurs and a whip." Rapid and continued expansion was the only answer to internal rot, drift, and decay. The Big Twelve corporate behemoths agreed, and backed the ISP with their immense wealth and weakly regulated political power. The discovery and exploitation of new markets and resources would pay for the expansion, they argued, without the necessity of imposing additional Imperial taxes. Local governments could assume the burden of dealing with purely internal matters; if they failed to deliver, well, people could always vote with their feet. In such a vast empire, there would always be pockets of depression and discontent, but as long as the Empire itself remained sound, local failures would not matter.

But they mattered a great deal to the people directly affected by them, countered the Loyal Opposition, as embodied by Jimmy Karno's People's Progressive Alliance and the potpourri of smaller parties aligned with it. The PPA had been out of power for more than twenty years, but had a not-unrealistic hope of putting together a majority coalition in this year's elections. Karno—a crafty, gregarious hothead—wanted to put the brakes on Imperial expansion and devote more resources to improving the lot of the Empire's 3 trillion citizens. Most of them reaped no benefit from planting the Imperial flag on distant worlds, and many suffered under the yoke of incompetent or oppressive local governments that were in cahoots with or in thrall to the Big Twelve. Their only hope for a better future lay in an activist Imperial Government dedicated to internal improvements—or so Karno and his allies argued.

Mingus, supposedly above politics in his role as Dexta Secretary, knew that Karno was right, although often for the wrong reasons. Demagogues and rabble-rousers like Karno *had* to be right at some fundamental level if they were to gain any traction with the general population, who instinctively knew when they were being screwed but seldom knew whom to blame. On the other hand, minions of the status quo, because they enjoyed the advantages that always accrued to entrenched power, could afford to be wrong—up to a point. The eternally dangerous question remained: *Where was that point?* To Mingus, it looked as if the Empire was rapidly approaching it.

So this year's elections could be pivotal for the fate of

the Empire. The pundits all said that it was too close to call, and Spirit knew what would finally happen. Whatever the outcome, Dexta would be required to sweep up the debris and put the pieces back together again in a semblance of working order. Mingus idly wondered, as he sometimes did in moments of doubt, if he was getting too old for this shit. Perhaps he was, but he had come to consider the task of running the Empire his personal responsibility, and he knew that he could never turn his back on it. And he had no desire to live long enough to see what would become of the Empire if he retired. *Après moi, le déluge*, he told himself. The truly frightening thing was, he was probably right.

When Singh had steered the meeting through the major items on the agenda, Lord Nepali begged her indulgence. He was a well-rounded nabob from Kathami, a prosperous world in nearby Sector 7, and spoke in a curious singsong voice that belied his reputation as a vicious political operator. He cleared his throat politely and began to speak.

"There is a matter of some importance," Nepali said, "that does not appear on the formal agenda, but which, I believe, demands our most earnest attention. I refer to the plight of my close personal friend, and honored Imperial diplomat, Lord Kenarbin. It has been three weeks since we received word of his abduction by the bandits of Denastri, and yet, we have heard nothing from Secretary Mingus, or from the Government, concerning his fate. I would like, most respectfully, to inquire—"

"Excuse me, Lord Nepali," Singh interrupted, "but I don't believe this is the proper—"

"I disagree, Madame Prime Minister. I most emphatically disagree. I will not allow this matter to be swept under the rug. I must insist upon explanations, Madame Prime Minister. Secretary Mingus, would you tell us, please, just what has the Department of Extraterrestrial Affairs done to rescue Lord Kenarbin?"

"Everything that we can do, milord," Mingus replied simply.

"And what, Mr. Secretary, is that supposed to mean?"

"It means precisely what I said, Lord Nepali." Mingus stared resolutely at Nepali, determined not to be drawn into a public discussion of such a delicate matter.

"I take that to mean that you have done nothing at all," Nepali responded.

"As milord is well aware," Mingus said with more patience than he felt, "rigid Imperial policy, dating back centuries, forbids any negotiations for the release of hostages. Within the confines of that policy, we are doing whatever we can to secure the return of Lord Kenarbin. If milord desires more detailed information, I would be happy to arrange a private briefing."

"So that you can pull a cloak of secrecy over the whole affair?" Nepali demanded. "It won't do, Mr. Secretary! It won't do at all. With all due respect to Imperial policy, I must point out that Lord Kenarbin is not just *any* hostage. He is the father of our dear Lady Patricia, and the grandfather of young Prince Henry, heir to the Imperial Throne! What does it say about our Empire that it cannot protect such a person? How are we to be seen if we meekly submit to such an outrage, merely to conform to an antiquated policy that never anticipated so blatant and contemptible an action? For the sake of our Emperor, for the sake of his beloved Consort and child—indeed, for the sake of the Empire itself—we must act!"

Lord Nepali went on, at considerable length, to describe the actions he had in mind. Apparently, he envisioned striking a bargain for the release of Lord Kenarbin, and, having secured it, carpet-bombing the entire planet of Denastri into oblivion. Mingus tuned him out and focused, instead, on Charles, who wore an expression of intense and genuine pain on his handsome face. Emperors, like other men, were capable of the most basic of human emotions—even love.

Two years earlier, Charles had attempted and failed to win the return of his ex-wife, the glamorous and popular Dexta official Gloria VanDeen. Mingus didn't know the details of her rejection of his offer of remarriage and elevation to Empress, but he had sensed a profound change in Charles following the episode. He could have any woman in the Empire except for the one he wanted most, and the realization must have seared his soul in some deeply painful way. The private man, Mingus supposed, must have surrendered some essential part of himself to the public figure; Charles had been thwarted, but Charles V could not be. Under pressure to produce an heir, he had wanted Gloria for his Empress and the mother of his son. Denied his desire, he had swiftly turned in another direction and taken Lady Patricia as his Consort. Not Empress, but Consort. Some Emperors never married at all, and were content to sire their successors with Consorts; Charles, it seemed, would be one of them. He didn't need an Empress, he didn't need Gloria, he didn't need love.

And yet, he seemed to have found it anyway. Mingus could not gauge the depth of Charles's feelings for Lady Patricia, but he suspected that it was considerable, and had probably come as a surprise even to Charles. It happened that way sometimes, for some men. And whatever his feelings for Patricia, there was no doubt about his intense attachment to young Henry.

The last time Mingus had seen them together, the Imperial Heir had cutely puked on the shoulder of his Imperial Dad. Charles had merely laughed, and Mingus, a veteran of five marriages and many children, considered it the most human moment he'd ever seen Charles experience. For a moment, Mingus almost liked him.

Now, Lady Patricia was in anguish over the fate of her father, and Charles, the man, was clearly at odds with

Charles, the Emperor. What Charles would gladly do for the woman he loved, Charles V could not do. Man and Emperor were trapped together in a golden web that circumscribed his actions as surely as it bound his heart. Charles was no less a hostage than Kenarbin, and no conceivable negotiation could free him.

Mingus returned his attention to Lord Nepali, who was now berating Defense Minister John Drum for the inexcusable failures of his department. "You say the population of Denastri is 1 billion?" Nepali inquired rhetorically. "And just how many troops have we deployed there, Minister Drum?"

Drum, who had what Mingus considered the worst job in the Government, gritted his teeth, and replied, "As Your Lordship is aware, we have assigned the Fifth Imperial Marine Division to Denastri. Including support personnel, that comes to some 18,000 men and women. But allow me to point out that the native Denastri government forces, which we are training and equipping as rapidly as possible, number some 145,000 troops, as well as—"

"Eighteen thousand!" thundered Nepali. "Eighteen thousand, to subdue and control a population of 1 billion? Can no one in the Defense Ministry *count*? How do you explain such a disparity, Minister Drum? How do you justify it?"

"Milord," Drum replied, "as you are well aware, we are stretched very thin in Sector 14—"

"And in twenty-three other Sectors!" Jimmy Karno butted in. His flat, harsh voice contrasted with the cultured tones of Lord Nepali; it was a voice that was more appropriate to the dockworker he had once been than the Parliamentarian he had become.

"Mr. Karno—"

"Don't shush me, Edie," Karno told the Prime Minister. "Lord Nepali has had his say, and now I'll have mine." Karno glared across the table at the rotund Lord.

"I've known Bill Kenarbin for forty years," he said, "and I consider him a friend. No one here is more eager than I am to secure his safe return. And I'll tell you how we can do that. You know the answer as well as I do, milord. We remove all 18,000 of our people from a world where they should never have been sent in the first place!"

That produced a noisy hubbub and angry objections, but Karno plowed onward, and his dockworker's voice gradually overcame the uproar. "Why are they there? Why have we sent 18,000 of our finest young people 1053 light-years to a world no one ever heard of until a couple of years ago? I'll tell you why. It's so we can dig up some rocks and convert them to cash to fill the corporate coffers of Imperium and KemTek and Servitor! No other reason, milord, no other reason—unless it's to satisfy the thirst—the lust! —for glory of a few fat, greasy politicians who would rather use our limited resources to kill aliens than serve our own people! Of *course* we're stretched thin in Sector 14! We're stretched thin *everywhere*! How could we not be, given the insane, self-destructive expansionist policies of this Government?"

Mingus leaned back in his chair and sighed as the inevitable storm of protest erupted. Trust Karno to hit the exposed nerve of the Empire. The fate of the popular Kenarbin would make a handy issue for the PPA in the coming election.

Mingus pulled a pen from his pocket, and before he had removed its cap, an eager aide had placed a blank sheet of paper on the table in front of him. *Knock it off, Jimmy,* Mingus wrote. *The last thing we need is political grandstanding on Kenarbin.* He folded the paper, wrote Karno's name on it, and handed it to the aide, who scurried over to where Karno was holding forth. Karno looked at it, quickly scribbled a response, and handed it back to the aide, who returned the paper to Mingus.

Blow it out your ass, Norm! it read. *I'll be in NY next week. How about some golf?*

Mingus smiled, looked over at Karno, and nodded. They had been friends for seventy years, and in all that time, Karno had never figured out how to cure his slice.

The debate raged on. Mingus felt a rumbling in his stomach and wondered again about the sushi.

As the meeting broke up and people drifted off to the buffet, one of the Emperor's aides approached Mingus; Charles wanted to have a word with him. Mingus found him standing alone on the upper tier, staring down into the shadowed depths of Shackleton Crater. Ice-mining machinery was moving around on the floor of the crater like aimless glowworms.

"Sorry about Nepali and Karno," Mingus said. "Edith has never gotten the hang of running these meetings, I'm afraid,"

"She may not have to much longer," Charles said, turning to face him. "Karno could win on the Kenarbin issue. It's the kind of thing that can turn an election. I tell you, Norman, the thought of Karno as PM is enough to keep me awake at night. Not that I don't already have enough on my mind these days."

"How is Lady Patricia holding up?"

"She tries to put on a brave face, but I know it's killing her. She's not used to this sort of thing. She always led a pretty sheltered life at Court."

"She's Bill Kenarbin's daughter," Mingus pointed out. "She'll be as strong as she has to be."

Charles nodded. "She's only twenty-one," he said. "Sometimes I wonder if I did her a favor by choosing her."

"I'm certain that she thinks you did, Charles. What's more, you did yourself a favor."

The Emperor smiled a little. "Even a blind hog finds the occasional acorn," he said. The smile faded. "Norman? I need to ask you for something. Something difficult."

"I'm at your service, Highness."

"Maybe not this time. I want him back, Norman. I want my son to have a grandfather and Trish to have a father. This is tearing me up inside. I've never . . ." He trailed off and shook his head.

"It's different when you have a family," Mingus said.

"Isn't it just? I had no idea, I truly didn't. I never really knew my own parents. Just as well, probably. My father was an idiot, and my mother . . . well, you knew her."

"It isn't easy, being a Hazar. They meant well, Charles."

"I don't want somebody telling Henry the same thing about me someday, Norman. He was a bastard, but he meant well. Spirit! It's not enough just to *mean* well. I want to *do* well. For both of them."

"What do you want from me, Charles?"

The Emperor looked the Dexta Secretary in the eye and said, "I want you to send Gloria to Denastri and get him back."

Mingus was genuinely shocked by the Emperor's words. He wanted to ask if he was serious, but there was no doubt that he was.

"I know what you're going to say, Norman. You can't do it officially. I understand that. But, dammit, Gloria gets *results*!"

"She does," Mingus agreed.

"I wouldn't ask this if there were any other way. You know that."

"I do." Mingus returned Charles's steady gaze, and for a few moments, neither of them spoke.

Charles ran a hand through his dirty blond hair and shook his head. "She's infuriating and impossible, but somehow she always gets the job done. She wouldn't do it if I asked her, but maybe you can find some appropriate excuse to send her to Denastri. From what I hear, the Dexta staff there are at each other's throats. Isn't that the kind of thing she's supposed to handle? Strategic interventions, and all that?"

"It is," Mingus said, giving a small nod. "To tell you the truth, I've even considered it myself. She might be able to knock some heads together and at least get everyone on the same page. But as for Kenarbin . . . I can't ask her to do that, Charles. Not officially, and not even unofficially."

"Well, could you at least *suggest* it?"

"When a Dexta Secretary makes a suggestion, a Level IX can hardly avoid taking it as an order. No, Charles, I can't ask her, and I won't suggest it. There's only one person who can ask her."

Charles nodded and took a deep breath. "Then," he said, "I suppose I must."

· 3 ·

Gloria signed her name on the napkin for the young woman and offered her a warm smile. The woman returned it and said, shyly, "Thank you, Ms. VanDeen."

"You're very welcome," Gloria told her. "Have a nice evening."

The woman returned to her own table, proudly clutching her souvenir, and completely ignored Gloria's dinner companion, who grimaced in mock pain. "Didn't even recognize me," he said. "Serves me right. First rule of my profession is never to let yourself be upstaged by dogs, children, or a devastatingly beautiful woman."

"It's probably the hump," Gloria suggested. Her date this evening was Jeremy Pendleton, a famed classical actor who was currently in rehearsals for a new production of *Richard III*. As part of his "process," Pendleton found it necessary to wear a fake hump strapped to his back, everywhere he went—even in bed.

"You must think I'm crazy," Pendleton said. "Many people do."

"Not crazy. Just a little eccentric."

"But it really is necessary, you know. I can't merely *play* Richard, I must *inhabit* him. The hump is the key to the man's character. It made him different from other people. It isolated him." He gave Gloria a wry smile as he gazed at her. "We all have our own humps, of course. You certainly do."

Pendleton might have been referring to Gloria's round, perfect breasts, almost entirely revealed in her airy summer dress, but she suspected that his reference was more metaphorical than morphological. "Some people think I'm crazy, too," she said.

The actor shook his head. "Not crazy. But different? Absolutely. Gloria VanDeen, Sweetheart of the Empire, ex-wife of the Emperor, Avatar of Joy, daring and courageous Dexta Tiger, heroine of Mynjhino, savior of New Cambridge, glamorous, gorgeous, enticing—"

"Blah, blah, blah. Jeremy, you're reviewing me as if I were a play."

"Or appraising you, as a work of art."

"Then save your plaudits for my parents, or the genetic sculptors who cooked up my sexual enhancements. I'm their creation, after all."

"Nonsense. We all create ourselves, every minute of every day. All the world's a stage, you know. Our lives are a performance, as who would know better than I? Some lives are hits on Broadway, and some close in New Haven. Yours, I suspect, is destined for a long and successful run on the Great White Way."

"Well," Gloria mused, "I suppose I've had a killer first act. Alarums and excursions all over the place."

Pendleton raised one eyebrow. Gloria wondered if he had spent hours in front of a mirror, learning to do that. "But you're worried about the second act?"

"Not worried, exactly. But I do seem to have begun it. Things are definitely different now. Spirit, it's been more than two years since anyone tried to kill me! Makes a girl wonder if people still care."

"Remember what I said about being upstaged by babies?"

Gloria sighed. "Prince Henry, you mean."

"People are always captivated by the Next Big Thing. When you first burst upon the scene four years ago, you were something new and unexpected, a real-life heroine of the Empire, impossibly sexy and brave and glamorous. Then Charles took his Consort and produced his cute little heir—and suddenly, you were yesterday's news. Does that bother you so much?"

"It doesn't *bother* me at all," Gloria protested. "In fact, I was relieved. If anything, I think I overplayed my part at first, and I was ready to get out of the spotlight. But, to be honest, I suppose I do feel a little . . . neglected. All that attention can be heady stuff. The last couple of years, I've just been doing my job like a good little bureaucrat. And I think I've been doing it pretty well. But . . . Spirit, I'm twenty-seven already, practically an old woman! I feel like I'm over the hill."

Pendleton chuckled and reached out to caress Gloria's right hand. "When I was just starting out," he said, "I did *Hamlet* and got rave reviews. I was a sensation, and people couldn't get enough of me. Next time out, I played Biff Loman in *Salesman,* and hardly anyone noticed. And yet my performance in *Salesman* was ten times better than what I did in *Hamlet.* The point is, *I* knew it, even if no one else did."

Gloria groped for something profound to say in response, but was rescued from the necessity by the arrival of her assistant and best friend, Petra Nash, and her date. Gloria introduced Pendleton, then everyone got seated and the waiter came and poured more wine. They were meeting in a trendy little exoethnic restaurant on Manhattan's Upper West Side, near Columbia, where Petra was taking courses for an advanced degree in government administration. Her date was one of her professors—a frizzy-haired, mustachioed historian named

Albert Fenlow. Gloria had met him a few times and found him interesting, if a bit didactic. But Petra liked him, and that was all that mattered.

"Sorry we're late," Petra said. "Class ran long. We got into this fascinating discussion about the Second Interstellar War."

"Ah, yes," said Pendleton. "Gripping tale, that. I played General Valerio in a vid once."

"Saw that," Fenlow said. "Enjoyed your performance, but your scriptwriter was an idiot."

"Was he, now? Well, I just did it for the money. I'm afraid I can't vouch for the authenticity of the thing."

"It made a hash of the chronology. I mean, the Glonci didn't use bio weapons until *after* Praxna, and Valerio never—"

"Why don't we order?" Gloria suggested. "I'm starving."

"I recommend the sautéed pseudoscallops," said Fenlow. "I come here all the time. One of the few benefits of Empire. For us, anyway."

The restaurant featured cuisine from the distant world of Krunkul and was staffed by immigrants from there; most of the waiters were young students at Columbia, five feet tall and covered with soft golden down. They were unfailingly polite and spoke Empire English with a lilting, melodic accent.

"Have you tried that new Pakuli restaurant over on Ninety-seventh?" asked Pendleton. "Gloria and I were there the other night. They've got some kind of spicy lamb thing that's astonishing. And I've always enjoyed Zinoothi cuisine, as well. Sort of Mexican-Chinese, with a touch of Italian. Always something new and delicious at the exoethnics."

"Yes," Fenlow agreed. "We'll eat our way through the entire galaxy before we're through."

"Albert sees the exoethnics as a metaphor for Imperial policy," Petra explained. "How'd you put it?

We're insatiable gourmands, milking the galaxy, skimming the cream, and tipping the help if the service meets our standards?"

"If all we took were a few tasty morsels," Fenlow said, "it wouldn't be so bad. Unfortunately, our appetite isn't so limited. The truth is, we're not simply gourmands, we're gluttons."

"But I notice you eat here, too," Gloria pointed out.

Fenlow gave her a slightly guilty grin. "When in Rome—and we are—eat what the Romans eat."

"*Ave Imperator*," Pendleton said grandly. "We who are about to dine, salute you."

They ordered and chatted amiably, sipping wine and enjoying the warm early summer evening. Gloria and Petra smiled privately at each other while letting their dates bat the conversational ball back and forth—the intellectual and the artist, being self-consciously intellectual and arty to impress their ladies.

Their meals arrived, preceded by little green capsules that their waiter insisted they take before beginning. Alien cuisine often required a neutralizing agent to combat the inconvenient and sometimes disgusting side effects of an unfamiliar biochemistry. But with proper precautions, humans could enjoy tasty and exotic fare from hundreds of Empire worlds.

Food, inevitably, became the main conversational theme. Gloria and Petra, in their travels on behalf of Dexta, had encountered a number of delicious native dishes. "I think my favorite," Gloria said, "was a fruit they have on Mynjhino. Sort of a cross between a mango and a watermelon, but a little chewy. Dexta has been trying to get them to export it, but so far, they've refused. The Myn have a religious taboo against sending products of their land off-world."

"They'll give in, sooner or later," Fenlow predicted. "Eventually, you'll be able to enjoy their forbidden fruit with your breakfast every morning. Native cultures simply can't stand up to Imperial pressure."

"Some of them do," Gloria objected. "The Myn are very committed to preserving their traditional ways. So are many other cultures."

"Undoubtedly, but in the end, it won't matter. Take the Krunkuli. When they were absorbed into the Empire, about a century ago, they were insular and xenophobic. Didn't want to have anything to do with the Imperial culture and economy. But gradually, we won them over with our methods, media, and muscle. Now, they export a few items like platinum, chromium, and our dinner. In return, they import computers, skimmers, fusion reactors, drugs, and everything else you can name. They're completely integrated into the Imperial economy and couldn't live without us."

"Is that so awful?" Pendleton asked. "Seems like a good deal to me, for all concerned."

"From a Terran perspective," Fenlow said, "that's a defensible position. But look at it from their side. See our waiter? He came here to get an education of a kind that isn't available on Krunkul. A Terran education. He'll learn a smattering of Terran law or engineering, then return to his homeworld. He'll become one of the Krunkuli elite, if he isn't already. And then what? He's not Terran, but he's no longer truly Krunkuli. We've acculturated him—by design. He'll live a life separate and distinct from that of the common Krunkuli. They'll resent him, he'll look down on them, and bit by bit, the traditional culture will erode and fragment. It's already happening. A nativist movement is developing, and one fine day our young waiter will find himself forced to choose between the old ways and the new. He'll get his throat cut, or join the nativists when they start cutting Terran throats. Then we'll send in the Marines to back the elite, Krunkul will be devastated, and we'll have to do without our delicious pseudoscallops for a while. No matter. We'll just find a different, trendier exoethnic restaurant and go on with our lives as if nothing had happened."

"He's right, Gloria," Petra said. "That's almost exactly what happened on Mynjhino."

"Not really," Gloria said. "Mynjhino wasn't devastated."

"Only because *you* were there," Petra insisted. "Think what would have happened if Servitor had gotten its way."

"Mynjhino was a special case."

"They're *all* special cases," Fenlow said. "Each world is unique. And yet, they are all part of the same inexorable pattern."

"So what would you have us do, Albert?" Gloria asked, feeling a little exasperated. "Abandon the Empire?"

Fenlow shook his head. "Far too late for that. We can't abandon the Empire. But we can change it."

"Ah!" cried Pendleton. "Another vote for the PPA. I have to say, they make some sense. But that Karno fellow is a little hard to take."

"Karno's just another ruling-class stooge," Fenlow said. "He talks a good game, but when you get right down to it, he's not going to do anything that would deprive his constituents of all the goodies the Empire provides. Liberals have always been in favor of liberty, equality, and fraternity, but only as long as no one is seriously inconvenienced in the quest to achieve them."

"You'd prefer the Jacobin alternative?" Gloria asked.

Fenlow smiled. "The Jacobins and Bolsheviks were bloodthirsty idiots, but they did have the right idea about how to deal with crowned heads. No offense intended."

"None taken," Gloria assured him politely. She knew a lot more about crowned heads than Fenlow did.

"I'm not suggesting that we sharpen the old guillotine, Gloria," Fenlow said. "I'm not an ideologue, and, historically, violent revolutions of that sort seldom achieve their stated goals. Usually, it's just the reverse. Try to impose Utopia at the point of a sword, and what you wind up with is Bonaparte, Stalin, or Fukajima."

"So what's the answer?" Pendleton asked.

"I'll let you know," Fenlow said with a smile, "just as soon as I figure it out. We historians have the advantage of not being required to be practical. We get by with being *des*criptive, rather than *pre*scriptive."

"We don't have that luxury at Dexta," Gloria told him.

"And that's why I'm comfortably ensconced in the groves of academe. I let braver souls like you and Petra fight my battles for me." Fenlow reached over, put his arm around Petra, and gave her a squeeze.

"I had to kill a spider in his kitchen last week," Petra said, grinning. "Albert's afraid of them."

"I am *not* afraid of spiders," Fenlow protested. "I merely respect their right to pursue an independent lifestyle, uninfluenced by human chauvinism."

Gloria's wristcom beeped. She turned a little in her chair, away from the others, and answered.

"Gloria? It's Norman Mingus. I wondered if you would care to join me for dinner tonight at my home. There's something I'd like to discuss with you."

"Uh . . . Norman? I'd love to, but the fact is, I'm right in the middle of dinner with some friends."

"Ah. Of course, the time difference. Forgive me. I've been on Luna all day, and that always scrambles my sense of time. I apologize for the interruption. Perhaps tomorrow, then?"

"No, no, it's all right, Norman. Tell you what. How about if I join you in an hour or so for coffee and dessert?"

"That would be wonderful, but I don't want to impose on you and your friends."

"It's no imposition at all, Norman," Gloria assured

him. "Really. Does your cook still make that delicious cherry cobbler?"

"He does, and if he knows what's good for him, he'll have some ready by the time you arrive. But please, do take your time and enjoy your evening." Mingus clicked off and Gloria turned back to her friends.

"I take it this means you won't be coming home with me tonight," said an obviously disappointed Pendleton.

"Duty calls, I'm afraid." Gloria leaned over and gave him a peck on the cheek. "Sorry."

"Damned Imperial tyrants!" Pendleton snorted dramatically. "You've got the right idea, Albert, my boy. Off with their heads!"

Gloria stepped into the Transit ring at Dexta HQ in Manhattan, and stepped out of it into Idaho. A familiar Security man waved her through with a smile and a minimal scan; in her flimsy evening wear, it was obvious that she was not carrying any concealed weapons. She crossed the yard to the house, breathing deeply in the thin, brisk mountain air. A faint afterglow of pink and orange highlighted the peaks to the south and west.

Mingus greeted her at the door and Gloria gave him a kiss on his cheek. She thought he was looking well these days; she had been worried about him following their painful and revealing sojourn on New Cambridge, two years earlier. But Mingus had slowly rallied, and now seemed as healthy and vigorous as any 133-year-old man had a right to be. They went upstairs to the third-floor deck and settled in on a comfortable couch while Mingus's cook personally served them coffee and cobbler.

"I apologize for spoiling your evening."

"Not at all, Norman," Gloria assured him as she dug into the dessert. "It was just a casual double date with Petra. We went to a little Krunkuli restaurant on the Upper West Side, near Columbia."

"Krunkul!" Mingus smiled.

"You know their cuisine?"

"Their cuisine and their planet. Krunkul was my first off-world assignment, back in 3111—no, 3112, I think. I was twenty-five and a newly minted Level XIV, full of fire and ambition. Krunkul had just joined the Empire, and I was determined to plunge into the assignment and dazzle the natives with Imperial goodwill and efficiency."

"I wish I'd known you then," Gloria said. "You must have been a dashing young man."

"On the contrary, I was a gangly, awkward young oaf. First day there, I took a walk through a native market, showing my willingness to mix and mingle with the indigs, you see. Gobbled down some of the local delicacies and spent the next three days belching and farting uncontrollably. Made quite an impression on my coworkers, I can tell you."

Gloria laughed. Somehow, the thought of a gauche and fumbling young Norman Mingus made the man even more appealing.

A thin crescent moon shone down on them from the glittering night sky. Gloria pointed to it. "Spent the day up there, did you? Oversight meeting?"

Mingus nodded. "I really ought to take you along to one of them," he said. "If you truly want my job someday, you should see some of its more tedious aspects."

"I don't know. I think it would be interesting."

"If you think spending a day with babbling politicians is interesting, you still have much to learn. Of course, with elections coming up, they're even more garrulous and feather-brained than usual."

"Who do you think will win?"

Mingus shook his head, then took a sip of coffee. "No idea," he said. "The ISP's core is pretty solid, but Karno and the PPA have been nibbling away at the margins. It may well come down to the minor parties. If the ISP fails to win a majority, Karno could cobble together some sort of half-assed coalition Government. But without a mandate of their own, the PPA wouldn't be able to get much done. We'd probably just stagger along for a couple of years until one of the minor parties bolted and forced new elections."

"You don't think Karno would be an effective PM?"

"Jimmy's a good man," Mingus said. "A bit hotheaded and obstinate, but he's smarter than the average pol. Still, the qualities that make him a good Minority Leader would work against him if he ever achieved power. He'd never be able to deliver on all the promises he feels free to make in his current role."

"Petra's date said pretty much the same thing tonight," Gloria noted. "He's a Columbia history professor. Albert Fenlow."

"Fenlow? Know his work. Did a rather good book on William II a few years back. He dealt quite well with the personalities, although he totally misinterpreted the dynamic within thirtieth-century Dexta. Academics never quite grasp the realities of a bureaucracy. They tend to rely too heavily on the published and documentary sources. Only to be expected, of course. They spend years digging through the musty old records and imagine that what people wrote about what they did is the same as what actually happened." He gave Gloria a meaningful glance. "Of course, we both know that isn't necessarily true."

Gloria nodded in agreement. On New Cambridge, two years earlier, Mingus had told her the long-hidden truth about events that had unfolded at the beginning of the war with the Ch'gnth, more than half a century earlier. At the same time, Gloria had learned the unpleasant facts surrounding Charles's rise to power in 3213. History was what the historians wrote; reality was what actually happened.

They sat in silence for a while. Gloria knew Mingus

had something on his mind but felt content to wait until he was ready to bring it up.

"You've been doing good, solid work with the OSI these past few years," Mingus said at last. "You really have turned the Office of Strategic Intervention into a Fifth Quadrant, of sorts."

"We try," Gloria said humbly.

"You do more than try. You succeed, for the most part. OSI has, what, about a hundred staffers now?"

"A hundred and seventeen. But don't tell the Comptroller. She thinks it's still just 105. We've got a dozen new people off the books. A little creative book-keeping, until we can straighten things out for the next Quarterly Allocation."

Mingus smiled indulgently. "You're getting pretty good at this. Your success in Dexta is not simply a function of your personal bravado and sex appeal. I'm glad to see that you understand that. However . . ."

He paused, and Gloria turned to stare at his aristocratic features and subtle blue-gray eyes. "Yes?"

"However, a situation has arisen that may call for some more of your bravado. I hesitate to make this assignment, Gloria, because the problem may prove intractable, and is inherently dangerous. Nevertheless, action is clearly called for, and I can think of no one better qualified to tackle this mess."

"Which mess?"

"Denastri."

Gloria nodded slowly. "That's a mess, all right."

"The Dexta office on Denastri is in chaos. Some people are in outright rebellion, others are quitting, and no one seems to have a handle on the situation. Freya Benitez, the Imperial Secretary, is out of her depth. Governor Blagodarski has complained about her performance, and I gather that the Marines are extremely displeased with her. The Corporates seem satisfied, since she tends to grant them all the leeway they require, but her UnderSecs are squabbling and probably actively plotting against her. I would like you to go to Denastri and attempt to restore some order to the Dexta establishment on that world."

"I see. And what about the insurgency?"

Mingus shook his head emphatically. "Not your problem. I would prefer that you stay out of that side of things, to the extent that you can. Of course, you'll need to consult with Blagodarski and General Ohashi about the diplomatic and military aspects, but your mission is limited to the Dexta situation. Get things straightened out as quickly and efficiently as you can, then come home."

"All right."

"As a Level IX, of course, you'll be senior Dexta rep on the planet—indeed, in the whole McGowan Cluster. Under the OSI Charter, you'll have full authority to do whatever you think needs doing."

"Just how far can I go?"

Mingus smiled. "You can't shoot anybody," he said, "even if they need shooting. Beyond that, I'll back you in whatever you decide. I don't think you should take a full team with you, however. We don't need more Dexta people there; that would only add to the confusion."

"Understood. I'll just take Petra, if that's okay with you."

"Ms. Nash? Of course."

"Norman? What about the military situation on Denastri? Just how bad is it?"

"About as bad as it can be, I'm afraid." Mingus sighed wearily. "We don't have half the troops we need there, but no more are available at the moment, nor are they likely to be. The new government we installed after the Occupation has minimal support, and they've been dragging their feet about recruiting an adequate native force. The natives are split three ways, and the local politics seem to be murky, at best. I'll have a full briefing book prepared for you, and you can study it en route. But, again, I emphasize that the military dimensions of the Denastri situation are not your responsibility."

"And the diplomatic dimensions?" Mingus had made no mention of Lord Kenarbin, and the omission was obvious and glaring. Gloria had her own reasons for being glad that he hadn't mentioned Kenarbin—reasons that had nothing to do with Imperial policy. Nevertheless, Kenarbin's abduction had become a major issue in the Empire, and Gloria didn't see how she could ignore it.

Mingus stared at the dark mountains in the distance. He didn't say anything for several moments.

"What?" Gloria wanted to know. "What aren't you telling me, Norman?"

He turned to look at her. "Gloria," he said, "I think you should go to Rio tomorrow."

"You want me to see Charles?" Gloria was taken aback by the prospect. She hadn't seen Charles—hadn't even had any contact with him—in more than two years. Not since she had foiled Lord Brockinbrough's assassination attempt and learned the ugly truth about the Fifth of October conspiracy . . . and the ugly truth about Charles.

"It's a delicate matter," Mingus said. "I don't think I should say any more about it. But see him, Gloria. For his sake, and the Empire's."

Gloria wanted to say no. Mingus could ask her to go to dangerous, faraway Denastri, and she would do it without a second thought. But asking her to go to Rio . . . *Spirit*!

"I believe it's necessary," Mingus told her.

Gloria smiled gamely. "Then I'll have to go, won't I?" But her smile quickly faded, and she joined Mingus in staring silently at the dark and distant peaks.

·4·

Rio was hot and sticky. The Security people at the Residence gave her a scan that was far more than perfunctory, then ushered her in. As Gloria walked across the grounds to the main building, she took in the familiar sights of Sugar Loaf and the needle spire of the Spiritist Mother Church. When she was married to Charles, before he became Emperor, Rio had been their principal home, although they had spent most of their time together cruising throughout the Empire in his yacht. And she had spent much of her childhood here, as well, growing up at Court in the hazy, dreamlike, decadent days of old Darius.

She had dressed for the tropics in a low-slung lacy band skirt and a minimal halter top. Of medium height, with arresting turquoise-blue eyes, a long Dura-styled blond mane, and a cocoa-colored complexion that spoke of her six-continent genetic blend, Gloria would have attracted attention even in a parka and mukluks; she usually wore considerably less than that. In the past couple of years, however, she had consciously muted her Tiger stripes a bit, perhaps in guilty reaction to her flirtation with—well, addiction to—the dangerous, pleasure-intensifying drug Orgastria. She had kicked the drug and reined in her enhanced sexuality following the tragedies of New Cambridge; but, like Richard with his hump, Gloria couldn't avoid being what she was. Today, she didn't feel like trying.

Charles, damn him, still evoked the Tiger in her and made her want to push the limits, just because she could. With his own sexual enhancements, Charles—with or without Orgastria—was a lover of overwhelming power and appeal. He was a selfish, cold-blooded bastard, too—but few, if any, of her many paramours could match his sexual virtuosity. She had walked out on him long ago, with no regrets, but could not resist looking back over her shoulder now and then and contemplating the life she had left behind. Even now, knowing the truth about how he had become Emperor, Gloria still felt a painful twist in her heart—and other organs—when she thought of him.

She entered the Residence and walked through the main hall, surrounded by memories. Ghostlike, they swam before her, speaking to her in dim, echoing voices of a time of innocence and expectation, of youthful exuberance and untempered passions. Handsome men and beautiful women danced about her to forgotten melodies, swirling through an uncomplicated life with grace and elegance. No painful memories, then—no burning bodies on Mynjhino or slaughtered friends on Sylvania; no pungent whiff of her own burned hair from an assassin's near miss on Cartago. Reality had not yet intruded on the delicious gaiety of life. There was only the moment, and the prospect of all the joyous, carefree moments yet to come. With Charles. And before Charles, Kenarbin . . .

Gloria banished the ghosts and concentrated on *this* moment. As the Chamberlain escorted her to the office where the Emperor awaited her, she steeled herself for the coming encounter. Mingus thought she should see him, and she had seldom been able to say no to Norman. He wouldn't have made the suggestion if he hadn't thought it important, so here she was. But she didn't like it.

Charles met her at the door, and the Chamberlain swiftly departed, leaving them alone together in the glittering, opulent office where the Emperor attended to the affairs of state. This was the very heart of the Empire, where the fate of trillions was determined and the future of humanity plotted with the cold exactitude of a starship's navigation computer. The first draft of history was written here; in this very room, Gregory III—and three other Emperors—had been assassinated.

The Emperor stood before her, handsome and resplendent, his watery blue eyes fixed on her. *He's aged,* she thought.

"Hello, Glory," he said simply. "Long time, no see."

"Hello, Charles. Congratulations . . . about Henry, I mean. You must be very proud."

"Thank you, I am. You should stop by the nursery before you go. He's the spittin' image of his old man. He's not housebroken yet, but then, neither am I, really."

Gloria couldn't help smiling. "Still peeing on the potted palms, are you?"

"Only when sufficiently drunk. Which isn't very often, these days, I hasten to point out. I'm a responsible family man now. If you don't believe me, just read the propaganda the Household cranks out. Every word of it's true."

"I never doubted it."

"And what about you, Glory? Still finding fulfillment as the Empire's most glamorous bureaucrat?"

"Don't you know? Or have you finally stopped having me followed?"

"I'll never stop keeping tabs on you," he replied, "but

let's just say that the leash is a little longer now. Your independence is an accomplished fact. I recognize and accept that."

They fell silent and stared at each other, standing three or four feet apart. A safe distance.

"Norman said I should come to Rio, so I came," Gloria said. "Your move."

"A bold opening gambit. Should I sally forth a knight to meet it, or castle and cower behind my rook?"

"Why not just tell me what you want?"

Charles frowned. "Norman didn't tell you? No, I suppose he wouldn't have. He has a precisely calculated sense of propriety. But surely you can guess."

"He wants to send me to Denastri," Gloria said.

"And that suggests nothing else to you?"

Gloria refused to help him. "Should it?" she asked.

"Well, it damned well ought to," Charles snapped, betraying emotion for the first time. "You're not going to make this easy for me, are you?"

Gloria walked past him and strolled deeper into the cavernous office. If anyone had suggested to her that the movement was designed to give Charles a better view of her minimally covered posterior, she would have denied it. But Charles was right; she wasn't going to make this easy. Why should she?

Charles trailed after her. "There are things I can't say, or shouldn't. Like it or not, I'm Emperor every second of the day. But I'm also a father, and I have a woman in my life who means a great deal to me. She's in pain, and so am I, dammit. You know what I want you to do, Glory."

A fat antique globe caught her attention. She stopped next to it and examined it carefully. Seventeenth century, probably. Familiar continents looked strangely distorted; Australia and Antarctica were nowhere to be seen. She gave the world a gentle shove and watched idly as the days spun past.

She looked up at Charles. "What makes you think I can do it?"

"You seem to be able to accomplish most things that you set your mind to," he said.

"They're aliens, Charles," she reminded him. "My tits and ass won't have any effect on them."

"You've got more going for you than that exquisite body, Glory. You've got a devious, calculating brain, and a strong and courageous heart. You really are an extraordinary woman, in case I never mentioned that before."

"Flattery will get you nowhere, Chuckles."

"What do you want from me, then? Do you want me to get down on my knees and beg?"

Gloria cocked an eyebrow. "Would you really do that?"

"Would you really make me?"

She thought about it for a moment, then said, "No, I don't suppose I would."

"Good, because I wouldn't do it. I'm the fucking Emperor. I command, I threaten, I manipulate, but I don't beg. Look, Glory, you're going to Denastri anyway, aren't you? Why can't you see your way clear to . . . to *deal with* the situation?"

"What could I do that you can't, with your Marines and plasma bombs? What could I offer the Denastri that would make the slightest difference?"

Charles scratched his closely cropped beard for a few seconds. "I didn't say it would be easy," he conceded. "And I'm afraid that I have no productive ideas on the subject. I had hoped that you might."

"What do you want from me, Charles?" Gloria demanded. "I can't work miracles."

He approached a little closer to her, but observed the unspoken distance between them. "You saved my life on New Cambridge," he said. "I count *that* as a miracle."

"It was no miracle, Charles. It was just luck, or

maybe self-preservation. They were trying to kill me, too, you know."

"Well, whatever it was, I'm standing here today because of it. Did I ever thank you for that?"

"No," she said, "you didn't."

"Well, I'm thanking you now."

Gloria dismissed it with a curt nod. "Some people save Emperors," she said, "and some people kill them."

"And both types are represented here, aren't they?" Charles gave her a caustic frown.

Gloria had belatedly learned that Charles had been a passive accomplice in the Fifth of October Plot that had killed Gregory III, two of his sons, and three of his nephews, leaving the throne to Charles. His cousin Larry—Lord Brockinbrough—had orchestrated the plots and counterplots that had left a stageful of dead and eternally silent conspirators; but that had not been the final act of his drama. Two years ago, he had attempted to assassinate Charles as well, which would have made his son, Gareth, the new Emperor. Gloria had managed to stave off disaster, but learning of Charles's involvement in the Fifth of October Plot had permanently altered her relationship with the man who had once been her husband.

"Are you going to hate me forever because of what I did—or didn't—do?"

"I don't hate you, Charles. I know you too well to hate you. I know exactly what you are. Does Trish?"

The Emperor stared at Gloria in icy silence for a long moment. "No," he said at last, "she doesn't. With Cousin Larry and his detestable offspring dead, you and I are the only ones left who know the truth."

"Is that supposed to comfort me? You could snap your fingers and reduce the total from two to one. Maybe you will someday."

"I don't deny the possibility."

"Is that it, then? I should help you because if I don't, you'll have me killed?"

Charles spun around and stomped away from Gloria, then turned again and glared at her. "Why must you always overdramatize everything? You're enjoying this, aren't you?"

"Not really."

"The hell you aren't! You're as big a bitch as I am a bastard, Glory, and don't try to deny it. I know *you* too well."

Gloria gave him a grim smile. "Guilty knowledge," she said. "A wonderful thing, isn't it?"

"All right, you know what happened on the Fifth of October. You know I was a passive accomplice to murder. So what? Can you honestly deny that I'm a better Emperor than Gregory?"

"Gregory's dead," Gloria pointed out. "That makes the comparison a little one-sided, don't you think?"

"And are you so pure? In case you didn't realize it, I know about your little debt to the zamitat. You'll spend the next century paying them off and telling yourself that it was all justified because it seemed necessary at the time. So I'm an assassin and you're an accomplice to organized crime. We're both criminals, Glory. Show me somebody in this fucking Empire who *isn't!*"

"Out of 3 trillion, there must be one or two."

"At a maximum. Let me know when you find them. In the meantime, are you going to help me with this or not?"

Gloria looked down at her toes. She wiggled them.

"I'll think about it," she said.

Gloria wordlessly walked past him, opened the door, and left the Emperor alone in his office. During the entire interview, no one had spoken the word "Kenarbin."

In the main hall, she immediately encountered Lady Patricia, who must have been waiting for her. Gloria approached her and offered a warm, genuine smile, which was returned by the Imperial Consort.

They had known each other years before, when Gloria was a blossoming teen and Trish was a freckle-faced, gap-toothed little girl. She had grown up to be a spectacularly beautiful and elegant young woman. Her long auburn hair framed a brown-eyed face, with full red lips and a peaches-and-cream complexion. She was taller than Gloria now, slim, lithe, and graceful. Thanks to the adoring media, she was even better known to the masses than Gloria had been at the peak of her fame.

Gloria reached out and took Trish's hands in hers. "Hi, Trish."

"Gloria. It's been a long time."

"Still putting lizards down the back of people's dresses?"

Trish laughed. "I'm sorry for that, I really am. I'm afraid I was a bit of a scamp."

"Scamp? You were a little monster! I'd have wrung your neck if I'd caught you."

"Well, you have to understand—I was a woman scorned. I had a huge crush on Charles, and when you took him away from me, well, I just had to get even."

"And now, you have," Gloria said as she released Trish's hands.

Trish's smile became slightly brittle. "A dream come true," she said.

"He's a selfish, coldhearted bastard, Trish," Gloria told her. "If you don't understand that yet, you will in time."

"Maybe that's how he was with you. He's not that way with me."

"Sorry," Gloria said, feeling a bit abashed. "I didn't mean to be nasty. I just met with him, and I guess I'm still under his magical spell."

They looked at each other in silence for a moment,

then Trish brightened and asked, "Would you like to meet Henry?"

"Love to," Gloria said.

They walked along together through ornate corridors, then went up an elevator, chatting idly about matters of small consequence. Trish asked about life in Manhattan, and Gloria responded with polite inquiries about life in the Residence. Trish had spent her entire life in Rio and admitted envying Gloria her travels. "Charles says that when Henry's old enough, we'll take a grand tour of the Empire," she said, a little wistfully.

The nursery was the size of a small gymnasium, cluttered with toys and cribs and medical equipment. Aside from the two beefy Security men at the door, two nurses were in constant attendance, and a physician was never more than a room away. Nothing bad would ever happen to the young prince.

The Prince was currently crawling around a crib with aimless determination, intent upon an infant's mysterious errands. A nurse picked him up, despite a mild protest from the Prince, and carefully handed him to Lady Patricia. Henry made a happy little squeal and nestled in his mother's arms.

"He's adorable," Gloria said.

"I think so," Trish said. "Every baby is, of course— but especially mine. Would you like to hold him?"

"Uh . . . sure." Gloria's experience with babies was minimal; she was always afraid she would drop them. She took the tubby little prince in her arms and hefted him up to her shoulder. He had Charles's eyes—watery blue, alert, and suspicious. He frowned a little, so Gloria gave him a kiss on his cheek. He seemed to like that, so Gloria kissed him again on the other cheek.

"It's never too early to suck up to a future Emperor," she explained.

"Oh, he'll be a hundred years old before he's Emperor."

"Like the first Henry," Gloria said, instantly regretting it. Henry I had been the son of Victor the Great, who had ruled for seventy-six years, the longest reign of any Emperor. When Victor finally expired, Henry, at the age of 104, served as Emperor for all of three days before being assassinated by his impatient son, Henry II, who was, himself, dispatched by an assassin two months later. It was 2676, the Year of the Four Emperors—an eventful and storied episode in Imperial history.

Trish noticed Gloria's embarrassment and quickly tried to allay it. "People always ask us why we chose that name," she said. "Charles insisted on it. He said it was a perfectly good name and deserved another chance. And, anyway, no matter what some people say, history doesn't really repeat itself."

"I'm sure it won't," Gloria quickly agreed. "He's a handsome young devil, isn't he?"

"He has his father's eyes, and I think he has his grandfather's chin. You knew my father, didn't you, Gloria? I know he was a friend of your parents. How are they?"

"Thriving. Dad's off on another of those round-the-planet yacht races somewhere in Sector 9, and Mom's with him, probably plugging leaks and repelling boarders." She took a closer look at young Henry and realized that he did bear a resemblance to Lord Kenarbin. Henry began to squirm, and Gloria handed him back to his mother.

"Do you get to see them very often?" Trish asked.

"Not as often as I'd like. It's been about six months, I think. Between my job and Dad's seafaring, we're not on the same planet at the same time very often."

"I know the feeling," Trish said. "Dad's always got some diplomatic mission . . ." She trailed off. Her eyes began to mist up, and she quickly turned away from Gloria and handed Henry to one of the nurses. Trish walked over to a window and Gloria, reluctantly, followed her.

Lady Patricia wiped her eyes.

"I'm so sorry about what's happened, Trish," Gloria said softly.

"We always knew it could happen," Trish said, her voice sounding husky and unsteady. "Mom is in seclusion and refuses to see anyone. And I . . . I just carry on, the best I can. An Emperor's Consort can't be weepy and emotional, you know. Stiff upper lip, and all that. And I have Henry to keep me occupied."

Trish turned and looked into Gloria's eyes. "Is it true?" she asked. "You're going to Denastri?"

Gloria nodded. "I am," she said. "Dexta business."

"I see." Trish looked disappointed, as if she had expected something more.

"Trish—"

"I understand about Imperial policy, Gloria," Trish insisted. "Really, I do. I mean, if we started negotiating for hostages, we'd never see the end of it, would we? Terrorists and bandits all over the Empire would start grabbing our people, and it would turn into ever so much of a mess, wouldn't it? And we just can't have that, can we?"

Lady Patricia's voice broke, and she whirled around to hide her face.

Gloria listened to Trish's quiet sobs for a moment, then tentatively reached out and put her hand on the young woman's shoulder.

"I'll do what I can, Trish," she said.

·5·

The Dexta Flyer hummed along through the spooky realm of Yao Space, carrying Gloria and Petra on their eleven-day journey to Denastri. The tiny vehicle consisted of little more than a fusion reactor, a Ferguson Distortion Generator, and a cramped cylindrical compartment with room for two people and their luggage. For Gloria and Petra, interstellar travel had become a familiar, humdrum experience; as usual, they had stripped off their clothing to save on laundry and spent most of the time in their bunks, reading or sleeping.

Petra had loaded her pad with books from the Required Reading List for her courses at Columbia. Once a flighty, wisecracking, inexperienced assistant, Petra had become more of a partner to Gloria, aside from being her closest friend. Cute and diminutive, with straight brown hair, mischievous green eyes, and a sexy girlish body that was more attractive than she realized, Petra was the product of poverty and a broken home in Weehawken, across the river from the splendors of

Manhattan. After a painful and difficult start at Dexta, she had become Gloria's assistant four years earlier.

Dexta was, by design, a competitive and frequently hostile environment, where simply surviving was a major accomplishment. In response to the junglelike conditions, over the centuries a distinct set of bureaucratic species had evolved. There were fierce, proud Lions, the natural leaders; seductive Tigers; anonymous, workaday Sheep; Pack Dogs, who savaged the weak; and Lap Dogs, who attached themselves to powerful and protective superiors. Gloria was a natural Tiger, and Petra had become her Lap Dog. She had made a brief foray as a Tiger, but found the experiment unsettling and had gladly retreated back to Dogdom.

Petra had been notoriously unlucky in love, and her relationship with Fenlow struck Gloria as another retreat, of sorts. Fenlow was safe. He wouldn't get himself killed by hostile natives on some backwater world, or be taken from her by the machinations of a wealthy, powerful family. Gloria didn't think that Petra was in love with Fenlow, but the relationship was probably just what she needed at this point in her life. At twenty-nine, Petra was settling into a long-term commitment to Dexta and attempting to improve herself with her studies at Columbia. She had already earned advancement to Level XII, and seemed determined to accompany Gloria in her rise to ultimate power within Dexta. That was the plan, at least.

While Petra pondered the hoary wisdom of scholars, Gloria dug into her briefing book on Denastri. She had followed the story in the media, giving her a sketchy overview of the situation, but in-depth analysis proved to be dauntingly complex.

Civilization had arisen on Denastri some forty-seven thousand years ago, as nearly as anyone could tell. It had progressed rapidly, and within ten thousand years, the Denastri had achieved star travel. They were, it seemed, a race given to deep physical and metaphysical thought, and had developed a means of transluminal flight that was different from the version employed by Terrans. Humans had fabricated the Fergusite crystal as a means of focusing fusion energy inward, upon itself, rupturing the fabric of normal space to create a bubble of Yao Space that squirted from star to star at astounding velocities; Gloria's Flyer traveled a hundred light-years per day, the fastest means of interstellar transport available for human passengers.

The Denastri, in contrast, had found a more subtle means of motion between the stars. Utilizing string harmonics, they had managed to stretch normal space, rather like a rubber band, storing up energy that was released all at once. The energy from each "snap" was enough to propel a vehicle forward at about one-third of a light-year per day, for distances of five or six light-years, before the energy dissipated and the ship dropped back into normal space at a subluminal velocity. Then, the whole process had to be repeated. The method allowed the Denastri to reach the nearby stars of the McGowan Cluster within a month or two, but could not be employed for longer distances due to the prohibitive fuel requirements. Thus, the Denastri had built no large stellar empire, as the Terrans did thousands of years later, but had managed to establish themselves on a dozen planets in the Cluster, ten to twenty light-years from their homeworld.

As the millennia passed, the cultures of the colony worlds diverged from that of the mother planet, and conflict erupted. For thirty thousand years, the denizens of the McGowan Cluster had been battling one another, in ever-shifting alliances and tides of military fortune. In consequence, the Denastrian civilizations had exhausted themselves and slipped backward from the heights they had once occupied at a time when humans were still honing their hunting-and-gathering skills.

The Terrans had first made contact with the McGowan Cluster some eighty years earlier. After a lengthy interruption during the war with the Ch'gnth, contact had been restored in recent decades, with tentative trade and cultural ties being established between the Empire and a few of the Denastrian colony worlds. Then, five years ago, in another surge of internecine hostility, the Denastri had struck once again at one of their offspring worlds, destroying a few Empire trade vessels in the process. The Empire had been obliged to respond, and three years ago, the Navy had demolished the inferior Denastri fleet, overthrown the government, and sent an occupation force to restore order and bring Denastri into the overarching embrace of the Terran Empire.

The Denastri were a curious species, human enough to seem deceptively familiar but fundamentally alien and impenetrable. Males and females were so different from each other that, to Terrans, they almost seemed to be separate species; little was known about the females. The males came in six distinct varieties, or castes, according to the order of birth. Unlike Earth, on Denastri it was the Firstborn who were lowest in rank, and the Sixthborn who were the highest. Members of each caste occupied a distinct, strictly delineated place in society; in fact, individuals didn't even have names, as such. Rather, each was identified by a long series of honorific titles, which the translation software rendered in a convenient shorthand. Thus, the current Premier was known to Terrans as "3A-27-12J," which signified that he was a Thirdborn member of Superclan A, 27th Lodge, 12th Nest, 10th Line.

The Denastri Firstborn were low-ranking artisans and tradesmen. The Secondborn were scholars, physicians, and scientists. The Thirdborn, with whom the Terrans had the most contact, were the managerial class, business and government leaders. The Fourth- and Fifthborn were warriors, enlisted men and officers, respectively. The shadowy Sixthborn, little seen by humans, were priests and mystics, who conducted the complex and arcane rituals that unified Denastri society in ways that humans only dimly comprehended. As they came of age, the Sixthborn directly absorbed the wisdom and knowledge of their fathers, who then died in an elaborate sacred ceremony. In effect, the Sixthborn became their own ancestors.

Only the Sixthborn were permitted to reproduce, which they did just six times in their lives, although Fifthborn were sometimes enlisted to produce more warriors. The Denastri apparently took no particular pleasure from sex, and reproduction was a matter of cultural ceremony rather than biological urge. For the females, however, reproduction was a deadly obligation. The birthing process always resulted in one male and three female offspring—and the death of the mother. The females were barely half the size of the males, and could not survive the lengthy and demanding Denastri version of pregnancy.

The males, apparently, didn't survive very long, either. The Empire hadn't been on Denastri long enough to have good statistics, and the Denastri hadn't bothered to keep any, but it seemed that the average life span was only about thirty years. Thus, not all Sixthborns lived long enough to complete their reproductive cycle; in consequence, there were many Firstborn but few Sixthborn. The likely reason was that the Denastri hadn't taken very good care of their planet. Nuclear and chemical waste abounded, and the many wars had left a legacy of a high background radiation count. As a result, the surface of the planet was a bleak, barren terrain, bereft of all but the hardiest vegetation; most agricultural production took place underground.

Females who were not selected for reproduction by a certain age—and thus, survived—became the "old maids" who were exclusively responsible for all agricultural production. They fed the males selected foods, according to the order of their birth, resulting in distinct physical differences between each caste. Firstborns had

sallow yellow skin and were barely five feet high. Fourth-
and Fifthborn warriors were brawny, well over six feet,
and had an orangish tint to their flesh. The Sixthborn
were crimson-colored and nearly seven feet tall. Terrans
could thus identify members of each caste simply by
looking at them. Differences between members of the
different Superclans were much more subtle, but readily
apparent to the Denastri, if not to humans.

For convenience, the Terrans had labeled the three
Superclans A, B, and C, but the true clan names had
deep significance for the Denastri: Strong Rock Rising
High from the Plain; Delightful Water Flowing Down
from the Hills; and Eternal Wind Blowing Free Through
the Sky. A, B, C—Rock, Water, Wind.

The politics of the three Superclans were infuriat-
ingly complex to Terrans, but revolved around differing
interpretations of the rituals performed by the Sixthborn.
Superclan A (Rock) was the most open and cooperative,
and the Terrans had accordingly installed them as leaders
of the new government. Superclan B (Water) generally
tried to ignore the humans, but would cooperate if com-
pelled to do so. The members of Superclan C (Wind)
were unremittingly hostile to humans and led the insurgency against the Occupation—although it seemed that
As and Bs were sometimes involved, as well.

The planet consisted of three main continents, and on
each, the population mix was about sixty–thirty–ten.
Before the arrival of the Empire, Superclan C had dominated the world from its ancient capital city on the continent of Lataka, where the Cs were in the majority. The
Terrans had overthrown the Cs and installed the As as the
new leaders, which made them, in effect, a minority government on Lataka, where the insurgency was centered.
There was only sporadic resistance on the other two continents, which were dominated, respectively, by As and Bs.

Denastri was an ancient world, 8 billion years old,
whose geological fires had long since ebbed. Mountain-

building had ceased, and now erosion ruled. The highest peaks on Lataka, in the Southern Hemisphere, were worn-down nubs to the north of the capital city of Enkar, just two thousand meters above sea level. The Denastri had incautiously denuded their land, adding to the erosion problem, and few trees remained to oppose the cold, strong winds that swept across the continent. A broad, flat, empty plain stretched southward from the capital, eventually sloping into the sea, two thousand five hundred kilometers away.

Two billion years earlier, when the local star was brighter, that plain had been home to a vast tropical rain forest. Then the star cooled, and the forest died off and was covered by the alluvial runoff from the steadily diminishing mountains. As the sediments accumulated, the remains of the forest compressed and congealed and formed a thick layer of what the Terrans called HCH, or Highly Compressed Hydrocarbons. The stuff was similar to coal, only better. But the Denastri physicists had discovered nuclear energy early in their history, and their civilization had made scant use of the HCH. Being better physicists than chemists, the Denastri had never explored the potential uses of their greatest resource. And now, what the Denastri had failed to do, the Terrans would.

Imperium had already begun mining the huge HCH deposits south of the capital, and KemTek was in the process of setting up refineries that would extract every usable molecule from the black, carbon-rich rocks. Synthetic materials of every description and a million profitable uses could be produced from the riches hidden beneath the bleak, dun-colored plains of Lataka. The considerable cost of conquering and occupying Denastri would be repaid a thousandfold over time. It was only a question of suppressing the insurgency and getting on with business. It should have been easy.

Only it wasn't.

* * *

Gloria looked up from her pad and rubbed her weary eyes. Across the narrow aisle, Petra was stretched out on her bunk, staring at her own pad.

"The Denastri are weird," Gloria announced.

"Everybody's weird," Petra replied. She looked at Gloria, smiled, and added, "Except you and me . . . and sometimes I'm not too sure about you."

"I'm only weird when I want to be," Gloria protested. "What I want right now, I think, is some dinner, and maybe a couple of glasses of that DryWine goop."

"That just proves you're weird. Make mine a double."

Gloria crawled out of her bunk and took a couple of steps forward to the food locker and the 'wave. She dug out two packets of chicken à la wallpaper paste, got them cooking, then mixed two glasses of the DryWine concoction. Petra joined her in the tiny galley, clinked glasses with her, and swilled down a big gulp of the purple fluid. "Ahhh," she sighed in ersatz satisfaction. "The Dexta life! Glamour, adventure, and gourmet comestibles! Who wouldn't envy us?"

After dinner and a couple of glasses of the potent DryWine, Gloria decided to tell Petra about her unspoken mission to rescue Lord Kenarbin. Petra ought to know, she figured, just in case something unfortunate happened. She was sure she could trust Petra with the secret; she had even confided some details of the Fifth of October conspiracy to Petra, certain that she would never say anything about it.

"Charles and Trish never actually *said* anything, but it was clear that they wanted me to try. Norman didn't say anything, either, and I don't really know where he stands on this. But the whole situation is a huge black eye for the Empire. If we can't protect someone as important as Lord Kenarbin, it makes us look pretty bad."

"Do you know what you're going to do?" Petra asked.

"I have no idea. I guess I'll just have to wait until we get there and see what's possible—if anything. Whatever I do, it will have to be secret. I can't be seen doing anything that looks like negotiations."

"Well, there is one obvious way to get him back."

"Oh? And what's that?"

"You heard what Karno said the other day, didn't you? Just pull *everyone* out. We had no business being there in the first place."

Gloria sipped some more of the DryWine, then stared across the table at Petra. "That's pretty simplistic, isn't it?"

"Maybe. But that doesn't make it any less true."

"People on the other worlds in the Cluster might disagree," Gloria pointed out. "The Denastri have been a threat to them for millennia."

"And vice versa. It's their fight, not ours."

"So we should just stand back and let our trade partners get attacked by the local bad guys?"

"We could protect our trade," Petra maintained, "without invading and occupying Denastri. What good have we really done? Spirit, Gloria, we only have 18,000 troops there to pacify and occupy an entire planet!"

"You're forgetting the new Denastri government's forces. We've trained and equipped 145,000 of them so far. Anyway, our technological advantage acts as a force multiplier. The insurgents are using old chemical weapons; they don't even have plasma technology."

"They do now," Petra pointed out. Lately, plasma weapons supplied to the government army had been turning up in the hands of the insurgents.

Gloria pursed her lips. "That's a problem," she conceded. "But the fact is, we're committed to Denastri. We're not going to pull out."

"But we *should*," Petra insisted. "The expansionist policy is killing us! Denastri is a perfect example of the whole problem in miniature. Do you realize that if we push the Frontier out just a hundred light-years, that would increase the total volume of Empire space by a *third*? Albert calls it 'Imperial overreach.' He says it's the thing that brings down every empire, sooner or later."

"Oh, really?"

"Absolutely. Albert says that Napoleon could have maintained a stable, enduring empire between the Pyrenees and Poland. Instead, he extended the war into Spain, then invaded Russia, and that doomed him. The same thing happened to the Americans after they started picking fights halfway around the world. Albert says that the more territory you dominate, the more you have to defend. He says that, in the long run, our whole policy is self-defeating."

"Is that so? Well, let me remind you that you and I don't make policy. We just carry it out."

"That's the classic bureaucratic response," Petra said. "If what you're doing isn't working, do more of it. Albert says—"

Gloria abruptly got to her feet. "I think I've heard enough from Albert for one night. I'm going to get some sleep."

She dimmed the lights, walked a few steps aft, and slipped between the sheets of her bunk. She rolled over, away from Petra's side of the ship, to face the blank curving hull of the Flyer. Petra, it seemed to Gloria, had been a lot easier to get along with before she became a scholar.

On the morning of the eleventh day of their trip, the Flyer automatically docked at the new Denastri Orbital Station. Gloria and Petra transferred to a shuttle and descended to the southern continent of Lataka. From above, it looked bleak and forbidding, and no less so from the surface. As soon as they emerged onto the dock, a squad of burly Marines hustled them into a waiting

APC. The armored vehicle quickly rose a few feet off the ground, then followed a zigzagging course toward the capital city of Enkar, a few kilometers distant.

"Why so low?" Gloria asked the sergeant in charge of the squad. "Wouldn't we make better time if we flew higher?"

"We'd also make a better target, ma'am," the sergeant answered, and Gloria was sorry she'd asked.

The outlying towns surrounding the capital looked dismal and impoverished—low dun-colored buildings probably made of brick or adobe, crumbling with age and apparent neglect. The streets were filled with Denastri of varying sizes and hues, most of whom completely ignored the APC as it zipped past them. The few who watched it, peering out from beneath hooded robes, looked hostile and suspicious to Gloria's eyes, but she realized that it was foolish to try to project human emotions onto alien faces. No one shot at them, at least.

Enkar was more impressive. Except for a few soaring towers, it was hidden behind a thirty-meter-high wall that made it look like a city Crusaders might have encountered two thousand years earlier. The wall was studded with more modern-looking observation points, where a few Marines were visible among the native troopers. Extending for several kilometers, the wall was the same drab dun color as nearly everything else on the planet, and, according to the briefing book, had been built some twelve thousand years ago. Over the centuries it had served to keep out many different waves of invaders—but not the Terrans.

The APC paused briefly at what appeared to be the main gate, where a substantial contingent of Marines stood guard. Gloria examined the faces of the sentries, wondering if she might recognize any of them. The Occupation Task Force mainly consisted of the Fifth Imperial Marine Division, which was the same unit that had dispatched a company to Mynjhino, four years earlier. But there had only been two hundred troops in that company, and it was unlikely that she would encounter any of them here. She had been named an honorary member of the First Regiment—First of the Fifth—and still felt a deep sense of comradeship with them; she intended to look up the unit if she had the opportunity. But it might be stationed on one of the other two continents, so she wasn't optimistic about the chance for a reunion.

Inside the city, buildings looked newer, or better maintained, and there were some interesting architectural flourishes, including high, arching bridges between buildings and over canals. Here and there, civic gardens bloomed in meticulously groomed public squares. The streets bustled with pedestrian traffic and odd-looking three-wheeled vehicles, but there were Empire-built skimmers in evidence, as well. Enkar was older than Babylon, but it was active and alive with commerce and culture, as evidenced by blocks-long markets and a huge, ornate structure that reminded Gloria of an opera house.

The Imperial Compound was a city-within-a-city, complete with its own wall. This wall was of Dura-steel mesh, ten meters high, and topped by an electronic sentry system that unleashed plasma bolts on any intruder larger than a fly. Marines in dress uniforms manned the main entrance, where the blue-and-gold Imperial flag fluttered in a stiff breeze. Gloria noticed a number of armored vehicles and combat-ready Marines prowling the street surrounding the Compound. As the APC entered the Compound, the sergeant seemed to breathe a sigh of relief.

The APC halted and settled to the pavement, and Gloria and Petra emerged to find themselves surrounded; the insurgents had failed to spring an ambush, but the media had them cornered. Amid the confusion of shouted questions and probing imagers, Freya Benitez, the Imperial Secretary, led them to safety in the main building of the Consulate—a modern, Terran-built structure of glass and steel.

"Sorry about that," Benitez said once they were inside. "Ever since Lord Kenarbin was abducted, we've had a flood of media reps. And I'm afraid you're going to have to meet with them anyway. We've scheduled a briefing in a few minutes."

"No problem," Gloria assured her. "I'm used to it."

"First, though," Benitez said, "I'll take you upstairs and introduce you to the Governor and General Ohashi. They're pretty eager to meet you, too."

A few minutes later, Benitez made the introductions in a small anteroom just off the main auditorium. Gloria thought Governor Blagodarski looked haggard and distracted, while Ohashi was stiff and reserved, all spit and polish. She asked them if there had been any new developments.

"Politically," Blagodarski said, "the government is still spinning its wheels. We've been trying to get the three Superclans to cooperate better, but they continue to resist our best efforts. The idea of a coalition is still new to them, and the representative from Superclan C keeps threatening to pull out of the talks."

"I see." Gloria turned to Ohashi. "And the insurgency, General?"

"About the same. Scattered incidents. We lost seven more people last week. That's about average."

"And Lord Kenarbin?"

"Nothing," said Blagodarski. "Haven't heard a thing. Do you have any new instructions from Earth?"

Gloria shook her head. "It's become a political football in Parliament," she said, "but, of course, Imperial policy is fixed."

Blagodarski looked disappointed. "I was rather hoping they might . . ."

"They won't," Gloria said flatly. She had already decided not to let Blagodarski know about her secret mission. She turned to Benitez. "As you know, I've been sent here to see about the Dexta situation. Just how bad is it?"

"What have you heard?" Benitez asked cautiously.

"That people are at each other's throats, that factions have formed. Secretary Mingus is seriously concerned."

Benitez took the news stoically, but Gloria knew that Benitez probably had visions of her Dexta career going down the toilet. Which it was.

"I'll give you a full briefing later," Benitez said. "It's not really as bad as you may have been led to think. For the moment, though, I think we should go in to brief the media. Keep it general and upbeat. You know the drill."

Gloria smiled. "Oh, yes, I know the drill."

A swarm of about fifty media reps had gathered in the auditorium. Gloria gave them a friendly smile as she trooped up to the stage with Benitez, Blagodarski, and Ohashi. The media could be irritating, but they had treated her well throughout her career. She knew what they expected of her, and had come prepared; she was dressed in a navy miniskirt and a gray jacket buttoned at the waist—businesslike but sexy. As she ascended the stage, she noticed a number of Marines in the back of the auditorium and in the wings. Quite a few Dexta staffers seemed to be kibitzing, as well.

A Dexta Public Affairs Officer emceed the session. "The Governor, Ms. VanDeen, General Ohashi, and Secretary Benitez will be making brief statements," he said. "However, inasmuch as Ms. VanDeen has only just arrived, we will not be taking any questions today." A chorus of groans and protests arose from the media reps, but the PAO managed to quiet them by promising that a full media briefing would be scheduled within the next day or two. Then he introduced Governor Blagodarski.

Gloria could tell immediately that the relationship between the Governor and the media was strained. The faces of the media reps looked skeptical and contemptuous, and Blagodarski looked and sounded suspicious and wary. He made a few pro forma remarks, then formally welcomed Gloria to his planet. Blagodarski turned the microphone over to Gloria as quickly as he decently could, looking like a tired old farmer who had just finished slopping his hogs.

Smiling and sounding bright and glad to be on Denastri, Gloria said as little as possible. She mentioned that the Emperor and Secretary Mingus were both keeping a close watch on the Denastri situation, and that her mission here did not signal any change in Government policy. "Basically, I'm just here to observe, consult, make recommendations, and report back to Earth. When I know more about the situation on the ground here, I'll have more to say, and I'll be happy to take your questions at that time."

Still smiling, she stepped back from the microphone and let the PAO introduce General Ohashi. The general also welcomed her, then read from a prepared statement that was evidently the usual daily update from the Occupation Task Force HQ. As he spoke, Gloria looked around and spied a familiar face waiting in the wings to her right. She rushed over to the side of the stage and cried, "Alvin!"

Tech Sergeant Alvin Hooper grinned at her. He had saved her life on Mynjhino with some timely moves, and Gloria threw her arms around him and gave him a hard, happy hug.

"I was hoping you'd be here!" Gloria kissed him on his ebony-toned cheek.

"Glad to see you, too, ma'am," he said.

"What about the rest of the company? Are they—"

There was a sudden roaring sound, and Gloria felt herself being thrown into the air. And then, she felt nothing at all.

· 6 ·

Someone was shining a light in her eyes. Gloria groggily tried to focus. She seemed to be in a hospital bed, attended by a doctor and two medtechs. She looked down at herself and was relieved to discover that nothing was missing.

"Ms. VanDeen? I'm Dr. Renoir. How are you feeling?"

"Uh . . . you tell me. How *am* I feeling?"

Renoir smiled. "Pretty good, I trust. We kept you sedated overnight, purely as a precaution. You've suffered a moderate concussion, but it's nothing to be concerned about. There were some lacerations to your right shoulder and arm, but we've administered nanomeds, and you should be as good as new in a few days." Gloria checked her arm and found it swathed in bandages, feeling sore and stiff.

"What happened?"

"There was an explosion," Renoir told her. "A bomb."

"What about . . . the others?"

"We've notified the appropriate people that you're awake, and they'll be along in a few minutes. They'll explain everything. In the meantime, are you hungry?"

Gloria realized that she was, and said so. In short order, she was propped up in bed and served a plateful of watery scrambled eggs, bacon, toast, and a cup of weak tea. Hospital food—a universal constant. She picked at the food and fretted about what had happened.

As she finished the meal, Petra and a Marine officer came into the room. Petra rushed over to her and gave her a gentle hug and a kiss on her cheek. "The doctor says you're going to be fine," Petra assured her. "But you had us worried for a while there."

"Sorry. Petra? What the hell happened? The doctor said it was a bomb."

Petra nodded gravely. "Planted under the stage. If you hadn't gone over to see Sergeant Hooper . . ."

"And the others?"

Petra shook her head. "The Governor, General Ohashi, and Secretary Benitez were all killed, along with seven of the media people and the PAO. Another couple of dozen injured, five seriously. Gloria? This is General Matabele."

"Ma'am," the officer said, tilting his head toward her. He was tall and thin, with high cheekbones and dark, deep-set eyes; he looked to be of Indo-African descent. "Hope you're feeling better."

"Thank you, General. Uh . . . are you in charge now?"

Matabele shook his head. "No, ma'am," he said. "You are."

Gloria quickly looked at Petra, who nodded in confirmation. "Gloria, with the Governor and the ImpSec dead, there's no one left higher than a XIII. There's not even an UnderSec for Admin—she resigned a month ago. You're *it*."

"We sent off a courier to Earth," Matabele said, "but it will be at least eleven days before we get a response, and that will probably just confirm the obvious. Until they can send us a new Governor, as Acting Imperial Secretary, you would automatically become Interim Governor, as well."

"I see," Gloria said slowly. It was hardly welcome news, but she'd filled the same role on Mynjhino, four years earlier. But Denastri was a mess, and now, suddenly, it was *her* mess. "And you command the Marines now, General Matabele?"

"Yes, ma'am. I was second to Steve Ohashi as Occupation Task Force Commander, so I take his place. We were already short two colonels on our TO, so we'll have to do some reshuffling of division and regimental command, but we're covered. But I'll be taking my orders from you, ma'am, if you have any."

"Not at the moment. And, General, I'm sorry about the loss of General Ohashi."

"Thank you, ma'am. He was a good man, the best CO I've ever served under. This should never have happened."

"How *did* it happen? I saw at least three layers of security coming in. How could they have planted a bomb in the middle of the Consulate?"

"We'd like to know that, too, ma'am," Matabele said. "We're working on it. The Nasties have a pretty elaborate organization inside the city."

"Nasties?"

"The Denastri, ma'am. It's what we call 'em."

"Not anymore, General," Gloria said. "I don't want to hear command personnel using that term. I realize that the troops will still use it, but try to discourage it. Is that clear?"

Matabele straightened and stiffened. "Yes, ma'am," he said.

Gloria looked around. Soft, vaguely orange-tinted light was filtering in through a window. "What time is it?" she asked.

"About ten," Petra said. "The doctor says you can leave here in about an hour. I'll get some clothes for you. We've already moved your things into the Governor's Residence."

"I see." Gloria reached up and ran her hand through her hair. She felt a substantial bump on the back of her head, but it didn't hurt much. She tried to organize her thoughts.

"Petra? I'm appointing you Acting UnderSec for Administration. I realize it's a job for a XIII, but . . ."

"No problem. Any orders, Madame Governor?"

Gloria frowned at Petra's use of the title; that was going to take some getting used to. But she realized that it was important to restore, as quickly as possible, a sense of order and continuity. She would rather not have moved into the Governor's Residence, but that, too, was a symbolic necessity.

"I'd like you to call a meeting of all UnderSecs for, say, two o'clock. General, I'd like you and your senior people to attend, as well."

"Very well, ma'am."

"And Petra? See if you can get the senior Corporate people to come, too. We might as well get acquainted with all the players as soon as possible."

"Check. Anything else?"

"Not . . . no, wait. Was Alvin Hooper hurt in the explosion?"

"He's fine."

"Good. Tell him he's my new military aide. With your permission, General."

"I'll see to it, ma'am," Matabele said: "I take it you know him?"

"From Mynjhino. He saved my life."

"Yes, ma'am. Let's just hope that he doesn't have to do it again."

"My thought exactly," Gloria told him.

✿   ✿   ✿

Gloria wandered around the Governor's Residence, feeling very much alone. Every trace of Governor Blagodarski's presence had already been removed, except for some old books on a shelf in the bedroom. They seemed to be reprints of classics, for people who wanted to read them in the classic format: Plutarch, Aurelius, Lao-tse, Gibbon, Swift, Voltaire, Adams and Jefferson, Xi Qan. Had Blagodarski been trying to commune with great minds of the past, or was he merely seeking escape from the sprawling complexity of the thirty-third century? People had less to think about in those days, so perhaps they thought about the things that they did think about more deeply. *Easier then,* she thought. *Simpler.*

She flexed her wounded arm and found it functional but slightly painful. Another narrow escape, another near miss. *Spirit, how many times?* It didn't bear thinking about. Not now. Later maybe, late at night after some drinks. Some of Norman's prized Belgravian whisky, perhaps. She wondered if she could find any of it on this miserable planet. Maybe Alvin would know. That was the kind of thing Marines always seemed to know.

Interim Imperial Governor again. She'd held the post for a couple of months on Mynjhino, and might very well hold it at least that long on Denastri. It would take six days for the robot courier to reach Earth and, even assuming rapid decision-making at the other end, another six days to get a response. If Charles immediately appointed a new Imperial Governor, it would still take him or her eleven days to reach Denastri via Flyer. But ImpGovs generally traveled with an entourage, which meant a Cruiser instead of a Flyer. A Cruiser would take sixteen or seventeen days to make the journey. Realistically, then, she couldn't expect a replacement for at least three to four weeks. And if Charles dragged his feet or had trouble finding someone who was willing to handle such a hot potato, she might wind up holding it herself for a month or two.

Gloria sat down on the edge of the governor's bed and stared off into space. Responsibility, she thought—a funny thing. You wanted it, you worked for it, and when you got it, you wanted more of it. Then, still more. And yet, it weighed you down, pulled at you like a high-gravity world. Denastri was just .89 G, but it felt like much more than that. A third of the population was hostile, and the other two-thirds—who could say? Aliens were alien. It said that in the Dexta training manuals she'd pored over seven years ago, when she was a brand-new Level XV. *Spirit—seven years, already?*

Aliens were alien. She hadn't even met any of them yet. That would have to be corrected. She would need to schedule a meeting with the Premier as soon as possible, tomorrow, maybe. The Premier—3A-27-12J. What the hell kind of name was that? What kind of being was he? How could she hope to understand him?

And yet, her real problem would not be the Denastri. It would be the humans—squabbling bureaucrats, greedy Corpos, angry Marines. Humans weren't always easy to understand, either, but they were familiar. The glamorous, alluring, crafty Gloria VanDeen knew how to handle humans, oh yes. Just bat your big blues, flash a little skin, say the right words, and they'd fall all over themselves, trying to make you happy.

It had worked that way in the lower levels of Dexta, at least, and had even proven an effective strategy in dealing with the upper levels—up to a point. But she was a Level IX now, and swaying her shapely hips could take her only so far. The game was getting serious. This wasn't just some backwater world like Mynjhino or Sylvania. New Cambridge had been different—an emergency—and her many strategic interventions for OSI had, in truth, been pretty small potatoes. But Denastri was center stage, with an election and maybe the future of the

Empire hanging in the balance. And the responsibility—
the great, groaning weight of it —was all hers.

Governor VanDeen.

Petra, efficient as always, had already learned names
and faces, and stood next to Gloria at the entrance of the
conference room and made introductions as people filed
in. No introduction was necessary, however, for the last
man in.

"Delbert!" Gloria cried. She instinctively started to
hug him, but managed to restrain herself. Governors
didn't do that. She settled for clasping his extended hand
in both of hers and grinning at him. "Maj—uh, *Colonel*! I
was hoping you'd be here!"

He returned the grin. "Madame Governor," he said
with a little nod of his head, "it's great to see you again.
I'm very glad you're here."

General Matabele cleared his throat. "Colonel
Barnes," he said, "was CO of the First Regiment. After
what happened yesterday, I've promoted him to command of the division. I gather you know each other from
Mynjhino."

Gloria released her hold on Barnes's hand and
pointed to a service ribbon on his chest. "I've still got
mine," she said. "I wear it every Empire Day."

"*Semper Fi*," Barnes said. He was a stocky, solidly
built man, with short, spiky brown hair, a square jaw, and
steady gray eyes. He turned to Matabele and said, "The
Governor's an honorary member of the First of the Fifth,
General."

"We'll talk later, okay?" Gloria said. "Right now, I
think we'd better get started."

Gloria took her place at the base of a U-shaped conference table. Petra slid a piece of paper toward her,
showing who was sitting where. To the left were representatives of the Bank of Earth, Imperium, KemTek, and

Servitor, along with Matabele and Barnes. On her right sat the UnderSecretaries for Finance, Corporate Affairs, and Security. In addition to Petra, a Level XIV from Admin was also present.

She made a few general opening remarks, expressing regret for the recent losses they had suffered and determination to carry on. "As you may be aware," she said, "Denastri has become a major political issue in the Empire. The abduction of Lord Kenarbin and, frankly, my own presence have magnified the media attention, and consequently, everything that happens here will be viewed under a microscope. We can't let that become a distraction. I suggest that we all just concentrate on the work at hand and let somebody else worry about politics and the media."

She looked to her right, at the Dexta people. "Originally," she said, "my mission here was to deal with the Dexta situation. Obviously, that has changed. As Interim Governor, I'll be directly involved in everything that happens here. I've had a full briefing, but I need to get better acquainted with the situation on the ground. To that end, I'd like to go once around the table and have each of you give me a concise summary of your position, the major problems you face, and anything that you believe needs my immediate attention. Ms. Fujiwara, we'll begin with you."

Linda Fujiwara was a dapper, attractive woman with long black hair and a banker's precise, studied manner. Bank of Earth, she reported, was primarily concerned with integrating the Denastri economy with that of the Empire. Progress was being made, and a number of new corporate entities had been created, mainly to service the Empire Corporates. Native Denastri currency was still in widespread use, but the Imperial crown was gaining acceptance. The Denastri had no banks, as such, but relied on central repositories controlled by each of the three Superclans. They cooperated with one another and the BOE, but resisted large-scale economic planning. The major problem, in Fujiwara's view, was the lack of security, which undermined investor confidence and made it difficult to attract capital.

Imperium, represented by Dimitri Ramirez, was the major Corporate player on Denastri. They had set up a large mining operation one hundred kilometers south of Enkar, and had three giant Extractors at work, with more on the way. For now, they were simply stockpiling most of the HCH they dug up; the raw product was too bulky to be shipped economically. Full-scale production awaited the completion of KemTek's refinery, which was about two months away from startup. Gordon Overstreet, the KemTek rep, agreed that the main problem was security. A Transit had been established, allowing senior personnel quick and safe travel between Enkar and the mining facilities; but most workers, both human and native, lived on-site, in a rapidly expanding city known to the humans as Scooptown. Security there, the responsibility of Servitor, was proving to be a nightmare.

"We've got five thousand of our people out there," explained the Servitor chief, Sally Voelker, "surrounded by fifty thousand Nasties. Most of them are employed as service workers, which means they have pretty free access to the town and the site. We're trying to regulate that, but the government can't or won't let us do what needs to be done. The result is that we're losing people to insurgent attacks, both directly and through attrition. People don't want to work and live where they aren't safe."

"So you say you need better cooperation from the Denastri government?" Gloria asked.

"That, and a more active Marine presence." Voelker turned to Matabele. "I know you're stretched thin, General, but the mining is what it's all about. If Imperium can't dig up those rocks, we might as well just pack up and go home."

Matabele and Voelker stared at each other for a long moment, during which Gloria learned volumes. The Marine general glared at Voelker the way he might have looked at a French poodle that had just peed on his spit-shined boots. And Voelker made a plausible poodle; she was a small, shapely woman, with curling flame-colored hair and coldly seductive blue eyes. She seemed to be a Corporate version of a Dexta Tiger, clad in a deeply slashed blue dress that made Gloria feel downright conservative in her loose-fitting gray pantsuit.

"We recognize the needs of the Corporate community, Ms. Voelker," Matabele said at last. "However, we have many other commitments."

"Speaking of those commitments," Gloria said, anxious to forestall a confrontation, "could you give me a brief description of your deployments, General?"

"Of course, Governor VanDeen," Matabele said, averting his frosty gaze from Voelker. "As you know, we have a total of 17,600 combat and support personnel, in six regiments. First, Third, and Fifth Regiments are based in and around Enkar, including two companies at Scooptown. In addition, the Second Regiment is scattered around the southern fringe of the continent, based at various port cities. The Fourth is on the continent of Banako, and the Sixth is on Senka."

"Where they aren't needed at all," Voelker put in. "The insurgency is practically nonexistent on Senka, and there's nothing worthwhile up there, anyway. Those troops should be brought back here, where they're needed."

Matabele didn't even glance at her. "Superclan A is the dominant group on Senka, Governor," he said. "While there is little resistance on Senka, it would be politically impossible to withdraw our forces from that continent. That was Governor Blagodarski's position, anyway. The As are our only friends here, and if they thought we were abandoning them on their home continent, that would have a negative effect on the government here, which, as you know, is led by the As."

"I see," said Gloria.

"Governor —"

Gloria held up her hand. "Thank you, Ms. Voelker. We can discuss this in detail some other time. For now, I'm just trying to get an overview. General, just how serious is the resistance around Enkar? I mean, aside from terrorist attacks, like yesterday's. Who actually controls the territory?"

Matabele looked at Colonel Barnes. "The Colonel can give you the operational picture."

Barnes shrugged slightly. "It's not quite that straightforward, Gl—uh, Governor," he said. "Basically, we control the ground we're standing on, while we're standing on it. The rest of the time, the insurgents have a substantial measure of control."

"Just what are we talking about, here?" Gloria asked. "I saw a lot of suburbs surrounding Enkar. Do we control them, or do the insurgents?"

"In the immediate area," Barnes said, "I would say that we have effective control."

Gloria nodded. "I'd like to see for myself," she said. "Do you suppose you could arrange for a tour, say, tomorrow?"

Matabele and Barnes glanced at each other. "I wouldn't recommend that, Governor," Matabele said.

"General, I can't govern this world if I spend all my time locked up in the capital. If we have effective control of the area surrounding Enkar, then I should be able to make a quick tour. Would you see to it, please?"

"Yes, ma'am," Matabele said.

"Now, as to Dexta." Gloria looked to her right, where the bureaucrats quickly sat up straight. "We've had a number of reports that are, frankly, appalling. We've been hearing stories about factions and feuds, contributing to inefficiency and outright incompetence. I can tell

BURDENS OF EMPIRE • 75

you that Secretary Mingus is seriously upset by all of this—as am I. If it proves necessary, I won't hesitate to replace every last one of you and start over with a new staff fresh from HQ. For now, I'd like a brief overview. We'll start with Finance. Mr. Danelli?"

Frederick Danelli, a slick, dark-haired man of about thirty, gave Gloria a friendly, if slightly nervous, smile. "Governor," he said, "Finance is doing fine, contrary to what you may have heard. We're working hand in glove with BOE to integrate the local economy, and we're making substantial progress. We won't give you any problems."

"I'm glad to hear it," Gloria told him. "And Corporate? UnderSecretary Wong?"

Edgar Wong—a short, chubby, Buddha-like man— offered a placid smile. "No problems here, either, Governor VanDeen. The Corporates tell us what they need, and we try to provide it. That would be much easier if Security and Admin held up their end, but we—"

"Cram it, Wong!" The wiry young man sitting next to Wong looked ready to do physical violence.

"UnderSecretary McCray?" Gloria interceded. "I take it you have a dissenting opinion to offer?"

"Damn right I do, Governor. Security is doing everything it possibly can with the resources we have available."

"You did a swell job yesterday, didn't you, Jack?" Wong taunted. "They're still scraping pieces of Freya off the walls."

McCray started to lunge at Wong, but Gloria snapped, "That will be enough, gentlemen!"

McCray managed to restrain himself and returned to his chair. "I apologize, Governor, but I don't have to take shit like that from this fat bastard."

"I agree, Mr. McCray," Gloria said. "UnderSecretary Wong, your comment was completely uncalled for. And Mr. McCray, the next time you try to attack one of your coworkers will be the last. Is that understood? Look, people, we've just suffered a tragedy, and I know you've all lost friends. But if we give in to our emotions, we'll never get anywhere. I know it's a bad time, but let's try to be professional."

Wong nodded slightly and maintained his calm smile. "My apologies, Madame Governor. And to you as well, Jack. I was overcome by my deep emotions." To Gloria, Wong looked like a man who had never felt a deep emotion in his life, but his apology, if not necessarily sincere, was at least adequate.

Gloria turned to the last of the Dexta people, a thin, tired-looking young Level XIV named Gina Swenson. "Ms. Swenson," she said, "I know that you were next in line to serve as UnderSec for Admin, but Petra and I have worked together for years, and I wanted her in that slot."

Swenson gave her a wan smile. "It's okay, Governor," she said. "I understand. I don't mind."

"Nevertheless," Gloria continued, "I want you to work closely with Petra. Your experience here is valuable. Is there anything you'd like to say?"

She shook her head. "Not really. Just that things are a mess here. Everything you heard is right. It's been . . . awful." A tear rolled down the young woman's cheek, and she quickly turned away from Gloria.

Gloria couldn't think of anything to say. She was saved by the arrival of a Level XV she didn't know. The aide whispered in her ear, and Gloria got to her feet.

"Thank you all for coming," she said. "I'll be talking with each of you, individually, in the next few days. But right now, I'm afraid I'm needed elsewhere. It seems that the Denastri Premier has come to pay a call."

Gloria met 3A-27-12J outside the Governor's Residence, where a swarm of media reps recorded the scene. She made a brief statement, expressing regret over the events of the previous day; mainly, she just wanted to show everyone that she was all right and that the Imperial Government was still functioning. The Premier, through his translation software, also made a short statement that was a little vague but conveyed the appropriate sentiments.

Inside, Gloria conferred with the Premier alone in an ornate, lavishly appointed drawing room. The Denastri was about as tall as Gloria and, it seemed to her, moved with a fluid grace as they sat down next to each other on a divan. They were not an unattractive species, but the vertical eyes and piscine mouth took some getting used to, and the drooping triangular ears looked faintly comical.

The Premier spoke first, and Gloria's pad rendered his words as "We are mostly sad regarding your appearance as Imperial Governor, Terran female. Governor Blagodarski was respectable in our eyes and will be regretted. You are not for long, yes?"

Gloria thought she grasped his meaning. "I am the Interim Governor, Honored Premier. A permanent Governor will be assigned as soon as possible. For now, I have the same authority and responsibilities as Governor Blagodarski."

The Denastri listened to the translation and flicked his nictitating membranes back and forth a few times. "You will feed the Marine general, yes?"

That one stopped Gloria for a moment. Feed? Instruct? "General Matabele and the Marines will take their orders from me," she said.

The narrow slits of the alien's eyes seemed to widen. "This is—*unknown word*—among Terrans?" he asked.

"I am the senior representative of the Empire on this world. In a case like this, it is standard procedure for me to assume the Governorship."

The Premier seemed confused. "You feed the most exalted Emperor?" he asked.

Gloria couldn't help smiling at that. "Well, I used to," she said. "I mean, Honored Premier, that the Emperor has sent me to Denastri to help your people and restore order to your beautiful world. We must bring an end to the violence and destruction."

"Yes. A goodness. Not for much time, yes? A Terran Thirdborn will come?"

"As soon as possible," Gloria agreed.

The Premier stared at her. "A strangeness," he said. "This humble Thirdborn is mostly in awe of the great Terran Empire, but understanding is—*possible meanings include 'hungry' and 'lacking.'* "

"What don't you understand, Honored Premier?"

"A great strangeness," he said. "Terrans are different. This is understood by this humble Thirdborn, but Firstborns and Secondborns will be empty. Fifthborns will be hungry. Exalted Sixthborns must find wisdom of this."

Gloria tried to take it all in. "You're saying that other Denastri won't understand, and you must consult with the exalted Sixthborn of your clan? But what won't they understand?"

"You are woman. Female. Yes?"

Gloria nodded. "Yes," she said.

"A great strangeness," said the Premier of Denastri. "You are—*succession of unknown words.* Yes. A great strangeness."

I'll buy that, Gloria thought.

· 7 ·

The Fifthborn looked down at Gloria and bowed his head. "This humble Fifthborn," Gloria's pad translated, "is cognizant of the great honor of escorting the revered Imperial Governor. All of my clan bids you a gratifying welcome to our world."

"Thank you, General . . . uh . . . 5A-46-9C," Gloria replied. "And I look forward to seeing your people and your world."

Carrot-colored and six and a half feet tall, the Denastri officer wore a dun-colored hooded robe that was distinguished by three orange lightning bolts angling downward from his shoulders to his waist. A plasma pistol was holstered on a wide black belt. In his right hand, he carried what looked like a riding crop or, perhaps, a swagger stick. He looked formidable and efficient.

"The general's troops will lead off," Colonel Barnes explained. "We'll be taking a lap around the exterior of the Compound, just to give you a look at the city."

"And then we'll go outside the walls?"

"If you insist." Barnes didn't look very pleased by the prospect.

"I do," Gloria assured him.

Barnes sighed. "You're the boss," he said.

"I'm the Governor. Relax, Delbert, it'll be fine."

They got into the back of a long limo skimmer, along with Sergeant Hooper and a Denastri Fourthborn, who was a little shorter and a more subdued tone of orange than his general. Barnes and the Denastri commander spoke a few words into their wristcoms, and the procession got under way. Half a dozen Marine vehicles surrounded the limo, and up ahead, a hundred or more Denastri troops trotted along in formation, Terran plasma rifles held at port arms.

It seemed like a major operation for what was supposed to be no more than a brief tour, but Gloria accepted the necessity. Having just lost one Imperial Governor, the Marines and the Denastri Home Guard were not about to risk losing another.

There were not many Denastri to be seen in the streets, and those she did see were backed up against the walls of buildings, giving the procession a wide berth. Nearly all of them were short, sallow First- and Secondborns, peering out from beneath their hooded robes in what looked like apprehension and suspicion. Gloria tried to imagine herself in their place, and decided that she would probably feel suspicious, too. Who were these arrogant, pushy invaders who had arrived so suddenly and upset the established order? What did they want and why were they here?

Barnes provided a running commentary, pointing out sights of interest. The immense building she'd seen upon arrival turned out to be not an opera house, but a religious shrine, the holiest in all of Lataka. It was the home base for Superclan C, but currently under the control of Superclan A. "Imagine Hindus taking over the Vatican," Barnes said, "or Baptists occupying the

Spiritists' Mother Church in Rio. It's the source of a lot of resentment."

"I should think so," Gloria said. "Can we stop and take a look inside?"

"An impossibility of great completeness, Honored Governor," said the Denastri general. "Request to yourself by exalted Sixthborns is of necessity, almost."

"Access by invitation only," Barnes amplified. He pointed at a large building off to the right, apparently trying to change the subject. "That's the headquarters of Enkar Trust," he said. "It's sort of a holding company for a bunch of small factories and service industries that we've managed to establish. They do business with Imperium and KemTek, and they've actually been quite helpful."

"Who runs it?"

"Superclan A Thirdborns, of course."

"Only As?"

"They employ some Bs and Cs, but the As are in charge. That's true of practically everything."

"Sounds like another source of resentment."

Barnes nodded. "Before the Occupation, the Cs ran the show here. We've upset the applecart, and the locals aren't very happy about it. We try to get the As to be more equitable in the distribution of wealth and power, but their cooperation is, well, grudging, at best."

The Denastri general said something short and emphatic. Gloria's pad said only, *"Unknown word. Possibly pejorative."*

They came to one of the vast, open markets that Gloria had seen earlier. "Stop," Gloria said. "I want to get out and take a look around."

With seeming reluctance, Barnes issued the appropriate order. The limo halted, and Sergeant Hooper sprang out of his seat and opened the door. Gloria stepped out and took a deep breath; she wrinkled her nose at the sudden infusion of a thousand pungent, unfamiliar scents. Before her, long tables were spread out, sagging under the weight of fruits, vegetables, nuts, and berries.

From her briefing book, Gloria knew that the Denastri were primarily vegetarians, although they did consume some shellfish and crustaceans. There were no large animals left on the planet; the last of them had disappeared millennia ago. Indeed, aside from a few birds, the Denastri were virtually alone on their world. A team from the Imperial Exo-Paleontology Survey was at work, cataloging the vanished species of Denastri.

Gloria strolled over to one of the tables and idly hefted a melon. "Don't eat anything," Barnes warned her.

"I know," she said. The native foodstuffs of Denastri were entirely inedible for humans. Everything the Terrans ate had to be imported, at considerable expense. There would never be trendy Denastri restaurants on Manhattan's Upper West Side.

Standing near one of the tables, Gloria saw, for the first time, a Denastri female. She had seen images of them, but seeing one in the flesh was a bit of a shock. The female was barely four feet tall and almost spherical in shape. Her body was hidden under a flowing robe and her face all but concealed within the recesses of a shadowy hood, but Gloria could sense the impassive gaze of her vertical almond eyes. As she looked around, she noticed a number of other females, each apparently tending her own table of produce. She also noticed that the customers, all males, were segregated by caste; there seemed to be tables exclusively for Firstborn, Secondborn, and Thirdborn.

"Females are responsible for all the agricultural production," Barnes explained. "The agplexes are outside the city, on and under the plains. There seems to be some complex system of distribution, according to caste, but to tell you the truth, we don't really understand it.

The Denastri are reluctant to talk about it, and we haven't pushed the issue. In fact, they rarely even mention the females."

Gloria nodded. "Yes," she said, "I got the impression that the Premier was a bit nonplussed to find himself dealing with a Terran female."

"That's an understatement," Barnes told her. He glanced at the Denastri officer, who was several paces away, then quietly said, "Our friend the general is amazed that we're willing to take orders from you. He considers that, well . . . degrading. You should try to avoid giving him any direct orders."

"If I want anything, I'll go through you."

"That would be best."

"How do the civilians feel about having a female Governor?"

"Who the hell knows?" Barnes shook his head. "The Thirdborn seem to be able to accommodate themselves to our barbarian ways pretty well, but the First- and Secondborn—it's anybody's guess."

"Let's find out, then," Gloria said. She walked over to where three Firstborn were standing, watching her in frozen silence.

Gloria took her pad out of a pocket and hit a switch that would translate and audibly transmit her words to the Firstborn, who would not have their own translation devices. She smiled and said, "Good morning, gentlemen. How are you today?"

The three Firstborn seemed to cower, in evident shock and bewilderment. They said nothing.

"I'm Gloria VanDeen, the new Imperial Governor," she said, then paused as the pad rendered her words into Denastrian. "Are you shopping for food? It looks delicious."

One of the Firstborn angrily, it seemed, spat out a few words. "Terran female!" the pad translated, adding helpfully, *"Tone conveys shock, possibly outrage or confusion."*

Gloria tried again. "These melons look like food we have on Earth," she said. "We call them cantaloupes. What do you call them?"

A female suddenly dashed over, interposing herself between Gloria and the Firstborn. "Know your place, Terran female!" she cried. "Food is *unknown word*. Food!"

"I'm sorry," Gloria told the female. "I was just —"

The female screeched at her. "Improper! Improper! *Unknown word*. Food!"

The Denastri general suddenly stepped between them and savagely swiped his swagger stick across the face of the female. The force of the blow bowled her over, and she literally rolled into the Firstborn, who jumped out of the way as if trying to avoid a cannonball.

"General!" Gloria shouted. "Stop it."

The Denastri general whirled around and faced Gloria. His fishy mouth dropped open, and his nictitating membranes blinked furiously for a moment. Then he angrily stomped away, back to the limo.

"Big mistake, Gloria," Barnes said softly as he took her arm and maneuvered her away from the market table. "You've publicly disgraced him."

"But—"

"Just get back in the limo and keep your mouth shut . . . Madame Governor. Let me handle this."

As the convoy got under way again, Barnes tried to soothe the feelings of the disgruntled Denastri general, but didn't seem to accomplish much. Finally, the general addressed Gloria. "Honored Imperial Governor," he said, "this humble Fifthborn is understanding of difficulties between your people and mine. Strangeness is mostly all the time. Food is—*unknown word*. Improper to speak of it for Terran female to—*pejorative adjective*—Firstborn Wind-clan. Denastri female—

unknown word. Feeding of selves is—*unknown word, possibly 'sacred'*—obligation. Terran female must not interfere. Honor of yourself, myself, made unclean by your words to this humble Fifthborn. Understanding strangeness, this humble Fifthborn—*indeterminate phrase, possibly 'makes allowances.'* Exalted Sixthborn will make clean. A goodness."

"He understands and forgives you for your ignorance, I think," Barnes said. "But he'll need some sort of absolution from a Sixthborn to recover his honor. And try not to mention food, if you can help it. It's a sensitive subject around here."

Gloria nodded toward the general. "I apologize for my improper behavior, General," she said. "I did not intend to dishonor you in any way."

"*Unknown word,*" said the general.

At the main gate, the convoy came to a halt and everyone got out of the limo. Barnes gestured toward a waiting APC. "We'll switch to more appropriate transportation," he explained.

"What do you mean?" Gloria demanded. "I won't be able to see anything from inside that thing. And nobody will be able to see *me.*"

"You'll be able to see fine," Barnes told her. "There are some ports, and plenty of viewscreens. As for being seen . . . well, it's better if you're not."

"But the whole point of this trip is to show the flag," Gloria protested. "We need to let the population see that we can't be stopped by terrorist attacks. They need to see that there's still an Imperial Governor."

"There won't be if you stay in that limo," Barnes said.

"I thought you said we'd be traveling through areas where we have effective control."

"We will. But there's a big difference between 'effective' and 'absolute.'"

Annoyed, Gloria dug in her heels. "Dammit, Delbert," she said, "we can't let ourselves be intimidated. I want to stay in the limo. I'm willing to take the risk."

"Maybe you are, but I'm not. I have my orders, and they don't include suicide missions in unarmored limos. If you want to change my orders, you'll have to go through General Matabele. And he'll just tell you the same thing." He smiled and gestured again to the APC. "After you . . . Madame Governor."

Gloria scowled, then accepted the inevitable and boarded the APC. A moment later, the gate opened and the APC glided forward. Outside the city, an entire armored convoy was waiting to escort her through the suburbs. Overhead, nimble Marine SALs (Sea-Air-Land vehicles) skittered back and forth like nervous hawks.

She couldn't see much through the ports, but an array of viewscreens gave her limited vision in every direction. Ahead, Marine vehicles were strung out for a kilometer, slowly skimming down a long, sloping road that led to the river, perhaps three kilometers distant. Ramshackle dun-colored buildings lined the roadway, with connecting cross streets trailing off into dense, jungly neighborhoods. Clusters of Denastri gathered at some of the intersections, staring at the procession in glum, wary silence.

"Can I get out and talk to them?" Gloria asked.

Barnes didn't quite laugh. "I wouldn't recommend it," he said.

"Unwise," the Denastri general said. "Lowborn— *pejorative adjective*—Wind-clan. Honored Imperial Governor must remain safe."

"They're all Cs here?" Gloria asked.

"Most of them," said Barnes. "There are some A and B neighborhoods—ghettos, really—down by the river. I was hoping—"

On the forward viewscreen, a column of oily black

smoke suddenly erupted from the road. Gloria heard a dim rumble penetrating the thick hull of the APC.

"Shit," Barnes muttered.

"*Expletive*," the Denastri general echoed.

Barnes quickly shooed away a Marine technician and took his seat at a command console. "Javelin, this is Archer. What's happening?"

"A mine," came the reply. "And we're taking some small-arms fire from the left."

"Hightop, this is Archer. What can you see?"

An officer in one of the SALs reported, "Archer, we've got a concentration of Nasties at Charlie Six. Maybe twenty that we can see."

Ahead, another explosion, bigger than the first, detonated directly beneath an APC. As Gloria watched, the vehicle pinwheeled into the air and came down in a crumpled heap.

"Archer, Javelin! RPG fire from the right!"

"Hightop!" Barnes shouted, anger in his voice. "You are green! Repeat, you are green! Take 'em out!"

"Rodge, Archer."

On a viewscreen, Gloria saw a brilliant blue-green bolt of plasma flaring from the belly of one of the SALs. An instant later, a second SAL fired, then a third. The sharp, distinctive crack of the plasma discharges echoed through the streets. It was impossible to see what, if anything, had been hit.

"Javelin, Archer. What's your status?"

"Archer, we got one APC out, another burning. Still getting small-arms fire from both sides of the road."

"Deploy immediately, Javelin."

"Wilco, Archer." On the forward viewscreen, Gloria saw Marines boiling out of the APCs lined up along the road, like hornets swarming out of a nest. Helmeted, with self-regulating camouflaged body armor that exactly matched the dun color of the buildings, the troops charged to each side of the road and were quickly lost from view behind the low, crumbling structures. Another cloud of black smoke churned upward from the suburban sprawl. Plasma cracks sputtered continuously.

The APC suddenly rocked violently, almost spilling Gloria from her seat. Through a port, she saw a yellow streak slicing through the air, and the APC lurched again.

"Archer, they're behind us!" came a cry over the com. In abrupt confirmation, an explosion knocked the APC immediately behind them over onto its side.

"Longbow, Archer!" Barnes bellowed. "Deploy!"

There was no immediate reply.

"Longbow! Report!"

"Archer, Hightop. Longbow's out. Repeat, Longbow is out."

"Roger, Hightop. You are clear to fire at will. Repeat, fire at will!"

"Rodge, Archer! We're burnin' 'em!"

Meanwhile, the Denastri general was speaking into his own wristcom. The translation software was valiantly attempting to follow his torrent of words, but Gloria could make no sense of it. She could barely hear it above the rising din of battle. She turned the translator off and looked at Barnes.

"Delbert . . . ?"

"Sit tight, Gloria," Barnes said. He turned and looked at her, offering a thin, bleak smile. "Enjoying your tour, Madame Governor?"

Barnes quickly swiveled around and barked out more orders, while the com crackled with terse, intense voices. Through the ports, Gloria saw a swarm of Denastri Home Guard troops surrounding her vehicle. They blasted away at everything in sight, and the symphony of plasma cracks reached a crescendo; it was like being inside a thunderstorm.

On both sides of the road, buildings collapsed as plasma beams sliced through them. More explosions rocked the APC, and clouds of smoke blinded the viewscreens. Gloria didn't know what was happening, only that chaos was engulfing the world around her. She wanted to scream.

"Delbert! Can you get us out of here?"

"Working on it, Madame Governor," he said. Barnes turned again and fixed his gaze on her. "That's the problem with these little excursions. Getting out is never as easy as getting in."

Another explosion jolted the APC, rocking it back and forth like a rowboat in a hurricane. Gloria had faced death before, but never like this. It had always been . . . *personal*. But battle, she realized, was entirely impersonal, and that made it worse, somehow. An RPG or a plasma beam didn't care that she was the Imperial Governor, or that she was smart and brave and beautiful and beloved by billions. They didn't care that she was Gloria VanDeen. They didn't care at all.

"Javelin, Archer," Barnes said. "Report status!"

"We got at least nine KIA, maybe a dozen wounded. But we've established a perimeter, and we're collecting our people. If Hightop can cover, I think we can start a withdrawal."

"Copy, Javelin. Get your people out of there, Ben."

"Archer, Hightop. Can do. And we've cleared out a path behind you. DHG has established a corridor."

"Copy, Hightop. Good work, Judy." Barnes craned his neck and shouted to the Marine at the controls in the front of the APC. "Lieutenant! Skip and zip!"

"Roger *that*!" cried the young man.

The APC rose a few meters into the air, swiveled around its central axis, then darted forward, toward the gate to the city. In a blur, Denastri troops swept past the ports, still firing, almost randomly, into the shattered remains of the suburban neighborhood. More plasma bolts rained down from above, providing a searing covering fire for the fleeing APC. Almost before Gloria realized what was happening, the vehicle glided through the main gate and settled to the ground. Barnes remained at the command console, barking more orders, while Sergeant Hooper led Gloria out.

Before returning to her limo, Gloria paused just inside the open gate and stared back at the chaos she had escaped. For more than a kilometer along both sides of the sloping roadway, every building was now a heap of smoking rubble. Fires had broken out in the neighborhoods to the left and right, and a pall of dark, oily smoke was forming over the area. SALs still darted in and out of the smoke, firing at targets only they could see. The DHG troops along the road were finding targets of their own as the Marine APCs made their way back to the city, leaving behind a smoldering junkyard of expensive hardware.

All this, for a sightseeing tour!

Spirit, she thought, *what have I done?*

·8·

Gloria sat at her desk in the Governor's office and tried to concentrate on Dexta personnel files, without much success. Events of the morning refused to leave her mind.

Sergeant Hooper entered the office, holding a piece of paper. "Got those casualty figures you asked for, ma'am," he said. "Official numbers haven't been released yet, but I got a friend over at Task Force HQ."

"Let's hear them, Alvin."

"Yes, ma'am." He looked down at the paper. "Seventeen KIA, thirty-three wounded. We also lost five APCs, seven damaged, and light damage to two SALs." He looked up at her.

Gloria registered the statistics and tried not to think about what they meant. "Go on," she said.

"DHG's reporting twenty-eight KIA, eleven wounded, and fifty-five missing."

"Why so many missing?"

Hooper shrugged. "Marines don't leave people behind, ma'am," he said. "DHG folks don't seem to get that."

"I see. Anything else?"

"Yes, ma'am. We figure we killed eighty-six Nasties."

"We don't call them that anymore, Alvin. They're insurgents."

"Yes, ma'am," Hooper said. "Eighty-six insurgents."

"How can we know that?" Gloria asked him. "I didn't see anyone taking the time to count bodies."

"Best number we got, ma'am," Hooper explained. "Means we killed at least fifty or sixty of 'em, maybe eighty or a hundred. HQ needs a definite number, so . . . eighty-six."

Gloria nodded. "And civilian casualties?"

Hooper hesitated. "Hard to say, ma'am," he said.

"Alvin?"

"Yes, ma'am. They figure three to four hundred. Maybe five. Hit those neighborhoods pretty hard, ma'am."

"Yes," she said, "we did, didn't we?" She took a deep breath.

"Ma'am . . . ?"

"I screwed up, Alvin. Matabele and Barnes warned me, but I just wouldn't listen. I had to take my little sight-seeing tour. Show the flag. Show them Gloria VanDeen was in charge. Spirit!" She brushed some hair away from her face. "Next time, I'll listen to them."

"Ma'am? Can I say something?"

"Anytime you have something to say, Alvin, say it."

"Yes, ma'am. Twenty-seven years in the Corps, I seen a lot of officers. Most of 'em good, some of 'em bad. But good or bad, every one of 'em makes mistakes. Bad officer makes a mistake, one of two things happens. Either he refuses to admit he made a mistake and just goes on makin' 'em, or he lets it get under his skin and gets to where he can't make any decisions at all. Worst thing for an officer, ma'am. Officers *got* to make decisions. Even a bad decision is better than no decision."

"And the good officers?" Gloria asked.

"Good officer makes a mistake, he does what you just

did, ma'am. Admits it. Recognizes it. Learns from it. Doesn't make the same mistake again."

Gloria gave him a crooked smile. "Well, we'll see about that, I guess. Alvin? You've been in combat before, haven't you?"

Hooper nodded. "Now and then, ma'am."

"Is it always like that? Confusing, I mean?"

"Every time, ma'am."

"I just don't see how anyone can . . . can *function*. Know what to do."

"Training helps," Hooper said. "And Marines get lots of training. It's what we mostly do. And some of it's just instinct, I guess. Never thought about it much, ma'am. Moment comes, you just do what you gotta."

"Even if you're afraid?"

"'Specially if you're afraid. Can't just sit there, bein' scared."

"That's what I did this morning."

"You didn't have any choice, ma'am. Wasn't anything for you to do, 'cept sit there and take it."

"I've never been so scared in my life," Gloria said. "I thought I was going to wet my pants. You ever feel like that, Alvin?"

"No, ma'am, can't say as I have. O' course, couple of times, after it was all over, I threw up pretty good. Strikes everyone different, I guess. Ma'am? You got nothin' to be ashamed of. Anyone tells you they weren't scared in combat, ain't *been* in combat."

Gloria grinned at him. "Alvin," she said, "can I promote you to general?"

"Oh, no, ma'am. Can't do that. Generals just command the Corps; sergeants *run* it. Start makin' generals outta sergeants, Corps would just fall apart." He returned her grin. "Will there be anything else, ma'am?"

"Not right now. Thanks, Alvin." Hooper started to leave, but Gloria thought of something. "Wait, Alvin. I need a favor."

"Name it and it's yours, ma'am."

"You think there's any Belgravian whisky on this planet?"

"Just might be," he said after a moment's thought.

"Think you could get me a bottle?"

"No, ma'am." He winked at her. "Get you a whole damn *case*. You're the Governor, after all."

"Uh . . . I don't have any cash handy, but —"

Hooper shook his head. "That ain't how scroungin' works, ma'am. You just leave everything to me."

Gloria grinned at him. "Wilco, Sergeant. And Alvin, on your way out, could you tell Petra I want to see her?"

"Yes, ma'am." Hooper made a crisp military exit, and a moment later Petra walked in. Gloria motioned to a chair, and Petra sat down next to the big desk.

"I think you should marry Alvin Hooper. He may just be the best man I know."

"Whatever you say, Madame Governor. I'll get right on it." Petra's smile slowly faded as she looked at Gloria. "Pretty rough this morning?"

"Petra? I killed five hundred people this morning."

Petra slowly nodded. "That's what happens in wars, isn't it? People get killed. Why should your war be any different?"

"It is my war, isn't it? On Mynjhino, I was trying to *stop* a war. Here . . . Spirit, I'm not sure what I'm supposed to be doing. I may be in over my head."

"What do you want me to say, Gloria? You're taller than I am. If it's over your head, it's *way* over my head."

"No wisdom from Albert?"

Petra frowned. "I don't think you'd want to hear it."

"Try me."

"I think Albert would say that what happened this morning was inevitable. As long as we're here, things like that are bound to happen. Imperial powers always wind up massacring the locals, whether they intend to or not."

"Sometimes the locals win," Gloria pointed out.

"And then, they usually massacre each other. If we walked out on Denastri now, the As would slaughter the Cs."

"Probably," Petra agreed. "Albert said something once about how empires always suffer from what he called 'the illusion of control.' If you're big and powerful, you naturally think that you're in control of the situation. Usually, it just means that you don't really *understand* the situation."

"Unknown word," Gloria said ruefully. "Possibly pejorative."

"Huh?"

"Nothing. Maybe I should just concentrate on the things that I *can* control. Petra, I want you to set up meetings tomorrow with each of the UnderSecs and their top people. We'll start with Finance, then Corporate, then Security. I'll finish with you and Admin."

"Good idea," Petra said. "I get the impression that everyone around here is just kind of holding their breath, waiting to see what you do."

"And what do *you* think I should do?"

"I think you should go with what you're good at."

"Meaning?"

"Kick some butts."

Gloria nodded. "One of my best things," she said. "I've always thought so."

Gloria dined alone in her quarters that evening, then opened a bottle of Belgravian whisky, courtesy of Alvin Hooper, and did some slow, serious drinking. She didn't quite manage to get drunk, but the whisky provided a much-needed anesthetic. In less than three full days on the planet, she had been bombed, wounded, confused, and frightened out of her wits. And caused the death of four or five hundred people, Terran and native. The VanDeen Administration was off to a flying start.

Technically, this was not a war. The war, such as it was, had ended three years earlier, almost as soon as it started. This was the inescapable sequel to war—occupation. So far, more people had died in it than in the war. More were going to die.

She sipped whisky, stared at the walls, and tried to understand what was happening. Getting into these things was always easier than getting out, according to Delbert. Smart man, Delbert. She had been surprised but very pleased to find him here. They had become close friends back on Mynjhino, although circumstances had prevented them from becoming anything more than that. This time around, maybe there would be an opportunity to form a deeper relationship.

Lord Kenarbin was a smart man, too. Maybe he could have negotiated a way out of this mess, but he never got the chance. Did that task fall to her, now? She didn't think so. As Imperial Governor, her job was to administer the planet and carry out Imperial policy—which was determined in Rio and on Luna, not on Denastri. She had no real authority to make deals with anyone. And what could she possibly offer, anyway? She couldn't sell out the As to appease the Cs. And what did the Cs want? What would they settle for? Would they settle at all?

The whisky eased the pain, but offered no answers. Eventually, she gave up the quest and picked a book from the bedroom shelf. Swift. She read until her eyes grew heavy, then went to bed and dreamed that she was Gulliver, tied down by Lilliputians. The Lilliputians all wore hooded robes and spoke a language that made no sense.

The next morning, Gloria returned to the Compound hospital to have her bandages removed and receive a final checkup. Thanks to the nanomeds, her wounds had nearly healed, with only a little residual redness to mark the trauma. Her arm and shoulder were still a little stiff, but there was no pain worth mentioning.

She felt pain of a different kind when she forced herself to visit the ward where the Marine casualties were being treated. A doctor led her on a brief tour, offering concise, clinical comments on the damage that had been done and the treatment being performed to heal it. Four of the Marines were scheduled to be transferred to the naval hospital on Kandra Four, where they would spend long, painful months having limbs regenerated.

The Marines were all cheerful and glad to see her. She had made certain of that, at least, by dressing in her Tiger mode—minimal miniskirt and a very sheer silk shirt, unbuttoned to her waist. Sometimes her sexy, scandalous reputation could be a burden, but other times it was a definite asset. The Marines certainly seemed to think so, and the doctor said that she was better medicine than anything he could prescribe.

One young Marine, his face half-hidden by bandages, told Gloria that he had been with her on Mynjhino. She sat down on the edge of his bed and clasped his hand, which produced a storm of hoots and whistles from the other beds in the ward. "Finch, Corporal Michael T.," the Marine said. "Guess I'm a little hard to recognize right now, ma'am."

"Nonsense. I'd know you anywhere, Michael. You were on the perimeter, the morning Major Barnes took me on that tour."

Finch smiled, although it must have been painful for him. "That's right, ma'am. Told these clowns about it, but they didn't believe me."

"They're just jealous. How are the rest of my old comrades from Bravo Company? Is Captain Zwingli here?"

"Captain Zwingli got killed last month, ma'am." When he saw the look of pain on Gloria's face, Finch quickly added, "But most of the rest of the Company's okay. Haddad finally got his sergeant's stripes."

"Did he? That's great. And you'll get yours one of these days, too, Michael."

Finch shook his head. "No, ma'am," he said. "My enlistment's up in three months, and I'm getting out. Wanted to see the galaxy, and I've seen it. Don't think I want to see any more of it. Goin' back to my dad's farm on Shiva Prime."

"Sounds wonderful. Thank you for your service, Michael. The Empire's very proud of you, and so am I." She leaned forward to give him a kiss on his undamaged cheek, then quickly got up and walked out of the ward before anyone could see the tears in her eyes.

Her meetings with the Dexta staff proved to be painful, too, in an institutional sense. Frederick Danelli and his Finance people struck her as smug and complacent, pleased with their own performance and contemptuous of everyone else's. That was typical of Finance people throughout Dexta. They controlled the flow of money, which was self-evidently the most important thing that anyone could do. Working closely with Bank of Earth also gave them a leg up on possible post-Dexta careers. A substantial portion of Dexta staffers opted out after ten or twelve years and stepped into lucrative positions in the private sector, where a Dexta background was viewed as valuable training. Consequently, Dexta people who should have been scrupulously regulating banks and industries often spent more time and energy buttering them up. Danelli's staff was no exception.

Edgar Wong's Corporate Affairs staff also fit the pattern. As was often the case, his people tended to adopt the attitudes and personality of their chief. That was particularly unfortunate in this instance, Gloria thought, since Edgar Wong was a consummate ass. His tactless comment to McCray the other day proved to be typical of his personal style. Wong was older than the usual Level XIII, nearly forty, which suggested that he had managed to offend or annoy most of his previous superiors and didn't seem to care whether he did or not. He had carved out a comfortable spot for himself in the Dexta hierarchy, and seemed content to spend his career as a tinpot dictator, exercising his limited authority in an unlimited way.

Some Dexta people were empire builders who tried to extend their power as high and as far as their talents permitted. Others settled for being small-town bullies, like Kevin Grunfeld on Sylvania, only with more polish. Wong was one of the latter. He ruled his little Corporate satrapy with a mixture of arrogance and deftly applied sadism; he reminded Gloria of Hector Konrad, the Level X who had devoted himself to making her life miserable when she was a XIII back in Sector 8. Wong's staff, out of fear and ambition, had shaped themselves into faithful mirror images of their boss. The result was that the Corporate Affairs office on Denastri was a contemptible nest of strutting, self-important, self-promoting young jerks.

If they were back at HQ in Manhattan, Gloria would have transferred the lot of them and started over from scratch. But that wasn't possible on Denastri, so she was forced to work with what she had. The disturbing thing about them was that they approached their jobs as if they *were* in Manhattan, making few concessions to the very different conditions on Denastri. Unlike the Finance people, whose work brought them into regular contact with the natives, the Corporate staff dealt almost exclusively with Imperium, KemTek, and Servitor. The Denastri were of no consequence, except to the extent that they facilitated or impeded the desires of the Corporates.

Satisfying the Big Twelve was a major function of

Corporate Affairs offices throughout Dexta. Staffers who favorably impressed the corporate behemoths could look forward to attractive job offers; those who frustrated them could expect no such rewards and were likely to be shunted aside within Dexta, often landing in dead-end positions where they could do no further harm to Corporate interests. Norman Mingus, Gloria knew, regarded Corporate Affairs as the biggest institutional thorn in his side, but even Mingus was limited in his ability to improve the situation. The Big Twelve were simply too powerful to be cowed by mere bureaucrats.

On Denastri, keeping Imperium, KemTek, and Servitor happy meant that the Corporate Affairs office was frequently at odds with Security, Administration, and the Marines. Life would have been much easier for them if Security and the Marines kept the natives out of the way and Administration established and enforced regulations favored by the Corporates. Wong took their failures to do so as a personal affront. He also seemed to regard Gloria as a mere interloper, of no real consequence except as a figurehead representing Imperial power. The true purpose of the Imperial presence on Denastri was obvious to Wong: they were there to dig up HCH. Anyone who did not contribute to that goal was a fool.

Jack McCray's Security team stood in sad and stark contrast. Entrusted with the responsibility of preserving the safety of the Imperial Compound and all who lived and worked in it, Security was overwhelmed by forces beyond their control. The Marines were ultimately responsible for everything that occurred outside the Compound's wall, but they had an entire planet to occupy and couldn't be everywhere at once. The bomb at the briefing was a tragic reminder of that fact. McCray and his people were devastated by their own lapses and yet powerless to prevent such episodes. Far from being complacent or insular, Gloria thought that her Security people were shell-shocked and fatalistic.

McCray, a wiry, compact, overwrought young man, reminded Gloria of some of the junior Marine officers she had seen. He looked older than he was, staggering under the weight of responsibility, stretched thin by duties that were inherently impossible to perform without suffering losses. If Finance or Corporate dropped the ball, no one even noticed; but when Security was less than perfect, people died.

Security was whipsawed by unrealistic and frequently impossible demands from Corporate and the obdurate reality of the insurgency. Wong had evidently been giving McCray a hard time, and it seemed to Gloria that the young man was near the breaking point. She didn't really know what to do about it other than to offer him support and encouragement. But she knew she would need to keep a close eye on him.

The problems in Administration proved to be more philosophical than practical. Admin tended to attract bright young intellectuals who were enthralled by the theory and practice of government. They knew the *Dexta Code* chapter and verse, but could also cite the Code of Hammurabi, the *Federalist Papers,* or the Eridani Compact with equal facility. Attrition and tragedy had stripped Admin of its leaders, leaving a residue of idealistic, opinionated XIVs and XVs, now under Petra's gently applied authority.

"Denastri is a disaster, and it's going to get worse the longer we stay," maintained one of them—a dark-haired, sharp-nosed young woman named Cassandra Pascal. "We should pull back and establish a Protectorate over the whole McGowan Cluster instead of trying to integrate every planet."

"Yeah, right," mocked Hansi Veblen, a young man from a moon of Colfax Seven. "And just how long do you think it would be before the As wiped out the Cs? We've got a responsibility here, like it or not, and we've got to see this thing through. We need to work closer with the Thirdborns and get them to accept Imperial guidance. Once they're committed, they can bring the others around."

"Whose Thirdborns?" demanded Wallace Wintertree, a member of the ruling family on Trevose Secundus. "Sure, the Thirdborn As will go along. But what about the Bs and Cs? You can't even get them to listen, much less cooperate."

"You won't get *anyone* to listen," objected Francine Jaleel, "until you do something about the Corporates. Why should the Denastri listen to us when they can see that Imperium and Servitor are really in charge?"

"Then we have to show them that *we're* in charge," responded Hakim Lone Pine, a Yemeni-Sioux from the fractious world of Raven Two. "Bring in more Marines and do what should have been done in the first place. Dammit, you can't coddle the Nasties. Political power grows from the barrel of a gun, and it's about time we made those bastards realize it."

Gina Swenson didn't say anything. She just sat there looking sad.

The debate went on for an hour, until Gloria grew weary of it. She felt as if she were auditing one of Albert Fenlow's classes. She thanked everyone for their contributions, then retreated to her office and consoled herself with a couple of fingers of Belgravian. This job, she reflected, was enough to drive a woman to drink.

Petra strolled across the Compound, just stretching her legs, wrapped in one of the dun-colored hooded robes that the Consulate acquired from the natives. Hers was sized for a Secondborn; it was a substantial, rather heavy garment, made of she knew not what, and it kept her warm on this cold and breezy world. The wind never stopped howling across the open, empty plains, and the sky was always a dirty yellow. It was easy to understand why the Denastri carried on most of their agriculture underground. She had seen a lot of planets in the past few years, but never one as grim and depressing as Denastri.

Gloria hadn't done much butt-kicking at the meetings, which Petra found mildly surprising. Mostly, she had simply listened to the complaints and theories, offering few comments or suggestions. Of course, it was helpful to know precisely which butts needed kicking. In time, Gloria would sort it all out.

At least, Petra hoped that she would. Gloria usually got things right, but this time around, the right answers might prove elusive. She seemed to be taking yesterday's fiasco pretty hard, and Petra wondered if Gloria's confidence had been shaken. That was a troubling thought. Gloria had her ups and downs, like anyone, and had made more than a few mistakes in her time, but she had always managed to come out on top—somehow. There were times when Petra was frankly in awe of her friend and counted herself as privileged to be so close to such an extraordinary person.

Yet Petra was also aware of Gloria's shortcomings: her confidence and determination could border on pigheaded obstinacy, her ego sometimes ballooned to impressive dimensions, and her capacity for self-indulgence was boundless. Her genetically enhanced sex drive was often as much a curse as a blessing, and her stunning beauty sometimes blinded Gloria as much as it did those around her. There were times when that beautiful butt of hers could stand a little kicking, too.

History, Petra had lately learned from Albert and her other professors, was, above all, a matter of contingency. Sometimes, the grand, impersonal forces of history all turned on the flaws and foibles of a single individual—a Caesar, a Washington, a Hazar. On Denastri, it might very well come down to Gloria. Petra honestly didn't know if that would turn out to be a good thing or a bad one.

Off in one corner of the Compound, some Marines were playing softball. Petra paused beyond the right field foul line and watched the strong, healthy young men and women performing the familiar rituals they had brought with them across the light-years. Humans always seemed to find a way to turn a patch of even the most alien world into a little slice of home. The crack of bat on ball and the chatter of the fielders sounded the same everywhere, and Petra found herself feeling a touch of homesickness.

"I'll buy the peanuts if you'll spring for the Cracker Jacks."

Petra turned and saw the grinning face of Bryce Denton. She threw her arms around him and almost knocked him over with the force of her hug.

"Bryce!" she cried. "What are *you* doing here?"

"I heard you were going to be here, so naturally, I just had to get myself assigned to Denastri. The fact that it happens to be the biggest story in the Empire had nothing to do with it."

Denton was a rep for ENS, one of the leading news organizations in the Empire. His coverage of Mynjhino had given his career a major boost and helped turn Gloria (and even, briefly, Petra) into a media phenomenon. He and Petra had indulged in a temporary but very satisfying fling on Mynjhino, but had not seen each other in the four years since then. Denastri suddenly looked a lot better to her. Albert Fenlow was far away, and neither one of them pretended that the relationship was serious. It was a perfect moment for Bryce Denton to drop back into her life.

"Spirit! What a surprise!"

Denton grinned at her. "Of all the towns in all the galaxy, I walk into yours, eh, kid?"

"I can't tell you how glad I am that you did." Petra

stared into Denton's vid-friendly face, then pressed her lips against his in a kiss that went on for some time.

As they disengaged, Denton explained that he had just arrived and was eager to plunge into his new assignment, and that drinks and dinner with the beautiful and charming UnderSecretary for Administration might be an ideal way to begin his work. That struck Petra as a pretty good idea, too.

One of the Marines clouted a long foul ball that conveniently rolled right up to them. Petra picked it up and threw it back to the right fielder.

"You throw like a girl," Denton observed.

"I do *lots* of things like a girl," Petra told him.

"Lucky me," said Denton.

· 9 ·

If it had proved impossible for Gloria to venture even a kilometer beyond the gates of Enkar, traveling ten thousand kilometers to the opposite side of the planet turned out to be a breeze. A Marine LASS (Land-Air-Sea-Space) vehicle safely lifted her out of the Compound the next morning, then soared upward on a suborbital trajectory that deposited her and a small contingent of staff on the continent of Senka forty minutes later.

Senka—where 60 percent of the population belonged to Superclan A, the Rock-clan, and just 10 percent to the hostile Cs, the Wind-clan—was relatively safe ground, and the Imperial Governor was welcomed by the local authorities with a respectful ceremony witnessed by crowds of curious, if restrained, onlookers. Following the formalities, Gloria was ushered into an ancient palace, where she met with a gaggle of Thirdborns, who assured her of the continuing loyalty and support of the people of Senka. The *pejorative adjective* Wind-clan troublemakers were no more than a minor nuisance, easily dealt with by the DHG and their Imperial Marine allies.

Gloria cautiously broached the possibility of withdrawing some of the Marine contingent and transferring them to Lataka, where they were needed. The Thirdborn officials paled at the prospect and immediately contradicted everything they had already said, earnestly warning Gloria that paring down the Marine commitment to Senka would necessarily lead to calamity and chaos. Nor would it be safe to transfer any more of the DHG forces. Despite their professed loyalty, Gloria got the impression that the As of Senka saw Lataka as a problem for the Terrans to deal with. They were happy to be back in charge of the planet, after eleven hundred years of rule by the Wind-clan, but they were equally happy to let the Imperials do all the heavy lifting.

The small Dexta staff, whom Gloria met later, seemed refreshingly ordinary. Isolated from the factions and feuds of Enkar, they pursued their everyday tasks with humdrum efficiency. Gloria, pondering personnel changes back in the Compound, scouted the Senka staff for possible replacements. If she shipped a couple of the worst malcontents to the boonies, it might serve to get the attention of the rest.

That evening, Gloria was the guest of honor at a banquet hosted by the Corporates. There was no HCH on Senka, so the continent was of minimal interest to Imperium and KemTek, but Servitor was providing financial services, infrastructure assessment, and security specialists. Bank of Earth was also active, putting down Imperial roots in the virgin soil. On Senka, unlike Lataka, people actually spoke of a long-term future and planned for it. Fully integrating Denastri into the Empire would take decades, even without the insurgency on Lataka, and the evident stability on Senka offered a glimmering vision of what the future might hold for a peaceful and united Denastri.

As she tried to sleep that night in a guest room at the Consulate, Gloria considered the great Paradox of Empire. *We fight wars to bring peace; we overturn civilizations to spread civility; we impose our rule to give freedom.* Senka was already a better place than it had been, thanks to the arrival of the Terran Empire. Not even the anti-imperialists, not even Albert Fenlow, could have denied it. The tyranny of the Cs had been replaced with an enlightened, progressive government—which would tyrannize the Cs the minute the Empire turned its back.

Governing indigs, Gloria decided, was like herding cats. They'd do what you wanted them to do, as long as it was what *they* wanted to do. But what *did* the Denastri want? The As seemed willing to sign on to all of the vague, poorly translated Imperial clichés about good government and fat profits, but she suspected that the Thirdborns she dealt with were mainly concerned with telling her what they thought she wanted to hear. And the angry rhetoric of the Cs was familiar enough—it echoed the outrage of every conquered people down through the ages—but ultimately unilluminating. The Cs apparently wanted a return to the *status quo ante bellum* and would settle for nothing less, even though it should have been obvious to them by now that there was zero chance of achieving that goal.

The Bs—the Water-clan—were harder to understand, but Gloria learned more about them the following morning when the LASS took her to the capital city of Banako, Denastri's third major continent, where Super-clan B held sway. Terran policy officially viewed the Bs as "moderates" and potential allies in the fight against the insurgency—but it was clear to Gloria that the Bs did not necessarily view *themselves* that way. If they did not seem to share the deep mutual antagonism of the As and Cs, it was probably only because the Bs simply wanted to be left alone.

With a 30 percent minority population of Cs on Banako, the majority Bs had no intention of stirring up trouble by cooperating with the Empire in suppressing the insurgency. For their part, the Cs of Banako preferred to vent their wrath against Imperial targets and the small minority of As on the continent; they generally left the Bs in peace. Gloria's attempts to get the Bs to become more actively involved in the fight met with impassive gazes and bland statements of insincere regret.

The Water-clan officials took Gloria on a daylong tour of their continent, where Denastri civilization had first arisen. She saw immense eroded petroglyphs, the sketchy remains of ancient cities, and a religious shrine commemorating events that had transpired there more than thirty thousand years ago. Gloria felt impressed, but frustrated in her hope of gaining a better understanding of the Bs. It was like trying to comprehend Earth history, culture, and politics based on a quick tour of the Pyramids, Mount Rushmore, and the Great Wall of China.

Imperium and KemTek had substantial operations on Banako, where heavy metals abounded. Servitor security specialists and a regiment of Marines protected the mines and spaceport facilities, and left the rest of the continent to the indifferent attentions of the Denastri Home Guard, led by B-clan Fifthborn generals. The insurgent forces—mostly but not entirely C-clan—took a small but steady toll from the Imperials with their bombings, ambushes, and acts of sabotage.

The situation was not exactly encouraging—Gloria saw no realistic hope of gaining the Bs active support—but it was not entirely to the Empire's disadvantage. The insurgency on Banako was, in a sense, self-regulating. The Bs would not clamp down on the Cs for fear of provoking a larger rebellion; and the Cs would not dare escalate the level of violence to the point where the Bs were forced to do something about it. The Empire could simply hunker down on Banako in secure defensive positions and accept a sustained but relatively low level of attrition. Nothing on Banako seemed to require an additional commitment of scarce Imperial resources.

She returned to Enkar that evening and learned that in her absence, three more Marines had been lost in an ambush just outside the city walls. *More low-level attrition*, she thought. Viewed as a whole, such losses were acceptable as long as the percentages remained low— except that each victim was one hundred percent dead. *Dear Mr. and Mrs. Smith, I am sorry to inform you that your son was attrited . . .*

Gloria paced around her bedroom, a frown on her face, a glass of Belgravian in her hand. She wondered if Mr. and Mrs. Smith would understand why their son had died. Perhaps they would; perhaps they held stock in KemTek.

In an empire of 3 trillion souls, the daily loss of a few Marines was hardly a cause for grave concern. Denastri, after all, was not the only planet where Imperial forces were engaged. Active military operations were currently under way on forty or fifty different worlds, and on some of them, the level of violence was considerably higher. Off in Sector 18, she knew, the Second and Third Marine Divisions were still cleaning up the aftermath of a bloody uprising on Dairen, where a hundred thousand civilians had died before the Marines arrived. And in Sector 1, a naval task force was busy chasing down a pack of marauding nomads who descended upon peaceful worlds the way the Vikings had plundered England, two thousand years earlier. Elsewhere, the Empire was coping with guerrillas, revanchists, religious zealots, political radicals, and at least one madman-with-a-following who claimed that he was the *third* coming of Jesus Christ.

Yet, somehow, Denastri seemed to matter more than the other problems. In part, that was due to the abduction of Lord Kenarbin, and even to Gloria's own presence; those were stories that the media could personalize, dramatize, and—when necessary—fictionalize. People who didn't give a fundamental damn about Denastri could be made to care about a missing Imperial legend or the perils faced by the sexy, intrepid Sweetheart of the Empire. But more was involved here than media hype. Most of the troubles on other worlds were occurring *within* the Empire and, in a sense, represented business as usual —a fixed and recurring cost of Imperial rule. But Denastri was the product of Imperial expansion, and that made it a political issue of supreme importance in an election year. Karno and the antiexpansionists could point to it and declare to the people of the Empire, "*Here* is your future! Do you like it? Do you want more of it?"

Yet the people would never really see the entirety of Denastri. They wouldn't see the peaceful optimism of Senka, or the uneasy equilibrium of Banako. Nor would they see the tyranny of the old deposed government. What they would see was the blood and death of Lataka, the mangled bodies and crumpled machinery, and—no doubt—the sad and mournful faces of Mr. and Mrs. Smith after learning that their son had died for the greater glory and profit of the Empire.

How could you convey the reality of war, in all its gruesome complexity? Did Thucydides get it right? Did Ernie Pyle?

They weren't available, but Gloria realized that their professional descendants were—just across the Compound at the bar of the Imperial Hotel. She decided that she didn't want to drink alone, so she threw on some jeans and a gratuitously revealing blouse and walked across the floodlit Compound to the hotel. There, she found Petra camped in the corner of a booth with Bryce Denton, along with a couple of other newsies. She happily greeted Denton and sat down to join them.

Introductions were made. One of the journalists was a young, dark-haired, subtly beautiful woman named

Hettie Pando; she was INP's ace correspondent, with a reputation as hot as Gloria's own. The other was a craggy, white-bearded relic named Elmo Hunt, who had carved an enduring legend for himself half a century earlier during the war with the Ch'gnth. Gloria had heard of him, of course, and expressed mild surprise to find him there.

"Thought I was dead, didn't you?" Hunt snickered. "Most people do. It always seems to disappoint them to be wrong."

"No," Gloria assured him, "I'm glad to see that you're alive and well. But Denastri must be pretty small potatoes for someone like you. I'm just surprised to see you here."

"Well, what can I tell you? It's a shitty little war, hon, but it's the only one we got at the moment. Best one, anyway. Name me another war where you get to see the Imperial Governor's tits!"

"Down, Elmo," counseled Hettie Pando, whose own attire was as revealing as Gloria's. "Forgive him, Governor VanDeen, he's been drinking."

"For ninety years," Hunt confirmed. "And in all that time, drunk or sober, I never saw the likes of you, Missy. Helen of Troy, Eleanor Roosevelt, and Mad Queen Nixata, all rolled into one. If I were a semilegendary, Hazar Prize–winning journalist—and I am, you know—I could write one helluva good book about you. Maybe I will."

"Oh, please don't," Gloria said.

"I want a percentage," Bryce Denton put in. "After all, I'm the one who made her famous."

Petra gently elbowed Denton's ribs. "Baloney. Gloria was already famous before you showed up. But," she added, "you did make *me* famous, for about twenty minutes."

"Fifteen," said Denton. "Don't exaggerate. That's *my* job."

Gloria looked at Hunt's famous, ravaged face. "Tell

me, Mr. Hunt, what do you think of our 'shitty little war'?"

Hunt frowned. "Shitty," he said. "Little."

"He gets paid by the word," Pando explained. "You just got sixty crowns' worth of adjectives."

"I'm amazed to discover that a vid-head like you even knows what an adjective is," Hunt said. "You and your Dura-styled tribe write on the wind, Ms. Pando—except for Denton there, who pisses his initials on the beach. But the printed word is eternal. You pander to the whims of the moment; I write for the ages."

Pando put her arm across Hunt's massive chest and squeezed him. "Don't you just love him when he's being pompous?" She pinched his cheek. "Isn't he just the cutest little legend?"

"Little? You have a short memory, Pando."

"Why? Did something memorable happen?"

"Evidently not," Hunt snorted, then took a healthy swig from his drink.

"Aside from being shitty and little," Gloria persevered, "what other adjectives can you spare for our war?"

Hunt thought for a moment. "Familiar," he said at length. "Doomed. Nobody ever really gets what they want out of a war. Except me. I get rich and famous. Other people get dead."

"You've seen a lot of wars," Gloria said. "How do you think this one will turn out?"

"I charge extra for prophecy, Madame Governor."

"Next round's on me," Gloria said, signaling for a waiter. She noticed that a half dozen other journalists had pulled a table over next to the booth and were kibitzing the conversation. Two of them were aliens; Denastri was a big story among the native populations of the Empire.

When the drinks arrived, Hunt briefly surveyed his growing audience, then held forth. "You can't run an empire on the cheap, Ms. VanDeen. Denastri's a bargain-basement war because that's the only kind we're willing to pay for these days. Your ex-husband isn't the worst Emperor I've lived under, but he's in the wrong century. Three or four hundred years ago, he'd have been Charles the Conqueror. Now, he's just Charles the Pimp. The Big Twelve point and say, 'We'd like that one, please,' and Charles delivers for them. Parliament pays the tab, because that's what they're there for, but the price always frightens them. So we end up sending kids out on a shoestring to places like this and expecting them to make all our dreams come true. Pathetic. Shameful."

"Elmo thinks any war with less than a billion casualties is a waste of time and ammunition," put in one of the newsies at the other table.

"I didn't say it was a waste," Hunt retorted. "Maybe these people needed liberating. Maybe they'll thank us for it someday. I wouldn't hold my breath on that, but it's possible. I've seen stranger things happen. But, you see, no one *likes* getting liberated . . . except Ms. Pando, here, who has been liberated by both sexes and at least a dozen different species. But liberating her has never been the problem—it's keeping her occupied afterward."

"My goodness," cried Pando, "first adjectives, and now, a metaphor! Before you know it, he'll be speaking in iambic pentameter."

"It was good enough for Homer, my pale-armed Goddess of Rumor and Innuendo. He thanked me for the advice, too. Idiot was going to do it in blank verse before I set him straight."

"So wise." Pando sighed in admiration. "So old."

"Getting back to the occupation—of Denastri, I mean—what do you expect will happen here?" Gloria was determined to glean some useful information from this encounter although she suddenly realized that Hunt was playing games. He had spent his life asking questions and thus knew how to avoid answering them. Hunt was letting Gloria try to interview him and probably enjoyed being hard to pin down.

"I expect shit will happen, Madame Governor," Hunt replied after a moment. "Great steaming globs of it."

"Could you be more specific?"

"Not really. Shit comes in many forms. But come it will."

"What makes you so sure of that?"

"If I said that it was my vast experience in these matters, someone would surely accuse me of being pompous. Instead, let me ask *you* a question, Madame Governor. What outcome do *you* see? Off the record, I assure you."

Gloria took a deep breath and said, "I'd say I'm cautiously optimistic that, in the long term, the insurgency will fade away and Denastri will enjoy an era of unprecedented peace and—"

"Horseshit. I expected better from you, VanDeen."

Gloria smiled sheepishly. "Sorry," she said. "You get to a point where you just sort of do that automatically. What do I really think? I think the insurgency will drag on for another three years, maybe five. Eventually we'll wear them down, but a lot of people are going to die in the meantime. We'll probably still have troops here— and still be taking casualties—twenty years from now."

Hunt nodded. "I see. You're an optimist, then."

Gloria hadn't thought of it quite that way. She cocked an eyebrow at Hunt and said, "I take it that you are not?"

"Saints and Spirit preserve us, Ms. VanDeen! When you've seen as many severed limbs and blackened entrails as I have, optimism comes to seem a perverted indulgence of the naïve and foolish. I'm known for my clear-eyed realism, my vaunted compassionate skepticism, my unflinching devotion to—"

"Self-promotion," Pando interjected. "Would you

like to see the citation for his Hazar Prize? He carries the clippings in his pocket."

"You're becoming annoying, my dear Hettie."

"And you're becoming an accomplished bore, dear Elmo. Of course, you've had so many years of practice."

"An accomplished boar, you say? Yes, I remember you calling me your Wild Boar last night in the throes of passion."

"I called you a pig."

"Close enough. At least you didn't call me an accomplished *boor*. I might have resented that."

Gloria smiled, leaned back, and just listened for a while as the newsies fenced and parried, deftly slicing up one another with cynical abandon. She liked journalists, for the most part, and envied them their raucous camaraderie. The best of them shared a long-standing mutual respect combined with cutthroat competitive instincts and egos the size of small asteroids. They covered wars for a living, and that made them special, somehow, because they, alone, didn't *have* to be there. And they knew, better than anyone, even the generals, what war was all about. Elmo Hunt was said to have covered more than a hundred different wars during his storied career. Even a young woman like Hettie Pando had probably covered a dozen of them. Gloria wondered how they did it, and why, but suspected that it was the kind of thing that they didn't talk about much, either among themselves or to outsiders.

As the evening wore on, Gloria became the subject of a dirty limerick contest. "There once was a gal named VanDeen," Hunt extemporized, "who humped like a fucking machine. You could tell with one feel, her tits weren't quite real . . ." Hunt attempted to demonstrate, and while he was doing so, Pando beat him to the fifth line.

"And her blueprints were considered obscene!"

Gloria took it in good humor and managed to respond in kind. "Said Pando when fucked by old Hunt, 'I thought you beyond such a stunt. You've labored all week, to find what you seek, and mistaken my ear for—' "

The newsies erupted in guffaws before Gloria reached the inevitable conclusion. "Not bad, for a fucking bureaucrat," Hunt admitted.

"We have our moments," Gloria said modestly.

"You have more than your share of them, kid," Hunt told her. "Word is, you could have been Empress a couple of years ago. Why'd you settle for this?"

"Empresses are rarely permitted to get falling-down drunk with a bunch of degenerate journalists," Gloria pointed out.

"Well, there's that." Hunt fixed his gaze on her. "You really think you can make a difference?"

Gloria shrugged. "I can try."

Hunt lowered his voice so only Gloria could hear him. "You're here to get Kenarbin back, aren't you?"

"And if I am?"

Hunt took a sip of his drink, then idly scratched his beard for a moment. "You met any of the local femmes?" he asked her.

"The Denastri females? Just one, I'm afraid."

"You might make it a point to meet some more of them," Hunt suggested.

"Why? Do you know something?"

Hunt shook his shaggy head. "Just a feeling," he said. "Things around here don't add up right. There's a missing piece somewhere."

·10·

It was butt-kicking time. A couple of No-Regrets tabs had somewhat dissipated Gloria's hangover, but the excesses of the previous night still left her feeling surly and combative. She took it out on a Level XIV named Clifford Xumi, whom Gloria had identified as the most obnoxious of Edgar Wong's acolytes.

"I'm transferring you to Senka," Gloria told him.

"*Senka?*" Xumi protested. "You can't be serious!"

"Mr. Xumi," Gloria said with more patience than she felt, "as you continue your Dexta career, you will find that when Imperial Governors make staff decisions, they are invariably serious. You leave today."

Xumi continued his protests. Gloria ignored him and pressed a button on her desktop. An instant later, Sergeant Hooper entered the office; he must have been listening just outside the door.

"Sergeant Hooper," Gloria said, "please see that Mr. Xumi has a place on the Marine shuttle to Senka. I believe it departs in about an hour. Have a pleasant trip, Mr. Xumi." Xumi started to protest again, but discovered that Hooper had a firm grip on his upper arm and was swiftly escorting him out of the Governor's office.

Half an hour later, Edgar Wong arrived, a scowl distorting his smooth, Buddha-like features. "Governor VanDeen," he stormed, "this is an outrage! You cannot take my best people away from me."

"Of course I can," Gloria informed him.

"I should have been consulted."

"Perhaps. In any event, the decision has been made."

"But I need Xumi!"

"Yes, I hear he's very skilled at bullying junior staff and scooping up perks from the Corporates. Now, he'll have the opportunity to exercise those skills on Senka. Meanwhile, I've transferred a Level XIV, Myra Schoenweiss, from Senka to replace Xumi here. She seems to possess a knack for leadership. We might find that necessary, should we be forced to make any more changes around here."

That brought Wong up short. He stood in front of Gloria's desk and stared at her, as if uncertain who she was. "Am I to take that as a threat?" he said at last.

"Take it any way you like, Mr. Wong."

"You're only the Interim Governor, you know," Wong reminded her. "And I am not without influence."

Gloria raised an eyebrow. "And should I take *that* as a threat, Mr. Wong?"

"The Corporates won't like this, Ms. VanDeen," Wong assured her. "I have a very good relationship with them, and they will not take it lightly if you attempt to run roughshod over existing arrangements here."

"I'll deal with the Corpos, Mr. Wong. In fact, I just received an invitation to a reception they're holding Thursday night. If they have any problems with my decisions, they can take it up with me then. And as for those 'existing arrangements,' I intend to conduct a very thorough review of them in the coming days. I have already discovered in my files no less than twenty-seven complaints about you and your smug little minions, from Security, Admin, and the Marines. I'll be sending you the complete list later today. I'll expect a written response to them no later than Friday."

"You're playing with fire here, VanDeen."

"That's *Governor* VanDeen to you. Mr. Wong."

Wong nodded and gave her a cold smile. "My apologies," he said. "*Governor* VanDeen. But what I said still goes. My job—and yours, *Governor*—is to keep the Corporates happy. Not the drones in Admin or Security, not the natives, and not even the Marines. What the hell do you think we're *doing* here, for Spirit's sake? We're here to get the HCH. Nothing else matters."

"I won't debate policy with you. But you're quite right, the HCH *is* important. In fact, I would like to get a closer look at just what's happening in that area. To that end, I want you to go out to Scooptown today, Mr. Wong, and spend the next couple of days there putting together a thorough report on the state of operations, with particular attention to relations between the Corporates and the Denastri. I'm especially concerned with employment practices and security arrangements. According to the information I already have, it seems that Imperium, KemTek, and, particularly, Servitor have been in violation of a number of existing regulations regarding the rights of indigenous peoples. I'm referring specifically to the *Dexta Code*, Chapters 32 and 33, as well as the *Imperial Code*, Chapter 27, Subsections B, C, and D. I'll expect you to address that in your report."

"This isn't Manhattan, Governor VanDeen," Wong said. "It's not even some established, stable Empire world. It's the Wild West, Governor. It's Peshawar under the Raj, and we're surrounded by Apaches and Afghans. You can't fight them with the *Code*! While you're busy citing chapter and verse, they'll sneak up behind you and slit your pretty throat for you."

"Better them," Gloria said, "than my own people."

Wong shook his head. "You're temporary," he said. "I'll still be here, long after you've gone back to the flesh-pots of Manhattan. Do what you think you have to, Governor, but don't delude yourself that it means anything. In the end, the Corporates will get whatever they want. It's my job to make that happen, and I'm very good at it."

Gloria smiled pleasantly at him. "Mr. Wong," she said, "we're *all* temporary. Have a nice time in Scooptown."

"You want me to go to *Scooptown*?" Petra asked, a note of disbelief in her voice.

"I need to know what's going on out there," Gloria said. "I can't go myself—it would be too big of a disruption, and I don't want to set off any more pitched battles. But if you go along with Wong, as UnderSec for Admin, I'll have a pair of eyes and ears out there."

"And it'll be my eyes and ears—and ass. Isn't it pretty dangerous there? Bryce was just out there, and he says we've got police-state security in Scooptown, and it *still* isn't enough to prevent attacks."

"You and Wong will have a platoon of Marines around you. Plus, there's Servitor security. You can take the Transit and be back here by nightfall. I think you'll be as safe there as you are here, probably safer."

Petra nodded dutifully. "If you say so," she said.

"How's it going with Bryce?"

Petra brightened. "Oh, you know. Same old Bryce. Emotionally, he's still about ten years old, chasing after fire engines. But he's sexy and funny, so I make allowances. What about you? How's it going with Colonel Barnes?"

Gloria shook her head and frowned. "I haven't had five minutes alone with him since I got here. He's busy,

I'm busy. Maybe I'll get to spend some time with him at that reception the Corporates are putting on."

"Well, if Colonel Barnes is too busy, there's always Elmo Hunt."

Gloria laughed. "The man of my dreams—and his own, I think. But I don't want to have a knife fight with Hettie Pando over him. Hey, Petra? Have you seen many Denastri females around the Compound?"

Petra thought for a moment. "Not many, now that you mention it. Except there are some that serve food to the male Denastri who work here. I think they've got some kind of kitchen over in the Admin building."

"Have you talked to any of them?"

"Well, no, not really."

"Neither have I," said Gloria. "The only one I've encountered was the one who bawled me out at the market. If you get a chance, try to strike up a conversation with one of them. I'd like to learn more about them."

"Will do. Anything specific in mind?"

"No. It's just sort of a missing piece. That's what Elmo Hunt says, anyway. You have to trust the instincts of a man who's seen a hundred wars."

That afternoon, Gloria met with Jack McCray and some of his Security people. She didn't go out of her way to kick additional butts; Security was already demoralized. But she made it clear to them that she expected better performance from all concerned. There had been no progress made on the bombing the day of Gloria's arrival.

"There are seventy-three regular Denastri workers who have access to the Compound," McCray said, "and every one of them gets a full scan when they enter. It just isn't possible that one of them could have smuggled in that bomb."

"Could they have done it in pieces? One small component at a time?"

McCray shook his head. "No way."

"Does that figure of seventy-three include the females?" Gloria asked him.

The question seemed to surprise McCray. "Uh, well, no, it doesn't. There are about two dozen of them, I think, and each of them gets a scan, too. All they bring in is food."

"That leaves us just two possibilities, then, doesn't it? Either the bomb or its components came in via some route that we don't know about, or it was built inside the Compound using available materials."

"It's easy enough to build a crude bomb," said Elena Rossovitch, one of McCray's deputies. "Cleaning fluid, a few common chemicals . . . terrorists have been doing that for centuries."

"Then all you'd need is a place to put it together. Say, a kitchen?"

McCray caught Gloria's drift. "You think the females did it?"

"It's a possibility . . . and evidently one that you haven't investigated yet."

McCray shrugged. "It wasn't a high-priority item, but we'll get right on it. The thing is, it's tough even to communicate with the females. They have what amounts to their own separate language, and the translation software doesn't do a very good job with it. But I have to tell you, I just don't see the females as much of a factor. The males generally treat them with contempt or ignore them—except at mealtimes. Preparing and serving food seems to have religious implications although it's not clear exactly what's involved."

"I'd like a report on that, Jack," Gloria said. "If we're going to govern these people, we need to know more about them. I get the impression that the only Denastri we understand at all are the Thirdborn males. And I'm not sure we even understand *them* very well."

"Maybe you should meet with our staff exosociologist," McCray suggested.

"I didn't realize we had one."

"Dr. Mankato," Rossovitch explained. "She's been here for over a year, compiling data."

"Strange," said Gloria. "I don't think I've seen any of her reports in the files."

"There isn't one yet," Rossovitch said.

"Why not?"

McCray shook his head apologetically. "Well, she's an academic, you know what I mean? She's not in Dexta, just a contract worker from some university on New Florida. She probably has more detailed information about Denastri society than anyone, but we don't really get much input from her."

"Do you consult her at all?"

"Well, not much. Truth is, she's kind of . . . well, difficult."

"She's a pain in the ass," put in Rossovitch. "Her one and only concern is her own study, and she doesn't really give a damn about anything else. She's about ninety, and regards us as nothing but bothersome children."

"I'd like to meet her," Gloria said.

"I think she's over on Banako, at the moment," said McCray.

"Then get her back here as soon as possible."

"Yes, ma'am. But if you interrupt her studies, she won't like it."

Gloria silently sighed to herself. No one here seemed to like much of anything she did. Why should Dr. Mankato be any different?

"Just get her," she said.

Scooptown was spooky. When Petra stepped through the Transit ring into Scooptown, she was expecting a dusty, ramshackle mining camp, like Greenlodge back on Sylvania. Instead, she felt as if she had stepped into the workings of a vast, gleaming machine. The Transit ring was in Building #1, a large square structure that teemed and bustled like a street corner in Manhattan. Yet there was nothing random about the activity; humans, Denastri, and robots moved with purpose and planning, as if part of some elaborately choreographed stage production. A platoon of Marines abruptly fell into formation around Petra, Wong, and two of Wong's assistants, and officials from Imperium, KemTek, and Servitor appeared to greet them, seemingly from out of nowhere. And a hundred black-uniformed Servitor security troops formed a precisely spaced perimeter around the inner walls of the building. Petra, who had recently taken an elective course in Cinema History, looked around at the soaring metal towers and regimented masses and thought: *Metropolis*.

While Petra pondered the influence of German Surrealism, the corporate managers introduced themselves. They were, they emphasized, very busy men, and had little time for dog-and-pony shows for the sake of visiting bureaucrats. Wong expressed his sympathy and understanding and apologized for the necessity; the new Interim Governor, he stressed, had insisted on the meeting. The Corporate reps nodded wisely; they understood.

The ungainly procession made its way outdoors, and Petra, peering through the forest of Marines and Servitor people, got her first look at the sprawling site known as Scooptown. There were four main buildings, each as large as a sports arena, arrayed around a central plaza, where there were small shops, kiosks, and park benches. *A little patch of Earth,* she thought, remembering the baseball diamond in the Compound. The complex was a standard design, duplicating identical facilities on scores of other worlds. The dormitories were over there, the administration building over here, that was the factorium, and they had just left the central warehouse.

The pylons of an electronic fence ringed the site, and armored skimmers restlessly prowled the perimeter while Marine SALs stalked the skies.

There was only one entrance to Scooptown, and no one—human or Denastri—entered or left without a thorough scan. Petra watched while black-clad Servitor guards ran their instruments over a procession of Denastri Firstborns who had patiently queued up outside the gate. Petra would have described them as sullen-looking, except that *all* the Denastri she had seen seemed to look the same way.

"Each of them gets an ID pin as they enter," the Servitor manager explained. "Back in Control, their movements are monitored. If any Denastri enters an unauthorized location, we know about it immediately— not that it happens very often. The Nasties who work here know the rules and abide by them. We haven't had a serious incident inside the complex in six months. Most of the trouble comes outside, at the head of the mines or the refinery construction site."

"If *most* of it happens outside," Petra said, "then *some* of it must happen inside. Like what?"

The Servitor manager, whose name was Scoggins, gave Petra an impatient frown. "Minor incidents," he said at last. "Nothing to be concerned about."

"What sort of incidents?" Petra persisted.

"Minor scuffles. Misunderstandings. The kind of thing that happens at any facility as large as this."

"Could you be more specific?"

"Just your run-of-the-mill interspecies difficulties, Ms. Nash," Scoggins told her.

"Mr. Scoggins," Petra said, "we've had reports of Denastri being seriously beaten by Servitor people."

"Exaggerations. We respect the rights of the indigs, Ms. Nash. Servitor is committed to scrupulous adherence to all relevant regulations."

"Forgive me, Mr. Scoggins, but that's one of the

things we're here to look in to. Why are Denastri being mistreated here?"

"They aren't. Your reports are false or, as I said, exaggerated."

"Why would someone file a false report about such a thing?"

Scoggins shrugged. "We have several thousand humans here, Ms. Nash. It stands to reason that some small percentage of them will be unhappy. Despite the amenities we provide, Scooptown is—let us be honest—a pretty grim environment. People get antsy or frustrated, they nurse grudges and obsess over trivia. Minor incidents get blown out of proportion and assume great significance in the minds of a few malcontents or emotionally troubled individuals. We have a first-rate mental-health program and generally manage to nip that sort of thing in the bud, but there are always exceptions. I'm sure you understand."

"No," Petra said flatly, "I don't. You still haven't answered my question, Mr. Scoggins. Why are Denastri being mistreated?"

"Really, Ms. Nash," Wong interceded, "I think you're making mountains out of a few molehills."

"Maybe. But I still want to hear about the molehills. I saw one report of two Denastri Firstborn workers being stripped naked and beaten senseless by a bunch of drunken KemTek people."

"Yes, I'm familiar with the incident," Scoggins said. "A perfect example of what I'm talking about. The day of that incident, there had been a terrorist attack at the refinery site. Two of KemTek's people were seriously injured. That evening, some of their friends had a little too much to drink and took out their frustrations on a couple of Nasties who crossed their path. Unfortunate, but understandable, I'm sure you'll agree."

"The report said that the Denastri were also beaten

by Servitor security people after the KemTek drunks finished with them."

"An exaggeration, I'm sure," said the Servitor manager.

"And what was the disposition of the incident?"

"The workers were fined," Scoggins said.

"And the Denastri?"

"Dismissed, of course. Rightly or wrongly, the fact is that we can't have disgruntled Nasties roaming around inside the complex. There are fifty thousand natives out there beyond the fence, Ms. Nash. They've come here to work for us or, in the case of the females, to serve those who work here. There are more potential workers than jobs, so we don't have to employ anyone who might constitute a hazard. The Denastri who were unfortunately involved in that incident undoubtedly resented their treatment, so it was best for all concerned that we dismiss them."

"So, now they're out there in the native settlement, spreading that resentment?"

Scoggins forced a smile. "There's already more than enough resentment out there, Ms. Nash. Nothing we do in here is likely to add to it significantly."

Petra returned the smile. "I'm sure that's true, Mr. Scoggins. But you have it backwards. The question we should be asking is, can we do anything in here that will *lessen* the resentment out there?"

That seemed to strike Scoggins as a novel notion. He furrowed his brow for a few seconds, then looked at Petra. "Ms. Nash, *we stole their planet.* Of *course* they resent us. Nothing that happens in here, good or bad, is going to change that. Our operation here is geared to human and Corporate needs, not Denastri sensibilities."

Petra had no response to that. The procession moved onward and Petra followed along, wondering just how far the influence of German Surrealism extended. Scooptown, it seemed to her, was some sort of Corporate fantasyland where the only local reality that mattered was the rocks. Workers—both Denastri and human—were simply interchangeable parts in the machine.

From the roof of one of the buildings, she got a better view of the area. In the distance, she could see two of Imperium's immense Extractors—quarter-mile cubes that patiently devoured the landscape and exposed the rich, thick layer of HCH. The Imperium manager said that there was enough of the stuff to keep them busy for the next thirty years. Meanwhile, KemTek's refinery, in all its baroque complexity, was slowly taking form, while a spaceport was under construction along the bank of the broad, sluggish river that meandered across the empty plain. The Corporate investment here must have been huge.

Then, there was Nastyville, as it was known to the Terrans. A mile or so from the main gate, the native quarter sprawled along the riverbank like a fallen tree. Some fifty thousand locals lived in the low dun-colored buildings, with more arriving all the time. The Imperium manager explained that as the Extractors did their work, small, ancient villages dotting the plain had to be "reoptimized," resulting in the "labor resource centralization" of the population. In other words, as the Denastri's homes were destroyed, they were forced into what amounted to a refugee encampment where, presumably, they would reside for the next thirty years as the Terrans dug up their planet. Petra wondered what would become of them when the HCH was gone, but didn't ask.

She did ask about the dynamic in Nastyville. How did the As, Bs, and Cs get along? Swimmingly, Scoggins of Servitor assured her. Each group had its own neighborhood, and under the authority of an A-clan Regional Administrator—a Thirdborn with a retinue of Terran advisors—they were thriving in the rough-and-tumble boomtown. Naturally, there were unfortunate incidents, but Denastri-on-Densastri violence was none of Servitor's concern, unless it impinged on the Corporates' operations. DHG troops kept order, more or less, and the Marines stood ready to provide additional support should it be needed.

"I would think that Nastyville would be a prime breeding ground for insurgents," Petra said.

Scoggins casually dismissed her concern. "That's potentially true anywhere on the planet where two or more Nasties get together," he said. "It's actually convenient for us to concentrate the discontented element in once place."

"It must be convenient for the discontented element, too," Petra suggested.

The party was about to leave the rooftop when a bright flash from Nastyville froze them in place. A roiling column of dark smoke began to rise from the riverbank and, a few seconds later, the sharp crack of the explosion reached them. They all watched in silence for a moment, then Scoggins turned to them and smiled.

"Nothing to be concerned about. Happens all the time."

· 11 ·

Thursday morning, another bomb exploded, just outside the main entrance to the Compound. Three Denastri Home Guard troops and one Marine were killed. It was not a major or particularly unusual event, but it served to ratchet up tensions another notch, and it might have explained what happened that evening.

The Corporates' reception was held in a ballroom at the Imperial Hotel, where most of the upper-level executives resided. Formal affairs were rare in Enkar, so the occasion was regarded—especially by the executives' spouses—as a high point of the local social season. Glittering gems and stylish gowns were hauled out of storage, tuxedos were dusted off, and a twelve-piece Marine band was recruited for the event. Invitations had gone out to every major executive, senior Dexta personnel, Marine officers above the rank of captain, and selected media correspondents. A few high-ranking Denastri, including the Premier, were also invited, although only a handful of them actually showed up.

Gloria, after debating whether to play against her

image or to it, finally decided on the latter, and arrived in the ballroom wearing filmy low-slung harem pajamas and an open lacework vest, achieving her aim of being not quite nude and not quite *not* nude. That way she satisfied everyone; she gave the prudes and bluenoses something to harrumph about, and gave everyone else an erotically charged personal encounter with the famous Gloria VanDeen. And aside from fulfilling public expectations, she hoped to remind Delbert Barnes that she was still the same Gloria he had known back on Mynjhino.

She had been with Brian Hawkes then, and her relationship with Barnes had not been intimate, although it was clear that both of them wished it could have been otherwise. Gloria had come to admire and respect the second-generation Marine, who proved to be creative, flexible, and compassionate in the way he played his role on Mynjhino. She could not have succeeded there without his help. It occurred to her that the same might prove to be true on Denastri.

Gloria found Barnes, looking more attractive than ever in his trim dress blues, surrounded by a gaggle of Corporate execs, including Sally Voelker, the Servitor chief. All of them turned toward her as she approached. Barnes ran his eyes over her, grinned, and said, "Same old Gloria. Still improving the morale of the troops."

"I try," Gloria said. "I can't sing or dance, so—"

"Horseshit," rasped the familiar voice of Elmo Hunt. "Song and dance is what you Dexta types do best."

Gloria turned to her left and saw Hunt striding up, clad in his very nonformal, rugged correspondent, bushjacket outfit. But, next to him, Hettie Pando was decked out in an expensive designer original; Gloria knew it was expensive because it was precisely the same designer original that *she* was wearing. From an exclusive little shop on Thirty-seventy Street . . .

Pando and Gloria stared at each other in dismay. "Mr. Zhotay," Gloria said.

"I'll wring his neck, next time I see him," Pando vowed.

"I don't think that works with Hutumki," Gloria advised. "I think you have to grab them by their wattles."

"Mr. Zhotay, on Thirty-seventh Street, just off Lexington?" asked Sally Voelker. "Did the same thing to me a few years ago. I put out the word on him, but I guess it didn't do the job. The wattles, you say?"

"See?" said Hunt. "This is why all the truly civilized races turn their captives over to their women. You know the Cetongi, in Sector 14? Back in '87, I was—"

"Spare us, Elmo," Pando cut him off. "Save it for your memoirs."

"In which you will appear prominently, Hettie, my dear, in the chapter entitled, 'Castrating Bitches I Have Known.'"

"Darling Elmo! You *do* care!" Pando leaned over and gave Hunt a peck on his cheek.

"Why do I suddenly feel sorry for Mr. Zhotay?" Barnes asked.

"You feel sorry for everyone, Colonel," Voelker said. "That's your problem. Marines are supposed to be ruthless. Let Dexta handle the compassion."

"And Servitor, the ruthlessness?" Barnes and Voelker glared at one another for a few seconds. Gloria knew there had been problems between Servitor and the Marines, but she hadn't realized that they had spilled over into personal animosity.

"We do what we're paid to do, Colonel," Voelker said. "The shareholders insist upon it. If only the taxpayers would do the same."

"If the taxpayers gave the Marines the resources we need," Barnes replied, "there'd be no need for Servitor, Ms. Voelker."

"Yes, of course. General Matabele said the same

thing the other day. The same sad song the Imperial Marines have been singing for centuries. Just give us more of everything and we'll get the job done . . . eventually."

"They do, you know," put in Hunt. "Get the job done, I mean. Seen it dozens of times. The Government frequently sends them to do the *wrong* job, of course, but that's not the Marines' fault."

Voelker skeptically eyed the living legend. "And you think this is the wrong job, Mr. Hunt?" she asked him.

"Where does it say that in order to dig up rocks, you've got to conquer the people who live on top of them?"

"Sometimes that's the only way," Voelker said.

"And sometimes it's not," he responded. "Perhaps someday the Spirit will bless us with a government that can tell the difference."

That, inevitably, led to a discussion about politics and the election. Gloria exchanged a look with Barnes, and the two of them unobtrusively stepped away from the throng. They met at the bar, where a Denastri Firstborn served them champagne.

"The Corpos giving you a tough time?" Gloria asked him. Up close, Barnes looked drawn and weary.

Barnes managed a grim smile. "Goes with the job," he said. "As a regimental commander, I was shielded from a lot of it. Now, running the division, it all lands in my lap."

"Not all of it. Some of it lands in *mine*. Mynjhino was a snap, compared to this."

Barnes's weak smile turned into a grin. "Those were the days. Only *two* vicious races."

"And Servitor."

Barnes nodded. "And Servitor. Nothing a Marine likes more than guns for hire. They get paid better than our people, get all kinds of perks, and they get to play by a completely different set of rules."

"How so?"

"Look," Barnes said, pausing to wet his whistle with a sip of champagne, "if the Marines screw up, everybody immediately knows about it. We violate the *Code,* a complaint goes right up the ladder to General Matabele, then on to Quadrant and finally to HQ. A parallel complaint goes through the Imperial Governor—you, in this case—and back to the Household, Parliament, and Dexta. The General Staff acts quickly, and somebody gets called to account for whatever bad thing may have happened. But what if Servitor does something that's not strictly proper? If there's a complaint at all, whose desk does it land on?"

"Edgar Wong's," Gloria said.

"Where it dies. If, for some reason, it gets past Wong and back to Dexta HQ, it still belongs to Corporate Affairs."

"Where it's also likely to die," Gloria said, nodding.

"And if it does get beyond Corporate Affairs, it has to go to a formal Dexta Board, which must issue a Finding that Servitor is in violation of the *Code.* At which point the Board can order Imperial Marshals to enforce compliance."

"At which point," Gloria continued, "Servitor gets a writ and the whole thing winds up in the Imperial courts for the next five years."

"Exactly. If I start shooting Denastri babies tomorrow, within a month I'll be tried, convicted, and sentenced. Somebody from Servitor shoots those babies, and maybe five years from now, he gets a fine that the company will pay for him."

"So there's really no effective control on Servitor?"

"They can do pretty much whatever they want. Marines are stuck with outmoded concepts like service and honor. For Servitor, there's nothing but the profit motive. Five years from now, Imperium and KemTek will be turning a fat profit on HCH and Servitor will have fulfilled its contract and gotten paid. Money is literally all that matters to them."

"Making money," Gloria pointed out, "is why Corporates exist."

"And it's also why we're on Denastri."

Gloria didn't really want to talk shop with Barnes, but it seemed unavoidable. As she was trying to find a way to move their conversation to a more personal plane, Petra and Bryce Denton showed up. Petra had reverted to her modified-Tiger mode and looked cute and sexy in a midnight-blue gown that plunged in a wide V from her shoulders to her navel. Denton, in his tux, raised his champagne glass in a salute.

"Here's to the Mynjhino Veterans Society," he said. "May we all continue to profit from career-boosting disasters."

"A noble sentiment, Bryce," Gloria observed.

"Just realistic. If peace breaks out, Colonel Barnes will be selling pencils on street corners, and I'll be covering asteroid impacts on methane moons. You Dexta ladies will go back to counting paper clips. Fortunately for us, peace ain't about to break out—here, or anywhere else."

"Whew," exclaimed Petra. "You had me worried there, for a minute."

Denton extended his arm around Petra's shoulders and massaged her upper arm. He looked at Gloria and Barnes. "So," he said, "what's the deal with the Governor and the Jarhead? You two finally making some whoopee?"

Barnes's eyes narrowed as he peered at the slightly drunk journalist. "If we do, Denton," he said, "it'll be none of your damned business."

"Not so!" Denton airily objected. "If the Governor and a senior military commander are canoodling, that has direct policy implications. It would be a legitimate story."

Gloria and Barnes glanced at each other. Drunk or not, Denton had spoken the uncomfortable truth. If the Imperial Governor was in bed with the military—figuratively or otherwise—it would inevitably become grist for the media mill. Whatever the reality, it would look bad; and both Gloria and Barnes had risen high enough in their professions to understand the importance of appearances. Gloria felt like grabbing Denton by *his* wattles. Damn him!

Barnes evidently felt the same way. "Leave it alone, Denton," he growled.

Denton nodded elaborately. "As you wish, *mon colonel*. But even if *I* would never presume to take advantage of my close personal relationship with the principals simply in order to tell the people of the Empire the lurid truth about their leaders on war-torn Denastri, I can assure you that my brother and sister jackals would have no such scruple. I'd find a broom closet with a good lock on it, if I were you."

Barnes looked as if he would have liked to call in an airstrike on Denton. "'Jackals' is right," he spat. "Dammit, everyone's entitled to a private life."

Denton gave Gloria a skeptical look. "Is that true, Gloria?" he asked.

Gloria, from years of experience, knew that it wasn't. It annoyed her that Denton knew it, too. She pursed her lips, exhaled heavily, then said, "He's right, Delbert. Imperial Governors don't have private lives. This one doesn't, anyway."

As if to confirm Gloria's words, Sally Voelker arrived, eyebrows arched, and said, "Aha! What have we here? Ah, yes, you two know each other from Mynjhino, don't you? Well, the Marines are famous for getting everywhere first, aren't they, Colonel?"

"Delbert and I are old friends," Gloria said quickly, before Barnes could respond.

"How convenient for you," Voelker said. "Service above and beyond the call, eh, Colonel?"

Gloria wanted to yank Voelker's flame-colored hair out by its roots, but calmed herself with a long sip of champagne. Barnes, quietly steaming, said nothing and simply stared at the Servitor chief.

Bryce Denton leaped into the pregnant pause. "Ms. Voelker," he said, "maybe you'll have a little time later to answer some questions about what happened on Moho Five."

Voelker gave him a look that might have frightened a more sober man.

"You remember, Ms. Voelker. That little pirate base that Servitor cleaned up, over in Sector 10? Wanted to ask you—"

"You really are an idiot, aren't you, Denton?" With that, Voelker walked away without another word.

"She's right," Denton said glumly, "I am an idiot. She'll make me pay for that."

"So what happened in Sector 10?" Petra asked.

"Fraulein Voelker's last assignment," Denton explained. "Couple of years ago, Servitor was doing contract security for GalTrans in the Kettle Drum Nebula. Rough neighborhood, lots of hijackings. Then Servitor found the pirates' base and blew it into the middle of next week. A public service from your friends at Servitor."

"I seem to recall the story," said Gloria.

"The *official* story," Denton said. "But, intrepid journalist that I am, I have sources who tell a somewhat different story. Seems that pirate base consisted of one rusting freighter and a town full of wildcat settlers on a supposedly virgin moon. Seven hundred and fifty dead, mostly women and children. Next thing you know, GalaxCo arrives and sets up mining operations. And, strangely enough, the hijacking rate in the Kettle Drum Nebula remains unaffected."

"If you know that for a fact," Barnes said, "then why don't you report it? Are you afraid of Servitor?"

"I *am* Servitor," Denton said. "Apparently you forgot that ENS is a subsidiary of Servitor. My sources were deep inside the company, and nobody else got the story. I'd leak it to the competition, but they'd trace it right back to me, and Sally the Hun would have my liver for breakfast. But that's where she came from, folks. Denastri's her reward for a job well done."

Later, Gloria saw a Denastri Fifthborn standing alone near a wall. Barnes was busy with an Imperium exec, so Gloria wandered over to the Denastri. She wasn't sure, but she thought that he was the officer who had been with her on the morning of her disastrous sightseeing tour. She offered him a smile and said, "Good evening, General 5A-46-9C. I'm delighted to see you here. I trust you're having an enjoyable time."

Gloria had no computer pad with her, but the Fifthborn had his own translation device, and listened to its rendering of Gloria's words. Denastri never seemed to smile—or display any other identifiable facial expression—but the general tilted his head forward in acknowledgment.

"Exalted Governor VanDeen," the software said, "it is mostly pleasurable in the extreme to partake of Terran hospitality." Terran hospitality, in fact, was marginal; there was no Denastri-compatible food or drink available, and most of the humans seemed to go out of their way to avoid encountering the Denastri Fifthborn. Gloria couldn't help wondering if the invitation to the reception had been a calculated snub, designed to impress upon the Denastri leaders just how little they mattered to humans.

She attempted to make pleasant, sociable small talk, but found it an uphill struggle. The general's translation software rendered their banalities in strange and unexpected ways, and Gloria wondered if either one of them knew what the hell their conversation was about. When she commented on the remarkable constancy of weather on Denastri, the general's response came out, "The rain, in the main, is on the plain." Gloria suppressed an urge to burst into song.

"Tell me, General, do the Denastri have social events like this? Parties, and so forth?"

"My revered clan," the software replied a moment later, "engages in society of a form not dissimilar to Terran activity, but in ways of indescribable privacy, for example."

In other words, it's none of my business, she thought. "Do the different clans mingle?" she asked. The Fifthborn offered a look of blank incomprehension, so Gloria amplified. "I mean, do the Rock-clan, the Water-clan, and the Wind-clan get together at social occasions?"

It was hard to be sure, but Gloria got the impression that the general was shocked by the suggestion. "A wrongness of impossible completeness," he said after a moment, then added something that stumped the software. *"Idiomatic phrase,"* it reported, *"possibly analogous to 'A place for everything, and everything in its place,' or 'Each to his own.'"* Gloria took that as a negative response: no, the clans didn't mingle.

"So you don't get together socially? But surely, you interact economically and politically."

"Economic functions are—*unknown word*—of honorable necessity. Political functions enjoy order and possible usefulness. Our present government, gratefully imposed by Terrans, fulfills essential requirements in satisfaction of my revered clan, most likely. Other clans fear and obey, a goodness."

"But is it enough that the other clans merely fear and obey?" Gloria persisted. "A coalition requires more than mere obedience. Can't you work together, to achieve goals of common interest to all the clans?"

"Other clans fear and obey," the general repeated, without elaboration. "*Pejorative adjective* Wind-clan terrorists resist obedience and therefore require mostly fear, at least."

"I have spoken with your Honored Premier, 3A-27-12J," Gloria said. "He seems to understand the necessity of all the clans working together."

The Denastri Fifthborn moved his head in a way that, had he been human, Gloria would have interpreted as a gesture of contempt. "Thirdborn 3A-27-12J perceives Terran demands and attempts gratification. A function of necessity, almost."

"Yes, I understand that the Honored Premier must work closely with the Empire and attempt to comply with our guidelines. But to succeed, he needs your support. The support of the Denastri Home Guard."

The general seemed puzzled. After a moment, he replied, "Why should we lift up the Premier?"

Gloria presumed a software inadequacy, and tried again. "Support him," she said. "Stand behind him. Follow his lead."

This seemed to baffle the general even more thoroughly. "But he is *Thirdborn!*" he said at last, as if the explanation were obvious.

"Yes, but—"

"I am *Fifthborn!*" the general insisted.

"I understand," Gloria said, "but still, he leads your government, doesn't he? Surely, he deserves your support."

"I am *Fifthborn,*" the general repeated, with an air of finality. The more she learned about the Denastri, Gloria decided, the less she understood them. She dropped the subject and tried a new line of inquiry.

"General, have you or your people heard anything more about Lord Kenarbin?"

The general shook his head awkwardly, apparently in imitation of human gestures he had seen. "A disappointing sadness, at least," he said.

"You have no new information?"

"A sadness," he said again. Gloria could only agree with the sentiment.

As the evening wore on, Gloria danced and chatted with a succession of Marines, Corporate execs, and a few of her bolder Dexta underlings. She was used to being the center of attention, and appreciated the opportunity to pick the brains of people who had been on Denastri longer than she had and, presumably, knew more about it. Opinions ranged from "Pull out immediately," to "Get tough," to "Get tougher."

Some of the crowd, it became clear, were much more than half-drunk. Voices were raised, and here and there around the ballroom, arguments escalated into shouting matches. Off in one corner, young Jack McCray was going at it, jaw to jaw, with one of Edgar Wong's smug minions, and in another corner, a Marine major was bellowing at a Servitor exec. Gloria sought out Barnes.

"Maybe we ought to do something about this," Gloria suggested.

Barnes frowned. "They're just blowing off steam," he said. "Probably a good thing."

That proposition became debatable when McCray took a sudden swing and decked the man from Corporate Affairs, who rebounded from the floor and tackled McCray. Both of them wound up on the floor, grappling like drunken sailors.

"I didn't see that," Gloria said quickly, turning away from the action. She had already warned McCray about physical violence directed at his coworkers, and didn't want to be put in a position where she was forced to sack her chief of Security. But, as she looked toward the opposite corner of the ballroom, she couldn't help noticing that the Marine major and the Servitor exec had also begun exchanging blows.

"And I didn't see *that*," said Barnes.

It soon became impossible for either of them to pretend that nothing interesting was happening. Some critical mass seemed to have been reached, and within moments a general free-for-all had begun. For a brief instant, Gloria wondered if she should take advantage of the chaos and kick Sally Voelker's shapely ass, but dismissed the thought as unworthy of an Imperial Governor; anyway, Voelker seemed to have surrounded herself with a phalanx of beefy Servitor men and would have been difficult to reach. Instead, she retreated with Barnes to a neutral corner and watched, fascinated and horrified, as bodies went flying and noses got broken.

"We have to stop this!" she shouted to Barnes above the din.

"What did you have in mind?" he asked.

Elmo Hunt, she noticed, seemed to be enjoying himself immensely, and casually bashed a few chops with his elbow; he was evidently an old hand at these things. Most of the other participants seemed to make up in enthusiasm what they lacked in experience. No serious damage seemed to have been done yet, but if the mayhem continued, it was only a matter of time until someone got his neck broken. With an increasing sense of urgency, Gloria looked around in search of a solution. One turned out to be close at hand, on the wall just behind her.

Gloria hit the light switches, and the ballroom was abruptly plunged into darkness. After a minute or so, the thumps, thuds, and curses died away, and she turned the lights back on. When she saw the dismal scene before her, she was tempted to turn them off again. As Barnes waded into the scrum and attempted to sort out the bodies, she noticed General 5A-46-9C standing by a wall, his almond eyes impassively taking in the spectacle of his human overlords.

Mostly an embarrassment, she thought. *At least.*

·12·

The invitation was delivered by a Thirdborn aide to the Premier. He seemed nervous as he stood in front of Gloria's desk; possibly he had heard about the brawl at last week's reception and feared for his safety in the presence of the violent and unpredictable Terrans. Gloria couldn't say that she blamed him.

"The Rite of Continuation is a mostly sacred event of utmost importance to humble Denastri people," he explained. "In hope of increasing understanding between our humble selves and Honored Imperial Governor of glorious Terran Empire, we are completely begging the honored presence of your exalted self at the time and place of our example, it seems. *Unknown word, possibly 'foreigners'*—are mostly never seen at Rite of Continuation, for good and plenty reasons, we hope. Impossible exception to ancient customs is adequate fulfillment of humble Denastri desire for better sense of goodness between our different selves. Much honor to our humble selves, and to revered Imperial Governor, by your significant presence at our sacred Rite. If possible, your exalted self is mostly welcome and desired by humble Denastri, at least."

Gloria tried to take it all in. It seemed that she was being honored by an invitation to a sacred ritual that was rarely, if ever, witnessed by non-Denastri. She felt a distinct thrill when she grasped the significance of the invitation. Could this be a breakthrough?

"I am mostly pleased—" Gloria stopped herself. The problem with the translation software was that after hearing enough of it, you started to talk like it. She tried again. "Please tell the revered Premier that I am very honored by his kind invitation, and I will be delighted to attend the Rite of Continuation. It is a great goodness that your people and mine should come to know each other better. Please extend my gratitude to the Honored Premier."

The Thirdborn bowed and quickly departed, probably glad to have escaped with his life. Gloria leaned back in her chair and gave a low whistle. "Wow," she said to herself. She drummed her fingers on her desk and thought about the meaning of the invitation for a few moments. Then she hit a button on her desk and said, "Petra? Is Dr. Mankato back from Banako yet?"

"The exosociologist? I think she got in yesterday."

"Good. Ask her to come see me at her earliest con— no, better make that an order to report here in half an hour. From what I've heard, she might consider her 'earliest convenience' to be next year."

While she was waiting for Dr. Mankato, Gloria received word that the courier from Earth had finally arrived. When she viewed the message on her console, she found that it was about what she had expected. In a public statement, the Emperor expressed his regrets and condolences for the tragic losses suffered by "the people of Denastri," and his confidence that all Imperial personnel would carry on with their usual courage, determination, and professionalism. As for a new Imperial Governor, he had merely said that one would be appointed "in due course." Mingus had said much the same in his message addressed to every member of the Dexta establishment on the planet.

Mingus had also sent a private message to Gloria. "Charles," he said, "seems to content to leave you in place as Interim Governor for as long as it takes for you to carry out your mission. Your additional powers may facilitate things. I, of course, would like to get you back here as soon as possible, and I intend to prod him about naming a permanent ImpGov. However, I think you should plan on spending at least another month on Denastri, and possibly more than that. The fact is, Charles might have a hard time finding someone to take the job. News of the bombing has only intensified the political controversy over Denastri, and no one is eager to be associated with such a public failure. You'll just have to carry on as best you can for now. Let me know if there's anything I can do to help you."

Gloria was struck by the fact that even in his private message, Mingus had not mentioned Kenarbin. He was too wise and experienced to put anything in print that could come back to bite him. She also couldn't help noticing that both Charles and Mingus had deftly dropped the Denastri hot potato into her lap. "Thanks, guys," she said.

Dr. Doris Mankato arrived an hour later. She was a tiny, well-weathered woman in her nineties; with antigerontologicals and a little effort, she might have looked fifty, but she obviously hadn't made the effort. She wore spectacles—a rarity—and had short gray hair that she apparently tended with garden shears. Gloria ushered her over to a couch and a table bearing coffee, tea, and cookies. Without waiting to be asked, she helped herself to a cup of coffee and a chocolate chip cookie. Gloria sat down next to her and offered an ingratiating smile.

"I've been looking forward to meeting you, Dr. Mankato," she said.

"You pulled me away from my work," Mankato said. "My studies on Banako were very important, and it didn't help to be interrupted. I hope this isn't just some stupid formality, Governor."

"It's neither formal nor stupid, Doctor," Gloria replied. "I need your input."

Mankato brushed some cookie crumbs from her chin and looked at Gloria. "Well? What is it?"

Gloria paused and stared at the exosociologist for a moment. She decided that attempting to be nice just wasn't going to work with Dr. Mankato. This appeared to be one of those times when it would pay to be officious and high-handed.

"First, Doctor," she said, "as a general matter, I see that you have been on Denastri for fifteen months, and in all that time you have submitted just two preliminary reports amounting to a total of some three thousand words. You have a contract with Dexta, Doctor, and it requires regular and detailed reports concerning conditions on this planet. This is not some leisurely academic exercise. If you are unable to fulfill the conditions of your contract, I'm sure we can find another exosociologist who will."

Mankato met her gaze. "I see," she said. "You want to be a hard-ass about this."

"In a word," said Gloria, "yes."

Mankato nodded and offered something that might have been a smile. "Good," she said. "I get so tired of namby-pamby Dexta clods who don't know what they want and wouldn't recognize it if they saw it. Poor Freya let me walk all over her."

Gloria returned the smile. "That won't be a problem with me," Gloria assured her. "In one week, I want to receive a detailed report on your work to date, with particular emphasis on interclan relations and internal Denastri political conditions. I also want to learn as much as possible about the role of females in Denastri society."

"You don't want much, do you? I could give you a hundred thousand words on each of those subjects without even scratching the surface."

"Boil it down to about ten or twenty thousand words, if you would, Doctor."

"Can I use words of more than two syllables, or do you want the Busy Bureaucrats' Edition?"

"Use as many syllables as you think appropriate," Gloria said. "But if I get some piece of jargon-laden academic babble, I'll boot your gray old ass off of this planet faster than you can say 'Grant Proposal.' Are we clear on that, Dr. Mankato?"

Mankato took a sip of her coffee. "Good java," she said. "Cookies aren't bad, either. You'll do, Toots. Just testing the waters."

"I understand. Can I sweeten that for you with a little Belgravian whisky?"

"Belgravian? Hell, yes! All you can spare."

Gloria retrieved the whisky from her desk, poured a splash of it into Mankato's cup, then fixed a cup for herself. Mankato raised her cup in a salute. "Confusion to the bureaucrats," she said.

"And a plague upon academics," Gloria responded.

"Nice to know where we stand," Mankato said. "Heard a lot about you, VanDeen. Didn't believe half of it, of course."

"Which half didn't you believe?"

"The part about you screwing all the miners on Sylvania. Seemed excessive."

"No," Gloria lied, smiling, "that's the true part."

"Ah. Well, now that I've gotten a close look at you, I guess I can believe it after all. Avatar of Joy, huh? Someday, I'd like to do a study on the Spiritists. As religious fanatics go, they're rather interesting. Meantime, what can I do for you?" She took a long sip of her sweetened coffee and leaned back on the couch.

"I just received an invitation to attend something called a Rite of Continuation."

"Are you shitting me?" Mankato demanded.

Gloria shook her head. "Not at all. The invitation came from the Premier himself."

"Not likely," Mankato said. "He wouldn't have the authority. An invitation like that had to have come from the Sixthborns. Don't happen to know which one, do you?"

"I've never even met one of them."

"Figures. Still, that lickspittle Premier wouldn't dare issue an invitation like that. Thirdborns handle worldly matters. Religion is the exclusive province of the Sixthborn. It seems that one of them wants you to witness his death and resurrection. Interesting."

"Death? Resurrection?"

"I'm being anthropomorphic," Mankato explained. "By Denastri standards, it's neither death nor resurrection, just a natural transition. But by our standards, one Sixthborn dies, and another assumes his identity and place in the religious hierarchy. No Terran has ever witnessed the Rite, as far as I know. I want a full report. I'll give you a list of questions I want answered."

Gloria raised an eyebrow. "Will this be on the midterm?"

Three days later, fully briefed by Dr. Mankato, Gloria got out of the limo skimmer and slowly ascended the marble steps of the immense Temple of Eternal Goodness in the company of Premier 3A-27-12J. For the occasion, the

Premier was wearing a deep purple hooded cloak, and Gloria wore a slightly larger human version of the same garment. A large crowd of Denastri—mostly First- and Secondborns—had gathered in the streets to watch the event, but none of them were admitted to the Temple. What seemed to be an honor guard of Fourthborns stood at attention, flanking the main entrance.

Inside, the lighting was dim and it took a few moments for Gloria's eyes to adjust. The interior of the Temple consisted of one vast chamber, with a high, vaulted ceiling that reminded her of ancient European cathedrals. The walls were adorned with intricate friezes carved into the marble—very long ago, it seemed, from the blurred, eroded look of them. They apparently portrayed scenes from Denastri history, but it was impossible to glean any details based on what she could see. Soft, atonal music reverberated through the chamber; it could almost have been a Gregorian chant. The overall similarity of the scene to the religious and ceremonial sites of Terrans and other species struck Gloria as significant. *Maybe we aren't really so different,* she thought.

Row upon row of simple stone benches spread before her. Since she was with the Premier, Gloria expected to be seated near the front of the chamber, but was surprised when a Fourthborn ushered them to a spot on the left in the very last row. Looking around as she settled onto the bench, she noticed that there were only a few other Thirdborns in view. Ahead of her, the benches were occupied by Fourth- and Fifthborns and, far to the front, nearly a hundred meters away, a dozen or so rows of benches remained empty; apparently they were reserved for the Sixthborns, who had not yet arrived. At the center and right of the chamber, the benches remained unoccupied.

Gloria leaned over to the Premier and whispered, "Your Temple is very beautiful."

The Premier didn't look at her, but his software

whispered, "Silence is of a technical necessity, almost. Honored Governor is requested please to observe absence of speech, as this humble Thirdborn must bear responsibility for exceptional presence of unwanted intrusion, most likely." In other words, Gloria thought, *I went out on a limb to get you in, so shut up and don't embarrass me.*

And yet, according to Mankato, the invitation had to have been issued by a Sixthborn, and the Premier was no more than an intermediary. She wondered, not for the first time, just how much authority the Premier actually possessed within Denastri society. He seemed a competent and devoted public servant, but did that really mean anything on this world? He was merely a Thirdborn, after all.

Gloria heard a rustling sound and the shuffling of many feet behind her. She looked back and saw a solemn procession of hooded Fourthborns entering the chamber, but these wore cloaks of silvery gray. They ponderously moved forward and began occupying the benches at the center of the chamber. They had to have been B-clan, she realized. According to Mankato, religion trumped politics on Denastri, and even hostile C-clan leaders would be attending the ceremony. The B-clan Fourthborns filed in and were seated at the rear, then came a procession of the taller Fifthborns, who occupied the benches closer to the front.

Next came the C-clan, clad in cloaks of a deep russet. They filled in the benches on the far right. Gloria watched them closely, but could detect no obvious differences between them and the other two clans. But would a Denastri visiting Earth see anything to distinguish Spiritists, Christians, and Muslims?

When the last of the C-clan Fifthborns were seated, the music gradually grew louder and more energetic, almost frantic in its clashing harmonies and jittery rhythms. Gloria looked around but could see no musicians. Where did the music come from? Was it piped in? She couldn't tell.

The music reached a cacophonous crescendo, then abruptly ceased. A moment later, it was replaced by a high-pitched keening—almost a lost and lonely wail in the wilderness, like wolves in a snowstorm. To her surprise, Gloria realized that it was coming from everyone in the chamber, including the Premier, sitting next to her. She looked at him and saw that his almond eyes were closed.

From three alcoves at the far front of the chamber, the Sixthborns made their entrance. Even in their cloaks, they looked awkward and gangly, like impossibly tall, crimson-colored mantises. As the keening continued, they solemnly filed in and took their places on the benches to the front. Gloria, who considered herself immune to most forms of religious folderol—even that of the Spiritists, to whom she nominally belonged—couldn't help feeling a sense of awe. The Denastri had been performing these rites for thirty thousand years and more, and even an infidel outsider had to respect the reverence and devotion inherent in the event. Whatever nonsense the Denastri believed, they believed it very deeply.

One of the A-clan Sixthborn got to his feet and stood on an elevated altar. According to Mankato, this had to have been the most exalted of the A-clan—6A-1-1A, the equivalent of a pope or supreme lama. From so great a distance, Gloria was unable to make out his facial features, shadowed beneath his purple hood, but he carried himself with great solemnity and pride. He began to speak, and Gloria plugged in her earpiece and set her pad for direct transmission so as not to disturb those around her.

"The necessary moment has come," he intoned, "for the—*unknown word*—of our revered brother, 6A-7-14D. *Unknown word*—becoming—*unknown word*—as his fathers—*indeterminate phrase*—son and self, together in exalted—*unknown word*—*indeterminate phrase*—*unknown word.*" The software paused, as if to collect itself, then reported, "*Speaker is employing obscure vocabulary, possibly of archaic origin. Continue translation?*"

Gloria shut off the pad and removed the earpiece. The Sixthborn seemed to be using the Denastri equivalent of Latin, or some other ancient and sacred language.

The Denastri pope droned onward for another fifteen minutes. At one point, the entire congregation rose to its feet and Gloria followed suit. Then everyone sat down again and the Sixthborn continued the liturgy, or whatever it was. For all Gloria knew, he might have been announcing the results of last week's Bingo tournament.

Finally, two more Sixthborns rose and joined the speaker on the altar. These must have been the subjects of the ceremony, father and son—although, to Gloria, they looked identical. In fact, according to Mankato, in every meaningful sense, they *were* identical. The son had spent years absorbing the knowledge, experience, and very essence of the Sixthborn who had sired him. That process was now complete, and the father was about to die and the son would replace him in the Denastri hierarchy: 6A-7-14D was dead; long live 6A-7-14D.

One of the Sixthborns, presumably the soon-to-be-dead father, stepped forward, raised his arms, and began a rhythmic chant. The keening sound again erupted from the congregation; to Gloria's Terran ears it sounded mournful, yet she knew that the Rite of Continuation was considered a joyous occasion. That was not unprecedented, even on Earth. Gloria remembered reading about the ancient jazz funerals in the Lost City of New Orleans, where musicians simultaneously wept and capered, mourning the death but celebrating the life. The difference was that in this case, the beloved departed had not yet departed.

Then it was the son's turn to hold forth, and he did,

at even greater length than his dad. Out of curiosity and boredom, Gloria again tried the translation software, but was treated to another litany of unknown words and indeterminate phrases. Eventually, the son completed his ritual oration, and the pope followed with another half hour's worth of untranslatable pieties and profundities.

Eventually, all the necessary words had been spoken, and the father climbed onto a raised stone platform and stretched out, his hands clasped together over his breast. The pope withdrew a wandlike instrument from his cloak and handed it to the son, who stood behind the platform, raised his arms, and chanted some more while the congregation keened once again. Then he aimed the wand at his father's chest and a ruby-red beam of light appeared.

Spirit, Gloria thought, *they're killing him!* The laser sliced into the father's body as the keening reached a crescendo. Gloria had assumed that the death would be natural, and had wondered how the Denastri managed to regulate the moment of their own demise; it was a shock to discover that the process wasn't natural at all. She wondered what would happen if a father changed his mind and decided to stick around for a while. That probably never happened, she decided, and if it did, they would probably kill him anyway. The show must go on . . .

The laser beam carved a path through the head of the dead Denastri, then shut off. The son moved around to the front of the platform, his back to the congregation. Gloria couldn't see what he was doing, but after a few moments the son turned to face the crowd, his hands cupped together, holding a lumpy gray mass the size of a volleyball.

It was his father's brain.

The son tilted his head forward and began to eat. Gloria barely managed to avoid throwing up.

She watched in transfixed horror as the son ate his fill of his father's gray matter. Then the A-clan Sixthborns rose as one and filed up to the altar. The son held the dripping remains out to them and each, in turn, leaned forward to take a bite.

Gloria took a deep breath. Mankato had told her that the Rite of Continuation involved some unknown form of ritual cannibalism, but she had assumed that it was merely symbolic, like the communion of the Christian sects that symbolically consumed the blood and body of their messiah. But this was the real thing.

Aliens are alien, she reminded herself.

And maybe that was the message the Denastri had intended to convey to her with their invitation to attend this bloody ceremony. They must have wanted her to see for herself just how different their two races really were. The goal was not mutual understanding but an appreciation of the impossibility of such understanding.

The Empire was vast and diverse, and contained races of such bizarre opacity that not even the most determined exosociologists could hope to comprehend them. Generally, Imperial policy was to let such species tend their own gardens, and interactions were limited to the minimum necessary to maintain functional relations. But such a hands-off policy could never work on Denastri, where daily contact between humans and natives was unavoidable and essential to the overriding goal of extracting the HCH.

The ghastly ceremony brought home to Gloria at a visceral level the impossibility of the task she faced. The Denastri would not—*could not*—fully adapt to human modes of existence. And humans could never adequately comprehend the imperatives that drove a race that engaged in such behavior.

And yet, she thought, *here we are.*

When, at last, the ceremony was finished, Gloria stood next to the Premier on the marble steps outside the door of the Temple. He seemed nervous and anxious to be elsewhere, but Gloria insisted that they wait there as the congregation emerged.

"I want you to point out the leading C-clan Fifthborn," she told him. "Their top general."

The Premier looked aghast. "Exalted Governor!" he protested. "This would be mostly improper in the highest extreme! This humble Thirdborn cannot—"

"Just do it," Gloria told him curtly.

They locked eyes for a moment, then the Premier meekly nodded his head. "It shall be done," he said.

The procession filed out in dignified silence until, finally, the Premier pointed at the last of the C-clan Fifthborn. Gloria stepped in front of him and said, "Honored General, I must have words with you."

The tall, orange-tinted Denastri stared at Gloria for a moment, then tilted his head forward. The two of them moved to the side of the steps, away from the doors.

"Honored Terran offal," the Fifthborn said, "I trust you learned and profited from this experience."

"It was very educational," Gloria replied, "but we must speak of other matters. You are holding Lord Kenarbin. We want him back. I'm sure you know that Imperial policy forbids open negotiations for the release of hostages, but it might be possible for us to arrange something privately. This is a matter of the highest importance, and we are willing to discuss an accommodation that would be of interest and value to you and your clan."

The Fifthborn listened to the translation and said nothing.

"You know where to find me," Gloria said. "This could be a great opportunity for you, General. If you are wise, you and your clan may get some of the things you want. Don't miss a chance that may not come your way again."

The Fifthborn nodded slightly. "As you said, I know where to find you." He stared at her another moment, then turned and walked away.

·13·

The Marines were planning a Big Push—the latest in a series. Every few weeks, the Marines felt the need to flex their muscles and venture forth to impress the Denastri with Imperial might, and it was time for another such show of force. In any case, terrorist incidents had increased alarmingly around Scooptown. One attack had actually managed to do some minor damage to one of the immense Extractors, putting it out of service for two expensive days. More seriously, another attack at the KemTek refinery site had killed seven workers—two human, five Denastri—and delayed the whole project by at least a week. The Corporates were demanding action and the Marines were prepared to provide it. On the morning of the appointed day, Gloria joined Barnes in the Compound's Command Center to observe the offensive.

The Operations Room reminded Gloria of the control room of a vid network. There were monitors everywhere, with dozens of Marine personnel manning consoles arrayed in a broad horseshoe formation. Barnes took his station at a central console and Gloria sat next to him. They were joined by DHG General 5A-46-9C and a handful of his subordinates. The Denastri surveyed the array of equipment and humans surrounding them and seemed to fidget nervously. For them, Gloria figured, this must have been as strange and unsettling an environment as the Temple had been for her.

"This is going to be a combined operation," Barnes explained. "The goal is to clean out the insurgent bases in the native settlement along the river, a couple of klicks from Scooptown."

"Nastyville."

Barnes looked at her and nodded. "Right," he said. "Sorry about the name. It's what the Corporate people call it, and we're stuck with it."

"I understand," Gloria assured him.

"We'll be sending two companies and a heavy weapons platoon—about six hundred troops—straight down the main road between Scooptown and Nastyville. They'll be flanked by about a thousand DHG troops, who will move through the streets of the town. They'll be on foot, for the most part, so they'll have an easier time of it than we would with our big vehicles. There will also be about a hundred Servitor security people involved."

"What's their function?"

"Observation and reconnaissance. They'll identify suspected insurgent strongholds and tag them for future operations. Our immediate goal is to clean out known insurgent bases in the C-clan section of Nastyville, but long term, Servitor wants to establish a presence there. Sally Voelker is in Scooptown to oversee that end of things. We'll coordinate with them, of course, but they'll be peripheral to the main operation."

Barnes adjusted his headset and flicked a switch on the console. The face of a Marine officer appeared on one of the monitors.

"Ross? Communications check. How do you read me?"

"Five by five, Del," the officer reported. "We're all set here."

Barnes turned to Gloria. "That's Lieutenant Colonel Borisov," he explained, "the regimental commander. He'll direct operations from Scooptown. His exec, Major Hernandez, is with the column and will have tactical command. Captain Frost has Bravo Company, in the lead, and Captain Gupta will follow her with Dog Company and the weapons platoon. Easy Company's in reserve."

Gloria glanced up at the big monitors above them. On half a dozen screens, she saw views of the Marines assembled at Scooptown, the targeted areas of Nastyville, and the empty road between them. Dozens of APCs were lined up, awaiting orders, while the skies were dotted with Marine SALs, darting around like indecisive mosquitoes. From the airborne views, she saw Denastri civilians moving around in the narrow streets and alleys of Nastyville.

"All of this seems familiar," Gloria said.

"Your sightseeing tour, you mean?" Gloria nodded. Barnes shook his head and said, "The basic disposition of troops is similar, but the purpose of the mission is very different. We won't simply be targets this time. This is an offensive operation, and we'll have the initiative."

"Won't the insurgents know we're coming?" Gloria asked.

"Of course," said Barnes. "They always do. But we've got SALs covering the exits to the north and south, and across the river, to the east. If they try to run for it, we'll interdict. Actually, it's helpful that they know we're coming. The civilians will have time to get out of the way, so we can assume that any Denastri we encounter will be hostiles."

"That's a pretty big assumption, isn't it? I mean, those people *live* there."

Barnes shrugged. "In a firefight, you don't have

much time to pick and choose. Undoubtedly, there will be some civilian casualties—it's unavoidable in an operation like this. But we have to count on their own sense of self-preservation. They aren't idiots, and they'll take reasonable measures to protect themselves. If they stay in their homes and keep their heads down, they should be safe. We have a pretty good idea of where the insurgents are, Gloria. This isn't some random search-and-destroy mission. We've identified our principal targets and we aren't going to go house to house, except along the main axis of advance. The DHG will be protecting our flanks and should be able to deal with snipers and ambushes from the side streets."

Gloria looked at General 5A-46-9C, who had been listening to their conversation through his translator. "Your troops understand their role, General?" she asked him.

"Denastri Home Guard are prepared," he said. "We are mostly honored by confidence of respected Colonel Barnes and will most likely enjoy participation in this delightful event, especially."

Gloria wondered about his use of the words "enjoy" and "delightful," but figured it was just another idiosyncratic translation. She didn't have time to dwell on it, however; Barnes was back in contact with Borisov. "Anytime you're ready, Ross," he said.

"Rodge," said Borisov. "We are go. Major Hernandez, move 'em out."

The Battle of Nastyville had begun.

Like most battles, it started with marching and movement and a lot of nervous anticipation, but little action. The Marine column floated along the road to Nastyville, raising clouds of dust that obscured the ground-level view from the Command Center, but overhead views followed the slow, steady progress of the vehicles. To each side of the road, columns of DHG troops trotted along, keeping pace with the Marines. Squads broke away from the columns here and there to search the few ramshackle buildings along the roadside. There was no shooting, but one small structure burst into flames as the Denastri advanced.

A Marine Public Information Officer arrived a little later with half a dozen journalists in tow, among them Elmo Hunt, Hettie Pando, and Bryce Denton. A lieutenant got them settled in chairs behind Barnes's console and Sergeant Hooper brought coffee for everyone. For senior personnel and distinguished guests, at least, it was going to be a comfortable battle.

The newsies peppered Barnes with questions, basic and obvious inquiries designed to set the scene for billions throughout the Empire who would eventually watch the action in the security of their own living rooms. War had become a spectator sport centuries ago, when Mathew Brady first exhibited his photographs of the dead of Antietam, and the military had come to accept the necessity of putting on a good show for the people who paid for it all. Barnes was used to it and fielded the questions with just the right blend of professionalism and offhand humor. Gloria was also no stranger to the media, but modestly deflected the journalists' inquiries, explaining that she had no role to play here other than that of observer.

"But the Marines take their orders from you, don't they?" one of the newsies persisted.

"Only in terms of broad policy," Gloria replied. "The conduct of their operations is entirely up to them."

"So assaults on civilians are part of Imperial policy?"

"This is *not* an assault on civilians," Gloria said firmly.

"The hell it isn't," muttered Elmo Hunt.

"You know better than that, Hunt," Barnes told him. "We don't target civilians. But if the enemy is sheltered in a civilian area, then that's where we have to go to engage them. Some collateral damage is inevitable, but we make every effort to keep it to a minimum."

"Yeah," said Hunt, "that's what Tamerlane told me, just before he sacked Damascus."

The Marine column had advanced to within half a kilometer of the outskirts of Nastyville when the first combat erupted. A bright green plasma bolt burst forth from a building to the right of the road, slicing into the lead vehicle. The Marines responded instantly, and in the Command Center they watched from several angles as three APCs returned fire and a SAL swooped in low to administer the coup de grace with a spread of rockets. The offending structure vanished in a billowing orange fireball. The DHG troops to the right of the road hesitated, then sprinted forward and spent a minute firing wildly and ineffectually before order was restored.

"Where'd they get plasma weapons?" one of the journalists asked.

"Where do you think?" Bryce Denton said, glancing meaningfully in the direction of the Denastri general. He ignored the newsies and spoke rapidly into his headset.

Barnes said nothing, but listened intently as reports from the Marines filtered upward through the chain of command. They all watched as APCs on the road moved ahead, past the now-crippled lead vehicle. Medics swarmed over it and quickly extracted the living and the dead; then a skimdozer switched on its mass-impellers and shoved the hulk off of the road. The column continued, seemingly unaffected by the loss. Two Marines were dead, three more had been wounded.

Turning to 5A-46-9C, Barnes said, "General, can you get your troops to advance more rapidly? They should be a hundred meters ahead of the column."

"It shall be done, Colonel," the Denastri officer replied. If he resented being prodded by the Marine, he showed no sign of it. He issued the necessary commands, and a minute later, the Denastri infantry began moving forward again. To Gloria, they seemed a little reluctant, and they slowed to a walk again almost as soon as they had cleared the head of the column.

When the column reached the edge of Nastyville, it halted abruptly. "Del," Borisov reported, "we're getting indications of mines up ahead. It'll take a couple of minutes to clear them."

"Rodge," said Barnes. "Take your time, do it right."

The DHG troops veered away from the road and crouched behind some small houses as a specialized Marine vehicle crept forward and probed the road ahead with pencil-thin plasma beams. A miniature volcano suddenly erupted from the roadway, showering the area with dirt and debris and flattening two buildings to the side of the road.

"Collateral damage," Elmo Hunt commented.

"Can't make omelets without breaking some eggs," said Bryce Denton. "How do you like your eggs, Gloria? Scrambled or fried?"

Gloria gave him a dirty look, then turned back to the monitors. The column was moving again, and the Denastri troops filtered into the town, cautiously searching the roadside buildings and setting fire to a few of them. One of them must have contained munitions, for it disappeared in a thundering explosion that brought the column to a halt again as Marine ambulances moved in to pick up wounded DHG troops who had been too close to the scene.

Barnes leaned back in his chair and told an aide to get him some more coffee. "We're already fifteen minutes behind schedule," he said.

"Reminds me of the road to Arnhem," said Hunt. "At least you don't have to worry about bridges."

"I suppose you were there, too," Barnes said.

"Course I was," Hunt replied. "Told Monty it would never work, but did he listen? Pompous ass never listened to anyone. Now Hannibal, there was a general who could take advice. 'Double envelopment's your ticket,' I told him just before Cannae. Worked like a charm, too."

"Elmo's also the one who told Lee to charge Cemetery Ridge," Hettie Pando said. "Weren't you, sweetie?"

"Nonsense. I was nowhere near Gettysburg that day. I was in Vicksburg with my friend Sam Grant. Both of us blind drunk."

The Marine column steadily penetrated deeper into Nastyville, pausing now and again to engage in desultory firefights with scattered pockets of resistance. At one point, the DHG troops to the left of the road called for assistance from the weapons platoon, which lobbed in a few rounds of ordnance that effectively pulverized half a dozen buildings. This was not exactly a surgical strike, and collateral damage within a hundred meters of the road was extensive, but Gloria noticed in the overhead views that life elsewhere in Nastyville seemed unaffected. Denastri came and went at an unhurried pace, and on a parallel road a kilometer to the north, three-wheeled transports were bringing in loads of melons and other foodstuffs, as they would on any normal day.

Resistance stiffened when the column had reached a position no more than a few hundred meters from the river. The Marines paused, and Barnes listened intently to reports from the SALs and communications between Borisov and the officers on the scene. Finally, Borisov checked in with Barnes.

"Del? Captain Frost wants to execute Plan Baker."

"I heard. It's your call, Ross."

"Rodge. If you have no objections, we'll go with Baker."

"Copy that. Go at your discretion."

"What's Plan Baker?" Hettie Pando asked.

Barnes swiveled his chair around and looked at

her. "We have a number of options prepared," he explained. "What we do depends on the actual conditions we meet. In this case, Baker is a response to moderate opposition. You can see the SALs taking position now."

A monitor displaying a ground-level view showed four SALs lining up above each side of the road. They hovered in place for a minute, then lit up the screen with a sudden exhibition of dazzling pyrotechnics. Plasma cannons peppered the roadside buildings between the column and the river with high-energy bursts that quickly made a shambles of every structure in the immediate area. Simultaneously, the APCs of Bravo Company sheared off to the left and right, snaking around the shattered buildings or, in some cases, plowing straight through them. Dog Company then charged directly up the roadway, making a beeline for the river. When the vehicles arrived there a minute later, they opened up and disgorged squads of Marines, who swiftly established a secure perimeter around the main concentration point. Plan Baker had taken less than five minutes to execute.

"Nicely done, Ross," said Barnes. "Pass along my compliments to Hernandez, Frost, and Gupta."

"Rodge. We'll be ready to execute Phase Two in about five minutes. Just need to get the DHG elements into position."

"Impressive," Gloria commented.

Barnes gave her a smile. "Our people are good at what they do," he said.

"What's Phase Two?"

"Now that we've established our forces in the heart of the C-clan area, we'll spread out along the river and flush out any insurgents who are still there. The DHG will set up a perimeter inland and catch any of them that try to escape. Bravo Company will mop up inside the perimeter. The SALs will observe and direct fire from the weapons platoon. Basically, we'll be cleaning out a semicircle a kilometer in radius from the edge of the river."

"And a month from now," said Hettie Pando, "the insurgents will be back and you'll just have to do it all again."

Barnes nodded. "If necessary," he said. "In this kind of war, you don't simply conquer territory and occupy it. We don't have enough troops on the ground to do that, in any case. The goal is to kill insurgents, disrupt their operations, and make them pay a high price for continued resistance. Even if the insurgents don't get the message, the local population will. Hopefully, their support for the insurgents will erode and the overall level of resistance will decline."

"Right out of the Counterinsurgency Textbook," Elmo Hunt observed. "It worked so well for Napoleon in Spain and the Americans in Southeast Asia, why not just keep doing it? Maybe someday, you'll even get it right."

"Dammit, Hunt," Barnes snarled, "we *do* get it right. You were on Hexam Four thirty years ago and *saw* it work. I read your book."

"Sure," said Hunt, "it works—if you have enough troops and the patience to see it through. On the Hex, we did. Here, we don't."

"That's a matter of opinion," said Barnes.

"Bullshit, Barnes. It's a matter of *numbers,* and you know that as well as I do. Counterinsurgency only works if you have overwhelming numbers and the time to apply them effectively. Even then, it's dicey. Depends on what kind of local population you're dealing with."

"Plus," put in Bryce Denton, "you don't have the time, Colonel. There's an election in less than three months."

Barnes refused to rise to the bait. "If the civilian leadership wants to change Imperial policy," he said placidly, "the Marines will do whatever is required of us."

"He's *good*," cooed Hettie Pando. "Isn't he good, Governor?"

"General Matabele, Colonel Barnes, and the entire Marine complement are doing an outstanding job on Denastri," Gloria replied.

"She's good, too," Hunt said.

Phase Two was initiated, and the Marines moved forward. An intense firefight broke out a few hundred meters north of the road and an entire city block had to be leveled before progress could resume. Small bands of insurgents took to their heels and were spotted by the overhead SALs, which directed DHG troops toward their targets. The native troopers were less efficient than the Marines, and at one point they opened fire on each other, but the problems were sorted out before any great damage was done. Within an hour, the Marines had made contact with the DHG on the perimeter, resistance flickered out, and Borisov declared the area secure. Despite all the action, most of the buildings within the perimeter were still standing.

"Not quite as tidy as we had hoped," Barnes said to the journalists, "but I think you'll agree that collateral damage was minimal. By this afternoon, most of the civilians will have come out of their holes, and they'll probably start rebuilding tomorrow."

"The ones that are still alive, anyway," said Denton.

"Civilian casualties have been light, according to the initial reports. Probably less than a hundred."

"And the insurgents?" Denton asked.

"Hard to tell at this point," Barnes admitted, "but I think we probably put several hundred of them out of action, one way or another. DHG's reporting 120 POWs."

"And what will become of them?" asked Pando.

"That's up to the DHG." Barnes glanced uncertainly

at General 5A-46-9C. "We've established guidelines, but it's their world, their people."

"In other words," said Hunt, "the C-clan insurgents will be treated to the tender mercies of their A-clan friends and neighbors."

"What about our casualties?" Gloria quickly interceded. She didn't want the newsies to get into a discussion of interclan relations.

"Our casualties have been light for an operation of this nature," said Barnes. "Six Marines KIA, a dozen wounded."

"Was it worth it, Colonel?" Denton asked.

"That's up to your audience to decide, Denton," Barnes answered. "After all, they're the ones who sent us here." Barnes and Denton stared at each other for a long moment and said nothing.

As the Marines and DHG troops began pulling out of the area, sandwiches and coffee were brought into the Command Center and the journalists and Marine personnel enjoyed a leisurely lunch while keeping one eye on the monitors. "Lousy grub in this war," commented Elmo Hunt. "The best was in Paris after the Liberation. Those Frogs knew how to cook."

"It can't be helped," said Barnes. "Our nearest supply center is on Prisma, 150 light-years from here."

"Long way to go to deliver a liverwurst and Limburger sandwich," said Hunt. "At least, I *think* that's what this is."

"Oh, *yuk!*" cried Hettie Pando. "You have no taste, Elmo."

"That's why I'm so fond of you, my dear."

Another journalist pointed a finger at one of the monitors. "Who are *those* guys?" he asked.

Barnes looked up at the screen. "The ones in black, with the utility skimmers? Servitor security people."

"And what are they doing?"

Barnes took a closer look and frowned. "Not sure," he said. "Let me check with Scooptown."

Before he could, a series of explosions ripped through the riverfront of Nastyville. When the smoke cleared, they saw that every building in the area had been destroyed. The destruction—systematic and thorough—continued a moment later with another series of detonations a hundred meters back from the river.

"Lieutenant!" Barnes barked at a Marine. "Get me a link to Servitor!"

"Yessir!" The face of Sally Voelker quickly appeared on Barnes's console.

"Voelker, what the hell is going on there?" Barnes demanded.

"Oh, hello, Colonel Barnes," said Voelker, smiling sweetly. "That was a lovely little operation this morning. Tell your people we appreciate their efforts."

"Never mind that. Just what are your people doing?" As he spoke, another set of explosions leveled more of Nastyville.

"Oh . . . that?" Voelker asked. "Just doing our job, Colonel. You did yours, and now it's our turn. I'd love to chat, but I'm afraid I'm a little busy at the moment. Have a wonderful day, Colonel."

Voelker abruptly broke the link. In the Command Center, Barnes and the others watched in stricken silence as Servitor went about its work.

·14·

Petra didn't think she'd ever seen Gloria so angry. As Sally Voelker, Gordon Overstreet of KemTek, and Dimitri Ramirez of Imperium filed into the conference room, Gloria greeted them frostily and asked them to be seated. She hadn't raved or cursed since the events the previous day in Nastyville, but Petra found that a little unsettling, in itself. Instead, her voice had taken on a hard undertone and she seemed to be expending a great deal of energy simply to keep her rage contained. Not unlike a rumbling volcano, Petra thought.

Voelker must have noticed Gloria's mood and moved to preempt the imminent eruption. "Before you get up on your high horse, Madame Governor," Voelker said, "let me remind you of a few salient facts. Terrorist incidents in the Scooptown area have increased by 40 percent since you took office. Work has been delayed, property has been destroyed, lives have been lost. The Marine operation yesterday was a step in the right direction, but without additional measures, it would have accomplished little. What we did was a necessary and appropriate adjunct to the military operation. Servitor is not here simply to look good for the media. We're here to get results."

Gloria gave her a level, uncompromising gaze. "You are here, Ms. Voelker—and Mr. Ramirez and Mr. Overstreet—because the Empire has granted your corporations a concession to conduct operations on this world. That concession includes provisions specifying a rigid adherence to all relevant standards enumerated in the *Imperial Code*. If you fail to abide by those standards, the concession can and will be suspended or revoked."

Ramirez stifled a chortle. "Oh, come on, Madame Governor," he said. "You don't seriously think you can overturn our concession, do you? It was negotiated at the highest levels of government, and not even your friends and relations in the Household would consider revoking it. Not for a second."

"We've already invested hundreds of billions of crowns here," Gordon Overstreet calmly pointed out. "The Empire wants and needs that HCH, and we're going to provide it. If there have been technical violations of the *Code*, there are established procedures for dealing with such matters."

"In other words," said Voelker, "don't think you can threaten us."

Petra felt a sudden chill as Gloria sucked in her breath and stared at each of the three executives in turn. She had seen Gloria handle recalcitrant Corpos before, and it wasn't always pretty. On the other hand, this was no penny-ante game; the stakes were incredibly high.

Gloria visibly reined in her rage and spoke in even, measured tones. "Let's discuss those technical violations, if we may," she said. "Yesterday, Servitor personnel deliberately destroyed an estimated five hundred structures in the Denastri settlement known as Nastyville. In the process, they killed or wounded some two thousand Denastri civilians."

"*Civilians?*" Voelker snorted. "Governor, there's an old saying—Mao or Zhonti or someone—that the people are the water in which guerrillas swim. Sometimes it's necessary to drain the pond."

"You didn't drain it!" Gloria shouted, erupting at last. "You boiled it!"

"Whatever works," Voelker said. "Anyway, if the Nasties had put up more of a fight, the *Marines* would have done exactly the same thing that we did. We just saved them the trouble."

"And created a hell of a lot more trouble. Spirit! We just got a formal protest from the Premier! Even that meek little Thirdborn and his pathetic excuse for a government are outraged. How in hell do you expect to conduct operations here if you go out of your way to alienate the very people you have to work with?"

"Ms. VanDeen," Overstreet said, "we don't have to work with them. *They* have to work with *us*."

"And what is that supposed to mean?"

"It means," Voelker declared, "that we *conquered* this fucking planet. Or had you forgotten? We didn't come here, hat in hand, begging for cooperation. We overturned a corrupt and tyrannical regime, and now we're in charge here. They do what we tell them to do, or suffer the consequences. I'd have thought that would have been clear to you."

"What's clear to me, Ms. Voelker," Gloria responded, "is that your actions yesterday were a deliberate and blatant violation of the *Code*. However we got here, and whatever our goals, we are obligated to abide by the law. My job is to see to it that we do—all of us. The Terran Empire is a civilized and responsible body, not a band of rapacious barbarians."

"There are a couple hundred conquered races that

might give you an argument on that point, Governor," Ramirez said.

"History is written by the winners," Overstreet added. "We won here."

Gloria shook her head. "What you people don't seem to understand is that we could still *lose* here. We simply don't have the resources to run an airtight totalitarian occupation."

"Right," said Voelker. "And that's why you need Servitor's help. If the Empire can't or won't do what's necessary on Denastri, Servitor is willing and able to step into the breach. You need us, Governor."

"And just what do you think is going to happen when the Empire hears about this outrage? There's an election in less than three months, and this could be just what Karno and the Progressives need to put them over the top. The antiexpansionists will have a field day with this."

Overstreet dismissed the suggestion with a wave of his hand. "Governments come and go," he said. "We've been around for centuries, and we're not going away. The Big Twelve run this Empire, Madame Governor— we always have and we always will. Not even that loud-mouth Karno and his gang of idiots can change that. If they win, it will be an inconvenience, easily corrected."

"Maybe you aren't aware," Ramirez said, "that Imperium has already contributed several hundred million crowns to the Progressives. They may snap and snarl a bit, but they won't bite the hand that feeds them."

Petra listened, wishing that Albert Fenlow could hear this. It would confirm all his darkest suspicions about the Empire and the Big Twelve—not that it would make any difference. Being right, she realized, wasn't enough.

Gloria ran her hands through her hair and sighed. "History. Politics. Money. You've got it all covered, don't you? The Big Twelve paint the Big Picture. I won't argue the point, but I would remind you that the devil is always in the details. No matter how broad the brushstrokes, in the end, it always comes down to people. You killed a hell of a lot of them yesterday, Ms. Voelker. I'm not going to let you kill any more of them. Effective immediately, Servitor's operations are restricted to protecting the personnel and property of Imperium and KemTek, and their immediate surroundings. There will be no more excursions into Nastyville or any other Denastri cities, towns, villages, or settlements. Your personnel will no longer be involved in any Marine operations. If there's something specific that you think needs to be done, you will submit a proposal directly to me, and if I think it's appropriate, you will be permitted to carry it out—but only under strict government supervision. And if I don't like what you're doing, I'll put a stop to it. This is still a military Zone of Occupation, and I have the authority to take any measures I deem necessary and proper to assure the safety and well-being of both Terran personnel and the indigenous population. Fuck with me again, Ms. Voelker, and I'll clap you in irons. That goes for the rest of you, and everyone who works for you. Is that perfectly clear?"

"Oooh," cried Sally Voelker. "I'm scared to death!"

Petra looked at Gloria's ferocious expression, then at Voelker, and said, "You oughta be."

Gloria invited Petra into her office and asked if she wanted a drink. Petra declined, but Gloria poured herself a healthy slug of Belgravian. She seemed to be drinking a lot lately, not really to excess, but enough to concern Petra. Gloria had sworn off the dangerous Orgastria after the tragic events on New Cambridge, and these days she didn't seem to indulge much in jigli, the powerful erotogenic herb from Mynjhino. But Petra knew that Gloria had an addictive personality and was inclined to overdo her pleasures. She was certainly addicted to sex, although she apparently hadn't had much opportunity to indulge herself in that area since leaving Earth, more than a month ago. Though, for her own part, Petra had no complaints on that score.

Settling onto the couch next to Petra, Gloria took a sip of her drink and sighed heavily. Petra thought she looked tired and careworn, and had every right to. Wearing two hats, as both Imperial Governor and Imperial Secretary, Gloria had a heavy workload and problems coming at her from every direction—the Denastri, the Marines, the Corporates, and her own fractious Dexta staff. Petra tried to ease Gloria's burdens in her role as UnderSec for Administration, but there was a limit to how much she could accomplish. Much of what needed to be done could only be done by Gloria.

"Is there anything I can do for you?" Petra asked.

"You could shoot Sally Voelker," Gloria suggested.

"Sorry. My gun's in the shop. Best I can do is throw some rocks at her."

"The hell of it is, she's right. I can't revoke the concession, and we *do* need Servitor. If I take drastic measures against them, I'll simply be overruled by the Powers That Be back on Earth. Even Norman wouldn't back me if I got too tough with the Corpos. The last courier from Earth included a long memo from Corporate Affairs reminding me that my principal responsibility here is to facilitate the operations of Imperium and KemTek." Gloria took another swig of her drink and sighed again.

"You need a break," Petra told her. "Why don't you go find Colonel Barnes and commit some indecent acts?"

"Would that we could. He's out in Scooptown today, picking up the pieces. Then he's off to Banako tomorrow to inspect the troops there, or some damn thing. If anything, he's even busier than I am. Anyway, we've got to be careful. Neither one of us can afford to have Bryce and his friends turn us into an item."

"Why not? I mean, you're still Gloria VanDeen,

Avatar of Joy and Everybody's Sweetheart. You're *supposed* to be sexy and outrageous. Just look at yourself. I've got more buttons undone than you do! There's something unnatural about that."

Gloria laughed. "Probably," she agreed. "But as Imperial Governor, I can't be seen to be in bed with the military. Voelker would make a lot of hay out of something like that. It wouldn't hurt me much, I suppose, but it could really damage Delbert's career. He'll never get his star if the General Staff thinks he's indiscreet. They don't like it when their officers wind up in the tabs."

"Well, I still say you need to do something to relax. Go play some softball with the Marines. Hey, I know—maybe we could start a Dexta team."

"We'd get our asses kicked."

"So what? It'd be fun. You could pitch, and I'd be a very-shortstop. And maybe somebody would bean Edgar Wong."

"You talked me into it. If you can get things organized, I'll play ball. In the meantime, have you made any contact with the Denastri females?"

Petra shook her head. "I've tried. But they almost seem to be afraid to talk to Terrans. And the translators don't work very well with them. They seem to have their own language."

"Well," Gloria said, "maybe that report from Dr. Mankato will shed a little light on the subject. There's something going on with the females that we just don't get. And what's the deal with the food? If it all has to be grown, prepared, and served by the females, who's feeding the insurgents? Do they have their own ag complexes? If they do, where are they? The Marines don't seem to know, either."

"I know there's a major agricultural complex about twenty kilometers from here," Petra said. "You can see the food carts coming in at the main gate every morning.

But the Denastri don't seem to want to talk about food. Apparently there's some sort of taboo associated with it."

"I can almost understand that, considering what they ate at that ceremony." Gloria shook her head at the memory and took another drink.

"Have you gotten any feedback from the C-clan about Lord Kenarbin?" Petra asked.

"Not a word. They've had him three months now, and haven't made a single demand—haven't even mentioned him. We don't even know if he's still alive."

"You knew him, didn't you?"

"Years ago," Gloria said.

"Did you like him?"

Gloria didn't quite laugh. "Like him?" she said. "I was in love with the son of a bitch!"

Bryce Denton slid his hand under Petra's unbuttoned blouse and massaged her small round breast. Petra endured and enjoyed it for a moment, then slipped free from him. "C'mon, Bryce," she protested, "people are watching."

Denton looked around. They were standing in the evening shadows, pressed up against a column outside the entrance to the Imperial Hotel, where they had spent the past few hours drinking and carousing with the other media reps. "I don't see any people," he said. "Just Denastri."

"They count," Petra said, looking toward a few of the Firstborns who worked in the Compound. They seemed to take no notice of the humans or what they were doing, and walked past them without a second glance.

"Since when?" Denton asked scornfully. He made another move toward Petra, but she swatted his hand away.

"It's true, isn't it?" Petra asked, suddenly waxing philosophical. "They really don't count to us, do they? I mean . . . they *do* . . . but not really. If Servitor had killed two thousand humans yesterday, there'd be an unholy uproar about it. But they were only Denastri, so it's an interesting news item, but not much more than that. You should have heard Sally Voelker today. She sounded as if she were discussing dead farm animals."

"They might as well be," said Denton. "They're humanoid, but they ain't *human*. We're as different as clams and giraffes. I hear they don't even enjoy sex." Denton ran his forefinger down Petra's sternum, then made another try for her breast. Petra didn't resist as he toyed with her left nipple.

"Sort of makes you feel sorry for them," she said.

"They don't even know what they're missing."

"If you keep that up, they'll find out. Come on, let's go up to my room."

"What? And deny the poor Denastri an opportunity for education and enlightenment?"

"You're a real missionary, aren't you?"

"The missionary position, you mean? Well, if that's what you want—but I had something a little more exotic in mind."

Denton demonstrated what he had in mind, in great detail, when they finally made it to Petra's room. He was a playful and inventive lover, not as fiery as poor Ricky on Mynjhino or as boyishly sincere as Pug Ellison, but a lot more fun than Albert Fenlow, who tended to be stolid and rather academic in his approach to carnal matters. Petra hadn't had enough lovers in her life to avoid comparisons of that sort and wondered if quantity somehow improved quality. She'd have to ask Gloria about that sometime, she decided. In the meantime, Bryce Denton was all a lonely bureaucrat far from home could ask for.

When they were finished—for the moment—they lay back against the pillows and idly caressed each other. It always amazed Petra that men could take such interest in what seemed to her to be a rather small and ordinary body. Even during her occasional excursions into Tigerdom, it seemed strange that merely flashing a nipple or baring her bottom could provoke such an extravagant response from the male of the species. They were prisoners of their reflexes, she supposed. At any rate, she was glad that she belonged to a species that behaved that way. Did the Denastri females know joy? Or did they dread sex, knowing that it must inevitably lead to their deaths? So strange, so sad . . .

"Just what *did* Sally Voelker say about the Denastri today?" Denton asked.

"She compared them to fish in a pond."

Denton nodded. "Right out of the *Little Red Book*," he said. "People like Voelker and the Servitor crowd understand terrorism better than the terrorists do. They'd be good at it if they wanted to change sides. Hell, they *are* terrorists—they just dress better."

"Gloria agrees with you, I think. I've never seen her so angry."

"What's she going to do about it?"

"She's imposed strict limitations on what they can do," Petra said. "No more joint operations with the Marines, no more raids on Denastri settlements."

Denton gave a derisive snort. "Does she really think that will make any difference?"

"Probably not," Petra conceded. "All she can really do is huff and puff and make threatening noises. She may be in charge here, but she doesn't really have a free hand. She's in an impossible situation, when you think about it. She's answerable to Dexta, Parliament, and the Household, and all of them are pretty much in the pockets of the Big Twelve. Anything she does here will be reviewed back on Earth, and they don't even know what's really going on here. All they care about is the HCH and the elections."

"Latest poll has it even-steven," said Denton. "When

the Nastyville story gets back there, it might even tip it to the Progressives."

"Do you really think so?" Petra asked eagerly.

Denton looked at her carefully. "You sound like you want them to win," he observed.

"Don't you?"

Denton shook his head. "As a journalist, I'm supposed to be neutral in thought, word, and deed. That's a crock, of course, but it sounds good. Anyway, I'm not even registered to vote. From my point of view, I think Karno would make better copy than the ISP fuddy-duddies, so I suppose it would be a good thing for me if the Progressives won. But I doubt that it would make much difference to the Empire—or the Denastri."

"That's a depressing thing to say."

"The truth usually is. Petra, my love, you need to control your dangerous idealistic impulses. They'll just get you into trouble."

Denton poked a finger into her navel, then massaged her belly. Petra ran her hand through Denton's hair. "I'm really glad you're here," she said. "It makes all of this a lot easier. Poor Gloria doesn't even have anyone. That must be a first for her."

"What about Barnes? You mean she and the warrior prince still haven't gone on maneuvers together?"

"Thanks to you and your charming colleagues, they can't risk it. Gloria says it could really hurt Delbert's career."

"She's probably right about that," Denton mused. "Bit of irony there, don't you think? For once in her life, Glamorous Gloria can't do the thing she's best at. Until now, she's probably gotten every man she's ever wanted."

"Not always," Petra said. She was silent for a moment, then said, "She was in love with Lord Kenarbin."

Denton's eyebrows shot upward. "What?"

"When she was young. I don't think they've seen each other in years. In fact, I think she kind of resents him. But it must really complicate things for her. I mean, she came here to free him, but—" Petra stopped abruptly, realizing she'd said too much.

Denton propped himself up on one elbow and stared at her. "Are you serious? They sent her here to get Kenarbin back?"

"I didn't say that," Petra insisted.

"Yes, you did. Do you have any idea what that means? Spirit, Charles must really be desperate about Kenarbin. It figures, I suppose—I mean, he must be under a lot of pressure from Lady Patricia and her family to get him back. Enough to get him to violate Imperial policy. Damn, that's one hell of a story!"

"Bryce," Petra warned, "Don't you *dare*!"

"Is Gloria negotiating with the insurgents?"

"No, she's not. They haven't even responded to—" Petra grimaced. Dammit, she'd done it again!

"Then she's made an offer?" Denton demanded.

"All she did was make a tentative contact with a C-clan general," Petra said defensively. "It wasn't *anything*!"

"The hell it wasn't."

"Bryce, you cannot use this!"

Denton lay back against the pillows and stared at the ceiling.

"Bryce, I'm warning you, don't use this!"

But Denton was no longer listening to her.

·15·

Two days later, Gloria sat down at her desk, sipped her morning coffee, and checked her computer console for new business. She found the file overflowing with thirty-eight new documents that demanded her attention. One of them, she had been expecting—Dr. Mankato's long-awaited report on Denastri's population, culture, and society. The other thirty-seven were from Servitor.

With a growing sense of anger and frustration, she clicked through the mass of Servitor material. Sally Voelker, with finely calculated obedience, had taken Gloria's new directive quite literally. Servitor had to check with the Governor before embarking on any new projects or operations? Very well—here they were. A technical team needed to service the external pylons in the security fence surrounding Scooptown? Check with the Governor. Someone needed to go into Enkar and take delivery on a shipment of shovels and other tools for Denastri workers at the KemTek refinery site? Check with the Governor. A search had to be instituted for three missing ID pins at the Servitor office on Senka? Check with the Governor.

Most of Gloria's anger was directed at herself. She'd walked right into this one.

Voelker's slavish, punctilious compliance was among the oldest of bureaucratic ploys, and she should have seen it coming. She'd done something similar once or twice in her Dexta career: If an order makes no sense, obey it to the letter. Properly viewed, almost any directive could be used to generate a blizzard of superfluous paperwork for the person who had initiated the order. The Boomerang Effect.

Servitor, it now seemed, was going to request Gloria's approval for every last thing it wanted to do, no matter how trivial. Gloria leaned back in her chair, sipped some coffee, and considered possible responses to this bureaucratic assault. The obvious one was simple surrender. Rescind—or at least, refine—her directive; loosen the leash, bow to the inevitable, and let Servitor go about its business without direct Imperial oversight. That, of course, would create new ambiguities and loopholes, which Voelker would exploit to the max. In the end, little or nothing would have changed.

Gloria knew that the smart thing to do would be to give in and let Voelker have her little triumph. This was the bureaucratic equivalent of trench warfare, and there was nothing to be gained by going over the top and charging madly into no-man's-land. On the other hand, Voelker's barrage seemed to cry out for an appropriate response, and Gloria was not without artillery of her own.

She got up from her desk, walked out of her office, and strolled through the corridors of the Dexta complex, attracting the usual amount of attention from passersby. Feeling combative and defiant, she decided to attract *more* than the usual amount of attention and adjusted the smart fabric of her dress to an eye-popping minimum opacity and undid a couple more buttons for maximum effect. This was one of those occasions when a true Tiger needed to show her stripes. Intimidation could take many forms, and Gloria had not gotten to where she was by being shy about her assets.

Edgar Wong's assistant gulped when he saw her, and even Wong himself was momentarily speechless. Gloria greeted him, leaned over his desk to give him a good view, and tapped a few keys on his console to bring up the appropriate files.

"Your friends at Servitor," she said, "have dropped this mess in my lap. I'm dropping it in yours, Mr. Wong. Have fun."

"But . . ." Wong stammered for a moment as he surveyed the files.

"What we have here is thirty-seven different requests for government approval of new Servitor initiatives. Each of them will require a thorough review from the Corporate Affairs staff. I expect that at least half of them will turn out to be defective in some minor detail or another. Do you understand what I'm saying, Mr. Wong?"

"Uh . . ."

"Let me make it clear, then. Servitor wants to snow us under with trivia. We are going to impress upon them that two can play this game. It's simple Newtonian physics, Mr. Wong—every action produces an equal but opposite reaction. However many headaches Servitor creates for us, your assignment is to produce an equal number of headaches for them. I'll expect to see your detailed response to all thirty-seven Servitor requests by, let's say, tomorrow morning. And if at least twenty of them are not negative, requiring a resubmission of the request by Servitor, I'll know the reason why."

"But . . . but, that's ridiculous!"

Gloria smiled pleasantly. "Yes, it is, isn't it? You might mention that to your friend Sally."

Gloria strode out of Wong's office, feeling surprisingly

refreshed. Her next stop was Frederick Danelli's Finance office. "Mr. Danelli," she announced, "as you may be aware, we have received a formal protest from the Denastri government concerning the events at Nastyville. I want you to request from them a full accounting of the damage that was done to Denastri property by Servitor. You'll have to sort that out from the damage done by the Marines, so you'll need to get in touch with Task Force HQ and get an estimate of how many buildings were destroyed during the military operation. We have vids of the whole thing, so you may need to review them and actually count the number of structures involved."

Danelli stared at her for a moment, then nodded quickly and said, "Yes, ma'am."

"You understand what I'm after, Mr. Danelli?"

"I think so."

"Good. When you've got a final figure, I want you to issue a payment to the Denastri government covering the total amount of damage done by Servitor—not the Marines, just Servitor. Then send a bill for the same amount—plus 10 percent, to cover our own expenses—to Servitor. Try to get this done in the next two days. Servitor's payment to us should be receivable within thirty days, with penalties for being late. I think you'll find all the appropriate regulations in Chapter Twelve of the *Dexta Code*."

"Uh . . . yes, Chapter Twelve is correct." Danelli stared at her some more, openmouthed.

"Good." Gloria gave him a big smile. "Hop to it, Mr. Danelli."

Then, it was on to Jack McCray's Security office. McCray was still sporting the yellowish-purple residue of the black eye he'd acquired during last week's reception. She had carefully ignored the fracas; in a way, Delbert had been right. Everyone needed to blow off some steam, and while a full-scale brawl may have been a bit more than was strictly necessary, the end result was probably healthy.

"Jack," she said, "I'm concerned that some of Servitor's people may be a little hazy on Dexta regs concerning private security operations."

"A *little*?"

"Perhaps more than a little," Gloria agreed. "In any case, I think they could all benefit from a review. I believe that we have the authority to insist on a periodic examination in that area."

"Damn right we do . . . Madame Governor."

"Good. I think it's high time for such an examination. I believe that will require a seminar on the subject for every last one of Servitor's security personnel, including their top managers. Attendance, of course, will be mandatory."

McCray gave a gleeful chuckle. "Whatever you say, Madame Governor."

"Set that up as soon as you can, Jack."

"You know," he said, "I think we've got about eight hours' worth of old training vids around here somewhere."

"Perfect." Gloria gave him a friendly pat on his shoulder. "Oh, and Jack? A little advice."

"Yes?"

"Next time," she said, "lead with your left."

"You want me to *what*?" Petra gasped.

"You heard me, kiddo. You're the UnderSecretary for Administration, aren't you?"

"Well, yeah, but . . ."

"No buts about it, Petra. We've been too damn lax around here. A bomb blew up in our faces as soon as we got here, and ever since then, we've been playing catchup. I've been all buttoned-up and defensive, just waiting for the next disaster to strike. We've got to get out in front of things. Proactive. Decisive."

"I think you're right," Petra said. "And it's probably about time, now that you mention it."

"Past time. Administration isn't just another bureaucratic cubbyhole, Petra. It's got to be a positive, active process. We can't simply sit back and wait for the Denastri to get their act together. So I want you to sit down with their people and the Corporate people and work out an appropriate and effective set of administrative protocols that apply specifically to the situation on Denastri. Under my authority, you can grant waivers and exceptions, as necessary, and set up new guidelines and regulations governing both Corporate and government policy. You might bring in Linda Fujiwara from Bank of Earth, too. This concerns them, as well."

Petra nodded. "How soon do you want this done?"

"The whole thing will probably take months, but I want you to schedule a preliminary meeting for next week. I'll attend, but after that, it'll be your ball game, Petra."

"Oh—that reminds me. I've scheduled our first softball game. The Dexta Dragons versus the Media Maggots. I even found a factory in the city that can make us caps and T-shirts. We can get gloves, bats, and balls from the Marines." Petra grinned at Gloria. "Just call me Petra Doubleday."

"Fantastic. I assume you were able to recruit enough people to field a team?"

"More than enough. I just told everyone that you'd be our manager, and that in the interests of team solidarity, we'd all be showering together."

"Sounds good to me." Gloria laughed. "Now, if you'll excuse me, I think I need to go bone up on the infield fly rule."

The arcana governing pop-ups would have to wait; Gloria settled in at her desk and began reading Dr.

Mankato's report. The exosociologist had happily dispensed with the usual babble of her profession and produced a report that was straightforward, relatively concise, and even enjoyable to read.

"We know far less about the Denastri than we think we do," Mankato began, and went on to list a number of reasons why this was the case. Before she was halfway through the hundred-page document, Gloria was nodding thoughtfully and considering the implications of what Mankato had written. A good idea occurred to her, and she acted on it immediately. Invitations were sent out, and that evening she welcomed Dr. Mankato and Colonel Barnes to a private dinner in her residence.

"I've sent you a copy of Dr. Mankato's report," Gloria said to Barnes after introductions had been made, "but I thought you should hear this directly from her. I have a lot of questions, and you probably will, too."

The household staff she had inherited from the late Governor Blagodarski served them wine and dinner—a passable pot roast and some good Cabernet—then departed. Mankato talked nonstop as she munched and slurped (she must have been a hit at faculty dinners, Gloria thought), while Barnes mainly listened and made few comments.

"We flatter ourselves that we understand the Denastri," Mankato said, "because we've been through this kind of thing so many times before. They're generally humanoid in appearance, and that always engenders a false sense of confidence. We're the big bad Empire, and we've kicked alien asses from here to Aldebaran, with considerable success. We make allowances for the really weird species—remind me to tell you about the Guxalli sometime—but the ones that are not *too* different from us always make us think that under their scales or feathers, they're really just people like us. They're not. The profound biological differences between our two species guarantee, in themselves, that we will see the universe in fundamentally different ways. The biological differences inevitably create a cultural gulf that, in this case, is all but unbridgeable. We want different things. Humans want to get laid and get rich, in that order. Denastri want something else entirely."

"What?" Barnes asked.

"The honest answer to that question," Mankato said, helping herself to more wine, "is that it beats the shit out of me. But my tentative professional answer is that the Denastri seek a spiritual communion with a god, for lack of a better word, that embraces aspects of time, space, and a sort of cultural geometry. Take that Rite of Continuation you saw the other day, Governor. That was not simply a church service. That was, to the Denastri, a physical manifestation of their actual god, in form and flesh. Not symbolically, but really and truly. In some way that we don't really comprehend, to the Denastri, the Sixthborn actually *are* god. By the way, I still want you to tell me about that ceremony."

"Uh . . . maybe after dinner," Gloria said. Just thinking of it was enough to ruin her appetite.

"Anyway," Mankato continued, "the precise form of that ceremony was necessary to create the spatiotemporal conditions required to manifest the essential, underlying *godness* of the Sixthborn. That's why it was necessary for all three Superclans to be present, even though they seem to hate each other's guts out in the real world. We tell ourselves that if we weren't present to prevent it, the As and Cs would annihilate each other, but, of course, that just isn't so. Obviously, they didn't do that in the thirty thousand years before we got here, so there's no reason to suppose that they'd do it if we left. Nevertheless, that's one of the excuses we use to justify our presence here. In fact, they *need* each other to create this cultural geometry upon which the manifestation of their godness depends. Follow me?"

Barnes frowned. "I think so."

Mankato shook her head. "No, you don't," she said. "Don't worry about it, though. I don't understand it either. I'm just telling you what I *think* is going on. I may be totally wrong. I've only been here a year; ask me again in ten years, and I may give you a completely different answer."

"That's encouraging," Barnes muttered.

Mankato ignored him. "Now, as to these wars the Denastri have been fighting with their offspring worlds in the Cluster, they're religious wars, but not in quite the same sense as, say, the Thirty Years' War. They aren't simply arguing over what language to say Mass in. It's a bit more like the Muslim-Christian conflicts, with fundamental cultural differences at stake, but that doesn't really capture it, either. Allah, after all, is simply a later version of the old Judeo-Christian Jehovah. The differences between the Denastri and their offspring revolve around this spatiotemporal-cultural geometry I've been talking about. The forms of rite and ceremony evolved by the offspring cultures are fundamentally at odds with the geometry required by the native Denastri—they deform the necessary shape of the universe, if you will. They actually warp the very *form* of the godhood, in ways that are profoundly disturbing to the Denastri—and, presumably, to their god, itself. Like shaving Jesus's beard, or hacking off one of Vishnu's arms. But, as far as I can tell, *none* of that applies here on Denastri. The three Superclans are all on the same page as far as god is concerned. The differences among the As, Bs, and Cs are trivial and superficial, and don't really matter very much to the Sixthborn. In a sense, the war matters a lot more to us than it does to them."

"Then why do they fight?" Barnes asked.

"On the purely temporal plane, they squabble over economics and politics, the same as we do. They've been doing that for thousands of years. But, again, that's trivial to them. Wars come and go, one clan gets the upper hand for a while, then the others do. It's really no big deal. But the real reason they're fighting now is because *we're* here. Our very presence on their world distorts this necessary geometry. They are all in complete agreement that our presence here is an affront to the proper order of things. The only difference is in what the response should be. The As seem to think that they can live with us through a sort of limited appeasement. If they let us dig up their rocks, eventually we'll get what we want and go away. The Bs just try to ignore us, on the theory that if they do, we'll also ignore them. The Cs, who are also pissed off because we knocked them off their pedestal, think we have to be ejected as quickly as possible. They *all* want us to leave; they just differ on means and timing."

"If what you say is true," Gloria said, "then all of our attempts to set up a functional government under Imperial rule—"

"Are a waste of time. The longer we stay here, the more we'll upset the geometry I've been talking about. Eventually, even the As and Bs will get sufficiently sick of us and join the Cs in fighting us. Hell, some of them already have. You're not simply fighting the Cs, Colonel. You're fighting every Denastri who was ever born. Remember, the Sixthborn are, in effect, their own ancestors. Continuation isn't simply the name of one of their rites—it's a palpable reality to them."

"So what should we do?" Barnes asked.

"Isn't that obvious? We should get the hell off Denastri and leave these poor, strange people alone."

"But we can't do that," Gloria protested.

"Yeah," said Mankato, "I know. It's a bitch, isn't it?"

After several hours of discussion and the best part of a bottle of Belgravian, Mankato departed, and Gloria and Barnes snuggled together on a couch. Gloria kissed him, and Barnes responded the way a Marine far from home ought to respond.

"Four years," she breathed, between nibbles on his earlobe. "That's far too long to wait for something so good."

"I have dreams about you," Barnes said. "Hot, steamy, sweaty dreams."

"Dreams are nice. But this is better."

"Yeah . . . except . . ."

"No one knows we're here, Delbert."

"My staff does."

"Mine, too. But we can trust them."

"Can we? Dammit, Gloria, right across the Compound there are a hundred newsies who would put us on lead screens from one end of the Empire to the other, if they knew."

"I've been on those screens before, Delbert. It's not so bad."

Barnes pulled back from her. "Not for you, maybe," he said. "But for me, it could be a professional disaster."

Gloria looked at him carefully, reading the concern in his eyes. "I know it could be a problem for you," she said. "But would it really matter that much to those generals back on Earth? I mean, it would all blow over in time, wouldn't it?"

Barnes sighed, then reached for his glass of whisky and took a swig. "I don't know," he said. "Marines aren't exactly prudes, but you aren't just anybody. You're an Imperial Governor. Everybody knows who you are, and everybody would know who I am. Something like this could dog me for the rest of my career. Even if I got my star, there would be people in the Corps who would say I got it for . . . uh . . ."

"Fucking someone important?"

"Yes, dammit."

"That star's important to you, isn't it?"

"Gloria, my dad was in the Corps for forty years and

retired on a disability as a lieutenant colonel." He smiled. "Next time I see him, he'll have to salute me."

"And that means a lot to you?"

"It would mean even more to him. Yes, that star's important to me."

"I think I understand, Delbert. I want to run Dexta someday. But if making love with you meant that I couldn't . . . I don't know. I guess I'd have to think about that."

"We could keep it as quiet as possible," he said. "Stay cool and formal in public. Pretend there was nothing going on."

"We'd probably only be fooling ourselves. People would know. Somehow, they always do."

"Yeah, they probably would." Barnes stared into her eyes for a moment, then drew her closer to him. "But I think I'm willing to risk it."

"It's your call, Delbert. I'll play it any way you want. But you know what *I* want."

"The same thing I want." Barnes pressed his lips against hers, and within moments, Gloria's dress was off and she was fumbling with the buttons of his uniform. She had barely begun when Barnes's wristcom beeped.

Barnes groaned, hesitated, then pushed himself off Gloria and answered the call.

"Colonel? Captain Graves. Sir, we just got word that there's an explosion in the barracks at Scooptown. No details yet, but it looks pretty bad."

"Right. Thank you, Captain. I'll be there in five minutes." He looked at Gloria and shook his head sadly. "Duty calls," he said.

"But why does it have to call at a time like this?" Gloria demanded.

"War is hell," said Colonel Barnes.

· 16 ·

"I take it you've all read Dr. Mankato's report?" Gloria turned her gaze to each of the conference participants in turn—a wary-looking General Matabele, a haggard Colonel Barnes, and a major and a captain from their Intelligence staff. Each of them nodded.

"We need to rethink what we're doing here," Gloria said as she looked around the conference table. Unsurprisingly, no one disputed her statement. The explosion at the Scooptown barracks three nights ago had killed thirteen Marines and injured twenty-five. In the meantime, two more had died in an incident on Banako and another one just that morning in an ambush on a street in Enkar. The Marines, she knew, were willing to tolerate casualties as long as they believed that they were a necessary price to be paid in the course of fulfilling their mission. But on Denastri, no one quite believed that anymore. The nature of the mission was increasingly unclear, and progress impossible to measure. The Marines' morale was down, their anger and frustration rising.

"Governor," said Matabele, "I'm certainly in favor of reviewing our practices and procedures. Spirit knows, what we've been doing has not been achieving positive results. But if what you're suggesting is a change in our core mission here, I can't agree to that. Yes, I know what this Dr. Mankato says, but the Marines are not in the habit of taking their marching orders from academic thumb twiddlers. The Occupation Task Force takes its orders from the General Staff."

"And me," Gloria added.

Matabele looked uncomfortable. "Well, yes," he said, "in a limited sense. But I don't believe that you are free to redefine our mission."

"What if it *needs* redefining?"

"In that event, you'll need to make your case to the General Staff."

"Not to mention Parliament and the Household," put in Major Julia Morales, the Marines' head of G-2.

"And with an election coming up," said Captain Ken Hosagawa, one of the Marines' bright young staffers, "no one on Earth is likely to change policy until they see which way the wind is blowing."

"Quite right," Gloria agreed. "The new Government, if there is one, won't even be seated for six months. Even if Singh and the ISP retain power, they're likely to reshuffle the Cabinet, and that, too, would take at least six months. So the question for us to consider is whether we can afford to spend another half year doing the same thing that we've been doing. Major Morales, I assume you must have projections on Marine casualties in the next six months?"

"Yes, ma'am," said Morales. "If we simply project the current rate of loss, it comes out to about 300 KIA and 1,000 wounded. But the level of resistance has been steadily rising, so if we take that into account, it would be more like 500 KIA and 1,500 wounded."

"Two thousand casualties, then," Gloria said. "That's

about 11 percent of your total force? I'm no expert on military matters, but my understanding is that when a unit exceeds 10 percent casualties, it's generally taken out of combat and sent to a rear area for rest and refitting and to get replacements. Correct?"

Matabele nodded reluctantly. "That's generally the case," he said.

"So where does that leave us?" Gloria asked.

No one spoke for a moment. Then Captain Hosagawa cleared his throat and said, "Begging your pardon, ma'am, and General, but I think where it leaves us is somewhere up Shit Creek."

Matabele gave his subaltern a baleful look, but didn't say anything. After a meaningful pause, Major Morales said, "Actually, it's not quite that bad. Half of those injuries will be relatively minor, and we'll get those people back. So the net figure would actually be less than 10 percent. We can live with that."

"Can we?" Gloria asked. "What about it, Colonel Barnes? You haven't said anything yet. They're your troops. What will be the effect on them of that kind of attrition?" Gloria was sorry to put him on the spot, but knew that he would answer honestly.

"Can we live with it?" he said. "Yes, of course we can. But it won't help morale to have wounded troops hanging around the barracks, wondering when they're going to get hit again and not knowing what it's all supposed to accomplish. We'll manage, one way or another. But our relative strength and efficiency are going to decline dramatically in the next six months, General, unless we do something about it."

"I'm well aware of that, Colonel. But we're not going to get any reinforcements, so we must make do with what we have."

"What about the Denastri Home Guard?" Gloria asked. "Can we expect any significant increase in their numbers or combat effectiveness?"

Matabele shook his head. "In theory," he said, "we plan to train an additional fifty thousand DHG troops over the next six months. That would bring their total force level up to nearly two hundred thousand. The reality is that they're deserting almost as fast as we can recruit them. And the more weapons we give them, the more wind up in the hands of the insurgents. Frankly, there are a few DHG units that I don't trust at all. Their leaders don't strike me as reliable, and it's a major challenge just to communicate with them. I honestly don't know where their primary loyalty lies, but I doubt that it's to the central government."

"Which brings me back to the Mankato report," Gloria said. "If what she says is correct, then it really doesn't matter much what we do, from a military standpoint. The longer we stay, the worse the insurgency is going to become. Operations like the one at Nastyville simply create more guerrillas than we kill. And the DHG troops are not really on our side. The Mankato report implies that their primary loyalty, General, is to the Denastri race itself, and secondarily, to their Superclan. The government is essentially irrelevant. It's only there to deal with us. The very fact that it's headed by a Thirdborn means that the Fifthborn military leaders regard it as of minor importance."

"I think that's probably true," said Morales. "Mankato makes some valid points, and I think it's clear that she understands these people better than we do. A lot of our intelligence really doesn't make much sense, but it makes a little more when viewed in light of what Mankato says. Nevertheless, I don't see that Mankato offers any viable solutions to the military problems we face."

A heavy, brooding silence descended around the conference table. Finally, Barnes looked at Gloria and said, "Do you have something in mind, Governor?"

"Maybe," she said. "I'd like you to consider the possibility of suspending all offensive operations on Lataka and adopting a posture similar to what we have on Banako."

"You mean, just hunker down and wait to be attacked?" Matabele looked as if the very notion offended him. "Governor, that would be entirely contrary to the Marine philosophy. We don't go anywhere simply to serve as passive targets."

"Not to mention what it would do to morale," Morales added.

"That's just not realistic, Governor," said Barnes.

Gloria raised her palms in a defensive gesture. "I'm not suggesting that we do nothing at all," she said. "But maybe we've been trying to do too much. Everyone keeps reminding me that our *real* mission here is to dig up that damned HCH. Well, if that's the case, then why are we expending so much effort in doing things that don't contribute directly to that result? If the government is irrelevant and the DHG more of a hindrance than a help, why don't we just cut them loose?"

Matabele scratched his chin for a moment and gave Gloria a long, appraising stare. "I'm listening," he said.

Gloria looked around the table. "Look," she said, "I haven't thought this thing through, and I'm hoping you'll come up with angles I haven't considered. But I think there are a number of things we can do that will lower our casualties and reduce Denastri resentment. For starters, we could withdraw nearly all of our troops from Senka, except for maybe a small military liaison office of no more than a couple dozen people. They aren't really needed there, but the Senka leaders say they should stay because of what are, in essence, reasons having to do with internal Denastri politics. But Denastri politics are *their* concern, not ours. They don't really matter much, as far as our core mission is concerned."

Barnes was nodding as she spoke. "That's another

two thousand troops," he said. "We could certainly use them here, and they aren't accomplishing a damn thing on Senka."

"The Corporates have been bugging us to do exactly what you suggest, Governor," said Hosagawa. "But Governor Blagodarski said it was politically impossible."

"I know," Gloria said. "That's what I thought, too. We've been taking the conventional view until now, and the Empire always tries to play local politics for all they're worth. Generally speaking, it's easier and cheaper to work with the existing indigenous political system. But maybe that doesn't even matter on this planet. Maybe we should consider leaving all of that to the Denastri while we concentrate on what's important to *us*."

"I have to say, I like this, Governor" —Matabele flashed her a smile that seemed hesitant but genuine— "but how will this play on Earth?"

"If it works, they'll love it," Gloria assured him. "If it doesn't, I don't see how we'd be much worse off than we are now. For me, at least, Mankato's report puts everything in a new light. What she's saying is that we can never really hope to understand internal Denastri politics anyway, so why try? Instead of leaning on the central government to do things *our* way, maybe we should just back off and let them do things *their* way. Then we can stay focused on our own priorities."

"Can we really afford to do that, Governor?" asked Morales. "I mean, what happens if the Denastri government collapses without our active support?"

"We don't have to cut them completely adrift. But we could limit our direct involvement in their affairs. I just asked our UnderSec for Administration to schedule some meetings with them to work out a new set of procedures. But now, I think I see a better way to go. Instead of telling them what we are going to do and what we want them to do, maybe we should tell them what we *aren't* going to do. I mean, we've got experts and specialists looking over their shoulders in dozens of different areas, trying to get them to do things that we think they ought to be doing. We've been trying to get them to create a government that's compatible with standard Imperial methods and protocols. And they go along with that because they think they have to make us happy. What choice do they have?"

"So you're saying that we should just let them go off on their own, except in areas of direct concern to us?" Morales drummed her fingers on the table and thought about the idea.

"Why not?" Gloria said. "If, as Mankato says, our very presence on their world is fundamentally upsetting to their sense of order, then we're never going to come up with a Denastri government that satisfies both of us. Right now, what we have is neither fish nor fowl —it doesn't work well for either one of us. So why not let them work out something that makes sense to them and stop worrying if it doesn't make sense to us?"

"I don't know," Matabele said. "There's a certain logic to what you say, but I'm concerned about the possible consequences. We could wind up with a government that's entirely *too* independent, maybe even actively hostile to us."

"We could step in before it goes that far," Barnes pointed out. "It's all a question of the proper length of the leash. I admit, it could be tricky, but I think it's worth a try."

Matabele looked at Gloria. "Civil government is your bailiwick, Governor, not ours. If you really want to try this, we'll go along with it. But as for your original suggestion about ending offensive operations and just sitting here like ducks on a pond—that's totally unacceptable."

"I understand your objections, General. Let's give that one some more thought. Maybe we can simply scale back our offensive operations for a time. Could you come up with a set of plans for different levels of military activity, ranging from very active to very limited?"

Matabele nodded toward Captain Hosagawa, who gave Gloria a broad smile. "You want plans, Governor? Plans we got. Lots of 'em. We can do a study and select a few that meet your criteria."

"Excellent."

"Just don't expect us to beat our swords into plowshares, Governor," Matabele cautioned. "But we'll take a look at the options. In the meantime, how soon can we get those troops back here from Senka?"

"Not just yet, General," Gloria told him. "That's a card I want to keep in our hand for the moment. We'll play it at the right time." In fact, it was a card Gloria hoped to play in her purely hypothetical negotiations with the C-clan for the release of Lord Kenarbin, but she didn't mention that. If she handled this right, everything she wanted to do anyway might be sold to the C-clan as major concessions. She felt a little thrill deep inside as she considered the possibilities. For the first time since she'd come to this miserable world, she thought there might actually be a reason for hope. It felt good.

Gloria leaned forward and peered at the catcher's mitt. The sky was clear, the air was cool, and she felt invigorated and alive. She wore a blue baseball cap with the Dexta logo on it, a white T-shirt emblazoned with a purple fire-snorting dragon, and tight white shorts that she had carefully altered for minimal coverage. She scuffed the dirt of the pitcher's mound, scratched her nearly naked butt, and spat into the grass; she didn't really understand much about baseball, but she knew that it seemed to involve a lot of scratching and spitting. Hefting the softball in her right hand, she went into a graceful underhand motion and fired a high, hard one— clean over the backstop.

"Oops," she said with an embarrassed grin. The catcher retrieved the ball and threw it back to her. She dropped it, picked it up, and tried again. The batter, Hettie Pando, dived into the dirt, got up, glared at Gloria for a moment, then spat.

Two pitches later, Pando trotted down to first base with a walk and Jack McCray came over from his shortstop position. "You're a little wild today, Governor," he said. "Why don't we trade positions?"

"Well . . . if you think so."

"Trust me," he said, and took the ball from her hand.

Gloria got set in a crouch at her new position, the way the other players were doing, and tried to concentrate as McCray pitched to the next batter. Concentrating proved to be difficult, what with all the inane chatter coming from Petra at second base. She seemed to be chanting in some strange language: "Hey, batta batta batta, hum chuck kid!" Gloria wished she had her translation software handy.

As luck—or the baseball gods—would have it, the next batter hit a hot, bounding shot right at her. Gloria swiped her glove at it, missed, and the ball caromed off her shoulder and skipped away into short left field. She grimaced, rubbed her shoulder, then turned and trotted after the ball. By the time she reached it, Hettie Pando was streaking around second base and headed for third. Gloria knew what needed to be done, and fired a perfect strike that nailed Pando right between the shoulder blades. Pando went down in a heap and came up screaming. She charged at Gloria but McCray headed her off, and suddenly everyone was shouting and milling around in confusion. Gloria wondered what all the excitement was about.

Umpire Alvin Hooper walked over to her. "You haven't played this before, have you, ma'am?" he asked solicitously.

"Of course I have," Gloria insisted. "At summer camp . . . when I was eight."

Gloria suddenly found herself exiled to right field. She didn't like it there. Nobody hit the ball in her direction, it was hard to see what was going on, and worst of all, nobody could see her. She had hoped that a little exercise and a bit of calculated exposure might work off some of the unfulfilled sexual tension that had been building up within her, but standing there in right field, far from the action, didn't seem to be helping. She tugged her shorts down a little, scratched her bare butt again, and glumly waited for something interesting to happen. Everyone else seemed to be enjoying themselves, but baseball didn't strike Gloria as a lot of fun.

Five runs and three outs later, the Media Maggots were retired and Gloria ran into the bench and grabbed a bat. McCray approached her, looking dubious, and said, "You want to lead off, Governor?"

"Sure!"

"I think it would be better if we saved you for . . . uh . . . cleanup."

"Okay. When do I bat?"

"Ninth," he said.

Oh." Disappointed, Gloria took a seat on the bench and watched as Pee Wee Nash led off for the home team. "Hit a homer!" Gloria shouted.

The cagey Nash bunted instead, and dashed down the baseline with surprising speed, her short legs churning furiously. She was safe by a step and Gloria leaped to her feet and cheered.

Elmo Hunt, who was not playing, strolled over to the Dragons' bench. "How's it going, Governor?" he asked.

"We'll beat you bums," she declared confidently. "But I don't think I like it out there in right field."

"Nonsense. It's your natural position," he assured her. "And I know what I'm talking about. I'm the guy who convinced Babe Ruth to switch from pitcher to the outfield."

"Babe Ruth? Was she good?"

Hunt laughed and patted Gloria on the shoulder. "She was the best," he told her, then wandered away, snickering.

An inning later, Gloria took her turn at bat. She scuffed at the dirt in the batter's box, spat once more, and stared menacingly in the direction of the pitcher, Bryce Denton. Before he could deliver a pitch, Alvin Hooper called time and looked at Gloria. "Uh, ma'am? You're not holding it right. Put your right hand on top. Don't want to break your wrists."

Gloria tried it that way, but didn't see what difference it made. In any case, she flailed ineffectually at three straight pitches. She didn't see how in the world a person was supposed to hit a ball coming at her that fast. Stupid game, she thought.

The stupid game dragged onward for seven innings and the hated Media Maggots won by a score of 17–4. Well, it was just a game—and a stupid one, at that—but Gloria hated to lose at anything. She trudged disconsolately across the outfield toward the Governor's Residence, muttering to herself.

Bryce Denton caught up with her. "Better luck next time," he said cheerfully.

"Yeah, thanks," she said. She spat once more.

Denton, who had struck her out three straight times on nine pitches, said, "Sorry, Gloria. I didn't mean to make you look bad. And that also applies to what's going to happen at tomorrow's news conference."

Gloria stopped and looked at him. "What do you mean?"

"Just that we all have our jobs to do. You have yours, I have mine. I do what I have to do, but there's nothing personal about it. I hope you'll remember that. I still want us to be friends."

"Bryce, what . . . ?"

"Tomorrow," he said, then trotted away. She watched him go, then scratched her butt and spat again. The news conference? What was he talking about? Well, it probably didn't matter. News conferences, after all, were just another stupid game.

· 17 ·

As she approached the front steps of the Governor's Residence, Gloria noticed a cloaked, hooded Secondborn standing in her way. He clutched a piece of folded-over paper in his four-fingered hand and nervously, it seemed to Gloria, held it out to her. She looked into his dark almond eyes for a second, but the Secondborn quickly looked down at the ground and extended his arm toward her. She took the paper from him, and he darted away before she could stop him.

On the paper, in neat typescript, a short message was printed: "honored governor discussions of a privacy nature are possible you will be contacted."

"I'll be damned," she said.

She walked into her private quarters, went to the fridge, and opened a beer—another necessary baseball ritual, she knew, like scratching and spitting. She sat down on a couch, sipped her beer, and stared at the message.

It had to have come, directly or otherwise, from the C-clan Fifthborn she had spoken to outside the Temple.

As far as she knew, this was the first communication ever received from the insurgents. The implication was profound and exciting—Kenarbin must still be alive, or there would be nothing to discuss!

In her mind, at least, things were at last beginning to fall into place. She could make a concrete offer to the insurgents without actually giving away anything. For starters, she could offer to withdraw those two thousand Marines on Senka. That might cut both ways, though. Nothing much was happening on Senka, where the C-clan population was minimal and the insurgency nearly nonexistent. Returning those Marines to Lataka, where they could contribute to suppressing the insurgency, might not be viewed in a positive light.

Still, the offer could be presented as an Imperial concession, and even if the insurgents didn't like it, they might at least view it as a promising first step. But what about the second step?

Gloria finished her beer, stripped off her clothes, and took a long, hot shower. She hummed "Take Me Out to the Ball Game" as she stood under the hot spray, considering the possibilities. Matabele—and even Barnes—had resisted her idea of ending or severely restricting offensive operations. That much was to be expected. But they seemed to be in general agreement with the notion of altering the basic relationship between the Empire and the civilian Denastri government.

What she needed, she realized, was something that would look good to the insurgents without arousing the ire of the Marines and could be presented to the public as an essentially neutral, purely bureaucratic measure that was completely unrelated to the (hoped for) release of Kenarbin. The best bet might be to hide the concessions within the general administrative reorganization that Petra would be overseeing, coupled with an uncontroversial change in military policy.

She turned off the shower, stepped into the stato-dryer, then idly strolled around her quarters. Maybe it was just her imagination, but it always seemed to her that she thought better without any clothes on. For some reason, she suddenly remembered the first time she had been nude with Kenarbin, the first time she had made love with him. The first time with anyone . . .

William, Lord Kenarbin—Spirit, such a man! In her starry-eyed youth and inexperience, she had been in awe of him—and more than a little impressed with herself for having attracted the ardent attentions of a man who was nothing less than an Imperial legend. She was already well aware of the effect she had on the male of the species, but she had bided her time, waiting for just the right one. For a while she had been content merely to taunt and tempt the young men at Court in the overripe atmosphere of the final days of the reign of old Darius IV. She had even thought about offering herself to the Emperor, but by then it would probably have been an idle gesture. What she really wanted—conventionally enough, it now seemed to her—was a mature, handsome, confident, dashing man of the worlds who would sweep her off her feet and gently introduce her to the mysteries, joys, and sorrows of love: Kenarbin, in other words. She had written his name in her school notebooks, and he had written it on her heart.

The bastard!

"Fuck me, milord," she had said to him . . . and hadn't he, just! She had a good mind to let the old son of a bitch rot in whatever Denastri hellhole he was being held in—teach him a lesson. But that would never do, of course. There was Lady Trish to consider, and young Prince Henry. And Charles, an even bigger bastard than Kenarbin, in the end. She had started her carnal career with a couple of prize specimens, all right. What did that say about her? she wondered. And what had it done to her?

Considering the matter objectively, Gloria knew that

she was something of a slut. No other word for it. If she hadn't actually humped every miner on Sylvania, it didn't mean that she hadn't wanted to. And all those visits to null-rooms, floating and fucking with wild abandon, letting total strangers possess her for minutes at a time before giving way to the next shift. The Orgastria. The jigli. The public displays and private perversions, the desperate, grinding, unceasing *need*. Was she no more than a product and prisoner of those specially crafted genes, or was she something created by Kenarbin and Charles, so long ago? Or had she created herself out of all those raw materials? Gloria VanDeen, a self-portrait.

She gazed down at herself—the jutting nipples and exquisite navel and smooth golden flesh. How could anyone *not* want her? And how could she not want what *they* wanted? How had Elmo Hunt's limerick gone? There once was a gal named VanDeen, something something a fucking machine? Was that all she was, a biological mechanism designed for nothing but fucking?

Well, when you got right down to it, that was all that any woman—or man—amounted to. That was the whole point of evolution, wasn't it? Isn't my DNA lovely? Don't you want to help me make more of it? Wham, bam, thank you, ma'am, and let's crawl out of the water and climb those trees and maybe compose some symphonies and sonnets and build a starship or two.

Unless, of course, you were a Denastri female. Then the wham-bam had an unforgiving, fatal twist to it. We'll make one more of you, Honored Sixthborn, and no more of me. Except that each coupling produced one male and three females—was that a fair trade, then, after all? And what of those extra females, the ones who never mated and spent their lives feeding the males? Who the hell *were* they? What did *they* want?

And if you were one of them, what would you think of someone like, say, Gloria VanDeen?

"Very profound, Gloria," she said to herself. Maybe

she really did think better in the nude. Differently, at least. Strange thoughts for a strange world.

The news conference was a weekly chore that Gloria generally enjoyed. Sixty or seventy media reps crowded into the small auditorium, set up their imagers, checked their notes, hair, and makeup, cleared their throats, and prepared for the familiar ritual. In a way, the whole thing was as predictable and stylized as a Denastri religious ceremony, right down to the rather ghoulish symbolism, Gloria realized: they wanted to eat her brain. Nevertheless, Gloria enjoyed the give-and-take and the challenge of finding just the right words to say as little as possible or as much as necessary. It was always important to keep in mind the fact that her real audience was not the raffish collection of newsies who shared the room with her, but the billions throughout the Empire who would eventually see a five-second clip of her performance.

And it *was* a performance. Like her friend Jeremy, she strutted her stuff on a lighted stage, conscious of the effect of each gesture and nuance, playing her part with verve and vitality, inhabiting the well-practiced, much-rehearsed role of the fabulous VanDeen. She knew the public VanDeen the way Jeremy knew Richard, hump and all. There were certain expectations that had to be fulfilled or the performance would fall flat and her star would fade. Thus, she arrived at today's performance wearing a very sheer white blouse, wide open to her waist, and a knee-length burgundy skirt slit to her left hipbone. Her audience and critics expected as much, and she knew it would be foolish to disappoint them.

"First off," she said after the Public Information Officer had introduced her, "I want to thank all the Media Maggots who participated in yesterday's game. We all had a lot of fun, and I hear you had a fine time congratulating yourselves in the Imperial bar last night. On behalf of the Dexta Dragons, I hereby issue a challenge for a rematch, on a date to be determined. We intend to kick your butts." The Maggots responded to that with catcalls and hoots of derision. When they had calmed down, Gloria added, "Also, I want to apologize to Hettie Pando. And I promise to read the rulebook before the next game."

Gloria let her smile fade—put on her game face—and got down to business. "Today, before I take your questions, I want to announce a new initiative to be undertaken by the Imperial Government, in cooperation with the Denastri government, the Occupation Task Force, and the Corporate interests on this world. In the weeks ahead, we will be holding a series of meetings with the interested parties with the goal of establishing a new set of protocols and procedures specifically designed to meet the needs of Denastri. These meetings will be overseen by UnderSecretary for Administration Petra Nash. Up to now, we have rather slavishly followed the standard Imperial policies that apply to new Empire worlds. And while those policies have stood the test of time and have produced positive results on scores of worlds, the truth is that each world is unique and each requires appropriate adjustments to the standard procedures. That is especially true of Denastri. Frankly, our results to date have not been good. I believe that we can and must do better, and the time has come for a thorough and creative reexamination of our methods and procedures."

It was a minor bombshell, and the media reps turned to one another and whispered busily for a few moments as Gloria put her hands on the podium and leaned forward. She hadn't even mentioned any of this to the Denastri government or the Corporates yet, but figured it was best to get out in front of things and present them with a *fait accompli*. Once a policy had been presented to the media it became real, *de facto,* even if there was not yet any flesh and bone behind the public façade.

"I can't give you any specifics yet," she continued.

"All I can tell you for now is that we intend to conduct a thorough review of the situation in an attempt to identify and understand the causes and consequences of our various failures—as well as our successes. If we have done some things wrong on Denastri, we have also done some things right. I don't want to give you the impression that we are simply declaring our efforts here a failure and starting over. That's not the case at all. Rather, we are attempting to build on our achievements and, in close cooperation with the Denastri government and the Corporates, find appropriate ways of addressing and correcting our shortcomings. I caution you not to expect overnight miracles. This will be an incremental process, and may take many months to reach fruition. Nevertheless, I'm confident that, in the long run, our new initiative will lead to a stable, peaceful, and productive Imperial presence on Denastri."

She had, she knew, said practically nothing, but that was the name of the game. The media would draw the appropriate conclusions and decide for themselves how to tell their audience What This Means. That was the beauty of the thing; if you did it right, the media would fill in all the blank spaces and generate their own blizzard of speculation, comment, and analysis. Then, if it all blew up in your face, you could fall back to the time-honored, universal defense: I Never Said That.

The Q and A began. Gloria expertly fenced and parried with the media reps, cautioning against overinterpretation, unwarranted speculation, and unrealistic expectations. She carefully restated her announcement two or three different ways, each time adding a little spin to her presentation, designed to allow the reps to emphasize different angles in their stories. The net result would be a broad and necessarily vague array of reports, all of which would end the same way. What does it all mean? Only time will tell . . .

Bryce Denton got to his feet. Gloria suddenly recalled his little warning about not wanting to make her look bad. She hadn't given it any thought, having been distracted by the message from the C-clan. But Bryce was not a bad guy, and she didn't think that she had any reason to fear what he might say. She quickly discovered that she was very wrong about that.

"Madame Governor," he said, "a few days ago, I filed a story that will be arriving on Earth within the next two days. In that story, I report that, according to reliable sources close to the Imperial Governor, the true reason you were sent to Denastri was to negotiate with the insurgents to obtain the release of Lord Kenarbin. Since such negotiations would be contrary to long-standing Imperial policy forbidding negotiations for the release of hostages, I wondered if you would care to comment."

Gloria stared at Denton as an urgent buzz filled the auditorium. She was shocked and stunned by Denton's words. There was only one place Denton could have gotten that information, only one "reliable source close to the Imperial Governor" who could have told him: Petra. How could she have done that? How the hell could she?

"Madame Governor?" Denton prodded.

Gloria took a deep breath. "Mr. Denton," she said, "I don't know where you got your information, but I can state categorically that in my meetings with Secretary Mingus and His Imperial Highness before my departure for Denastri, neither one of them ever mentioned Lord Kenarbin. My mission here was to observe, consult, make recommendations, and restore order to the Dexta establishment on this world. Due to the tragic events that occurred on the day of my arrival, it became necessary for me to assume additional duties, specifically, to serve as Interim Imperial Governor and Imperial Secretary. I have been fully engaged in those tasks, and during my time here I have not entered into any negotiations, official or otherwise, concerning the release of Lord Kenarbin. Your story is incorrect, Mr. Denton."

"You deny that you're here to gain the release of Lord Kenarbin?"

"I can only repeat what I've already said. I never received any instructions regarding Lord Kenarbin."

"Whether or not anyone made specific statements concerning Lord Kenarbin," Denton persisted, "isn't it true that there was an unspoken understanding that you would attempt to achieve his release?"

"In my considerable experience with Secretary Mingus and His Imperial Highness, I have always found it to be the case that if they want something, they tell me what it is in no uncertain terms. I assure you, they do not rely on 'unspoken understandings.' "

"Nevertheless, Madame Governor," Denton said, "isn't it true that you have made what my source refers to as 'a tentative approach' to a C-clan leader regarding the release of Lord Kenarbin?"

So far, Gloria had managed to dance her way around the truth. Now, she had no choice but to lie.

"No, Mr. Denton," she said flatly, "it is not true."

"Not according to my source," he said. The hell of it was, everyone in the room was well aware of the identity of Denton's source. His affair with Petra was hardly a secret, and she was certainly "close to the Imperial Governor."

"Your source is mistaken, Mr. Denton. All I can say is that it is certainly the earnest desire of everyone here that Lord Kenarbin will be released at some point. Perhaps your source misinterpreted some comment I may have made in that area. We all hope for his safe return. But, as you have already said, rigid Imperial policy dating back at least five centuries forbids any negotiations for the release of hostages. I have no intention of violating that policy. I hope that answers your question, Mr. Denton."

"It doesn't," he said. "I stand by my story, Madame Governor." Denton sat down, and a dozen other reps leaped to their feet, shouting questions.

Gloria endured the storm, like a clipper ship captain lashed to the mast in the face of a hurricane: a nautical metaphor, courtesy of her father. But perhaps the wrong one; she felt as if she had just struck an iceberg.

Throughout it all, Gloria silently cursed Petra. How could she have done this? How could she have leaked such precious, sensitive, explosive information to Bryce Denton, of all people? Why not just shout it from the rooftops?

She found herself making repeated denials, each one sounding weaker and lamer than the last. If she admitted the truth, Parliament would hang her from the nearest yardarm (thanks again, Dad). Worse, Mingus and even Charles would be dragged into the whirlpool, with Spirit knew what damage to the Empire. If terrorists ever got the idea that they could get what they wanted merely by kidnapping the right person, no Imperial Governor, no Imperial Secretary, no Lord or Lady, would ever be safe. The Empire could not, *must not* negotiate for the release of hostages.

The story she had wanted to present today had already sunk without a trace. The Kenarbin story would be on lead screens throughout the Empire within days—and here on Denastri, as well. The insurgents would learn of it immediately, and what would that do to the "tentative approach" she had made to the C-clan general? Would they break off contact—or would they announce a confirmation that the contact had been made, thus adding to the discomfiture of their Imperial overlords and enemies? And what would it mean for Kenarbin himself? If the public disclosure meant an end to negotiations, would they decide he was no longer useful and simply kill him?

When the newsies had dredged the revelation for all it was worth, Hettie Pando got to her feet and said, "Madame Governor, if I might change the subject . . . ?"

"Please do," Gloria replied with total sincerity.

"I hesitate to bring this up," Pando said, "but, while your private life may not be fair game, in this case I feel it is a relevant and legitimate point of inquiry. Is it true, Madame Governor, that you have entered into an intimate relationship with a member of the Marines' high command? Are you and—"

"*Don't*, Hettie!" Gloria pleaded.

"But Governor—"

"Dammit, Hettie, I don't care what you say about me. But you could be doing serious damage to the career of an outstanding officer!"

"I won't mention any names, then," Pando said. "But given the animosity that exists between the Marines and Servitor, and considering the delicate state of relations between the Imperial Government and the Denastri, it strikes me as a serious matter if the Imperial Governor is literally in bed with the Marine leadership. This has troubling implications for Imperial policy, and—"

"But it isn't true!" Gloria shouted. And it wasn't! Their desires notwithstanding, she and Delbert had never managed to consummate their smoldering relationship. But how could she tell them that? And would they even believe it?

"You deny that such a relationship exists?" Pando asked with a skeptical sneer.

"I do," Gloria insisted.

"But Governor, you do have a certain reputation. And it is a well-known fact that you and a certain Marine officer have a close and long-standing relationship. Do you think it's appropriate—"

"I don't think this whole line of questioning is appropriate! Whatever you may think, you're wrong!"

Gloria angrily stomped off the stage, leaving a roomful of excited and titillated newsies to decide for themselves what was true and what wasn't. All things considered, only one conclusion was possible.

· 18 ·

Softball with the media was bad enough, but Gloria felt as if she had just engaged in a brutal game of rugby with them. She emerged from the scrum battered and bruised and feeling a medley of emotions that she couldn't even identify. Spirit, what the hell just happened?

She returned to her office, sat down behind her desk, pulled her ever-present bottle of Belgravian out of a drawer, and poured herself a stiff slug of the stuff. She gulped it down and poured another.

It was hard to focus on any particular point of outrage. How could Petra have blabbed to Denton? And Pando! Damn that woman, didn't she realize the damage she could be doing to Delbert Barnes? Why even bring it up? And what about Kenarbin? What would all of this mean for *him*? And for the Empire? And Denastri? Not to mention her own Administration—and her career! Spirit, would Mingus ever trust her again? And speaking of trust, how could Petra—Petra, of all people!—have betrayed her like that?

The second glass of Belgravian didn't help, and she barely noticed the third. Just when she was beginning to get a handle on this miserable world, it all exploded in her face like another terrorist bomb. And what could she do about it? How could she ever repair the damage that had been done? Maybe she should just hand in her resignation and go home. Let someone else pick up the pieces. Let someone else deal with the media and Servitor and the Marines and Edgar Wong and brain-eating aliens and . . . and *Petra*!

Loyal, steadfast, devoted, competent, funny, trustworthy Petra, the best friend she'd ever had or ever hoped to. They were going to spend the rest of their lives together, side by side, with Gloria running Dexta and Petra guarding the gate. Pals to the end.

The end. Spirit, was this it, then?

Gloria discovered that tears were running down her cheeks. The pain she felt was beyond description. No one had ever hurt her like this, not even Kenarbin or Charles. That was the problem with loving people. Let them get too close and they were sure to stick a knife in your back. And then twist it.

Even Petra. The cute little girl from Weehawken had turned out to be as scheming and disloyal as all the rest. What had she hoped to gain from her betrayal? Maybe a job with the media? Sure, why not? ENS could pay her a lot more than Dexta, and Petra had been poor all her life. It was easy to forget how much money meant to people like that.

She had always known, deep down, that Petra resented her. How could she not? Gloria was born with everything and Petra with practically nothing. Money, beauty, brains, a loving family, and glittering, endless possibilities. All Petra ever had was a father who deserted her, a brainless, snobbish shrew of a mother, and a shabby tenement in New Jersey. It was only natural, then, that someone like Petra Nash would envy and resent someone like Gloria VanDeen.

And, of course, there was the whole business of sex. Gloria, with her dazzling looks and extraspecial genes, enjoyed it to the hilt and had all of it she had ever wanted—with Emperors and Lords and famous and successful men from one end of the Empire to the other. Petra, cute but plain and small, always seemed to have to settle for doomed losers and second-raters like Bryce Denton and Albert Fenlow. No wonder Petra resented her! Everyone did, when you got right down to it. But Petra, closer than the rest, had better reasons. She'd probably planned this. Probably had it in her devious, envious little mind for years, waiting for just the right moment to slip it to her and bring down the great and glamorous Gloria once and for all. Of course she had. It all made perfect sense, now that Gloria considered the matter objectively, with a bellyful of Belgravian. The little bitch had hated her from the beginning!

The little bitch chose that moment to enter Gloria's office and hesitantly approach her desk. Gloria quickly wiped her face with the back of her hand, sniffed deeply, and tried to meet Petra's eyes. But Petra immediately looked away, then down at the floor.

"Gloria?" she said softly, shyly. Of course, she would play it this way. Abject and abashed. Just a poor little girl from Weehawken, so terribly sorry about her monstrous betrayal. Of course.

"I'm so sorry," she said. "I never meant to tell him. It just sort of slipped out."

"Of course it did," Gloria responded. "Oh, Bryce, darling, you looked so strong and manly striking out Gloria the way you did, and, oh, did I mention that she's here to free Lord Kenarbin?"

"It wasn't like that at all!" Petra protested.

"How was it, then?" Gloria demanded. "Did you just murmur it in the throes of passion, or did you plan the whole thing? Great way to give Denton's career a boost, wasn't it? I'm sure he'll express his gratitude in some appropriate way."

"Gloria! How can you say that?"

"How can *I* say that?" Gloria exploded. "How could *you* say that? Spirit, don't you realize what you've done? I thought I could *trust* you! Did you tell him about Charles and the Fifth of October, too?"

Petra stared at her in openmouthed amazement for a moment. "Spirit!" she gasped. "Of course I didn't!"

"No? Good. It could get us both killed, you know. My own fault, I suppose. It was stupid of me to tell you in the first place. Of course, that was when I thought I could trust you."

"But, Gloria . . ."

"And you may have gotten Kenarbin killed, too. Now that the secret is out, maybe they'll just decide that he's not worth anything to them and get rid of him. I can't possibly negotiate with them now, so they don't have anything to gain by keeping him alive. Did *that* occur to you when you just let it slip to that fucking weasel?"

Petra seemed to visibly deflate as she stood before her. "Spirit! I didn't . . . I never . . ."

"Didn't think of it, huh? Well, why should you have? What does Kenarbin matter, anyway? What's he to you? And what does it matter if our whole mission on Denastri goes down the drain? It's not *your* responsibility!"

Now tears were rolling down Petra's cheeks. Perfect. Nice touch, that.

"Gloria . . . *please!*" She was sobbing. Almost as if it really mattered to her.

"Do you have any concept of how much damage you've done?"

"But it was an accident! I swear to you, I never meant to tell him! And after I did, I *begged* him not to use it! But you know Bryce—"

"You bet your ass I know him! Don't *you* know him? Don't *you* know what he is?"

"Yes, but . . . but it was an *accident*!"

"Was it?" Gloria glared at Petra and gritted her teeth. "Or did you just want to impress good old Bryce with all the important secrets you knew? Well, I suppose it doesn't really matter whether you meant to tell him or not. The point is that you *did* tell him. And now we all have to live with the consequences . . . except maybe Lord Kenarbin, who might just *die* from the consequences."

"Oh, Gloria," Petra sobbed. "I'm so sorry!"

"Good. I'll make a note of that. UnderSecretary for Administration Nash expressed profound sorrow after getting Lord Kenarbin killed. A little addendum to the file. Speaking of which, we have a little problem to resolve, you and I. What the hell am I supposed to do with you? Now that I know I can't trust you, that creates certain organizational difficulties, doesn't it?"

Petra looked up, her chin quivering. "Gloria, you *can* trust me! I swear to you, it will never happen again."

"You're goddamned right it won't! I'm sending you home. Jack McCray can take your slot. He's competent, and I won't make the mistake of trusting *him* with anything important. My own damn fault, I suppose. I should never have trusted you in the first place."

"Oh, no!" Petra cried in despair. "Gloria, you can't do that."

"What the hell else *can* I do? What choice do I have? Forget about the fact that you betrayed *me*—you betrayed *Dexta*! There will probably be a Board of Inquiry after you get back to Earth. I'd suggest that you start looking for another job, Petra. Maybe Denton will hire you as his girl Friday. Of course, *he'll* know better than to trust you with anything more important than making coffee."

"Please don't do this to me, Gloria! *Please*!"

"You did it to yourself."

"I know, I know. But . . . please, Gloria! Don't decide this now. You're still angry, and you've been drinking. Just, please, wait a day or two. That's all I ask. After all we've been through together, you owe me that much!"

"Do I?" Gloria pursed her lips and stared at Petra for a long moment. "Very well, then," she said at last, "I'll hold off for a day or so. I wouldn't want to do anything rash, after all."

"Thank you," Petra said in a small, lost voice.

"Don't thank me. Today, tomorrow, next week, it'll still come out the same."

Petra wiped away her tears. "I'm sorry. I know I made a mistake. I guess I'm not perfect . . . like *you*." There was a sudden hint of defiance in the tone of her voice and the set of her chin.

"Oh, now it comes out! I've been expecting it. I know you've always resented me. I just never dreamed it went so deep! I should have known."

"That's not true, Gloria," Petra protested.

"Isn't it?" Gloria demanded.

"You know it isn't! Maybe I've envied you, and maybe sometimes . . . I . . . I . . ."

"Oh, just spare me. Just get out of here. Get out of my sight! I'll let you know when I've made my decision. Now get the hell out of here!"

Petra tried to say something in response, but the look on Gloria's face stopped her cold. Choking back another sob, she turned and walked from the room, softly closing the door behind her. Gloria watched her go, choked back a sob of her own, then poured herself another drink.

She spent the rest of the afternoon drinking and brooding. Finally, she flopped down on a couch and drifted off into a troubled, boozy sleep. Dreams came to her, hazy and ill-defined, brimming with anger and pain and confusion. When she awakened, it was dark. Early evening. A lost day. The worst day of her life.

Still feeling the effects of the Belgravian, she got unsteadily to her feet and wondered what she should do next. Petra? Kenarbin? Nothing to be done about them, now; they were gone. Lost. What else? Delbert. What about him?

It was so unfair! That poor man, suddenly dragged into a media morass, his career irretrievably damaged. Ruined, maybe. And they hadn't even done anything! They had behaved with all the upright rectitude that anyone could possibly have asked of them—and for what? So that Hettie Pando could have her little scoop? Naturally, she had to try to upstage Denton after his grandstand play. Can't let the competition get too far ahead.

At least she hadn't mentioned Delbert's name, but if she didn't, someone else probably would. Weasels, all of them! But maybe it wasn't too late to head them off. Maybe, if she could convince Pando to retract her story, the damage could still be limited. It was worth a try, anyway.

Gloria weaved her way out of her office and crossed the open Compound, the cold wind whipping at her flimsy blouse and skirt. She paused in the middle of the Compound and faced the gale, letting it knife into her like a thousand icy daggers. It seemed to help—sobered her up a little, at least. A few deep breaths and she was ready to face the media maggots again, this time in their own lair. She walked on, made her way into the Imperial, and found Pando and Hunt cuddled together in their usual booth. Without waiting to be asked, she sat down and joined them.

"Ah, Madame Governor," Hunt said; "somehow, I had a feeling you'd show up. Drinks are on me." He signaled to a Denastri waiter, who came over to the booth and poured Gloria a glass of whatever Hunt and Pando were having. It wasn't Belgravian, but it wasn't bad.

"Hettie," Gloria said, "you have to retract that story."

"Why would I want to do that?"

"Because, it isn't *true*, dammit!"

"That's not what *I* hear," Pando insisted.

"What you hear is garbage! Think about it. How the hell would anyone know?"

"I know you had a private dinner with him in your quarters the other night," Pando said.

"Yes . . . along with Dr. Mankato. Did your source happen to mention that?"

"Yes, as a matter of fact. And Mankato left an hour before Barnes did. Plenty of time for hanky-panky. Look, you're both single consenting adults, and ordinarily it would be none of my business what went on between the two of you. But if the Imperial Governor and the commander of the Fifth Marine Division are having an affair, that makes it a legitimate story."

"I know, I know—and that's precisely why nothing happened!" Gloria didn't feel it necessary to mention that something had been *about* to happen when they were interrupted by the emergency call. "We're both well aware of all the implications, Hettie. And neither one of us wanted to risk the damage this could do to his career."

Pando raised an eyebrow. "You really didn't do anything?"

"No!"

"Big mistake," said Hunt.

Gloria looked at him. "What do you mean?"

"I mean," said Hunt, "that you both forgot the first rule of war."

"And what's that?" Gloria asked him.

"First rule of war," he said, "is to gather ye rosebuds while ye may. Two minutes from now, a terrorist bomb could blow us all to kingdom come. And what good would your self-restraint and moral probity do you then? In war, if you see a chance to get a little of the good stuff, grab it with both hands! Sex, booze, loot—enjoy it while you can and don't waste your time worrying about it."

"He's right," Pando said, grabbing Hunt's hand and squeezing it. "This pompous old fool and I have been together for three wars now. No regrets, no hesitations, no rules. Well, *one* rule."

"What's that?"

"I go first," Hunt said. "We made a deal." He looked fondly at Pando for a moment. "I'm too damn old to bury another lover. Won't go through that again. That's our only rule, and I intend to hold you to it, Hettie, my love."

"And I shall be true to my vow, Elmo, dearest," Pando declared. "In fact, I'm looking forward to burying you. Standing over your grave, all dressed in black, weeping nobly, orating to beat the band. I've already got the eulogy half-written. Great stuff. You'll love it."

"I'm sure that I shall," Hunt said, then kissed the back of her hand. He looked at Gloria. "See? You and Barnes should profit by our example."

Gloria could hardly disagree. She sipped her drink and stared down at the tabletop.

"Listen," Pando said, "I won't retract my story. But I won't mention his name, and I'll put the word out around here. I can't guarantee anything, but I'll do my best to keep Barnes's name out of it."

"Thank you, Hettie," Gloria said quietly. "I appreciate that."

"Rough day for you, eh, kid?" Hunt shook his head slowly, almost apologetically.

Gloria gave him a crooked, downturned smile. "The roughest," she said.

"Our job is to comfort the afflicted and afflict the comfortable," Hunt said. "Sometimes that means hurting people, whether they deserve it or not. For what it's worth, I don't think you deserved it. Same thing with

Barnes. Fact is, I think he's one hell of a good officer. And I've seen worse Imperial Governors."

"Don't get all mushy on me, Hunt," Gloria said. "You'll ruin your image."

"Hogwash. My image is carved in granite."

"That's our Elmo," Pando said, smiling. "Granite on the outside, marshmallow on the inside."

Gloria noticed Bryce Denton walking toward them from across the barroom. He stopped outside the booth and looked at her. She met his gaze and felt the anger boiling up within her.

"It's not her fault," Denton said. "You want to blame someone, blame me."

"Oh, I blame you, all right, you incredible bastard! Don't you realize what you've done? They'll probably kill Lord Kenarbin now!"

Denton dismissed the notion with a frown. "If they wanted to kill him, they'd already have done it. The Denastri, as you may have noticed, take the long view. They'd think nothing of keeping him hostage for years. Decades, even."

"Which they probably will, thanks to you. I can't even *talk* to them now!"

"Wouldn't that be a violation of Imperial policy?" Denton asked.

"Oh, go fuck yourself!"

Denton shrugged. "I may have to," he said. "Petra says she never wants to see me again."

"The little idiot's finally wising up, is she? Not that it'll do her any good. She's finished at Dexta. You just killed her career, Bryce."

"I told you, it wasn't her fault."

Gloria seethed in silence for a moment. Before she could think of anything to say, Hunt intervened. "Go away, Denton," he said. "You've done enough damage for one day."

Denton started to leave, stopped, and turned back to

Gloria. "I told you before, it wasn't personal. The people of the Empire have a right to know if Imperial policy is being violated, and it's my job to tell them. But I'm sorry if I've hurt you and Petra. It's the last thing I wanted. But I still have to do my job." He stared at Gloria for another moment, then turned and walked over to the bar, where he ordered a double.

"He's right, you know," Pando said.

Gloria looked at her. "Oh, *please*."

"It's a fucked-up galaxy we live in, Madame Governor," Hunt told her. "I advise you to get used to it."

Gloria left the Imperial and wandered out into the Compound. She looked up at the unfamiliar stars; a dozen companion stars in the McGowan Cluster were brighter than any you could see from Earth. Orbiting them, other Denastri were probably looking back at her. Unless they were busy eating each other's brains. Hunt was right. The galaxy, with all its diversity and promise, was, at bottom, beyond comprehension and probably beyond redemption. She couldn't wait for the big black hole at its core to suck it all down into oblivion.

She felt another's presence and looked down from the stars to see a tiny round Denastri female standing next to her. The female peered up at her, from beneath her hood, and spoke a few words that Gloria could not understand. She reached into the pocket of her skirt and turned on the translation software in her computer pad.

"What did you say?" Gloria asked, then waited as the pad spoke her words again in the language of Denastri. The female responded.

"It is mostly important, Honored Governor," the pad translated, "that you come with me."

"What? Where? Where do you want me to go?"

"Honored Governor must come," the female repeated.

"But why?"

"Honored Fifthborn awaits," she said. "It is of a necessity." The diminutive female locked eyes with her for a moment, then turned and quickly moved toward the shadows at a corner of the Compound. Gloria hesitated, then followed her into the shadows.

·19·

Moving quickly, her short, stubby legs hidden by her long cloak, the Denastri female almost seemed to be rolling forward. Gloria broke into a trot to catch up. The female glanced back at her, then opened the door of a small supply shed backed up against one of the Compound walls. Gloria hesitated, looked around at the empty Compound, then followed her into the dark, cramped shed. The female closed the door, leaving them in total darkness.

"What . . . ?" Gloria stopped and listened. There were some soft metallic sounds, and abruptly, a dim glow flooded into the shed from below. Looking down, she saw the female gesturing toward a hole in the floor. A chain-link ladder led downward to a low, narrow passage-way. This, she figured, had to be how the insurgents had gotten their bomb into the Compound. Gloria wondered why they were letting her see it, but the female was urgently gesturing toward the hole.

"Honored Governor must go . . . *now!*"

In for a penny, in for a crown, she thought. She

crouched, probed for the ladder with her left foot, found
it, and began her descent. Reaching the floor, she looked
up and saw the female closing the hatch behind her. The
passageway was dimly illuminated and stretched off into
the indeterminate distance. She had to bend slightly to
keep from bumping her head. The female led the way,
and Gloria followed, wary but intensely curious.

Silently, they scurried onward through the bare rock
of the tunnel. Overhead light fixtures provided weak
pools of illumination every twenty or thirty meters, and
Gloria had to duck under them as she passed. They were
beyond the Compound walls now, she realized, somewhere under the alien streets of Enkar. She wondered
for a moment if this was such a good idea and briefly considered turning back. But after the disastrous events of
the day, she couldn't resist a chance to make direct contact with the insurgents. She'd probably never get an opportunity like this again.

After covering perhaps three or four hundred meters, they arrived at the end of the passageway, where another ladder awaited them. The Denastri female started
climbing it, toward a lighted area above, and Gloria followed. She emerged into a featureless rectangular room
with a higher ceiling and walls made of the familiar dun-
colored adobe-like substance that was so common in
Enkar. There was a single doorway, and the female
darted through it without even looking back to see if
Gloria was still with her. They went through another
room and another door, and Gloria found herself standing in the cold, open air of an empty street.

Not quite empty, she realized. An unlighted three-
wheeled Denastri vehicle rolled toward them and
stopped. A door popped open, and the female looked
back and gestured for Gloria to get in. She did, crawling
into the wide rear compartment of the vehicle. She was
no sooner seated then the door slammed shut, leaving

Gloria alone with the driver, a small, hooded Firstborn male. The vehicle suddenly lurched into motion.

Gloria leaned forward and said to the driver, "Where are you taking me?" He ignored her. Gloria sat back and watched in silence as the dark, ramshackle buildings of Enkar swept past. She felt increasingly uneasy about the whole thing but reminded herself that the locator transponder on her wristcom would permit Jack McCray's Security people to track her movements. And it seemed unlikely that the insurgents would try to do her any harm; they wanted to talk, after all.

They passed through the main gate of the city with barely a pause. After twenty minutes of seemingly random zigzags, the vehicle came to a halt in an empty open area. The door popped open and Gloria got out and looked around. The dark open area, she realized, was a ruin; it must have been the neighborhood that was flattened by the Marines during her brief, disastrous sightseeing tour. Another vehicle was waiting for her, along with three big Fourthborns. The first vehicle quickly departed, and Gloria started to get into the second one, but a Fourthborn stood in her way. He seized her left hand and quickly unlatched her wristcom.

"Hey, wait a minute!" The Fourthborn ignored her protests and slipped the wristcom into the pocket of his cloak. Then he gestured for her to get into the vehicle. Gloria reluctantly accepted the inevitable and got in. The insurgents weren't fools. The Fourthborn with her wristcom walked away, leaving her sealed inside the vehicle with a Firstborn driver and another Fourthborn sharing the backseat with her.

She tried conversing with the Fourthborn as they rolled away from the city, but he completely ignored her. Looking out the windows, she tried to identify landmarks, hoping to obtain at least some notion of their location, but soon gave up. They had left Enkar behind and were traversing the broad, featureless, windswept plain, headed Spirit-knew-where.

After perhaps thirty minutes, Gloria saw a cluster of buildings looming ahead. The vehicle came to a stop outside one of them, and she and the Fourthborn got out. It was colder and windier here, and Gloria shivered; her flimsy attire wasn't quite the thing for midnight skulking. The Fourthborn pointed to the door of the building and Gloria entered.

Inside, she found a nearly bare room with nothing inside it but a table, two chairs, and a Fifthborn. She wasn't sure, but she thought it was the general she had spoken to outside the Temple. She couldn't remember his "name," and decided it probably didn't matter. She nodded politely and said, "Honored Fifthborn, I thank you for agreeing to meet me." Her translation software rendered her words in the flowing language of the Denastri.

The Fifthborn tilted his head slightly forward. "Honored Governor of Imperial—*unknown word, possibly pejorative*. We shall speak." He gestured toward one of the chairs, and Gloria sat down. The Fifthborn remained standing for several moments, staring at her impassively, then took his seat.

"The first thing I must know," Gloria said, seizing the initiative, "is that Lord Kenarbin is alive and well. Can you assure me that this is so?"

"Terran offal still eats," said the general. His hood was back, and Gloria got a good look at his smooth, unlined, carrot-colored features. Denastri didn't live long enough to collect wrinkles, she figured. His dark topknot was meticulously threaded with strands of gold, red, and blue. The black wells of his eyes were unreadable, and his piscine mouth revealed no identifiable expression. Gloria wondered if Denastri could read human expressions any better than humans could read those of the Denastri.

"I am pleased to hear that he is well," Gloria told him. "If any harm were to come to Lord Kenarbin, it would have the most serious consequences for your people."

"My people are not your concern," he said flatly.

"You are wrong, Honored Fifthborn," Gloria said. "I am the Imperial Governor, and my concern is for all of the people of this world—Rock-clan, Water-clan, Wind-clan, and Terrans. Denastri is now a part of the Terran Empire, and His Imperial Highness cares for the well-being of all his people."

She had never seen a Denastri laugh before, but the Fifthborn's reaction certainly reminded her of a contemptuous guffaw. "You lie, of course," he said. "Imperial Highness is mostly a—*unknown word, possibly pejorative*—and his Honored Imperial Governor is no more than his—*unknown word, possibly referring to Firstborn servants*. Nevertheless, we talk."

"Yes," Gloria said. "Talking is better than fighting."

"One and both. A muchness, most likely."

Gloria had no idea what he meant by that, but pressed onward. "We can stop the fighting, honored Fifthborn. The Denastri have much to gain from peace."

"Terran offal gain more, take everything if Denastri do not—*unknown word*—that which is theirs. Imperial Marines are gluttons who never stop eating. A wrongness of great completeness, almost."

"And the insurgents kill innocent Terrans and Denastri," Gloria pointed out. "Surely, this is also a wrongness."

"Highest exalted—*unknown word*—demand necessary purification. Terran presence on Denastri is mostly upsetting in the extreme. Honored Wind-clan Fourthborn and Fifthborn must do what is necessary to—*unknown word, possibly 'cleanse'*—our delightful world. This is of highest necessity, almost."

"Yes," Gloria said, "I understand that Terrans disturb

the necessary order of things on your world. But that is not our desire. Tell me, what can we do to improve the situation? What can we do that will help restore the proper order?"

"This humble Fifthborn wishes to know, especially of importance, when Terran offal will leave Denastri."

"We aren't leaving," Gloria said.

"You will leave," he said confidently. "When the black rocks are eaten, you will leave."

"It will be many years before we have eaten all of the black rocks. A lifetime, for a Denastri."

"But then, you will leave."

"Even then, the Empire will not abandon Denastri. But," she added, choosing her words carefully, "when the black rocks are gone, the Imperial presence on Denastri will probably be reduced."

"The Marines will leave then?"

"Most of them, yes. The only reason there are so many Marines on Denastri now is because you are fighting us. If you stop fighting, most of them will leave. Even before the black rocks are eaten. There is no reason to wait so long."

The Fifthborn listened to the translation, then leaned back in his chair, as if pondering her words. Then he leaned forward again and said, "You are here for the black rocks. You will not leave until you have eaten them. This is mostly true all the time. Honored Governor cannot deceive this humble Fifthborn."

"I have no wish to deceive you, Honored Fifthborn. But you are right, the black rocks are the main reason we are here. They are of great importance to His Imperial Highness."

"They are of great importance to Imperium and KemTek, most likely."

"Then you understand the situation, Honored Fifthborn."

He nodded slowly and folded his hands together, a

very human gesture. "This humble Fifthborn," he said, "is mostly—*unknown word, possibly 'imagining'*—a different—*unknown word, possibly 'world,' or 'reality.'* In that—*unknown word*—Denastri eat the black rocks especially for themselves. Imperium and KemTek are not—*unknown word*. Can this be true, most likely?"

Gloria silently cursed the translation software, not for the first time. It was so damnably hard to be sure what they were actually saying! Yet the Fifthborn's words seemed, at least, to be suggesting something of great potential importance. If only she could be sure . . .

"Honored Fifthborn," Gloria said, "please forgive the inadequacy of our translation device. Sometimes it is very difficult to understand the true meaning of your words."

"This is mostly true, in the extreme, Honored Governor," the Denastri agreed.

"Nevertheless, I think I understand. Are you suggesting that the Denastri could mine—eat—the black rocks without the direct control of Imperium and KemTek? That you could deliver the black rocks to us?"

"If a meal is eaten, what does it matter which female prepares it?" Gloria sensed that the Fifthborn had just quoted some ancient Denastri proverb.

"Honored Fifthborn," she said, "without our technology and experience, it would take a very long time for the Denastri to mine the black rocks. It may not matter who prepares a meal, but it matters a great deal when it is eaten. Would you be willing to accept our assistance in mining the black rocks if we left you in control of the operation?"

"Too many cooks spoil the broth," said the translation software. That stopped Gloria for a moment.

"I think I understand," she persevered. "You are concerned that Imperium and KemTek would still want to control the operation even if the Denastri were formally in charge?"

The Fifthborn didn't seem to understand the translation. He seemed to frown, then said, "Honored Governor is mostly correct, this humble Fifthborn wonders especially. Imperium and KemTek are always hungry, most likely. They will desire Marines to force Denastri to eat the black rocks in their mostly proper way, at least."

"If you stop fighting us, Honored Fifthborn, the Marines will not be needed. Imperium and KemTek can be dealt with, I assure you."

"And Servitor? Is it not true that Servitor is the—*unknown word*—of Imperium and KemTek? They eat without honor."

Gloria nodded. "They do, indeed, Honored Fifthborn. But Servitor can be handled, as well. They are only here to protect the people and property of KemTek and Imperium. If the fighting stops, they will not be needed here and they will leave. This, I promise. Even if some small number of Marines must stay, Servitor will leave when the fighting stops."

"A goodness," said the general. "But Marines must leave."

"Most of them will," Gloria assured him. "A few must stay, because that is the way of things in the Empire. It is the necessary order for Terrans. But those who stay will not fight the Denastri unless the Denastri fight them."

The Fifthborn idly tugged at one of his drooping, triangular ears for a few moments. "Honored Imperial Governor," he said, "has given this humble Fifthborn much to eat. It is of a necessity to consider most thoughtfully, at least. A goodness, perhaps. Other Fifthborn and exalted Sixthborn must share in this meal."

"You need to consult your other leaders? I understand, Honored Fifthborn."

"A goodness, perhaps," the general repeated.

Damn right it is, Gloria thought. Spirit, had she just made a breakthrough? Could it really be that simple?

She reminded herself that *nothing* on Denastri was simple. The consultations with the other leaders might very well produce nothing but more delay and confusion. And even if the C-clan leaders signed on, how would the A- and B-clan leaders react? This might be progress, or it might not be anything at all. Whatever it was, it would require an abundance of patience to see it through. But there was another matter that might be resolved immediately.

"Honored Fifthborn," she said, "I believe that we have made a good beginning here tonight. I am very hopeful that, in the end, we will achieve a great goodness for both your people and mine. But there is something else that we must discuss. It would be a goodness if the exalted Wind-clan leaders would make a small gesture to demonstrate their honor and sincerity. Releasing Lord Kenarbin would be such a goodness."

The Fifthborn pursed his fishy lips slightly. "But Honored Imperial Governor cannot talk of such a thing, mostly. This humble Fifthborn knows this to be true. Honored Imperial Governor said this to—*idiomatic phrase, literal translation is 'scrap-eaters.'* "

Scrap-eaters? The newsies! For once, the translation got it exactly right.

"You heard the news conference today?"

"Denastri watch and listen to Terran offal. 'Long-standing Imperial policy' mostly forbids this. Scrap-eaters have said this. Honored Imperial Governor has said this."

"Yes, it is true," Gloria conceded. "We cannot have formal negotiations concerning Lord Kenarbin. But words are not really necessary, are they? You know what we want."

"It is mostly understood," the Fifthborn agreed. "But this humble Fifthborn cannot make—*unknown word*—at this time and place—*indeterminate idiomatic phrase, possibly equivalent to 'on the spur of the moment.' "*

"You need to consult with others about Lord Kenarbin?"

"Honored Imperial Governor must speak in own self, most likely. *Unknown words*—have proper—*unknown word, possibly 'jurisdiction.'* Your honored presence is of a necessity, almost."

"I must speak to someone else?" Gloria asked him.

"Most likely. Honored Imperial Governor will please excuse this humble Fifthborn for necessary time, why not?"

"Of course, Honored Fifthborn." The Denastri got to his feet and left the room, leaving Gloria alone. She took a deep breath and let the air out slowly. This was getting interesting.

It got considerably less interesting as Gloria sat alone in the room and waited for what seemed like an hour or more. "Patience is of the highest necessity, most likely," she said to herself.

Still, the conversation with the Fifthborn had produced surprisingly positive results—assuming she really understood what he had said. He had seemed to offer the faint glimmerings of a deal. But would the insurgents really stop fighting if the Denastri were offered nominal control of the mining operation?

The Denastri were not a primitive race—they had built their own starships, after all. Presumably, they could be trained to operate the Extractors and refinery equipment. That would still require a substantial Corporate presence on the planet, but if the overall level of Terran involvement could be reduced, that might at least mollify the insurgents. The necessary shape of things—the spatiotemporal-cultural geometry—could be at least partially restored in the short run. And in the long run—and the Denastri took the long view—they could look forward to a day when the HCH would be gone and the Terrans with it. Perhaps the Denastri would be willing to tolerate a small, mainly symbolic Imperial presence on their world after the mining operations were completed. And meanwhile, maybe they could be made to see the advantages of releasing Kenarbin.

The Fifthborn finally returned and beckoned Gloria to join him outside. "Honored Imperial Governor must meet—*unknown word*," he said, pointing to another building. Gloria followed him to it and entered the structure, which was broad and spacious and contained dozens of parked vehicles that vaguely resembled utility skimmers. She realized that they were the food carts she had seen in the city. Perhaps this was a warehouse or distribution center of some sort.

She followed the Fifthborn down a gently sloping ramp, emerging on a lower level of the building. A sort of tramway extended along a wide passageway, with a series of small cars lined up at the entrance. The Fifthborn led her to the first car and gestured for her to get in. She did. The Fifthborn joined her, fiddled with some buttons on a control panel and, quite suddenly, they were in motion. They shot through the passageway at a considerable velocity, the acceleration pushing Gloria back against the cushioned seat.

"Where are you taking me, Honored Fifthborn?" Gloria asked.

"It is of a necessity, Honored Imperial Governor," the Fifthborn replied with opaque courtesy.

"Yes, but where . . ." Gloria broke off. The insurgent leader obviously wasn't going to tell her any more than he thought she needed to know, which wasn't much. She told herself that it really didn't matter.

The journey continued in silence for ten or fifteen

minutes before the car slowed to a stop in another warehouselike structure. Gloria followed the Fifthborn up a ramp. She noticed a large number of short, squat Denastri females here, more than she had ever seen in one place before. She wondered if this could be one of the agricultural complexes, where the females tended the crops and prepared food for the males.

They walked along a series of featureless corridors until they arrived at what seemed to be their destination. It was another windowless room, similar to the one in which she and the Fifthborn had first met. In it, there was a table with just one chair and, along one wall, what seemed to be a Marine field cot with a couple of blankets on it. Gloria wondered why it was there and turned to look at the Fifthborn.

"Honored Fifthborn," she said, "will the Denastri leaders you spoke of be meeting me here?"

"Honored Imperial Governor must wait," said the Fifthborn. "Here you will eat. Your needs will mostly be observed in utmost regard of your honored self, almost. It is of a necessity."

"Yes, but—"

"It is of a necessity," the Fifthborn repeated. "Fear is not required. Honored Governor will be fed in proper time and order. Good night, sleep tight, and don't let the bedbugs bite."

"*What?*"

The Fifthborn gave her a minimal nod, then turned and marched quickly from the room. Behind him, a door panel slammed shut. Gloria tried to slide it open, but it wouldn't budge.

She paced around the small room for a minute or two, running her hands through her hair and trying to stay calm. Finally, she sat down on the edge of the Marine cot and stared at the blank walls. It gradually dawned on her that she was being held hostage.

·20·

Governor VanDeen was gone.

The Residence staff noticed her absence the following morning and notified the Governor's Office. Sergeant Hooper, in turn, informed Dexta Security and the Occupation Task Force Headquarters. Within an hour, teams of Marines were scouring the Compound and the surrounding city streets. Squads of DHG personnel joined the search, but no one found anything, aside from a terrorist bomb that killed three of the Denastri troopers and five civilians.

Petra, after a sleepless, tearful night, learned of Gloria's disappearance when she arrived at her office. Stunned, she closed her door, sat down at her desk, propped her head up on her elbows, put her hands over her eyes, and cried some more. *Spirit,* she thought, *what next?*

In less than a day, her world had shattered. Her betrayal of Gloria—and, yes, it *was* a betrayal, she now realized—the media riot, her loud and angry break with Bryce, the end of her Dexta career, and now . . .

Guilt, shame, and confusion overwhelmed her. She had known dark moments in her life, but nothing that remotely compared with this. It seemed that she could take no action, think no thought, that didn't lead to more despair, more hopeless desolation. Even taking her next breath felt like an impossibly burdensome chore, and probably a pointless one. She wondered if she had gone mad.

It all kept coming back to Gloria. Gone? How could she be gone? Gloria had been the one enduring constant in her life these past years, the star she'd orbited. Gloria had rescued her from the hell of Dexta's lower levels, taken her on as assistant, Lap Dog, and best friend. She owed *everything* to Gloria, and had repaid her by betraying her trust and sabotaging a mission that came straight from the top—from Mingus and the Emperor! For all she knew, Gloria's disappearance might even be a result of what she had done. Maybe Gloria, trying to repair the damage, had gone charging off to set things right and gotten herself captured or—*Spirit!* —even killed. And it was all the fault of Petra Nash—brainless, disloyal, heedless, nattering, *stupid* Petra Nash!

"Stupid, stupid, stupid!" she chanted to herself.

One stupid little slip, and it had all fallen apart. Maybe Gloria was right. Maybe she *had* been trying to impress Bryce with all the supersecret stuff she knew. I'm not just *anybody*, Bryce darling, I'm someone special. I'm in the know! And maybe if you realize that, you won't abandon me or get tired of me or go off somewhere and get yourself killed. If you understand what a big deal I am, you'll stay with me for as long as I want you.

Important but stupid. Expecting Bryce to ignore the news she'd given him was like expecting a wolf to ignore a lamb chop, or a weasel to ignore . . . what did weasels eat? Everything, apparently. Ah, but it wasn't personal! Nosirree. It was his job, his profession. The people of the

Empire depended on him, and good ol' Bryce would never let them down.

But the people of the Empire, Petra realized, also depended on *her*, and she *had* let them down. They paid her to do a necessary and important job, which definitely did not include blabbing vital secrets to her bedmates. A Dexta Board of Inquiry? Why bother? Why go through that? She'd just resign when she got back to Earth and let Dexta sweep the whole thing under the rug. No reason to embarrass Mingus or the Emperor—or Gloria.

But Gloria was gone.

There was no avoiding the meeting that afternoon. Looking, she was sure, as bad as she felt, Petra entered the conference room and sat down with General Matabele, Colonel Barnes, and Jack McCray. They stared at her for a moment, then quickly looked away, as if afraid she would dissolve before their eyes. McCray reached out, squeezed her hand for a moment, and offered her an encouraging smile. She didn't quite manage to return it.

Matabele cleared his throat. "Ms. Nash," he said, "I realize that this is very difficult for you, but there are things we must discuss."

"I understand," she said. "Has there been any word . . . ?"

"Nothing new," Matabele said. "The last time anyone saw Governor VanDeen was about 2200 last night at the Imperial bar. She apparently did not spend the night in her quarters."

"And the search?"

Barnes shook his head. "She's definitely not in the Compound," he said. "Sniffers show that she walked across the central area, but it's difficult to pin down her precise movements. And we've being raising holy hell in the city, but no one claims to have seen anything and there's no physical evidence of her presence outside the walls. Of course, there are a lot of buildings to search, and maybe the sniffers will turn up something eventually. For now, we have nothing."

"Can't you track her wristcom?"

"It's not functioning," said McCray. "The computer record shows that it moved randomly around the city for several hours last night, then shut down entirely, right in front of the main gate. Obviously, it was removed. Meanwhile, we're interrogating every Denastri Compound worker, but you can imagine how that's going. Some of them may well be lying, but our equipment doesn't work very well on the natives. Threatening them doesn't seem to accomplish very much, either."

"What about the Premier and the Denastri government?" Petra asked.

"They are officially shocked and distressed," Matabele said. "Genuinely so, I think. Naturally, they blame the C-clan insurgents, and they are no doubt correct. I think we must assume that Governor VanDeen is now a hostage of the insurgents."

"They've had Lord Kenarbin for three months," McCray pointed out, "and in all that time, there hasn't been a peep out of them. I don't think we can expect them to make any statements or claims concerning the Governor."

"Where does that leave us?" Petra asked, although she already knew the answer.

"If she's in the city," Barnes said, "we'll find her eventually. But the insurgents know that, so my guess is that they've taken her somewhere else. It's a big planet, and most of it is beyond our effective control. Hell, we haven't even *seen* most of it."

"Maybe Dr. Mankato would have some ideas," Petra suggested.

"I already talked to her," McCray said. "She suggested that we concentrate on the females, but I don't really see how that leads us anywhere. Just communicating with them at all is damn near impossible."

"Well, there must be *something* . . ." Petra sniffed back tears and tried to maintain a grip on herself.

"We're doing everything we possibly can," Barnes said in a soft voice. "We'll get her back, Petra. I don't know how yet, but we will."

Petra fought for control, and no one said anything for a moment. Then Matabele cleared his throat again.

"In the meantime," he said, "we have an important matter to discuss. Ms. VanDeen was . . . is . . . both Interim Governor and Imperial Secretary. In her absence, those positions must be filled."

Petra looked at him. "So you're in charge now, General?"

He shook his head. "No . . . you are, Madame Governor."

Petra's mouth fell open in surprise. Was the man serious? Did he know what he was saying?

"You're a Level XII," McCray said. "That makes you the highest-ranking Dexta official on the planet. You automatically become Imperial Secretary, and in the absence of a permanent Imperial Governor, you become Interim Governor, as well."

"But that's ridiculous!" Petra sputtered.

"It's the law, Madame Governor," Matabele informed her. "Naturally, we will give you all the help and support we can, but as a matter of legal necessity, someone must fill those offices—and that someone is you."

"But I can't . . . I mean, how . . . ?"

"Petra," Barnes said, "I've known you for more than four years, and I can honestly say that you are one of the most capable and dedicated public servants I have encountered in my career. You were a rock on Mynjhino. I know you'll be as strong now as you were then."

"But that was different," Petra protested. "I mean, I wasn't in charge of anything then. I didn't have to make any decisions or give any orders! Spirit, I've never done anything like that!"

Barnes smiled at her. "Then you'll just have to learn on the job, won't you?"

"Yes, but . . ."

"Gloria would expect it of you," he said. "You know that."

She didn't know any such thing. Two days ago, Gloria might have expected it. But now? She was all set to give Petra's job to McCray! Maybe that was the right thing to do. Maybe she should just resign and let someone competent take over.

"You're the only one who can do it," McCray said, as if he had read her thoughts. "Aside from the legalities, who else is there? Edgar Wong? Gina Swenson? Me? If any of us tried to take over, there'd be open warfare among the staff, and you know that as well as I do."

"And you won't be alone," Barnes quickly added. "We'll be right here, every step of the way, for as long as it takes."

"Which should not be too long," Matabele pointed out. "We'll dispatch a courier to Earth today, and they'll know the situation here within six days. It may take them a few days to decide how to respond, but my guess is that they'll appoint a new Imperial Governor as quickly as they can. It's an eleven-day trip in a Flyer, so he or she ought to be here in about three weeks. Then you'll step down as Governor but continue to function as Imperial Secretary . . . until we secure the release of Ms. VanDeen."

"Three weeks?" Petra asked uncertainly. It still seemed a very long time to her, but maybe it wasn't impossible. They just needed someone to sit in the Big Chair; Matabele and Barnes would really be in charge. She supposed that she could pretend to be the Imperial Governor for three weeks if she had to.

"You can do it, Petra," Barnes told her.

"Well . . . for three weeks? Yes, I suppose I can try . . ."

"Excellent," said Matabele. "What are your orders, Madame Governor?"

In the morning, the door slid open and a Denastri female entered, carrying a Marine field ration packet and a bottle of water. She put them down on the table and turned to leave. Gloria seized her by her shoulder and held her in place.

"You must take me to the person in charge," Gloria told her. The female looked up at her but said nothing.

Suspecting that the female didn't even comprehend her words, translation or no, Gloria released her and strode to the door. There, she found a Fourthborn blocking her way.

"Who's your commanding officer?" she demanded. "I want to speak to him!"

The Fourthborn didn't respond.

"Dammit, I'm the Imperial Governor! You can't do this to me."

But they could, and did. The Fourthborn gently but firmly shoved Gloria out of the way so the female could get by. Then he stepped back and the door slid shut.

In her frustration, Gloria kicked the door but succeeded only in stubbing her toe. She took a deep breath and said, "Patience, Gloria. Patience." It was good advice, but she found it hard to accept. She paced around the room—the cell—for a minute or two, then plopped down on the chair and had breakfast.

The Marine ration packet was self-heating, so at least she had a hot meal, although beef stroganoff was not exactly her notion of a proper breakfast. The bottled water was tepid. Hadn't these damned people ever heard of coffee?

An hour or so later—without her wristcom, she had

no clear idea of how much time had passed—the door opened again and a female walked in and gestured to Gloria to follow her. Gloria did, eagerly, and they went out into the corridor, where two Fourthborns joined them as an escort.

There was not much traffic in the hallway, and all of it consisted of short, round, silent females. Some of them stared at her as they passed. Gloria knew she was underground and that the facility was apparently quite large, but it was impossible to tell anything more about the place from what she could see. And she didn't see much, for the journey proved to be brief. She had hoped she was being taken to see someone in authority; in fact, she was being taken to the bathroom.

The Denastri facilities were not dramatically different from the Terran equivalent. Gloria realized that she had no idea of how the Denastri tended to such matters. She remembered one of her college exosociology professors commenting that personal hygiene tended to be a very private subject for nearly all intelligent species. Fair enough; any alien reading Terran histories would find virtually nothing to tell them how Caesar or Napoleon went about taking a dump. In any case, Gloria managed to deal with the situation successfully, and was swiftly returned to her cell.

She sat down on her cot and pulled her computer pad out of her skirt pocket. Without the link to her wristcom she couldn't use it to communicate, but at least she had plenty to read. The pad was mostly filled with official reports and communiqués, including Dr. Mankato's initial monograph on Denastri culture. She'd already read it twice and started it a third time, but quickly lost interest. Mankato obviously knew a lot about the Denastri, but the report was mainly a discussion of all the things that she and other Terrans *didn't* know.

Idly scrolling through the pad's index, she discovered a trove of old novels that had been sitting in the device

for years. Most of them were gifts from her father—
heroic tales of ancient seafaring, of course, all the way
back to Jason and Odysseus. Dad regarded the invention
of the steam engine as one of the great tragedies in human history; *real* sailors relied on nothing but wind and
tide, and maybe the strong, lash-scarred backs of galley
slaves. Some life *that* must have been! She could identify
with the hopelessness those poor slaves must have felt; at
least no one was whipping her.

She found the complete set of O'Brian's classic
Aubrey-Maturin tales, which Dad had been urging her to
read for years. *The Count of Monte Cristo* might have
been more useful at the moment, but she settled for the
subtly enthralling story of O'Brian's daring blockhead
captain and his philosophical, lubberly surgeon. When
lunch was served, she was actually annoyed by the intrusion. Chicken-something. She wondered what toasted
cheese and "drowned baby" were like.

Dinner found her boarding a big Spanish xebec, and
she slashed and bashed her way through the spicy lamb
curry. The Marines seemed to eat pretty well in the field,
although apparently not quite as well as Royal Navy cap-
tains, give or take the occasional weevil.

After dinner, she was again led to the bathroom.
Taking her cue from Jack Aubrey, she decided it was time
to make a bold foray against daunting odds. Shouting,
"Death to the Corsican tyrant!" she made a break for it
and sprinted down the long hallway, leaving the
Fourthborns far behind. At the end of the corridor, she
came upon two ramps, one leading upward, one going
down. She decided on up.

As she reached the top of the ramp she skidded to an
abrupt halt. She found herself in the middle of a vast
open area that seemed to be an agricultural production
site. It was underground, but the air had a fragrant out-
door feel to it, and she saw that she was surrounded by
thousands of rows of grow-tanks under a bright array of

overhead lights. Plants that looked a little like corn and tomatoes were arrayed in leafy green ranks that seemed to go on forever. Tending them were busy platoons of Denastri females, none of whom paid her the slightest attention.

Gloria looked around, hoping to find another ramp that might lead her to the surface. She looked back and saw half a dozen Fourthborns racing up the ramp behind her. With no time to form anything resembling a plan, she started running again, threading her way through the rows of vegetation, dodging females she encountered along the way. More Fourthborns were converging on her from every direction. They didn't appear to be armed, but they were bigger than she was and outnumbered her fifty to one. She didn't think she had any Qatsima moves adequate to the occasion.

At last, the Fourthborns blocked every possible avenue of escape. Panting, Gloria came to a halt and confronted her captors with what she hoped was a dangerous, determined grin. "Okay," she said, "who's first?"

No one moved or spoke. After a minute or so, a Fifthborn showed up, said a few words to his troops, then approached Gloria and clamped his four-fingered hand around her upper arm. Gloria had left her pad in the cell, so she didn't understand the Fifthborn's words, but their meaning was obvious.

"Okay, copper," Gloria said. "I'll go quietly."

Back in her cell, she stretched out on the Marine cot and stared at the blank ceiling. Aside from providing her with a little exercise, her attempted jailbreak had accomplished nothing. No, she realized, she had learned a few things. As she had suspected from the beginning, she was in one of the Denastri agplexes, which Terrans had never seen before. The Denastri were as reticent on the subject of food as they were on defecation. She knew that the city of Enkar was virtually surrounded by such sites, which were located on and under the broad, seemingly empty plain. That meant that she had to be relatively close to the city.

A better-planned escape might be possible, then, assuming she could reach the surface and somehow make her way back to Enkar. Perhaps she could steal or hijack one of the food carts. Maybe if she could find one of the Denastri hooded robes, she could evade immediate detection and quietly take her leave of the facility. The females didn't seem to pay her much heed, in any case, although there seemed to be plenty of Fourthborn warriors close at hand.

But she wondered if escape was really her best option. What she really wanted was to find the person in charge—Fifthborn general? Sixthborn mystic? —and resume negotiations. The Fifthborn she had spoken with last night seemed willing to discuss not only Kenarbin, but the entire range of Terran–Denastri relations. Had it all been a ploy? No, that didn't seem likely. If the only goal had been to take her hostage, why bother to talk at all?

So—they wanted to talk. Maybe it would be best to wait here, quiet and complacent, until someone showed up and renewed the negotiations. But how long would that take?

In the meantime, the Compound must have been in chaos. She was the second Imperial Governor they'd lost in less than two months. They'd be frantic. And who was in charge now . . . ?

Petra!

Gloria felt a sudden stab of pain at the thought. Poor Petra! Thinking back on all the things she had said in her anger and outrage, Gloria felt physically ill. Spirit, how had it come to that?

It was an innocent, if stupid, mistake, Gloria realized. Petra would never have knowingly, intentionally leaked information that would compromise their mission. Not possible. Maybe Petra did resent her, and maybe she even deserved it at some level, but it was absurd to think that Petra had meant her harm. She felt ashamed of herself for subjecting her best friend to that insane torrent of abuse. How could she ever hope to make it up to her?

On the other hand, Petra's lapse was hardly trivial. Dammit, she should have been more careful, especially with a weasel like Bryce Denton. By now, half the Empire probably believed that Gloria had violated Imperial policy by entering into negotiations for the release of a hostage.

Which, of course, she had.

And now, there was *another* hostage.

Using the heel of her shoe, Gloria managed to carve a single vertical notch on the adobe wall of her cell.

One.

• 21 •

Petra kept busy handling the routine ImpGov/ImpSec chores that reached her desk and tried not to think too much about the big picture—yet that was her responsibility now, and she found that she could never really escape the enormous weight of it. She felt as if she were back on some burdensome high-gravity world like New Cambridge, where the planet never stopped tugging at her and her feet always hurt. This time, though, the pain centered in her heart.

She had refused to move into the Governor's Residence, but she awoke each morning to find two brawny Marines stationed outside the door of her quarters. That took some getting used to. The guards accompanied her everywhere, adding to her feeling of self-consciousness. It was as if she wore a flashing neon sign around her neck proclaiming her identity as Imperial Governor.

On the second day of her administration, Jack McCray informed her that his Security teams had found a tunnel entrance under a supply shed near the south wall of the Compound. Petra dutifully went to inspect it, although the point of the exercise escaped her. Yes, it was a hole in the ground. McCray told her that the tunnel extended some 350 meters into the city, where it ended beneath an abandoned shop.

"We think this is how they got the Governor out," McCray said. "It's probably also how they got that bomb into the Compound, although we can't be certain of that. If they have one tunnel, they may have more. We're checking the whole Compound, but it will take a couple of days to complete the search."

"Good work, Jack," Petra told him. She thought that was the kind of thing that Gloria would have said. As an underling, Petra had always appreciated compliments and recognition from her superiors.

"Thank you, Madame Governor," McCray replied.

The deference accorded her by the Dexta staff was another thing that took some getting used to. Even Edgar Wong treated her with a measure of reluctant respect when he entered her office to complain about all the additional work that Gloria's recent orders had created.

"We still have fourteen of Servitor's original requests to process, plus twenty-two new ones. You have to rescind those directives . . . Madame Governor."

"I think Gloria's idea was to get Servitor to stop sending in the requests in the first place," Petra told him. "Maybe you ought to take that up with them, Mr. Wong."

"But surely, the situation has changed," Wong objected.

"How so?"

"Well . . . you must realize that this whole exchange of directives and requests was simply a product of the personal . . . uh . . . rivalry between Governor VanDeen and Ms. Voelker."

"And now that Gloria's gone, we should just let Servitor go back to business as usual?"

"That's not what I meant."

"Yes, it is. Don't think you can push me around. Gloria's orders stand. That will be all, Mr. Wong." Petra looked down at her desk console and pretended to be busy reading something.

"But, Madame Governor . . ."

Petra looked up at him. "What? Are you still here, Mr. Wong? Don't you think you should get back to your office and start processing all those Servitor requests?"

Wong frowned but said nothing more. He nodded, then turned and left the Governor's Office. Petra watched him go and allowed herself a satisfied smile. Wielding real power, she suddenly realized, could be fun.

But it could also be a terrible burden. That was brought home to her when General Matabele arrived and informed her that Task Force HQ wanted to conduct an airstrike.

"We've developed solid intelligence that the Nasties—the insurgents—have a base on the south shore of Lataka. They've been operating freely in the area for some time now, and we've put together a traffic flow matrix from our IR sats that pinpoints—"

"IR sats?"

"Infrared satellites, Madame Governor," Matabele explained. "You see, they mainly move at night. We can track motion although, of course, we can't actually identify anyone that way. However, the flow data clearly correlates with insurgent activity, and it centers on a particular village about two hundred kilometers down the coast from the city of Matinka. If you'll call up a map on your console, Madame Governor, I can show you the precise location."

"That won't be necessary, General," Petra said. "But why do you need an airstrike? Can't you just send in ground troops and make certain that you've got the right spot?"

Matabele shook his head. "We simply don't have enough troops in the area, Madame Governor. If we're right, cleaning out that village on the ground would be a major operation and probably cost us a hundred casualties."

"But if you're wrong, you could be bombing a harmless village and killing a lot of innocent people."

"We don't think we're wrong, Madame Governor. This intelligence is reliable."

"Yes, but . . . why are you bringing this to me?" Petra felt uncomfortable with the whole thing and hoped that Matabele didn't want her to make some sort of decision about it.

"Before her disappearance, Governor VanDeen expressed her intention to limit offensive operations severely. No final decision was arrived at, but she did send us what she referred to as a set of preliminary guidelines governing such operations. They don't have the force of an actual order, but I didn't feel that we could simply ignore them."

"So . . . if Gloria were still here, you'd have come to her for approval of your airstrike?"

"That's right . . . Madame Governor."

"Do you think she'd have given her approval?"

Matabele offered her an ambiguous smile. "That's not for me to say."

In other words, Petra thought, *the ball's in my court. Swell.*

She leaned back in her big chair, behind her big desk, and tried to think clearly. This was precisely the kind of thing that, according to Dr. Mankato's report, would simply increase Denastri resentment without really accomplishing anything positive. At the same time, there was nothing theoretical about the insurgents' activities along the south coast of Lataka. According to the reports she'd seen, they'd been responsible for over two hundred civilian casualties and a dozen Marine deaths in the past month. Matabele's airstrike was clearly intended to put a stop to that.

Petra realized that whatever she decided, people were going to die as a result of her decision. Insurgents, innocent villagers, loyal Denastri, Marines . . . whatever was true, and whatever she decided, some of them were going to be dead because the airstrike was conducted— or because it wasn't.

She wondered what Albert Fenlow would say. The answers all seemed so clear-cut and obvious back on Manhattan's Upper West Side. There was a neat catch-phrase to cover every eventuality: Imperial overreach, military reflexive response, Terran racism, bureaucratic inertia . . .

"Is there any reason why we have to do this immediately, General?"

"There is no immediate military necessity . . . but Madame Governor, forgive me, but we can't simply postpone every decision until your permanent replacement arrives. We're in the middle of a war."

"I understand that, General. But would it make any difference if I took a day or two to think about this?"

Matabele hesitated, then nodded respectfully. "As you wish, Madame Governor."

"Thank you, General."

"And Madame Governor? If it helps, I imagine that Governor VanDeen would probably have wanted some time to think about it, as well."

The next day, Jack McCray presented her with a plan. He was clearly enthusiastic, and Petra found herself getting swept up by the beauty and logic of it.

"After they got her out of the tunnel," McCray explained, "they had to have taken her somewhere else. We don't know for sure, but it makes sense that they would have moved her out of the city. But where? Within a hundred kilometers of Enkar, there are scores of small villages and probably a dozen or more big agplexes. They could have taken her to any one of them, and we simply don't have enough troops or Security personnel to go around and check every one of them with sniffers to see if the Governor was there. And if we even tried to do that, we'd probably take hundreds of casualties. So what do we do?"

"You're about to tell me, I hope," Petra said.

McCray gave her a broad smile. "Damn right, I am," he said. "We can't check all those villages, but I think there may be a way to check the distribution centers for the agplexes. Each day, hundreds of food carts come into the city from those centers. What we want to do is plant remote sniffers on as many of those carts as possible. Then, when they go back to the distribution centers each night, we'll get data that should tell us if Gloria was present at any of those sites."

"Will the sniffers still work? I mean, it's been three days."

"I admit, it's a bit iffy," McCray said. "The problem is the damn wind. It never stops blowing, and any of Gloria's ID molecules that she released outside are probably scattered to hell and gone by now. But if she went *inside* one of those distribution centers, there ought to be a residual concentration at the parts per billion level that's still detectable. It ought to work."

This was the first hopeful news that Petra had heard since she took office. She didn't want to overreact to it, but the weight of her worries suddenly felt a little lighter.

"Sounds great, Jack," she said. "When can you get started?"

"Already in the works," he said. "The problem is that we don't have enough remote sniffers. We've got the Marine techs working on it, though. They need to make them small enough so that they won't be seen when we plant them on the carts. We can probably get a few of them in place today, but not enough to cover every distribution center. Unless we get lucky, we probably won't have good results before tomorrow night."

"Can't we just send people with sniffers to check out those sites directly? There can't be that many of them."

"Yes, but they're *food* distribution centers."

"Oh. Right." If Terrans just marched into a food facility of any sort, Petra realized, the Denastri would be outraged. Not just the C-clan, but the A- and B-clans would probably rise up in outright revolt if they thought the Imperials were violating the most sacred and private of Denastri customs.

"Once we've identified the *right* distribution center," McCray went on, "we can take action. But we can't just go barging into every one of them."

"I understand," Petra said. "Still, maybe it would be a good idea if we spoke to the Denastri government about this."

"Don't tell them about the sniffers!"

"No, of course not. We really can't trust them very far, can we?"

"Not where food is concerned," McCray said.

"Our loyal allies," Petra mused. "Okay, I'll set up a meeting with the Premier for tomorrow afternoon. We might already have some results from the sniffers by then, and even if we don't, it will be too late for anyone to check all of tomorrow's returning carts. If we get results tomorrow night, we should be ready to move by the following morning. If I can't get permission from the Premier, I'll at least be able to give him a general idea of our intentions. That way, it won't come as too much of a shock to them when we defile their sacred food supply."

"No matter what we do," McCray cautioned, "they're not gonna like this. Whatever we do is going to upset *someone*."

"Jack," Petra said, "I think you've just written my job description."

*   *   *

There were four notches on the wall now, and Gloria had endured any number of shipwrecks, broadsides, boarding parties, and weevils with her fictional friends. But she missed contact with real people—real humans. She missed a lot of things. Actual cooking. The occasional nip of Belgravian. Sex. The Early Blues music she loved. Walks around the Compound. Evenings at the Imperial bar. Sex. The satisfaction of work well-done. Sex.

It was amazing how often you thought about sex when you were confined and idle. Not that she'd had any since leaving Earth, nearly two months ago. She suspected that she had set a personal record for sustained abstinence but took no pride in the accomplishment. Elmo Hunt had been right about his first rule of war. She and Delbert ought to have screwed their brains out when they'd had the chance, and damn the media. Delbert, with his strong hands and solid, Marine-fit body, looking so incredibly virile and sexy in his trim dress uniform . . .

Gloria reached into her open blouse, stroked her right nipple for a moment, and allowed herself a little explosion of sexual release. *There. Feel better, Gloria?*

No.

Her enhanced genes made it easy for her to obtain such fleeting pleasures, but they didn't do a damn thing to relieve the ongoing tension of denial and isolation. Her captors, who supposedly took no pleasure at all from sex, probably didn't even realize the dreadful toll all of this was taking on their hostage. They gave her food, after all. What more could she need?

She needed a bath, for one thing. She had tried to explain that to the female who brought her meals, using the bottled water to demonstrate what she wanted. At the next meal, she had delivered two bottles. Gloria used the second to damp herself down a bit, but she didn't think it had helped much.

Life in captivity was a study in the basics: food, water, minimal hygiene. In theory, she could live here a hundred years with nothing more. And maybe she would.

No, that was ridiculous. Back in the Compound, she reminded herself, people were working night and day to find her. Sooner or later, they'd succeed. She had to believe that.

She wondered if Kenarbin still believed it.

Hell, by now the Bill Kenarbin she knew had probably seduced and ravished half the Denastri females in the complex. The old goat was certainly capable of it.

No, that wasn't fair. Kenarbin had been a thoughtful, generous, and compassionate man, loved and admired by all who knew him. If he took occasional advantage of his circumstances, well, who could blame him? And if an inexperienced and starry-eyed young girl fell under his spell, was that really his fault? Did she have any right to blame him for giving her exactly what she had wanted?

You bet, she did! The bastard!

She had gone over it in her mind a thousand times. A million. The harmless flirtation. The cautious, almost reluctant approach. The artful seduction. And then . . . out the door and gone, mission accomplished. On to the next conquest without so much as a fond farewell.

Well, maybe there had been a little more to it than that. Their affair had lasted nearly three weeks, after all. For Kenarbin, that probably represented a major demonstration of fidelity and steadfast commitment. If a brainless, sexually voracious blatherskite like young Gloria had mistaken it for something more than what it really was, whose fault was that?

For years, she had been damning him and forgiving him, practically in the same breath. Spirit, was she going to spend the rest of her life haunted by the memory of it? Why couldn't she just get over it?

But did anyone ever really get over their first love?

Maybe she just didn't *want* to get over it. Maybe the person she was now had been forged and defined by the person she was then . . . and by Kenarbin. All the men since . . . had she been comparing them all to the great Lord Kenarbin, perhaps subconsciously searching for a man to match him? None ever had, of course, although a few—Charles, to take one prominent example—might have come close for a time. Was that why there had been so many of them? Or was she just blaming Kenarbin for something that was really deep within herself—always had been and always would be? Had she made him the scapegoat for her own failings, her own untamed longings and extravagant passions?

And, now that she considered the matter, why did she have to *blame* anyone for what she was? Why couldn't she just accept herself as she was? Maybe there had been some unfortunate excesses along the way, but she could hardly say that she regretted being the fabulous, glamorous Gloria VanDeen, Avatar of Joy. In at least some ways, she was exactly the person she had always wanted to be—and how many people could say that? Maybe, instead of blaming Kenarbin, she should thank him . . .

Thank him? That bastard?

No doubt about it, life in captivity was having a devastating effect on her. She seemed to be losing her mind.

Sometime during the afternoon of the fifth day, a squad of six Fourthborns unexpectedly showed up and ushered her out of her cell. This was a break from the established routine, and Gloria allowed herself to hope that she was finally being taken to see someone in authority. The Fourthborns marched her along the corridor, then down a ramp to a lower level. She noticed another ramp leading to a still-lower level and wondered just how deep this complex went. The place seemed to be huge.

Instead of continuing their descent, the party doubled back along another corridor, then took a right turn at an intersection. There was a lot of activity here, with females coming and going in great numbers, but Gloria could make no sense of it all. However, she was beginning to form a conviction that this was not simply some nondescript agricultural facility; it was more like an underground city. Nothing in the reports she had read suggested the existence of such a buried metropolis anywhere on the planet. It was yet another indication of how little Terrans really knew about the Denastri.

The Fourthborns led Gloria into a small room with hallways branching off from it, perhaps an outer office of some sort. After a moment spent standing and waiting, a Denastri female emerged from one of the hallways. She wore the usual hooded robe and looked exactly the same as all the other females Gloria had seen, and yet there was something about her that seemed to command attention. The Fourthborns all stepped back from her, which was unusual in itself; normally, the males paid as little attention as possible to the females, scarcely even acknowledging their existence.

But this female, short and squat as she was, nevertheless seemed to carry herself with an air of authority, as if she were accustomed to receiving deference and respect from the males. She barely glanced at the Fourthborns, then stood squarely in front of Gloria and looked at her carefully. Most females refused to meet Gloria's eyes, but this one stared into them for at least a minute.

Gloria wanted to speak to her, but couldn't think of an appropriate way to address her. Finally, she simply said, "I'm Gloria VanDeen, the Imperial Governor. I have many questions."

The pad in her skirt pocket translated her words, but

she was surprised to hear a second translation issuing from the female's cloak. She had her own computer pad—something no other female Gloria had met possessed.

"Questions will be answered at a mostly proper time, Terran female," the Denastri said to her through the software.

"Yes, but when? I've been here for days!"

"Patience is of a necessity, Terran female. A—*unknown word*—approaches, a muchness. A ripening. A coming together of many—*unknown word*." The female unexpectedly reached out and touched Gloria's arm, rubbing the thin fabric of her blouse between two of her fingers. She said another unknown word, then turned and departed.

"Hey . . . wait! I want to talk to you!" But the female was already out of sight, and the Fourthborns clustered around her again and took her back out into the corridor. They marched along for a minute or so, then stopped in front of a door that slid open. One of the Fourthborns put his hand on Gloria's back and gave her a gentle shove into the room. The door immediately slid shut behind her.

Inside, with his back to her, was a tall figure in a typical Denastri hooded robe. Another Fourthborn? The figure turned to face her, and Gloria saw that it was not a Fourthborn. It wasn't even a Denastri.

It was Lord Kenarbin.

·22·

They stared at each other in frozen silence for a moment, then rushed into each other's arms. The soft, solid warmth of another human being was a blessing in itself, and the fact that it was Kenarbin took Gloria's breath away. She nestled against him and silently thanked the Spirit for this moment.

"Oh, Bill," she whispered, "you're *alive*!"

"Never more than now," he told her.

They released their hungry grip and moved back so they could look into each other's faces. His blue eyes hadn't changed, and if his craggy features seemed a little thin, he was still as handsome as he been so many years ago, when . . .

Gloria slapped him. Hard.

Kenarbin flinched and stepped back. His brow furrowed and he lifted his left hand to his cheek and stroked it.

"I promised myself I'd do that the next time I saw you," Gloria said.

Kenarbin nodded slowly. Suddenly, his features

softened into a smile, then a broad grin. And then he began to laugh. At first it was just a knowing chuckle, but soon he was laughing full force. He staggered backwards and sat down on the edge of a Marine cot—evidently this was his cell—and gave himself over to a rolling, unrestrained belly laugh.

Gloria watched him with a growing feeling of chagrin. "You weren't supposed to laugh, dammit!"

That produced another round of mirth. Kenarbin wiped his eyes and looked up at her. "What," he managed to ask, "*was* I supposed to do?"

"You were supposed to get down on your knees and beg my forgiveness. Or something. Not laugh, anyway. Damn you!"

Kenarbin tried to collect himself and got to his feet. He reached out and put his hands on her shoulders. Still chuckling, he leaned forward and planted a gentle kiss on her left cheek.

"I apologize for failing to meet your expectations, Gloria . . . yet again, I suppose."

"Bill, I—"

Kenarbin shushed her, then sank to his knees, looked up at her, and, with all the sincerity of a professional diplomat, said, "I beg your forgiveness, my lady. With all my heart."

Gloria looked at him in his pose and turned away. "Oh, get up, you look ridiculous."

"Thank you. That kind of thing is hard on the knees at my age." Kenarbin rose, Gloria turned to look at him again, and suddenly found herself laughing. Then they were in each other's arms again, alternately laughing and kissing.

"So," Kenarbin said at length, "they got you, too, huh?"

"Five days ago," Gloria said.

"Yes, the Abbess told me you were here, but she didn't tell me they were going to let me see you."

"The Abbess?"

"The head female. That's how the software translates her title. Seems appropriate, somehow."

"I think I just met her," Gloria said. "Bill? How are you? How have they treated you?"

Kenarbin shrugged. "They feed me," he said. "They haven't tortured me or anything. For the most part, they just ignore me. Every now and then, a Fifthborn comes in to sneer at me and tell me how many Terrans they've killed. But they don't matter. The Abbess is the only one who matters, and she's been quite pleasant, really. We've talked several times, and I've had a couple of short tours of this place. Tell me, what's going on outside? I know you're the Governor." He grinned at her again. "Not much of a surprise. I always knew you were headed for great things."

"Oh, yeah . . . this is great, all right. And things on the outside are about the same as they were when they abducted you. That caused a huge flap, Parliament is very upset about it, and Charles . . ."

"He sent you here to get me back?"

"Well, not officially. But, yes, that's why I'm here." She looked around at the small cell, a duplicate of her own. "Doing a great job of it, aren't I?"

"Oh, not so bad. You found me, after all."

"I saw Trish before I left. She's in a lot of pain, but I think she's holding up pretty well. And Henry's adorable. You must be very proud."

"Very," Kenarbin agreed.

"You've lost weight," Gloria said.

"Nothing I couldn't afford to lose. I do my exercises every day, and I have a lot of books in my pad. I manage. It hasn't been so bad. Boring, for the most part."

"Tell me about it. Maybe we can trade books. How do you feel about the Napoleonic Wars?"

Kenarbin smiled. "Aubrey? Or Hornblower?"

Gloria returned the smile. "Aubrey."

"Fred's been trying to get me to read that stuff for almost as long as I've known him. How is he? And Georgia? Haven't seen them in two or three years."

"Oh, they're fine. You know them. They never change."

"Of course they do. You don't see it, of course. Children never do. But I know they're very proud of you. So am I, if I may presume."

There was a moment of awkward silence as they stared at each other, across the room and across the years. Then Kenarbin said, "Forgive me for being such a poor host. Please, sit down." He gestured to the single chair. "I'm sorry I can't offer you anything to drink but bottled water. Every now and then, they bring me a can of warm beer. And a few weeks ago, I got half a bottle of bad wine." Gloria took the chair, and Kenarbin perched himself of the edge of his cot.

"Quite a mess we've gotten ourselves into, isn't it?" Gloria frowned.

"Denastri, you mean?"

"I was thinking of our personal mess, but yes, Denastri too. It isn't going well out there, Bill."

He nodded. "We don't begin to understand them. I've learned a bit since I've been here, and the more I learn, the more I doubt that we'll ever comprehend them fully. Hell, we've been here less than three years. We destroyed their fleet, then landed, knocked over the old government, installed a new one, and went about setting up business as usual. We've done it a hundred times and figured we knew the drill. But the Denastri are different from anything we've ever encountered."

"We've got an exosociologist, a Dr. Mankato. She's been here about a year and says pretty much the same thing. And I've seen some of it for myself. I attended something called a Rite of Continuation." Gloria grimaced at the memory. "The Sixthborn honor their fathers by eating their brains."

"Lovely," said Kenarbin. "But I don't think the Sixthborn really matter very much."

"They don't? I thought they were responsible for the whole show. Mankato says they manage what she calls their 'cultural geometry.' The essential order of time, space, and . . . well, everything else."

"That may be true, but we're only seeing part of it. It's like this place we're in . . . a lot of different levels. To pursue that cultural geometry metaphor, what we see is only the surface—two dimensions, like Flatland. But there's a third dimension, Gloria, and we're sitting in it. It's solid geometry, not plane. I think the females are really in charge."

"Not from what I've seen," Gloria objected. "The males either completely ignore the females, or treat them with contempt. I saw one Fifthborn hit a female with his swagger stick."

"And yet, down here, the few males I've seen all act subservient and respectful. Each of us has only seen part of the whole. You've seen the male-dominated surface. And from the day I arrived, I've seen nothing but the female-dominated interior. You don't realize it, but there are more Denastri living in this complex than there are in the entire city of Enkar."

"Really?" Gloria raised her brow in surprise.

"It makes sense, when you think about it. Consider—for every male who goes through the complete reproductive cycle, the result is six male offspring and twelve surviving females. In other words, there are twice as many females as males. And most of them are in places like this, where Terrans never see them."

"Yes, but this is just an agricultural complex, isn't it? I mean, the females are responsible for growing and preparing food for the males, but that's all they seem to do. They have no role at all in government, business, or religion, as far as I can tell."

"Which only proves that government, business, and

religion aren't very important to the Denastri—at least, not in the way they are important to us."

"What do you mean?"

"Try thinking of them as insects," Kenarbin suggested. "Of course, the Denastri *aren't* insects, so it's an imperfect analogy, but I think it might be useful."

"Go on."

"How much do we ever see of an anthill or a beehive?" Kenarbin asked. "Almost nothing, just the external shape of the thing and the programmed activities of worker ants or drone bees. But what's really important to the ants and bees is what goes on *inside* the hill or the hive. And that's all up to the queens."

"Yes, but —"

Kenarbin held up one hand. "I know. All a queen bee does is make more bees. And reproduction is entirely different for the Denastri. As I said, it's an imperfect analogy. The female Denastri care about other things— and don't ask me what, because I simply don't know. But whatever it is, it has very little to do with the surface activity that we think of as Denastri government, religion, and culture. Look, if you asked a drone bee what life is about, it would tell you that life is all about finding flowers and nectar. Ask the queen, and she'd tell you it's about something entirely different."

Gloria nodded. "Interesting," she said.

"I've been thinking about this a great deal," Kenarbin said. "I mean, what else have I got to do? I don't claim to understand what's going on here, but I do have a theory."

"Tell me."

"Well, we know that each newborn male grows up differently—Firstborn or Sixthborn—depending on what it's fed. They all start out the same, but the females control their development based on the food they give them. Maybe—and this is just theory; I don't claim to understand a tenth of what goes on around here—but maybe the control goes beyond physical development. Maybe the females control the *behavior* of the males the same way they control their development."

"That would explain why food is such a sensitive subject to them," Gloria agreed. Then she shook her head. "But it doesn't make sense, Bill. I mean, if the females control their behavior, then why don't they just turn *every* male into an insurgent?"

Kenarbin shrugged. "Maybe they don't want to, for some reason we don't see. Maybe the females have their own internal politics to deal with. But the fact is, all of the males get their food from the same source—right here, and other complexes just like it. A-clan, B-clan, C-clan, insurgents, loyalists—*all of them* get their food from the same source."

Gloria nodded. "We suspected as much," she said. "The Marines and Servitor have wanted to do something about it, but they've been reluctant to try anything because nobody wants to interfere with anything having to do with food. We could wind up provoking a revolt by all three clans."

"Undoubtedly. But it's not just the food. It's this place, and all that goes on here. The life below. The inner life of the hive. They've hidden that from us. And yet . . ."

Kenarbin trailed off and looked very thoughtful.

"What?"

"I don't know, maybe I'm just being fanciful. But sometimes I think that the whole reason they abducted me was to give me a glimpse of that inner life. Maybe I'm some sort of test case. They want to see if it's even possible for a Terran to understand what's important to the Denastri. Remember, we don't understand them, but they don't understand us very well, either. The Denastri have been a very isolated culture, out here in the Cluster. Aside from very limited trade with a few distant races, they really haven't had much contact with outsiders until we got here. We're as much of a mystery to them as they are to us."

"So . . . you think they want you to learn about them while they learn about you?"

"That's my guess. In fact, that's probably why they brought you to see me. They're certainly listening to every word we say. And I know they're curious about Terran females. The Abbess frequently asks me about them. They couldn't understand why we have a female Governor. From their point of view, that would be like sending a queen bee out of the hive to collect nectar. It probably confuses them."

Gloria smiled. "It confuses me, too, sometimes. Bill, the media know—or think they know—that I was sent here to get you released. And you know Imperial policy. It could turn into a real mess."

"They're giving you a tough time, Madame Governor?"

"Well, they were starting to, but then I got abducted before it really led to anything. And Bill? That first night, I talked with an insurgent Fifthborn. And he seemed to be offering something that looked like a deal. I think if we give the Denastri direct control over the mining operations, they might be willing to stop fighting us."

"He actually said that?"

"Not in so many words . . . not that it's easy to tell *what* they're actually saying. I got the impression that he was interested in the idea, but that it would have to be discussed with others. I thought he meant other insurgent Fifth- and Sixthborns, but if you're right, maybe it's something that would have to be decided by the females. Maybe you should mention it to the Abbess the next time you see her."

"I certainly will. But don't get your hopes up. My sense of it is that the war is not a big concern to the Abbess. Our *presence* here is important, but I don't think the details matter a great deal, as long as we leave the hive alone." He took a deep breath, scratched his nose for a second, and gave Gloria a weak smile. "On the other hand," he said, "maybe I don't even know what the hell I'm talking about. Cooped up alone for three or four months, you get some strange ideas."

Kenarbin got to his feet, walked over to Gloria's chair, and looked down at her. He ran his fingers through her hair. "You also find yourself getting very lonely."

Gloria gently removed his hand. "Don't, Bill," she said.

"Why not?"

"You know why not. Please, just don't."

Kenarbin backed away from her. "You're still mad at me?" he asked.

"I'm . . . I'm . . . dammit, I don't know what I am. Confused. I've been confused for all these years, and I'm *still* confused. Spirit, Bill, why did you do that to me?"

"Do what?"

"Leave me the way you did. Without even a word."

"I had a diplomatic assignment. You knew that."

"Yes, but why did you just . . . just *leave*? Didn't I deserve more than that? Or did I just not matter?"

"You mattered a great deal to me, Gloria. I thought you knew that."

"But how . . . why . . . ?" Gloria suddenly felt all the pain and confusion that she'd felt at the time. Kenarbin put his hand on her shoulder.

"Why didn't I give you a big farewell scene, you mean, like in the end of an old vid? You all tearful, me all manly and noble, with the engines warming up and time running out? Like that?"

"Yes, dammit. Like that!"

"Life isn't really like that, Gloria."

"Well, it *should* be!" Gloria found herself crying and, at the same time, laughing at herself for being so adolescent and stupidly romantic.

"It would have been wrong for us to play out that

scene, Gloria. It would only have convinced you that life really *is* like that, and you'd have gone through life expecting it to be that way. And you'd have been disappointed and hurt when it wasn't."

"Yes, but . . ."

"I know what I'm talking about, Gloria. Believe me, I know. I've played out that scene more times than I can count, and it was always a mistake."

Gloria abruptly rose and walked toward a corner of the small room, her back to Kenarbin. "Yes," she said, "I'm sure you have. Love 'em and Leave 'em Kenarbin. Find 'em, fuck 'em, and forget 'em, right?"

"Do you really think it was like that?"

She whirled around and faced him. "Wasn't it?" she demanded. "Wasn't I just the latest notch on the belt of the great Lord Kenarbin?"

"I think you know better than that," Kenarbin said softly, staring into her eyes. "At least, I always hoped that you did."

"But you never bothered to find out, did you?"

"What would you have had me do, Gloria? Pop back into your life at odd moments? That would have done more harm than good. But I did keep track of you. By the way, I think you were right—and lucky—to have divorced Charles when you did. You'd have made a lousy Empress."

"That's not what Charles thought. He even tried to get me back a couple of years ago."

"I know. Fortunately for all concerned—including the Empire—you said no."

"Fortunately for *you*, certainly. You wound up being the Consort's father and the next Emperor's grandfather."

Kenarbin nodded. "A stroke of luck," he agreed. "I'm pleased for Trish, of course. She loves him, and I think he's finally grown up enough to be considerate of her feelings. I never liked him, and I certainly don't trust him, but I expect he'll be decent enough to Trish, if only for Henry's sake. It's not easy, being the father of a beautiful young daughter, and I can only hope that he won't hurt her."

"That's rich," Gloria snorted. "Coming from *you*."

"What do you mean?"

"You know exactly what I mean! My father was your friend! How could you even look him in the face after what you did?"

"After what *I* did?" Kenarbin shook his head. "You mean, after what *he* did."

"What?" Gloria took an angry step toward him. "What do you mean by that?"

"Maybe it's time you knew the truth," he said. "Gloria, your father arranged the whole thing."

Gloria stared at him in stunned bewilderment. She opened her mouth to speak, but no words came out. Kenarbin went to her, put his hand on her shoulder, and guided her back to the chair. Gloria stared at him but didn't resist.

"A few minutes ago, you said that your parents never change," Kenarbin said. "But you didn't know them when they were young. I did. Randiest couple I ever met. Gloria, your parents have precisely the same genes that you do. Didn't you ever think about what that meant?"

"Well . . . yes, I suppose . . . but . . . well . . ."

"But they're your parents. But long before they were your parents, they were two hot, passionate, beautiful youngsters, walking around with the same genetic fireworks inside them that you have in you. I said they were the randiest couple I ever met, but they were also one of the happiest. That didn't happen by accident, Gloria. They had to work at it, and it wasn't easy for them. They felt all the same pressures and needs that you felt, and they made a lot of stupid mistakes and went through a lot of pain and heartbreak before they found each other and learned to live with their gifts. And when you came along, they knew exactly what you were going through, and hoped to spare you some of what they endured. So Fred asked me for a little help."

Gloria looked up at Kenarbin and tried to comprehend his words. She didn't think she'd ever been so surprised and shocked in all her life.

"The first time is supposed to be special, more so for a girl than a boy, I suppose. And Fred and Georgia wanted yours to be not just special, but *right*. Not some groping, fumbling encounter with some horny teenage stallion. Not just a physical experiment or an explosion of hormones. So they asked me to play the part . . . to be the wise, gentle, experienced older man who would carefully and lovingly introduce you to sex and love and life. I admit, I was more than willing to help. And I didn't do such a bad job of it, did I?"

"But . . ."

"But why did I leave you the way I did? Gloria, that was always part of it. Part of the plan. You see, your parents always knew you'd be hurt by love, the same as they were. The same as everyone is, one way or another. So I would love you, then leave you, and I was to do it in a way that, hopefully, would leave you a little wiser, a little better equipped to deal with all your genetic gifts and the problems they were going to cause. Think about it. With me, you experienced the best part of love, then you experienced a painful loss. But you didn't have to go through all the hateful, spiteful, desperate quarrels and backbiting that usually accompany the end of a relationship. I mean, I wasn't even there, was I? You got off easy, kid. It's time you realized that."

"But . . ."

"Plus," Kenarbin said, smiling, "you finally got to slap my face. What more do you want from life, Gloria? Whipped cream with cherries on top?"

Kenarbin took her by the hand and pulled her up to

her feet, then wrapped his arms around her and pulled her close. They stared into each other's eyes. Gloria wanted to say something, but couldn't begin to imagine what. Kenarbin spared her the necessity by pressing his lips against hers.

An instant later, the door slid open and two Fourthborns and a Fifthborn strode into the room. They pulled Gloria away from Kenarbin and marched her out the door. She didn't even have the chance to say good-bye to him.

Again.

·23·

Petra entered the Command Center, escorted by General Matabele, Colonel Barnes, and Sergeant Hooper. Alvin, a friend from Mynjhino days, was even more of a friend now and had done much to ease her burdens and worries since assuming office. They had spent a couple of long evenings together in her office, drinking and talking, and Petra had come to feel a deep admiration and affection for the smart, tough noncom. Maybe Gloria had been right—maybe she *should* marry him, although that might prove to be difficult, since she had learned that he already had three wives on three different planets.

Jack McCray was already in the Command Center and, to Petra's surprise, so was Sally Voelker. Today's operation concerned everyone and there was no way to exclude Servitor entirely, although their people would play no active role in what was about to happen.

They got Petra settled in at the central console, between Matabele and Barnes. She looked around and felt a little overwhelmed by the evident complexity of the place. The actual, physical levers of power surrounded her; to the Marines, power was not some abstract concept but an everyday, practical reality.

But power, Petra was learning, was a slippery commodity. It wasn't simply a matter of pushing a button or giving an order. Shit, the Marines were fond of saying, rolled downhill, but it also splattered right back up to the top. The flowcharts and organizational diagrams never mentioned that. Having power and using it were two different things. As Imperial Governor and Imperial Secretary, she possessed more power than anyone else on the planet, but using that power was a messy, almost mystical business. Strange and unexpected things could happen along the path between intention and result. It was like planting a garden blindfolded; you might think you were planting the seed of a beautiful flower, only to find that a prickly cactus had grown in its place.

She might have planted such a cactus yesterday.

The Honored Denastri Premier, 3A-27-12J, had come to the Governor's office to meet with the latest of his Imperial overlords. If the poor Thirdborn was confused by the procession of new Governors, Petra could sympathize. And the fact that this one was another Terran female hardly helped.

Petra sat next to him on the couch, watching his dark vertical eyes, trying to fathom their depths. If he had been human, she would have thought that he was nervous and perhaps even frightened. Well, why shouldn't he be? *She* certainly was. Although, throughout her career, she had technically represented the Terran Empire, this was different. Now, as far as the Premier was concerned, she *was* the Terran Empire. The words she spoke were not her own; they were the words of His Imperial Highness Charles V, Dexta Secretary Norman Mingus, Parliament, and 3 trillion citizens.

Her attempts to make small talk and put the

Premier at ease had not been notably successful. Most of his comments and questions had been concerned, if only tangentially, with the fact that she was another Terran female. He had come to accept, reluctantly, Gloria's role as Imperial Governor, possibly because he was aware that she had once fed the Emperor. But what did he make of Petra Nash, who was not much larger than a Denastri female and had not been sent here by the Emperor, but had come to power through no more than an accident? He seemed profoundly confused by this turn of events.

Petra had finally given up on the pleasantries and plunged into the day's business. "Honored Premier," she said, "I have important news. Our Security people have discovered evidence that may make it possible for us to gain the release of Governor VanDeen, and perhaps even Lord Kenarbin."

"Is this so?" asked the obviously surprised Thirdborn. "A strangeness, most likely."

"A strangeness? Well, maybe so. But a goodness, too, we believe."

"This humble Thirdborn mostly desires the return of honored Imperial Governor and exalted Lord Kenarbin, at least. Yes, a great goodness. *Pejorative adjective* Windclan terrorists will release them?"

"No, they will not release them," Petra said. "But we believe that we can rescue them. We think we know where the Governor was first taken on the night of her abduction. Tomorrow morning, we intend to send Marines there to set her free."

That news seemed to trouble the Premier. "Someone has told you this information? This humble Thirdborn is—*unknown word*. How can this be so?"

"No one told us, Honored Premier. But we have ways . . . technical means . . . of finding it out for ourselves. We are quite sure that we know where Governor VanDeen was taken." Jack McCray's hidden sniffer ploy had paid off, and a few of Gloria's ID molecules had been detected in one of the Denastri food distribution centers. This was the ticklish part.

"Honored Premier, I must tell you that the place where Governor VanDeen was taken is a food distribution center. I know that this is a sensitive and private matter for the Denastri, but it is necessary for us to send the Marines to that place and attempt to rescue the Governor. I hope that you will understand the necessity."

He didn't. Not at all. His nictitating membranes blinked furiously for a moment, then he abruptly got to his feet and raised both of his arms over his head. "A wrongness!" He was actually shouting. "A wrongness of—*unknown word*—completeness! Marines must not violate the—*unknown word*—of the—*indeterminate phrase*. A wrongness! A wrongness!"

Petra stood up and faced him. "Honored Premier, please understand. We mean no disrespect to the Denastri people and have no wish to violate your sacred customs. But surely you can understand that we must do everything possible to achieve the safe return of Governor VanDeen."

"*Unknown word!*" he cried. "*Indeterminate phrase!*"

"I'm very sorry that this upsets you so much," Petra said, trying to sound calm and soothing. "But the Marine operation will go forward. I am not requesting your permission or approval, Honored Premier. I am simply telling you what is going to happen."

"A wrongness," the Premier repeated, a little less frantically. "A wrongness of impossible completeness! Honored Terran-female-who-is-now-Governor must not do this! This humble Thirdborn is mostly begging your honored self, all the time!"

"Honored Premier, we are not attacking your agricultural production centers. This is only a distribution center, and we promise not to disrupt its normal activities any more than is absolutely necessary. Food will continue to be delivered to Enkar, I promise you. It is not our intention to interfere with Denastri customs. We respect your people and honor their customs, but we must do this. And we will."

"You must not!"

"I'm sorry, honored Premier," Petra told him, "but the operation will be carried out as planned."

The Premier closed his eyes and seemed to sigh. "A wrongness," he said. Even the androgynous voice of the translation software sounded sad. "A wrongness," it said again. "A wrongness."

A wrongness or not, it was about to happen. Dawn was coming up, and in a few minutes a LASS would rise from the Compound, carrying a full company of Marines to assault a food distribution center forty kilometers east of Enkar. A squadron of SALs was already airborne. Petra looked around the Command Center at all the monitors and flashing lights, feeling dazed by the sheer power about to be unleashed—at her order.

Barnes leaned over to her and whispered, "Don't worry, Petra. We know what we're doing."

"But what if—what if they kill Gloria when they see us coming?"

"I don't think they'll do that. What good would it do them? They must realize how we'd react to that. Anyway, we'll be in and out before they know what's happening. Relax, it'll be fine."

Relax? Was he kidding, or did Marines have a different kind of nervous system than normal human beings?

The appointed moment came, Barnes issued an order, and the LASS took off. Petra watched on one of the monitors as it hovered for a few seconds, rotated around its central axis, then lunged forward and disappeared in the glare of the rising sun.

The LASS moved swiftly. Less than three minutes had elapsed when a report came back: "Bench, this is Tackle. Target in view."

"Copy, Tackle," Barnes said into his headset. "We see it. Hold one, Tackle."

"Wilco, Bench."

Barnes pointed at a monitor on the console in front of him. "What the hell is that?"

Petra looked and saw a large, warehouselike building with a cluster of smaller ones surrounding it. Tiny dark forms dotted the area immediately in front of the large structure. They were lined up in neat, precise rows.

"Colonel?" said a captain at another console. "They appear to be Denastri troops."

"Give me a close-up."

One monitor zoomed in until the dark forms resolved into ordered ranks of Denastri Fourth- and Fifthborns, apparently standing at attention with their plasma rifles held at port arms.

"Those aren't insurgents, sir," said the captain. "They're DHG troopers!"

"Tackle, Bench," Barnes said quickly. "Hold position. Do not, repeat, *do not* engage!"

"Rodge, Bench. Holding position."

Barnes turned to look at Matabele. The general looked as surprised and confused as the colonel. Both of them turned their gaze toward Petra.

"Governor," said Matabele, "you didn't tell the Premier where we were going, did you?"

Petra shook her head. "No. Just that it was a food distribution center. But there are dozens of them, and I didn't say which one!"

"Maybe they've got troops at all of them," Barnes suggested. "Captain? Check it out."

"Yessir!" In an instant, overhead views from SALS and orbiting satellites zoomed in on half a dozen different distribution centers near the city. There was no sign of troops at any of them.

Barnes looked back at Petra. "Colonel, I swear I didn't tell him!" Petra was afraid that she had somehow screwed up again, but she was certain that she hadn't.

"Then how in hell did they know where we were going?" Matabele said.

"They knew, General," said Sally Voelker, "because they *already* knew where VanDeen had been taken." Voelker focused on Petra. "Madame Interim Governor," she said, "your tame Denastri government is in bed with the insurgents!"

Petra nodded silently, realizing that it had to be true. No other explanation was possible.

"The question is," said Barnes, "what do we do about it?"

"Isn't that obvious?" Voelker demanded. "For Spirit's sake, Colonel, you'll never have a better target! Look at 'em, lined up like tenpins! You could take them all out in five seconds!"

"And what then?" Barnes said. He looked at Matabele.

The general clutched the mike of his headset. "Captain, all commands!"

"Yessir!"

"All commands, this is General Matabele. Go to red alert status immediately. Repeat, all commands go to red alert status immediately. Stand by for further instructions." Matabele looked across the room at another officer. "Major Norton, brief them on what's happening here. We could be looking at a planetwide revolt."

Matabele turned back to Petra. "Madame Governor," he said, "we can go ahead with the operation as planned, if that's what you want. But it would mean engaging those DHG troops down there, with unforeseeable consequences."

"What are you waiting for, you fool?" Sally Voelker

was on her feet, practically frothing at the mouth in her intensity. "Hit them now!"

"Ms. Voelker," Petra said, her eyes narrowing, "kindly sit down and shut up."

"But you can't let them get away with this, dammit!"

"General," Petra said calmly, "if Ms. Voelker doesn't do as I said, would you please have her removed from the room?"

"Gladly." Matabele turned and stared at Voelker, who returned the stare for a moment, then sat down.

Petra looked at Barnes and Matabele. "What happens if Gloria's down there and we go ahead and attack?"

Barnes shook his head. So did Matabele.

"And it's my decision?"

"That's correct, Madame Governor," Matabele told her.

As life-and-death decisions went, it was an easy one. "Call off the operation, General," Petra ordered.

"Yes, ma'am." Matabele looked relieved.

"Tackle, Bench," Barnes said into his headset. "Return to base. Repeat, return to base."

"Rodge, Bench. Returning to base."

"Gentlemen," Petra said to the Marine officers, "we're going to have to think of something else."

Petra found one of Gloria's bottles of Belgravian whisky and poured drinks for her guests, then one for herself, and settled into one of the comfortable chairs in the drawing room of the Governor's Residence. General Matabele, Colonel Barnes, Jack McCray, and Dr. Mankato raised their glasses simultaneously, as if in a salute, and downed a healthy slug of the smooth, expensive whisky. Petra did the same.

After a long and contentious dinner, they had retired to the drawing room to pursue their disagreements in greater comfort, if not harmony. Petra had managed to hold her tongue and seldom spoke, content to listen to what her guests had to say. There were few points of agreement, many ideas, and no solutions.

The one thing that everyone agreed upon was that the Denastri government could no longer be trusted. It was now obvious that the government had been in collusion with the insurgents all along, although even that conclusion didn't seem to make much sense. The DHG troops had been fighting and dying in the war with the insurgents, and the government would be toppled if the C-clan were to regain power. Yet it was perfectly clear that the Premier had dispatched DHG troops to defend the distribution center against the Marines' assault. That could only mean that the Premier already knew which distribution center Gloria had been taken to on the night of her abduction. It didn't make sense, but there it was.

"It simply confirms what I've been saying all along," Mankato said when the point was raised once again following dinner. "We don't understand these people, and we should get the hell off their planet before this thing turns into an outright disaster."

"The Empire cannot just walk away from Denastri," Matabele repeated. "Aside from the immediate consequences, it would have catastrophic repercussions throughout the Empire. There must be fifty or a hundred different races who would take that as a sign that the Empire can be defeated. We'd have rebellions all over the place."

"Look," said Barnes, "we might just as well assume that we're staying and concentrate on that. When and if Parliament and the Household want us out, they'll tell us. In the meantime, we need to come up with a strategy to deal with our immediate situation."

"Well," said McCray, "it's obvious that the key to the

whole picture is the food. The insurgents are getting their food from the same distribution and production centers as the rest of the population. And if we can't trust the government or the DHG, we might just as well go ahead and seize those agplexes."

"With what?" Barnes asked him. "We've counted at least twenty-two of those centers within a hundred klicks of Enkar. It would take everything we've got to seize them and hold them."

"It could be done, I think," said Matabele. "But we'd have to go in hard."

"General, they'd be defended by both insurgents and DHG troops—and I don't think they'd just stand around waiting to be shot, the way they did today."

"Granted, but we'd still have the edge in firepower."

"Why do we need to grab all twenty-two of them at once?" McCray asked. "If we just grabbed a couple of them, that would make our point."

"It would also touch off a planetwide rebellion," said Matabele. "Certainly, there would be a full-scale revolt in Enkar. They only way to prevent that is to take *all* of the agplexes, or at least most of them. If we control the food supply, they wouldn't dare revolt."

"Idiots," said Mankato. "I'm sitting here listening to idiots."

"Dr. Mankato," said Matabele, "if you have a better idea, short of turning tail and running away, I'm sure we'd all love to hear it."

"Running away wouldn't be manly, would it?"

Before Matabele could respond, Petra cut in. "Dr. Mankato," she said, "I don't necessarily disagree with your general point. I think a complete, orderly withdrawal from Denastri is an option that needs to be considered seriously. But *I* can't order it, and if I did, in two weeks my replacement would probably just countermand it anyway. I think Colonel Barnes is right. We have to assume that we're staying and deal with that. I'd appreciate it, Doctor, if you could try to focus on that scenario for now."

"You want us to rearrange the deck chairs on the *Titanic*? Sure, why not? Sounds like fun." Mankato reached for the bottle of Belgravian and poured herself some more.

Petra looked at Barnes. "Colonel? What happens to Gloria and Lord Kenarbin if we seize some or all of the agplexes?"

Barnes didn't say anything for a moment. He looked at her with unmistakable pain etched on his features. "Petra," he said, "I know it's hard, but in light of what happened today, I just don't think we should count on getting them back."

"You're just giving up?"

"I didn't say that. I'm just saying that the odds have changed. Without the government and the DHG on our side, it's going to be much more difficult to get them back."

"But now we know where they are!" McCray interjected.

"We do?" asked Matabele.

"Well, more or less," McCray said. "We know what distribution center she was taken to, at least. And that center serves three of the agplexes. It makes sense that she'd be in one of those four places. And they're probably holding Kenarbin in the same place as Gloria."

"That's a big assumption, son," Matabele said.

McCray frowned and said, "Yes, Dad."

"Now, look here—"

"Don't try to pull rank on me, General! I'm not a Marine, I'm Dexta, and—"

"Gentlemen!" Petra raised her voice. "I'm not going to let this degenerate into some Dexta versus the military squabble. Okay? That's the last thing we need."

"Sorry," McCray mumbled.

"My apologies, Madame Governor," Matabele said diplomatically.

Without feeling much hope, Petra turned to Mankato. "Doctor," she said, "do you have any theories on why the government would voluntarily feed the insurgents? Why would they feed their enemies?"

"They don't! Get this through your heads, people—the government has absolutely nothing to do with food. That's entirely up to the females."

"Yes," Petra persisted, "but why would the females feed the insurgents?"

"Because that's what they do! That's their role in Denastri society."

"But why would A-clan females help feed C-clan insurgents? Don't the females have any clan loyalties?"

Mankato shook her head. "Frankly, I don't know. I haven't been able to determine whether they do or not. Possibly, at some level, they do. But not at a level that makes any difference as far as politics is concerned. The females don't seem to care about politics. They leave all of that to the males."

"Well, then," Barnes asked, "why do the males go along with allowing the females to feed their clan enemies?"

Mankato sighed in evident frustration. "Because it's not *up* to the males, dammit! It's not a question of their going along with it. It would never even occur to them *not* to go along with it! That's just the way things *are* on this planet!"

There didn't seem to be anything to say in response to that. Everyone concentrated on their drinks for a moment.

Finally, Petra said, "We know that the males would resist any attempt to seize the food centers. But if the females don't care about politics, how do you think *they* would react? Suppose we just took over but let them go on producing food?"

"Honey," Mankato said, "you still don't get it. None of you do. And neither do I. Denastri is a big black box, and we just stuck our hand into it. And whatever's in there doesn't like it. Do you really think we're going to get all of our fingers back?"

·24·

The door to Gloria's cell slid open and in marched four Fourthborns and one female—the Abbess. Gloria got to her feet and stared at the round, diminutive female, who returned her gaze in silence for a few moments. Then she said, "Terran female—come." The Denastri party turned and walked out of the cell, and Gloria followed them into the corridor.

Gloria walked along next to the Abbess, shortening her stride to keep pace, while the male warriors kept a discreet distance behind them. They went up a ramp to the agricultural level above, where hundreds of females but only a few males were in evidence. Still saying nothing, the Abbess led Gloria between leafy green rows of vegetation sprouting luxuriously from their grow-tanks. At last, they came to a long low tank where there seemed to be nothing growing but neatly arranged rows of bright yellow flowers with sharp, pointy petals. The Abbess stopped and gestured toward the flowers.

Gloria looked at them for a moment, then turned to the Abbess. "They are very beautiful," she said.

"Why are they beautiful, Terran female?" the Abbess asked.

The question surprised Gloria. She hadn't expected to get into a discussion of aesthetics. "Well," she said, "they have a pleasing shape and a bright, attractive color. To my eyes, they seem beautiful. Do the Denastri consider them to be beautiful, as well?"

"They are of the proper form," said the Abbess. "They reach for the false suns above and do what is required of them. Now, observe, Terran female."

The Abbess bowed her head forward and quietly said a few words that the translation software didn't recognize. Almost an incantation or a prayer, it seemed to Gloria. Then she reached down into the tank, probed into the soil with her four-fingered hands, and pulled up one of the plants. The stalk of the flower was attached to a fat, brown, melonlike growth about the size of a softball. The Abbess held it up for Gloria to see.

"The flower," said the Abbess, "is only a flower. It is not the fruit."

"I see," Gloria said. "I mean, Honored Abbess, that I understand. What we see on the surface is not necessarily what is most important. What lies below may have greater significance."

The Abbess listened to the translation and nodded. Her piscine mouth did not quite form a recognizable smile, but she seemed pleased. She returned the plant to the tank, carefully covering the fruit with the soil, then looked up at Gloria.

"Terran female understands, most likely. A goodness."

"I want very much to understand, Honored Abbess," Gloria said. "I hope that you will help me to understand your people, and perhaps I can help you to understand mine."

"Terrans are mostly different from Denastri. A great strangeness. Honored Lord Kenarbin also tells me that he wishes to understand, but he is only a Terran male and cannot—*unknown word*. Terran males have great hunger, it seems, for example. Terran females have same hunger, too? We watch and listen, but understanding is mostly empty."

Gloria tried to think. They had apparently observed the interaction between her and Kenarbin and must have found it confusing. Hunger? Could the Abbess mean sex?

"Honored Abbess," Gloria said, "as you must know, Terran biology is very different from Denastri biology. Reproduction is not simply a duty with us. It is a great hunger . . . for both Terran males and Terran females. We feel it mostly all the time."

"This we know," the Abbess replied, "but understanding is empty. Terran females are the same as Terran males, why not?"

"We are the same in some ways, and different in some ways," Gloria tried to explain. "It is a strangeness even to Terrans, sometimes."

"You are the same and not the same? We see Terran Fourthborns and Fifthborns, mostly Imperial Marines, no doubt. Yet some we see are also Terran females, even though they are also Marines. This is mostly improper and a great strangeness to Denastri. But not to Terrans, most likely?"

"Honored Abbess, Terran males and females do many of the same things. Yes, some Marines are females. And I am Imperial Governor, but also a female. This is not because I feed the Emperor. Sometimes Terran females feed the males, and sometimes the males feed the females. Sometimes we simply feed ourselves."

"Yes," said the Abbess. "We know this, we see this. In—*unknown word*—we ponder it, but still we are mostly empty. Terrans are mostly improper all the time, a great strangeness to the—*unknown word*—below. Terrans—*unknown word, possibly 'warp' or 'distort'*— the proper—*unknown word*. Some Denastri say this is because you are—*unknown word with negative connotations, possibly meaning 'evil.'* I, myself, am still hungry. Come, Terran female."

The Abbess led her to another ramp extending downward, followed by another descent to a still-lower level. Here, there were many females, but no males at all. In fact, the Fourthborn escort stopped at the bottom of the ramp and didn't follow them through the lower corridors. Gloria mentioned this to the Abbess.

"A wrongness of great completeness," the Abbess replied. "Denastri males must not—*unknown word, possibly 'pollute' or 'defile'*—the—*unknown word*—of the—*unknown word.*" That was not very edifying, but Gloria thought she got it.

"Only Denastri females may go to the lower levels?"

"It is so, Terran female."

"When I attended the Sixthborns' Rite of Continuation, I noticed that there were no Denastri females present."

"A place for everything and everything in its place," said the software.

They came to an intersection of corridors. The Abbess stopped and pointed down one of the hallways. "Here," she said, "is the place of ripening. Terran female may not see, but must attempt to understand, most likely. Oneness happens. Completeness is—*unknown word.* Denastri females depart and return three times, Denastri Sixthborn are continued, all the time. The proper shape of the world is maintained and renewed. A rightness of infinite completeness."

"It's your nursery!" Gloria cried out, suddenly grasping the words of the Abbess. "This is where Denastri are born—and the mothers die."

"Die, Terran female? You do not understand, most likely."

"I'm sorry, Honored Abbess. Perhaps I used the wrong word. I think it is often difficult for us to understand each other, but I believe I understand what you said."

"Plants die," said the Abbess. "Birds die. Perhaps Terrans die—this is a matter of much—*unknown word, possibly 'debate' or 'controversy'*—among the exalted—*unknown word*—below. But Denastri females continue. Sixthborn also continue, in their proper way."

"I think I understand, Honored Abbess. But Terrans *do* die. And so have many Denastri males on the surface, even if the Sixthborn continue. This is a great wrongness, Honored Abbess. You and I must find a way to stop the dying, stop the killing."

"Stop the dying?" The Abbess seemed puzzled. "The petals of a flower must fall in their proper way. The fruit must continue, but the flower only matters for its proper moment. That is the proper shape of—*unknown word*—all the time, Terran female."

"Yes, but many Denastri males are dying—killing each other and killing Terrans. Surely, Honored Abbess, this is a wrongness of great completeness!"

The Abbess was silent for a long moment, then said, "Flowers are only flowers, Terran female. I see that we do not understand each other, most likely. A sadness."

"But we must *try* to understand each other, Honored Abbess. If we fail, great harm will come to your people and mine."

The Abbess nodded. "An improper shape of—*unknown word*—has been ripening since the Terrans came. This is mostly true all the time. But flowers must bloom and die, Terran female. As long as the fruit continues, what does it matter how the flowers die?"

Gloria thought for a moment and remembered something. "Honored Abbess," she said, "a Fifthborn male once said to me, 'If a meal is eaten, what does it matter which female prepared it?' It seems to me that you are saying the same thing, only from the female point of view. Are you telling me that as long as the males and females perform their proper role in Denastri society, neither one really cares what happens to the other?"

The Abbess pondered this for a full minute before responding. "Terran female," she said, "perhaps understanding ripens between us. But a strangeness continues. I hunger."

Gloria tried again. "Honored Abbess, a Terran poet once said that no man—or woman—is an island, entire of itself. He said, 'Each man's—or woman's—death diminishes me, for I am involved in, uh, humankind.' But it seems to me that you are saying that Denastri males and females really *are* islands. As long as Denastri society and culture continue, the fate of individual males is not important to you. Is that so, Honored Abbess?"

"Many islands make a world, Terran female. It is the world that is important, not the islands."

"Ask not for whom the bell tolls," Gloria said, "because it just doesn't matter?"

"Understanding is ripening, most likely," said the Abbess.

The tour was evidently over. The Abbess led Gloria back to the upper level and the escort of Fourthborns rejoined them. There was no more conversation, but Gloria had the impression that the Abbess was deep in thought. If Gloria could understand the Abbess, maybe the Abbess could understand John Donne.

When they reached the door of her cell, Gloria turned to the Abbess and said, "Honored Abbess, I would like to see Lord Kenarbin again. It would be a great goodness."

"It shall be arranged, most likely, Terran female."

"Thank you, Honored Abbess. And . . . do you think I could get a bucket of warm water and some soap? And maybe some wine or beer? And coffee? Terrans have other needs than just food and water."

"Terrans have many needs," said the Abbess. "A strangeness. Perhaps they should have stayed on their own world."

"Perhaps so," Gloria conceded, "but the fact is, we are here on your world. And I could really use a bath."

"I shall attempt to complete your needs, Terran female. We shall meet again at the proper time. We have given one another much to eat today. Time and— *unknown word, possibly 'contemplation' or 'digestion'*— are of a necessity."

Gloria was about to enter her cell but stopped when she saw a Fifthborn and two Fourthborns rushing toward them down the corridor. The Abbess moved a few steps away from her and listened as the Fifthborn spoke to her. The conversation continued for some time, and it seemed to Gloria that the Fifthborn and even the Abbess were becoming greatly agitated. Finally, the Abbess dismissed the Fifthborn and walked back over to Gloria.

"A wrongness!" she cried. "A wrongness of infinite completeness ripens, Terran female! A wrongness!"

"So," said General Matabele, "we are agreed, then?" He looked around the conference table, where the Corporate leaders, Dexta UnderSecs, Marine brass, and the Imperial Governor had been meeting most of the day. Those who didn't nod in agreement at least offered no objection. "We will mount an operation to seize and occupy the distribution center and the three agplexes where Lord Kenarbin and Governor VanDeen are probably being held."

"General," Petra said, "I agree that we should *plan* the operation. That's all. I haven't agreed to execute it."

"I understand, Madame Governor," Matabele said.

"And I still want to clarify Servitor's role in this," Sally Voelker said.

"You and your people will be involved in the planning, Ms. Voelker," Matabele said wearily. He and Voelker had been crossing swords all day. "Have your people meet with my staff at 0800 tomorrow morning and we'll start thrashing out the details."

"Thank you, General," Voelker said politely.

"Not at all, Ms. Voelker."

"And each UnderSec should designate one of your people to attend," Petra added, "unless you want to go yourself. If nobody else has anything, I think we're adjourned."

As people were filing out of the room, Petra buttonholed Colonel Barnes. "Colonel," she said, "could you come to my office in a few minutes?"

"Certainly," he said. "Just give me a few minutes to get things squared away with my people."

Petra walked back to the Governor's office, flanked by her omnipresent Marine guards. Sergeant Hooper bounced to his feet as she entered and gave her a careful once-over.

"You look tired, ma'am," he said. "Rough one?"

"Alvin," Petra told him, "they just don't get any rougher. You want to be Governor?"

"Unh-uh, ma'am. My mama didn't raise no fools."

Petra smiled at him. "Mine did. Colonel Barnes is going to be here in a few minutes. When he gets here, could you bring us some coffee and doughnuts or something?"

"How 'bout some sandwiches? Got a supply ship from Prisma in this morning. Less than a week old and almost good enough to eat."

"Sounds great, Alvin."

Petra went into her office, approached her desk, then stopped when she saw her console blinking at her to announce the presence of more new material in her In File. She didn't feel like facing that, so she went over to the couch, kicked her shoes off, stretched out, and closed her eyes. When she opened them again, Colonel Barnes was standing next to the couch, a tray of coffee and sandwiches was sitting on the coffee table, and Alvin Hooper was leaving the room.

"Maybe we could do this another time," Barnes said.

Petra sat up. "No, no, we need to talk. Sit down and help yourself." Barnes sat next to her and poured coffee for both of them, then grabbed a ham sandwich and took a big bite.

"Colonel . . ."

"Petra," Barnes said, "we've known each other a long time. Don't you think you could start calling me Del . . . Madame Governor?"

"Not Delbert?"

"Only Gloria and my mother call me that. Never liked it much, but somehow, I don't mind it coming from them."

"Del it is, then," Petra agreed. "So . . . Del . . . tell me what you think about our great meeting. Does this thing have any hope of succeeding, or are we just going to get Gloria and Lord Kenarbin killed?"

Barnes took a sip of coffee before replying. "It has a chance," he said.

"A good chance?"

"A chance. I can't give you odds, Petra. Any military operation depends on a thousand different elements, any one of which can literally blow up in your face. Sometimes, you get lucky. Eisenhower got good weather in Normandy, Bryant got good timing at Savoy. On the other hand, the Spanish Armada got bad weather and Bonaparte got hemorrhoids at Waterloo. All you can do is plan for every contingency, then roll the dice."

"But how can you do that? How can you *know*?"

"You can't, unless you've managed to load the dice."

"Well, what about the plan, then? Do you think it's a good plan?"

"It will be, by the time we've whipped it into shape. The only part that really bothers me is that we've only got two LASSes. We can drop a company of Marines right on top of two of the targets, but for the other two, we'll need to use ground transport. Ideally, the LASSes will go in first and pull defenders away from the other two sites before the rest of our forces arrive. I'd feel better if we had another LASS, but you have to work with what's available."

Petra nodded. "We're stretched too thin, aren't we? I mean, not just here, but everywhere. I have a friend who calls that Imperial overreach."

"I wouldn't argue the point," Barnes said. "But grand strategy is above my pay grade. I'm just a Jarhead colonel."

"But someday, you'll be a general, Del. What will you say then?"

"You mean, if I were on the General Staff and somebody actually gave a damn about my opinion? I don't know. I console myself with the thought that it's not very likely that I'll ever make it that high."

"You never know. I mean, look at me—Imperial Governor Petra Nash! How likely was that?"

Barnes chuckled. "You've done okay so far, Petra," he said.

"I haven't really done much of anything yet. I just don't know if I'll be able to give that order when the time comes. Spirit, Del, just think of all the things that could go wrong! People could—*will*—die if I give that order. Not just Gloria and Kenarbin, but hundreds of Marines, and thousands of Denastri. You heard what people were saying at that meeting. We might wind up touching off a rebellion all over the planet!"

"We might," Barnes said. He looked down at his coffee and swirled it around for a moment. "Personally, I doubt it. But if we do, I think we'll be able to deal with it."

"I wish I could be sure of that."

"Nothing in life is certain, Petra. That goes double

for military operations. You just have to do the best you can."

"Yes . . . but . . . sometimes my best stinks!" Petra looked into Barnes's eyes. "Del, I really screwed up. I accidentally told Bryce about the Kenarbin thing. Gloria was *furious*! I don't think I've ever seen her so mad. She was going to send me home. She said I was finished at Dexta."

"I see," Barnes said. "Tell me something. Did you mean to say that to Denton?"

"No! Of course not."

"Well, there you are, then. Sometimes people say things that they shouldn't. You did. Gloria did. Whatever she said to you, I'm sure she regrets it now. Yes, you screwed up. That doesn't mean it's forever and always. Sooner or later, everyone screws up."

"Have you?"

Barnes looked up at the ceiling for a few seconds. "Oh, yes," he said. "I've screwed up. Long time ago, I was a green second lieutenant. My first time under fire, and I was scared and excited. Captain told me to take a hill. But I misread the map and led my platoon up the wrong hill." He looked at Petra. "I lost five men," he said, "taking the wrong hill."

Petra nodded. "And what happened?"

"The captain scalded my ass. Told me I was the worst officer in the history of the Corps. Told me I should be counting thumbtacks on Ultima Thule. And then, the next day, he told me to take another hill, and I took it. The right one, this time. And I lost five more men in the process. Petra, words really don't matter a hell of a lot. Forget about what you said and what Gloria said. It's what you *do* that matters. When the time comes, you'll do fine. And I promise you, Gloria knows that. She'll expect you to do what you have to do."

"Even if I get her killed?"

Barnes nodded. "Even then."

·25·

The Fourthborns led Gloria out of her cell and down the corridor toward a ramp leading to the upper level. She felt good this morning, oddly optimistic. For one thing, she had finally gotten her bath—a bucket of tepid water and a bar of Marine soap had done wonders for her outlook. And for breakfast, there had been a packet of scrambled eggs, sausage, and, *mirabile dictu*, a container of cold but caffeine-laden coffee.

Her optimism abruptly died when she reached the upper level. There, she found Kenarbin, the Abbess, a Fifthborn—and hundreds of armed Fourth- and Fifthborn Denastri. The place was crawling with them. The Denastri females were there as usual, tending the crops, but the formerly placid agricultural complex was now an armed camp, seething with menace.

"What's happening?" Gloria addressed her question to Kenarbin, but the Abbess answered.

"A wrongness ripens, Terran female," she said.

"Yes," Gloria said, "I can see that. Why are all these

male warriors here? I thought this place was off-limits to them."

"It is of a necessity," the Abbess replied. "Mostly all the time Fourthborns and Fifthborns may be here in proper way, almost. Now, they come in—*unknown word*—for reasons of uppermost completeness, most likely. Terrans come. An impossible wrongness!"

"Gloria," said Kenarbin, "I think the Marines are planning an attack on this place. Maybe they know we're here and think they can rescue us."

"Terran offal are—*pejorative adjective*—fools!" snarled the Fifthborn. Gloria couldn't be sure, but she thought it was the same one she'd met on the night of her abduction. "If Marines come, exalted Lord Kenarbin and honored Imperial Governor will not continue, most likely."

"He means they'll kill us," Kenarbin said.

"Yeah, I sort of figured that. But how do they know?"

"The Denastri seem to know everything that goes on in the Compound. Either they've got the place bugged, or those weird ears of theirs hear a lot more than we think they do."

"Honored Abbess," Gloria said urgently, "I agree, this would be a great wrongness. We must prevent this from happening."

"Terran female," said the Abbess, "the shape of — *unknown word*—has been—*unknown word, possibly* '*altered*' *or* '*transformed*'—in impossibly improper ways. A muchness." The Abbess seemed to sigh in resignation. "A sadness."

"Honored Abbess, we can prevent this! Just let us go. I'll order the Marines to cancel the attack."

The Fifthborn immediately clamped his hand on Gloria's shoulder. "Terran offal will not go," he insisted. "Proper honor of —*unknown word*—must be satisfied, most likely."

"But, Honored Abbess—"

"Terran female, your understanding is empty," the Abbess said. "Honored Fifthborn must keep—*unknown word*—for self, all the time. Denastri females must feed Fourthborn and Fifthborn in proper way, but this meal is not ours to eat."

"I think," said Kenarbin, "she's saying that we're not *her* hostages, but *his*. She *can't* release us, and he *won't*."

"Understanding of exalted Lord Kenarbin ripens," said the Abbess.

Gloria started to address the Fifthborn, but thought better of it. "You tell him, Bill," she said. "Maybe he'll listen to reason from another male."

Kenarbin gave it a try. "Honored Fifthborn," he said, "surely you must understand that the only reason the Marines are going to attack this place is because you are holding us here. If you release us, they will have no reason to attack. Your food and your females will be safe."

"Terran offal is a coward and a fool, most likely," the Fifthborn responded. "Honor is empty, most likely. This humble Fifthborn cannot—*unknown word, possibly 'defile' or 'pollute'*—himself. Once food is eaten, it cannot grow again."

Kenarbin frowned. "I don't know," he said. "I think he's saying that for reasons of personal honor, he can't back down. Maybe that's why there have never been any demands or conditions for our release. Maybe they never had any intention of releasing us at all."

"Terran offal grows wiser, most likely. The meal is eaten."

"That's it, all right," Kenarbin said. "To the Denastri, taking a hostage is not some conditional ploy. It's a statement of personal honor, somehow. Like counting coup, maybe. Once the deed is done, it would be dishonorable to undo it."

"So they intend to keep us here forever?"

"Terran female understands," said the Abbess. "It is mostly proper, all the time."

"But, Honored Abbess, Honored Fifthborn," Gloria protested, looking at each of them in turn, "it would be a great wrongness for you to keep us here now. If you don't release us, the Marines will come here, and many will die. Food will be destroyed! Food!"

"Marines will not continue!" the Fifthborn bellowed. "Not! Food is sacred—*indeterminate phrase. Unknown word*—of impossible completeness! Honored Denastri warriors will not permit it!"

"Honored Fifthborn," said Kenarbin, "your warriors are brave and honorable. But they cannot resist the Imperial Marines. Surely, you must know this. And it won't be just the Marines. Thousands of loyal Denastri government troops will join them in this attack. You and your men will be overwhelmed."

The Fifthborn made a noise that sounded very much like a contemptuous snort. "Terran offal will come," he said. "See with your own eyes what fools you are."

The Fifthborn led the party to another ramp. They walked up it, went through a door, and emerged onto the surface of the planet and the open air. Gloria blinked in the unaccustomed sunlight, took a deep breath, and looked around. They were standing at the edge of a broad field of vegetation that looked like stunted cabbages. Denastri females were moving among the plants, evidently going about their normal chores. But surrounding the field were hundreds of Fourth- and Fifthborn warriors, most of them carrying Terran plasma rifles.

"Spirit," Gloria gasped, "those are *government* troops!"

"Indeed," said Kenarbin. "What the hell is going on up here?"

"Terran offal eats, most likely," declared the Fifthborn. "Denastri are all together, a oneness of proper completeness. A muchness. Food is sacred to all. Terrans are fools."

"I think I get it," said Kenarbin. "The usual politics don't matter where food is concerned. The loyalists and insurgents may fight over politics on the surface, but when it comes to the safety of the hive—the life below—they're all on the same side."

"But they must know that in the Compound," Gloria said.

"You'd think so," Kenarbin agreed.

"Then why . . ." Gloria trailed off as the answer occurred to her. She stifled a laugh as the absurdity of it hit her. "Spirit! Bill, the Marines have to attack for the same reason that the Denastri have to resist. The same reason that the insurgents can't release us."

"Precisely," Kenarbin said, nodding his head. "The Empire can't back off, any more than the Denastri can. Both of them, for their own reasons, have to do something that makes absolutely no sense, even if doing it will destroy the very things they're fighting for."

Gloria looked at the Abbess, who had listened to their words. The Abbess looked as if she understood, but it seemed to have made no impression on her. "Terran female," she said, "the wrongness ripens in its mostly proper way. The shape of the—*unknown word*—is mostly a—*indeterminate phrase*—of impossible completeness. If the sun rises, it must also set."

"But you can't let this happen, Honored Abbess! You can *change* the shape of the . . . the . . . whatever the damned word is. It doesn't have to be this way!"

"If the sun rises," the Abbess repeated, "it must also set. It is rising now."

"Dammit, this isn't some exercise in celestial mechanics! We're not talking about the sun, or even plants and food. We're talking about the lives of you and your people—all of them, males and females. We're talking about the future of your civilization, Honored Abbess! If you allow this battle to take place, nothing will ever be the same."

"A great sadness of impossible completeness," said the Abbess. "But the shape of the—*unknown word*—is—*indeterminate phrase*. The meal is prepared; it must be eaten. You should not have come here, Terran female."

"But . . ."

Tears were welling in Gloria's eyes from frustration and despair. Kenarbin put his arm around her shoulders and pulled her close to him.

"I don't think you can reason with them, Gloria," he said softly. "Even if we really understood them, and they understood us, we've both backed ourselves into a corner. As a diplomat, I've seen it a dozen times."

"Well, then, *do* something about it!"

"What do you mean?"

"You said it yourself, Bill. You're a diplomat! You came here to negotiate with these people. Don't you think it's time you started?"

"Good news," Barnes announced as he entered the Governor's office.

"You're kidding," said Petra, who couldn't remember the last time she'd heard any news that could be described as good.

"No, it's for real. Call up Map 7C on your console and I'll show you." Petra did as Barnes asked, and he joined her behind her desk and poked a finger at a spot on the display. "That's where they are. It's an agplex, fifty-six kilometers east of the city."

"How do you know?"

Barnes smiled. "The Denastri government told us. They didn't mean to, but they did."

There had been no communications of any sort between the Denastri government and the Imperials since the day of the aborted raid on the distribution center. Both sides had withdrawn from normal contact and maintained a wounded, wary silence. In part, Petra realized, it was because neither government knew quite what to say to the other. No one wanted to initiate a sequence of events that would lead to an irreparable rupture, so each waited for the other to make the first move.

"So what happened?"

"The DHG has the same problem that we have," Barnes explained. "More places to defend than they have troops to defend them with. On paper, they have about 120,000 troops on Lataka, but in reality, they probably only have about 40,000 available to be deployed. But there are, we think, twenty-six agplexes and distribution centers surrounding Enkar. If they tried to defend all of them, that would be less than 2000 troops at each site, which wouldn't be enough to do them much good. So they've deployed them in a loose ring at every other site. That's still not really enough, but it might have been enough to keep us confused. But then, they got nervous."

"I know the feeling," Petra said.

"They tried not to be obvious about it, but we've been tracking everything they've done. They put about 2,500 troops at the other sites, but at *this* one, they've got at least 5,000, with more coming in. There's only one possible reason for them to do that."

"Gloria and Kenarbin are there!"

"Gotta be," Barnes agreed. "Unless they're playing games and trying to deceive us and get us to attack the wrong site. That's possible, but I just don't think they're that subtle. Like I said, I think they just got nervous."

"What does that mean for us?"

"It means we can concentrate our forces and hit that one site with everything we've got."

Petra didn't necessarily like the sound of that. "What if we're wrong?" she asked.

"Worst case," said Barnes, "is that we take out maybe 20 percent of their best troops and occupy one of their agplexes. At a minimum, that will substantially weaken them and give them something to think about. They'll know we mean business and can go anywhere we want."

"And Gloria and Kenarbin?"

Barnes shrugged. "If they aren't there, the Denastri will still want to keep them alive as a bargaining chip . . . as their hole card."

"Do the Denastri play poker?" Petra wondered.

Late that evening, Petra bundled up in her Denastri hooded robe—a very practical garment for the windswept environment—and walked across the Compound in the company of her Marine guards and her own thoughts. The Marines kept a discreet distance from her, and Petra was so used to them by now that she might as well have been alone.

She went up a stairway that took her to the upper level of the wall surrounding the Compound. Marines on duty there greeted her politely and she mumbled a response; she was obviously in no mood for conversation, and the Marines carefully avoided her as she entered one of the observation points that bulged outward from the line of the wall. From there, she could see the city of Enkar spread out around her, poorly lit and strangely silent. *Older than Babylon,* she thought.

History was finished with Babylon now, but Enkar endured, with new history still to be written. Some of it would be written in about thirty hours, when the Marine assault on the agplex east of town was scheduled to begin.

Everyone just assumed that it would happen. She had not yet approved the operation, but the planning went forward as if her ultimate approval was simply a foregone conclusion. And perhaps it was. How could she possibly say no?

She had canceled the airstrike that Matabele wanted to conduct, and Matabele had not objected. There was no need to stir up additional trouble at this point; there was already trouble enough.

The Denastri seemed to regard the aborted operation at the distribution center as a major victory. Even the presumably loyal A-clan members, who were no part of the insurgency, apparently took pride and satisfaction in the event. Petra had noticed that the Denastri workers who still came to the Compound—and there were fewer of them now—seemed to regard their Terran overlords with a mixture of contempt and insolence. And out in Scooptown, some of the workers had actually gone on strike. Work on the spaceport and freight terminal had come to a complete halt, and the Corporates were frantic. Servitor was threatening to take matters into their own hands if the Governor and the Marines didn't do something about it. Just what Servitor could do, however, was unclear. Killing recalcitrant workers was unlikely to increase production.

And how would the people of Enkar react if the Marines attacked one of their sacred agplexes? So far, there had been no overt signs of rebellion, although Marine intelligence reported that at several locations, large crowds of First- and Secondborns had collected; Matabele, Barnes, and McCray had all assured her that if the city erupted in riot and rebellion, the Compound would be secure. The plasma cannon looming next to her on the wall would see to that, she was told. Thousands of Denastri might die, but the Terrans would be safe behind their walls.

Thousands more would die if she approved the attack. Hundreds of Marines might die, as well—plus two more Terrans. No matter what Barnes said about bargaining chips and hole cards, it seemed inescapable to Petra that Gloria and Kenarbin would be killed—if not by the Denastri, then perhaps by the Marines. Friendly fire, it was called, an oxymoron for the ages. In the fog of war, anything could happen.

But the experts told her that it had to be done. Even Jack McCray, who always struck her as sensible, if excitable, insisted that the attack was a necessity. In the wake of the first, aborted operation, it was essential for the Empire to regain the upper hand and show the Denastri who was boss.

Petra laughed mirthlessly at the thought. *Who's the boss? I am!*

In her entire life, she had never held so much power or felt so utterly powerless. Did leaders always feel that way, or was it just because she was new to the job? Did Hazar hesitate before Golconda and ask himself if it was worth the price that would have to be paid? Did Caesar pause at the Rubicon and reconsider his options?

The events that unfolded on this insignificant planet in the next few days would, she knew, reverberate around the vast and mighty Terran Empire. Bryce and his tribe would file their stories, and 3 trillion citizens would hear the news and ponder its meaning. The coming election might very well turn on Petra's decision. The Voice of the People would be heard. Even the humblest Firstborns out there in Enkar could vote if they wanted to, and so could the mysterious, mostly unseen females, for the Empire was devoted to equal rights for all. They could choose between the haughty, grasping incumbents and the progressive, platitudinous opposition, secure in the knowledge that it wouldn't make the slightest difference to their lives.

She wished that Albert Fenlow were there. He would have a neat, logical, well-reasoned answer to everything, cross-referenced and footnoted. Here's how history works, he would say, and this is what the actors on its stage should do. When she got back to Columbia, maybe she could write a term paper on her experiences. "How I Spent My Summer Vacation," by Petra Nash, Imperial Governor (ret.).

Whitney Bartholemew, Jr. had known the right answers, too. Rich kid, rebel, mass murderer, and angry lover—he had history all figured out. Historic inevitability, the eternal clash of opposites, the Hegelian dialectic . . . what would Whit say if he were here? Of course, Whit couldn't say anything now, having been executed by an Imperial firing squad two years ago. Petra still felt a sharp pang when she thought of him, and her own stupidly impetuous attraction to him. A woman who went to bed with a monster was now going to decide the fate of millions? Did Hegel mention that history must have a warped sense of humor?

Petra suddenly thought of Jill Clymer, her former OSI colleague who had angrily resigned her Dexta position two years ago, back on New Cambridge, when she discovered that Gloria had been less than scrupulously honest. Jill firmly believed that government officials had a sacred obligation to Do the Right Thing, no matter what the cost or consequences. But how could you know what was right? How could you be sure?

Colonel Barnes said that you could never really be sure, but you had to roll the dice anyway. Dice? Hole cards? Did Barnes think it was all some kind of game? No, he was a Marine, after all, and knew better than anyone that it was not a game. He had known that ever since he led those Marines up the wrong hill. He had rolled the dice, and they had come up snake eyes for five of his men. And when he rolled a seven the next time out, five more had died. Do the Right Thing or Do the Wrong Thing, and people died, either way.

And one of the people who would die when Petra made her throw was Gloria VanDeen.

·26·

Gloria listened and said little as Kenarbin negotiated with the Abbess and the Fifthborn leader of the insurgency. He was experienced and expert, a master of nuance and subtlety, but he had never negotiated for higher stakes—his own life and Gloria's, the future of Denastri, and, perhaps, the future of the Empire itself. The drama played itself out in a small room, furnished with a single table, chairs for the Terrans, and two chairs shaped and sized specifically for the Fifthborn and the tiny Abbess. Females occasionally brought in food and drink, then wordlessly departed. Without her wristcom, Gloria couldn't measure the passage of time, but she figured that they had been at it all day and well into the night.

Progress was also difficult to measure; Gloria wasn't really sure that there had been any. Between the Fifthborn's prideful obstinacy, the Abbess's philosophical fatalism, and the profusion of unknown words and indeterminate phrases, it was hard to tell if Kenarbin had managed to accomplish anything at all. If nothing else, the exercise had been educational.

Among the things the Terrans learned was the reason why food production and most of the female population were located beneath the surface of the planet. The scraggly cabbagelike growths they had seen above ground that morning were a clue. In their long history of wars and environmental neglect, the Denastri had managed to turn the surface of their world into a contaminated wasteland where little would grow and nothing could flourish. Gradually, agricultural production was shifted to underground complexes like the one they were in, protected from the deadly world above. And since the females were responsible for the food, they embarked upon a subterranean life that left them increasingly separate and isolated from the males, who remained on the surface. Over the eons, two interlocking but distinctly different cultures emerged.

"It's like Wells's Eloi and Morlocks," Kenarbin said to Gloria. "Only instead of the elite and the workers, on Denastri it was the two genders that diverged and formed their own civilizations. As long as the food is delivered and the world below is protected, neither one cares very much what happens to the others. Your brain-eating Sixthborns are pretty much irrelevant to the females, and vice versa. But they respect each other's culture and come together on the only issue that really matters to both—food."

"We never paid much attention to food production," Gloria noted. "It was a sensitive topic, so we never really looked in to it."

"Right. We dealt exclusively with the surface civilization of the males, on the assumption that it was the *only* culture on the planet. So the females figured that we weren't really their problem. Now that we're suddenly a threat to both, each of them is trying to deal with the problem according to its own cultural precepts. The males must resist not only the threat to their food supply, but also the insult to their honor and the general disruption of their culture created by our presence on the surface."

"And the females," Gloria said, picking up the thread, "weren't concerned with the war or the insurgency because it never affected them directly—until now. But they can't tell the males what to do, and their own philosophical predisposition seems to be to accept the changed shape of their cultural geometry caused by the Terrans, even though they consider it a wrongness."

Kenarbin's brow furrowed. "I wonder if that's really true," he said. He turned to the Denastri female. "Honored Abbess, you speak of the shape of things whose meanings we don't understand. Has that shape always been the same, or has it changed over time?"

The Abbess thought for a moment before responding. "Exalted Lord Kenarbin," she said, "the shape of the—*unknown word*—is a oneness, mostly all the time. Yet the seasons pass, and there are new crops to tend. The world—*indeterminate phrase*—and we are a part of the world."

"So it does change? Then change in itself is not necessarily a wrongness? It can also be a . . . a rightness?"

"It may be so, most likely."

"Then perhaps the coming of the Terrans may be a rightness, even though you cannot yet see that. Perhaps, as the seasons pass and new crops are planted, our coming may bring a great goodness to your world."

"*Unknown word, possibly pejorative*," hooted the Fifthborn. If the word was unknown to the translation software, it was at least becoming familiar to Gloria and Kenarbin. It seemed to be the Denastri equivalent of "Bullshit!"

The Abbess remained placid. "Honored Fifthborn's understanding is mostly limited," she said. "A flower cannot be a fruit, even if it would." That produced a flurry of indeterminate phrases between the Denastri male and female, quite possibly pejorative.

"Bill," Gloria whispered, "is this doing us any good? Do we really want them arguing with each other?"

"We may," said the seemingly imperturbable diplomat. "I think this may be almost as difficult for them as it is for us. The males are dominant on the surface, the females are dominant here, and that's understood by both of them. But this situation is unique and forces them to deal with each other as equals. They may not know how to do that."

The Fifthborn and the Abbess sorted out their philosophical differences, or at least put them in abeyance. Kenarbin resumed his attempt to get the Abbess to see the Terran presence on her world as a possible rightness. Gloria realized that he was playing for time. If the Abbess could be persuaded to accept the possibility that the changing shape of things was not necessarily bad, perhaps she would see the necessity of letting them communicate with the Compound to delay the attack, even if the hostages could not be released. But the Fifthborn was having none of it. The hostages could never be released, and even letting them speak to the other Terrans would constitute a wrongness of impossible completeness. Even Kenarbin grew impatient with his obstinacy.

"If the Marines kill you and destroy this place," he asked, "how would that satisfy your honor?"

The Fifthborn refused to concede the possibility. "This humble Fifthborn will continue," he insisted. "And if—*indeterminate phrase*—then other honored Fifthborn and courageous Fourthborn will continue. Marines will *not* continue!"

"Honored Fifthborn, allow me to point out that we have already destroyed your fleet, removed your government, and occupied your planet. The Marines will most definitely continue, even if it means turning your lovely world to ashes. You cannot defeat us."

"Then we will—*indeterminate phrase, possibly having to do with death*—with honor and impossible completeness, most likely. Terran offal will—*indeterminate phrase*. Honored Sixthborn have said this."

"Death before dishonor," Gloria said unhappily.

The Fifthborn looked at her. "Terran female," he said, "understands, most likely."

The Terran female understood, all right, but she wished that she didn't. The Fifthborn was never going to release them or let them communicate with the Compound. The Sixthborns had assured him that this was the proper course, and nothing was going to alter that conviction. The Sixthborns, she reminded herself, didn't simply speak for the Denastri god—they *were* god.

A Fourthborn entered the room and conferred briefly with the male Denastri. The Fifthborn looked at Kenarbin and Gloria and said, "Marines will come with the sun. Words are—*indeterminate phrase*—Terran offal." And without another word, he left the room.

"Negotiations would seem to have broken down," Kenarbin said.

"A sadness," said the Abbess.

"No," Gloria said quickly, "a goodness!"

Both Kenarbin and the Abbess turned to look at her.

"Denastri males are fools," she said. "So are Terran males. Fortunately, we Terran females have ways of controlling them." She eyed Kenarbin. "Don't we, Bill?"

Kenarbin pondered this for a moment, saw where Gloria was going with it, and nodded. "Absolutely," he agreed.

"The hunger you speak of?" asked the Abbess.

"That's right, honored Abbess," Gloria said. "And even though Denastri and Terrans are different in many ways, I'm sure that you also have ways of controlling *your* males. Isn't that so, honored Abbess?"

"Terran female's meaning has not ripened," the Abbess cautiously replied.

"I'm speaking of food, honored Abbess. You control

your males with food, the same as we Terrans control our males with sex. This is mostly true all the time, is it not?"

The Abbess took a long time to respond. Gloria was playing a hunch, based on the theory that Kenarbin had offered when they first met. She knew the Abbess would be reluctant to discuss it, but perhaps the female solidarity angle would work. At last, the Abbess said, "Terran female understands. A muchness. But it would be a wrongness of great completeness for this one to say more." She looked up at Kenarbin.

"Bill," Gloria told him, "take a hike. It's time for some girl talk."

Kenarbin suppressed a smile and got to his feet. He solemnly nodded. "As you wish, Honored Imperial Governor," he said, then walked to the doorway and out into the corridor, where two Fourthborns were standing vigil with their backs to the room.

When he was gone, the Abbess said, "Terran females also have things they do not say to Terran males, why not?"

"Many things," Gloria agreed with a conspiratorial smile. "Just as Denastri females do not discuss the truth about food with Denastri males. You don't simply control their development with food, do you, Honored Abbess? You control their behavior, as well. The things they do and say and believe."

"Control? Terran female's word is not proper all the time."

"Influence, then. You guide them along the correct path. You help them to maintain the correct shape of the world."

"It is so, Terran female."

"Tell me more, Honored Abbess. Your secret is safe with me. We are both females."

Gradually, in her elliptical fashion, the Abbess took Gloria into her confidence. It was a great strangeness to Gloria, but in the end, it all made a kind of sense.

The food grown and prepared by the Denastri females had many properties, and over the eons they had learned how to manipulate them in very precise ways. Just as the physical development of the young males could be controlled by serving them the proper assortment of food, their mental development was also subject to the dictates of diet. Firstborn were not only physically small, but psychologically humble and subservient, while Secondborn developed a flair for creative thought. Thirdborn became obsessive-compulsives, devoted to the details and minutiae inherent in management and government. Fourthborn became fierce followers, Fifthborn grew into bold leaders, and Sixthborn were dreamy and otherworldly. Thus, each caste was prepared to play a specific role within Denastri society.

The influence of the food did not end when the Denastri males were fully grown. Though the control exercised by the females was far from absolute, they nevertheless had the ability to tweak the attitudes and behavioral patterns of the males through subtle and sophisticated changes in their daily menu. The details remained unclear to Gloria, but it seemed to her that the females were able to emphasize or deemphasize certain of the male traits, as required by the times. They could not fundamentally alter the males, but they could make them more or less of what they already were. Thus, in times of war, the warrior castes could be made bolder and fiercer; in times of peace, their aggressive tendencies could be toned down.

The males might have been aware of some of this, but apparently did not realize the full extent to which they were controlled by the females. Their contemptuous treatment of the females on the surface was simply a logical consequence of their assumption that they were in charge of everything except food. But the arrogance of the males was more than offset by the subtlety of the females.

"You could end the insurgency if you wanted to," Gloria said. "Isn't that true, Honored Abbess?"

"Why should we want to?" the Abbess replied. "The Terrans should not have come here. The proper shape of the—*unknown word*—can only be restored when they leave."

"But you know that we will not leave. At least, not until the HCH—the black rocks—have been eaten."

"This is mostly true all the time," the Abbess said, a hint of her sadness coming through in the translation.

"If you understand this," Gloria asked her, "then why resist us? In time, we will mostly go away and the proper shape of things will be restored."

"A flower can only be a flower," the Abbess said. "It cannot be anything else."

"You're saying that the Fourth- and Fifthborns must fight us, because of what they are? But, Honored Abbess, some of them *don't* fight us. Some of them have actually helped us to fight the insurgents—at least, they have until now."

"A proper balance must be preserved. The shape of the—*unknown word*—requires it."

"And you preserve this balance through the food you serve to the different clans?"

"It is mostly so, Terran female."

Gloria thought that she was beginning to understand. Some level of resistance to the Terrans was inevitable; the goal of the females was to maintain what they considered a *proper* level. Too little, and the Terrans would simply make themselves at home, stay forever, and permanently distort the proper shape of the world. Too much, and the Terrans would turn occupation into outright conquest, with devastating consequences for both the world above and the world below. But the proper level of resistance, with the proper balance, would make Denastri exactly what it had become for the Terran overlords—a costly and frustrating quagmire. Eventually, the Terrans would grow weary of it all, and they would leave.

The females believed that they could control the intensity of the conflict by manipulating the behavior of the three clans. And, until now, they had been remarkably successful. HCH and the greed of the Corporates notwithstanding, it was entirely possible that the resistance on Denastri could bring about a sea change in Imperial policy. The humble, hidden females of Denastri might just topple the Imperial government and swing the coming election to the antiexpansionists. Gloria wondered if the Abbess truly understood the extent of her influence.

The Denastri females might have succeeded, but they had made two fatal mistakes: First they had abducted Kenarbin; then they had taken Gloria. Perhaps the decisions had been made by the Fifthborn insurgent leaders, or perhaps they had been prompted by some deeper strategy of the females. Either way, the result was catastrophic. Suddenly, the level of violence on Denastri was no longer subject to the control of the females. Their actions had provoked an inevitable, reflexive response from the Terran warriors, which, in turn, produced an equally reflexive response from the warriors of Denastri. Male honor was at stake now, and no one was safe.

"Honored Abbess," Gloria said, "soon, the Marines will come, and there will be no going back. The male warriors—Terran and Denastri—will change forever the proper shape of the world. You and I must prevent this from happening."

"I fear it is so, Terran female. But time is hungry. The Fifthborn will not eat."

"You're saying it's too late to slip them a mickey?"

"Unknown word?"

"I mean, there's not enough time to give the warriors food that will make them change their plans."

"It is so, Terran female. The meal has already been prepared, and it will be eaten."

"But if you would just let us go, we could stop this tragedy before it happens!"

"Just as a flower cannot be a fruit, neither can a fruit become a flower."

"You can't just order the males to release us?"

"It cannot be done, Terran female, even though I wish it could be so. I trust you, Terran female. You are very strange, yet I believe that you truly desire to restore the proper shape of the—*unknown word*. It is a great sadness that we cannot."

The Terran female known as Petra Nash, Level XII Dexta official and Interim Imperial Governor of Denastri, walked into the Command Center, and if a pin had dropped, everyone could have heard it. Every eye turned toward her. She knew her place at the central console and went to it. "Alvin," she said, "could you bring me some coffee?"

Petra sat down and waited for her coffee as activity in the room gradually returned to its normal pace. Colonel Barnes sat on her left, General Matabele on her right. Sergeant Hooper brought coffee for each of them, and Petra took a slow, careful sip.

She felt surprisingly calm and focused. For some reason, she remembered the day when she had taken the Dexta Entrance Examination. She had felt the same way then. Her entire future was at stake, and the prospect of the ordeal had left her sleepless and frantic for days on end. Yet, when the moment finally arrived, she had somehow pulled herself together and faced the biggest challenge of her life with quiet determination and a cool, steady confidence that surprised her.

"General," she said, "have there been any changes to the plan since last night?"

"No, ma'am. Everything will go just the way we explained it."

"Colonel? Is everything in position?"

"All set, Governor," Barnes replied. "The SALs are already airborne, and the LASSes are fully loaded. The ground convoy is at position Able and reports they are ready to go."

Petra nodded. The Marines knew their business.

And she knew hers. She had done all the worrying, agonizing, and fretting it was possible for her to do. If there was any angle that she hadn't pondered, any option that remained unexamined, she couldn't imagine what it might be. She knew what had to be done, and knew that the Marines would do it.

And yet . . . and yet . . .

Imperial overreach. The illusion of control. Reflexive military response.

Gloria . . .

She suddenly felt her gorge rising and took a deep breath, fighting for control. Spirit, how could she do this?

How could she not?

Someday, maybe Albert Fenlow would write a book about it. He would list all the options that might have been tried, but weren't. He would identify the mistakes, note the successes, find meaning in the outcome, and wrap it all up in a meticulously reasoned analysis of Imperial policies and personalities of the early thirty-third century. Maybe he'd give her an autographed copy.

"Madame Governor?" said Barnes. "It's time."

The decision had already been made. There was no reason to hesitate. She didn't.

"Go," she said.

·27·

The chatter from the strike force was coming in fast and furious. The two Navy LASSes—the *Lydia Tarbell* and the *Iona Halekulea*—each packed two full Marine companies for the short-range mission, and two more companies were coming in via ground convoy, for a total of nearly fifteen hundred troops. Another two companies were waiting in reserve at the Compound and could be quickly picked up by one of the LASSes if the need arose. Intelligence estimated that the Denastri had close to seven thousand troops at the agplex, of which some five thousand belonged to the DHG. Given the disparity in firepower and experience, the Marine leaders believed that the Imperials enjoyed a decisive advantage.

Already, with the orange sun of Denastri barely above the horizon, observation SALs were loitering above the target, sending back crisp, detailed images to the Command Center. "They've been doing some digging," Colonel Barnes noted. For Petra's benefit, he pointed to some features on one of the monitors. "They've got discontinuous earthen berms on three sides of the complex now, and you can see where work has begun on the fourth side. And you can see rifle pits scattered all around the perimeter. This won't be as easy as it would have been the other day at the distribution center, when they were just standing around in the open."

"And the DHG troops have plasma weapons?" Petra asked.

"Most of them have Mark VI plasma rifles, but they don't have anything bigger than that. No cannon, and nothing specifically for air defense."

"So they can't really do any serious damage with what they have?"

"I didn't say that," Barnes replied, shaking his head. "They can't really hurt the LASSes, of course, with their magnetic shields. Mark VI's just don't pump out enough joules to penetrate. But the SALs are vulnerable if they get multiple hits simultaneously—their shields aren't strong enough to deal with that. As for the ground vehicles, it's pretty much the same as for the SALs. Plasma's potent stuff."

"So we'll take losses?"

"They can hurt us," Barnes affirmed. "But the SALs will keep up a constant fire from overhead and make them keep their heads down while the LASSes get grounded. You remember the old *Myrt* on Mynjhino, don't you?"

"Of course."

"Then you'll recall how a LASS is configured. As soon as they're down, the defense nacelles will pop open and we'll have four twin p-cannons pouring out fire while the ground troops deploy. The *Iona* will land on the north side of the complex and the *Lydia* on the west, so we'll be able to take all of their entrenchments by the flank. Then the ground convoy will arrive, shielded by the *Lydia*. That will give us a second wave of ground troops, and the armored vehicles will spread out to the left and right and begin the actual penetration of the complex."

"You make it all sound . . . *easy.*" Petra didn't know much about military matters, and Barnes's cool confidence was at once comforting and troubling. She couldn't help thinking that there had to be more to it.

"Combat is never easy, Petra," Barnes told her. "People are going to die out there today . . . ours and theirs. But our people are confident and experienced, while theirs are going to be nervous and uncertain. They've never been through anything like this. A few of them are probably veterans of their wars within the Cluster, but there was hardly any ground fighting in their war with the Empire. Once we took out their fleet, surface resistance folded up pretty quickly. The insurgents have been effective because they hit and run, before we can concentrate our forces. But this is different. It's going to be an old-fashioned stand-up fight, and the Denastri forces are pinned to a specific piece of ground that they have to defend. On the surface, at least, they'll be overwhelmed."

"What about below the surface?"

"That will be more difficult. We don't know what's down there, and we won't have armor or air cover once we get below ground level. At that point, it becomes a pure infantry battle. Rifles and grenades. But our people are the best in the galaxy, Petra. There's just no doubt about the final outcome of this thing." Barnes flashed her a reassuring smile.

"And what about Gloria and Lord Kenarbin? I know you explained all of that, but I'd like to hear it again."

"Of course, Madame Governor. We think there are four entrances to the subsurface—here, here, here, and here," Barnes said, pointing to small structures on each side of the agplex. "There may be more, but we're certain of at least these four. We've tracked their people going in and out of them for two days. Each of the four companies coming in on the LASSes has a picked squad of experts, specifically trained in this sort of thing. As soon as they hit the ground, they'll make a beeline for those four structures, with covering fire from the rest of their companies. Meanwhile, the SALs will take out the surface portion of those structures, so the hostage teams shouldn't have to fight their way in. They ought to be able to get into the complex itself within the first few minutes of the action, almost before the Nasties know what hit them."

"And then . . . ?"

"Then," Barnes said, "while the rest of the troops deal with whatever opposition we find down there, the hostage teams will fan out and start looking for Gloria and Kenarbin. I won't kid you—they'll need to get lucky. We don't know how deep this thing goes, and we have no idea where they're being held or what kind of guard they'll have around them. The hostage teams will be using nonlethal weapons—flash and concussion grenades, mainly—so that minimizes the chances that we'll hurt our own people. If we can find them, I think there's a good chance that we'll get them out safely. There are never any guarantees in this kind of operation, but if we didn't think we had the odds on our side, we wouldn't be doing this."

"Wouldn't we?" Petra wondered aloud. "I thought the point was to show the Denastri who's the boss. Show the rest of the Empire that we can't be intimidated."

Barnes shook his head. "That's grand strategy," he said. "They pay me to do tactics. But I honestly think we're doing the right thing, Petra—for whatever that's worth."

Petra reached for him and squeezed his hand. "Coming from you, Del," she said, "it's worth a lot."

"H minus five minutes," said a disembodied voice.

There *had* to be a way . . . Gloria was certain of it. She could tell that the Abbess wanted to find a way out just as much as she did. But something was missing, some essential link that could unite them in a common cause. Somewhere amid the confusion of unknown words and indeterminate phrases, a solution existed. But what?

"Honored Abbess, could you *let* us escape? Help us?"

The Abbess seemed taken aback by Gloria's question. She started to respond, then stopped.

"It's the only way, Honored Abbess," Gloria persisted. "There isn't much time left, but we could still stop the attack if you help us."

The Abbess slowly shook her head. "An impossibility of great completeness, Terran female. The meal must be eaten, even if the food is not ripe."

Gloria thought furiously. "But what if the food has not been properly prepared? Must the meal be eaten even if it would do great harm to those who eat it?"

"Food is always properly prepared, Terran female," the Abbess insisted with what seemed, even through the translation software, a degree of indignation. "It could not be otherwise."

"I didn't mean to criticize your cooking," Gloria quickly responded. "I just meant . . . Spirit, I'm not sure *what* I meant! Abbess, we're so close, we've come so far . . . don't let it all be for nothing! We can find an answer if we just try."

"I would that it were so, Terran female. I feel that understanding ripens between us, and yet the— *unknown word*—remains—*unknown word*. I cannot— *unknown word*—even if—*indeterminate phrase*. And yet—"

A shrill, warbling sound suddenly cut through the air. Gloria looked through the open doorway and saw Denastri males and females rushing past in both directions with evident urgency.

The Abbess got to her feet and moved swiftly to the door. She paused momentarily and looked back at

Gloria. She opened her mouth as if to speak, then shook her head sadly and turned away. The Abbess brushed past Kenarbin and the two Fourthborn guards and disappeared into the confusion of the corridor.

Gloria wanted to scream in frustration. They had been so close . . .

Kenarbin caught her eye. Gloria somehow understood what he was thinking and got to her feet.

Suddenly spreading his arms, Kenarbin stepped between the two Fourthborn and grabbed them around their waists, then dived forward into the room, carrying both Denastri with him. All three of them thumped to the floor at Gloria's feet.

She didn't waste time trying to think of a fancy Qatsima martial arts move that would answer, but opted for a more basic solution. She snatched one of the chairs, raised it high, then swung it down onto the head of the nearest Fourthborn with all the strength she could muster.

Simultaneously, Kenarbin rolled to his right, on top of the other guard. He drew his arm back, balled his fist, and smashed it into the jaw of the surprised Fourthborn.

Kenarbin grinned savagely. "Now *that's* diplomacy!" he declared.

They quickly dragged the fallen Denastri to each side of the doorway so that they could not be seen from the corridor. "Bill," Gloria said, "I need a hand with this guy's robe." With Kenarbin's help, Gloria unbelted the Fourthborn's garment and pulled it over his head, discovering, in the process, that beneath it the Denastri wore a sort of quilted long johns. Gloria got into the robe, fastened the belt, and found that it was much too large for her. That would help her hide under the hood, but the hem of the garment trailed along the floor. Kenarbin's own robe fit better, but the hood was large enough to let him adequately shield his face; he needed only to keep his hands out of view.

They ventured out into the corridor and turned left, with Kenarbin taking the lead. Gloria tried to avoid tripping over the hem of her robe and kept the hood pulled low over her face. There was a great deal of traffic in the corridor, with tiny females scurrying this way and that while Fourthborn warriors conveyed a sense of haste and urgency as they marched by. No one paid them any particular attention.

At the end of the corridor they turned right and began ascending a long ramp to the food production level above. Here, many females were hurrying down the ramp, hustled along by a few Fourthborns. They were obviously clearing the vulnerable females out of the upper level. Gloria wondered what was happening on the lower levels, where the Nursery area was normally off-limits to the males. Would the Denastri abide by their sacred customs even in the face of an emergency, or were all bets off?

As they approached the top of the ramp, they came upon a scene of seeming chaos. Warriors were everywhere amid the endless rows of grow-tanks and vegetation; the few remaining females appeared to be arguing with them or, perhaps, issuing instructions concerning the care of their precious plants. Scattered Fifthborns seemed to be trying to direct their troops, but to Gloria, there seemed to be no detectable order amid the teeming confusion of the vast agplex. To their right, the ramp leading to the surface was clogged with Fourthborns; some were going up, some were coming down. The whole scene reminded her of an anthill that had been kicked.

Kenarbin motioned toward the wall on their right, and they huddled there as the other Denastri went about their business. "I don't see how we're going to get up that ramp," he said.

"Maybe we can just push our way through, then run for it," Gloria suggested without much hope.

"We need some kind of distraction," Kenarbin said. He took a deep breath. "Maybe it's time for me to make a speech."

"What?" Gloria demanded.

"Look, I'll pull back my hood and start orating. That should get their attention long enough for you to sneak up that ramp."

"Not a chance, Bill," Gloria objected. "After everything I've gone through to find you, I'm not about to leave you here."

"It's the only way. You've got to get to the surface and call off the Marines."

"Bill, they'll probably just shoot you. Let me try it— maybe they'll hesitate to kill a Terran female."

"Dammit, Gloria, just —"

The sound of an explosion rumbled down from above. The Denastri froze in silence for a long moment. Then Gloria heard the strange, high-pitched keening sound she had heard at the rite in the temple. All around her, the males and females seemed to be wailing . . . and screaming? Was this the Denastri equivalent of panic? The chaos and confusion surrounding them seemed to redouble.

"This is our chance," Kenarbin announced and grabbed Gloria by her hand. She clung to the wall on her right and tried to disappear into the folds of her cloak, while Kenarbin simply kept his head down and bulled his way past all obstructions. The Fourthborns on the ramp paid them no heed.

They were within a few steps of the top of the ramp—Gloria could see the light from above and smelled the pungent fresh air—when a dazzling bolt of blue-green plasma slashed through the small building above. The thundering *crack-boom!* of the plasma discharge was so loud that she couldn't even hear the sound of the structure collapsing on top of her.

*   *   *

The SALs lit up the monitors with their display of pyrotechnics. As Petra watched in awestruck fascination, a brilliant grid of blue-green fire erupted from the agplex. Seemingly every structure in or near the kilometer-square field disappeared in a coordinated burst of Imperial firepower. It was, she thought with guilty pleasure, one of the most beautiful things she had ever seen.

As if echoing her thoughts, Barnes said, " 'It is well that war is so terrible, or we should grow too fond of it.' "

Petra recognized the quote. "Robert E. Lee at Fredericksburg," she said. "I never really understood what he meant until now."

"It's one of those things that soldiers know and no one else does," Barnes said as a second volley of plasma was unleashed.

Petra shook her head slowly and whispered, "Spirit! How can anything still be alive down there?"

Before Barnes could answer, beams of return fire began sparkling upward from the rows of stunted cabbage. Three of them converged on a SAL; it seemed to stagger in midair, as if it had been punched, then abruptly disappeared in an orange fireball. Above a far corner of the field, a second SAL took two hits and plunged, nose first, into the ground.

"Home Plate, Center Field," said an excited voice on the comm. "Picking up ground fire. Recommend we go to Squeeze Play immediately."

"Center Field, Home Plate," Barnes said into his headset. "Concur on Squeeze Play. Execute at your discretion."

"Rodge, Home Plate. Executing Squeeze Play."

Two seconds later, the SALs fired a coordinated volley of rockets that detonated in a precise checkerboard pattern covering the entire field. Following the initial explosive bursts, clouds of a gray-green fog began billowing upward from the ground, obscuring the view from above.

"Dugout One and Two," Barnes said with crisp authority, "this is Home Plate. Ground and deploy. Repeat, ground and deploy."

The colonel gave Petra a quick glance. "We're accelerating the sequence a little because of the ground fire," he explained. "The LASSes are going in now under the smoke cover. Better than just trading plasma volleys and taking losses that we don't have to." He pointed to the monitors on the console in front of them. "That's the *Iona* going in to the north, and that's the *Lydia* on the west."

As Petra watched, the immense Navy vehicles settled to the ground at the edges of the agplex. Defense nacelles on their dorsal surfaces opened up like blossoming flowers, and twin-barreled plasma cannons began peppering the shrouded field with lances of green fire. On the sides of the LASSes facing away from the fields, scores of Marines suddenly spilled out of the vehicles and, by platoons and squads, sprinted around them and charged to the perimeter of the agplex. There, they went to ground and started firing their rifles into the fog. Petra was surprised to see pencil-thin beams of plasma stabbing back at them from out of the haze.

General Matabele looked around Petra and gave Barnes a raised eyebrow.

"They're hanging in there pretty good," Barnes said.

"Yes, they are, aren't they? Colonel, maybe you ought to get some armor in there."

"Yessir," Barnes replied. "Bullpen, Home Plate. You are go for immediate deployment."

"Home Plate, Bullpen. Rodge on that. We're going in."

On an overhead screen, Petra saw the convoy of armored skimmers charge into view, splitting around the *Lydia* like a muddy river encountering an immense rock. The APCs paused just behind the first line of troops and disgorged a second wave of Marines, while beetlelike assault vehicles cautiously probed forward into the rows of cabbage. One of them immediately hit a mine and pinwheeled into the air, coming down in a smashed heap.

The smoke was drifting to the east, gradually clearing the view of the field. It was hard for Petra to make out the camouflaged Marines at first, but their rifle fire delineated the limit of their advance. Moving in short rushes under the covering fire of their comrades, they made their way into the first rows of vegetation, then went to ground and laid down more fire to shield the continuing advance. Here and there, explosions billowed upward, and over the com, she heard what sounded like an agonized scream.

It all seemed to be unfolding in slow motion, but when she checked a time display, she was shocked to discover that it had been less than five minutes since the opening salvo of the battle.

"Home Plate, First Base. We're at the west entrance. Bunt One reporting heavy resistance on the ramp."

"Rodge, First Base. Clear off that ramp before Bunt One attempts to proceed."

"Wilco, Home Plate."

Barnes turned to Petra. "That's the first of the hostage rescue teams, from the *Lydia*. Bunt Two, from the *Iona*, ought to be close to the north entrance. It may take a few minutes to get to the south and east entrances."

Petra gave him a wan smile. "Rodge," she said.

Smoke, fire, plasma, excited voices, desperate men and women fighting for their lives . . . Petra took it all in, appalled by the maelstrom that had been unleashed by her order. And somewhere down there, in the midst of it all, Gloria and Kenarbin were waiting to be rescued.

If they were still alive . . .

Someone cleared away a piece of debris and rolled Gloria over onto her back. She found herself staring into the surprised eyes of a Denastri Fourthborn. With no preamble, she balled her right fist and punched the Fourthborn in the throat as hard as she could. He clutched at his throat, made a gagging sound, and staggered away from her, back down the ramp.

Gloria got to her hands and knees and saw Kenarbin lying facedown, his legs pinned under a big metal beam. "Bill!"

Kenarbin turned his head. The expression on his face was somewhere between a grimace and a smile. "Madame Governor," he said.

"Are you hurt?" Kenarbin tried to answer, but his voice was drowned out by the thunder of a nearby explosion. Gloria didn't waste any more time on conversation. She wedged a shoulder under the uptilted end of the beam and pushed for all she was worth. Kenarbin wriggled forward a few feet and Gloria let the beam go.

"My legs," Kenarbin gasped. Gloria pushed back the folds of his robe and took a quick look, immediately wishing that she hadn't.

"Broken," she said. "Both of them."

Kenarbin nodded. "Get out of here!"

"Not a chance!"

"Dammit, Gloria, just leave me here and find a Marine!"

Gloria looked around. Through the shambles of the destroyed surface structure, she could see brilliant beams of plasma fire, coming from every direction. Smoke filled the air, and the din of battle never ceased. Twenty meters ahead, she could make out a smoking earthwork of some sort, with the charred bodies of two Denastri lying in it.

"Bill, I'm going to have to drag you. Just hang on."

"Nonsense! Just leave me here."

"Oh, shut up! I know how much you hate good-bye scenes, so we're not going to have one." Gloria grabbed his forearms and pulled the protesting Kenarbin forward a couple of meters. She kicked away some debris and pulled again.

Once free from the debris of the shattered building, their rate of progress improved slightly, but it still seemed an awfully long way to that trench. She kept low and tried to concentrate on the immediate task at hand, ignoring the battle raging all around her. *You just do what you gotta do,* Alvin had said. *Smart man, that Alvin.*

Kenarbin moaned in pain a couple of times, but gritted his teeth and held on to Gloria as she tugged him forward, meter by meter. An explosion detonated a few meters away, and Gloria fell over backwards; dirt and shredded cabbage rained down on them. She got up, renewed her grip on Kenarbin, and slowly backed her way toward the trench. At last, she stumbled into it, and Kenarbin managed to scramble his way forward and roll into the shallow excavation. He groaned again, but fixed his gaze on Gloria.

"Okay," he said, "*now* you can leave me. I'll be as safe here as anywhere."

Gloria poked her head above the rim of the trench and surveyed the scene. Off to her right, she saw some Denastri warriors in another trench, bobbing up now and then to fire their plasma rifles. Ahead, indistinct in the smoke, she saw some figures moving toward her. She ducked again and grinned at Kenarbin. "The Marines have landed," she told him.

"Then *go!*" Kenarbin urged her. "But take off that robe first. You don't want to get shot by our side."

"You just want to see my tits," Gloria said.

"That, too," Kenarbin agreed. Gloria unbelted the robe and wormed her way out of the garment, leaving her in her flimsy blouse and skirt, both of which had seen better days. But no one was going to mistake her for anything but a Terran female.

She leaned forward and planted a hasty kiss on Kenarbin's cheek. "Don't go away," she said.

Gloria darted around the end of the trench and made her way forward, keeping as low as she could. She could see the Marines clearly now, half a dozen of them, looking distinctly surprised at the sight before them.

"Terran female!"

The words were in English, but the voice was Denastri. Gloria stopped and turned.

Standing unsteadily, ten meters from her, was the Fifthborn insurgent leader. In his right hand, he clutched a plasma pistol; his left hand, arm, and shoulder were missing. Smoke curled upward from the scorched fabric of his cloak. His dark, almond eyes fixed on her, and he raised the pistol to firing position.

"Terran female! It is not over!"

But it was. Three plasma beams suddenly sliced into the Fifthborn warrior. The pieces of his body collapsed to the ground.

Gloria stared at his remains for a long second, then looked around to see the Marines converging on her.

"Lord Kenarbin is in that trench," she shouted, pointing. "Be careful with him, his legs are broken!"

Four of the Marines jogged forward toward the trench. Gloria focused on the wide-eyed sergeant standing in front of her.

"Sergeant, is your helmet cam working? Can you link me to the Command Center?"

"Yes, ma'am," he said, then spoke into his headset. "Home Plate, Bunt Three! Home Plate, Bunt Three!" He nodded to Gloria. "Link established, ma'am."

Gloria looked into the small, round lens in the sergeant's helmet. "This is Gloria VanDeen," she shouted. "Lord Kenarbin and I are safe. Cease firing and return to base! Repeat, cease firing and return to base! This battle is over."

·28·

"Governor Nash, I presume?"

Petra was at a window, staring out at the dun-colored expanse of the planet she ruled. She whirled around, saw Gloria standing just inside the doorway, and ran toward her. Abruptly, awkwardly, she came to a halt a few feet away from her. The look on Petra's face was almost tragic in its anguished blend of joy and uncertainty.

Gloria closed the remaining distance between them and held out her arms. They hugged, long and hard.

When they broke at last, Petra still looked overwhelmed by conflicting emotions. "Gloria," she stammered, "I . . . I . . ."

"It's okay, kiddo," Gloria told her. "You got me out."

"But I could have gotten you *killed*!"

"You did exactly what I would have done if our positions had been reversed. Petra, they were *never* going to let us go. They were going to keep us forever."

"They were?"

Gloria nodded. "Some kind of honor thing," she explained.

"Then . . . ?"

"You did the right thing. It turned out that way, at least, and that's all that matters."

"But . . . .but I still feel terrible about blabbing to Bryce the way I did. I was an idiot."

"Yes," Gloria agreed, "you were. And I feel terrible about the things I said. But I'll forgive you if you'll forgive me. Anyway, it's a moot point, now. Lord Kenarbin and I are free, and nobody had to break any rules. As far as I know, there's no Imperial policy forbidding hostages from negotiating for their *own* release. And, technically, we weren't released, we escaped. So everybody's off the hook . . . and you and I are still friends, aren't we?"

Petra grinned. "To the end," she said.

"Through thick . . ."

". . . and thin."

"All for one . . . ."

". . . and one for all."

"Good. I'm glad we settled that. And Petra?"

"Yes?"

"If you ever do anything like that again, I'll kick your butt from here to Weehawken. Understood?"

"Yes, ma'am."

Gloria smiled. "So," she said, "how did you like being Imperial Governor?"

"It was . . . uh, interesting. Educational. Gloria, I really want to have a long talk with you about it."

Gloria nodded. "Later," she said. "Right now, all I want is a long, hot shower, a change of clothes, a meal that isn't self-heating, and a good, stiff drink."

"I can handle that last one." Petra fetched the bottle of Belgravian from the desk, found some glasses, and poured the amber liquid into two of them.

"One more," Gloria said. "There's someone else I want to have a drink with." She pressed a button on the desk and said, "Alvin, get in here."

Hooper arrived seconds later, and Gloria handed

him the third glass. "Alvin," she said, "something you said really helped me out there today. About how in combat, you just do what you gotta do."

He gave her a wry smile. "In the Corps," he said, "we sergeants are known for our wisdom."

"To the Corps," Gloria said, clinking glasses with him, then with Petra.

"The Corps," said Hooper.

Gloria took her drink, then looked toward the window and the world outside. "A lot of good people died today," she said. "This has to stop."

Hooper shook his head. "It never stops, ma'am," he said. "It just changes places."

Two days later, Gloria faced the assembled Corporate, military, and Dexta leaders gathered around the conference table. "I want to thank everyone who worked so hard to set me free," she said. "Lord Kenarbin sends his thanks, too. The surgery went very well yesterday, and his legs should be fine in a couple of months. He will be staying on, by the way, and hopes to begin formal talks with both the insurgent leaders and the Abbess as soon as he's physically able. It's still too soon to assess all the consequences of the attack. Many of them are undoubtedly negative, but some may prove to have been positive. We've all had a rough time of it around here lately, but I think we've learned from the experience."

The knowledge gained, however, had not come without a price. Twenty-seven Marines had died in the assault on the agplex, and forty-nine more were wounded. The total of Denastri casualties would probably never be known with any certainty, but Task Force HQ had posted a figure of seven hundred. It had not been a large battle, as such things went, but perhaps it had been enough to tip the scales. Perhaps it would be the last battle on Denastri.

"We're not going to do this again," Gloria announced. "Effective immediately, I am formally suspending all offensive operations by the Marines—or by anyone else," she added, giving Sally Voelker a passing glance. "This policy change was under consideration already, but in light of what we have learned, I think it is not merely desirable, but imperative."

"You're making a mistake," Voelker mumbled. General Matabele didn't look very happy about it, either.

"That's possible," Gloria conceded. "Nevertheless, this is the new policy, and we will all abide by it. There is simply nothing to be gained by continuing pinprick assaults on a population of one billion that is entirely opposed to our presence here. Until now, we've pretended that Denastri was just another planet and that we could divide and conquer, as usual. Use our good, loyal Denastri to fight the bad, rebel Denastri. But that was always an illusion, a product of our own experiences and prejudices. The truth, as we now know, is that our very presence on Denastri is profoundly disturbing to every member of the Denastri race—A-clan, B-clan, C-clan, Firstborn and Sixthborn, male and female. They differ only in the strategy and means they use to oppose us."

"In that connection," Jack McCray interrupted, "we've just learned that the Denastri Premier, 3A-27-12J, has apparently been deposed. We don't really have anything solid, but the word is that the clan leaders are meeting to select some other Thirdborn. Too soon to say what difference that will make."

"None," Gloria said flatly. "Thirdborns don't matter. Get that through your heads. From day one on this planet, we've been dealing with the wrong people. Fifthborns matter, in some ways. Sixthborns matter a lot, but in ways that we can't really comprehend. And the females matter a great deal. As I tried to explain in my report, there are two related but distinct civilizations on this planet, and until now, we have entirely ignored one of them. That has to change."

"Big deal," Voelker muttered. "Seize the agplexes and it won't matter how many different civilizations they have on this fucking planet."

"Ms. Voelker," said General Matabele, "I would think that by now it would be abundantly clear that we don't have enough troops to do that."

"Then nuke a couple of them and we'll be able to walk into the rest of them." Voelker shook her head in frustration. "I just don't understand you people, I really don't. We finally know how to control these bastards, and you refuse to take advantage of it."

"Killing them is not the same thing as controlling them," Matabele replied.

"Hearts and minds." Voelker sighed. "You Marines always think you have to win their hearts and minds, when all that really matters is their asses!"

"And the HCH," put in McCray.

Voelker gave him a hard, level gaze. "You said it."

"Regarding mining operations," Gloria said, hoping to regain control of the meeting, "I trust you all noted the section of the report concerning my talks with the late Fifthborn insurgent leader. We didn't get a chance to pursue it, and I honestly don't know where Lord Kenarbin's talks might lead, but I think it's significant that the insurgents at least appeared to be receptive to the possibility of conducting extraction operations under nominal Denastri control."

"Not a chance in hell, Madame Governor," snarled Dimitri Ramirez of Imperium. "If you think we're going to turn over our operations to the Nasties, you're dreaming."

"If it results in continued HCH production," Gloria asked him, "what difference does it make who's in charge, Mr. Ramirez? If the meal is eaten, what does it matter who prepared it? Do you think it will matter to your board? Or your shareholders? If anything, it would probably increase production. The Denastri know that as soon as the black rocks are eaten, the Terrans will mostly leave."

"Eaten?" asked Ramirez.

Gloria ignored him. She turned to Matabele. "General, I want you to withdraw those two thousand troops on Senka immediately and bring them back here to beef up security around Scooptown. Hopefully, that will reassure our Corporate friends that we aren't simply abandoning them. You can also withdraw any of our people who have been involved in training the DHG. They aren't on our side and never really were."

"Yes, Madame Governor."

"You'll also step up security patrols in the area immediately surrounding the Compound. But there will be no more active patrolling in the rest of the city or beyond the walls. Understand, General, that I'm not asking your troops simply to be passive targets. All necessary measures will be taken to protect Imperial personnel and property. But we're not going to go into the Denastri neighborhoods just to show the flag and remind the natives who's in charge here. The insurgency isn't going to go away; in fact, it will probably intensify in response to our attack on the agplex, and it wouldn't surprise me if they started employing new tactics. So I don't want us frittering away our limited resources on operations that accomplish nothing and only add to Denastri resentment. We are going to keep our profile just as low as possible. Ideally, the average Denastri citizen of Enkar shouldn't even know we're here."

"We might as well not be," sniffed Voelker.

"That goes for Servitor personnel, as well," Gloria told her. "Tend your fences and keep the workers from stealing paper clips, Ms. Voelker, but stay the hell out of Nastyville. Is that clear?"

Voelker shook her head. "This won't last," she said.

"The new Imperial Governor should be here next week, and none of what you're doing is going to stand up."

"Be that as it may," said Gloria, "for the next week, I'm the only Imperial Governor you've got, and you *will* obey my orders." She slowly moved her gaze around the table. "Is that perfectly clear to everyone?"

As the meeting ended and people filed out of the room, Gloria buttonholed Colonel Barnes. "Delbert," she said, "I'd like you to come to my quarters for dinner tonight."

Barnes sadly shook his head. "Can't," he said. "I'm meeting all the regimental commanders tomorrow morning, and I've got to review—"

"Colonel Barnes!" Gloria snapped. "You will report to my quarters at 1900 hours. Or do I have to gig you for insubordination?"

"Uh . . ."

"This is official business, Colonel. It has come to my attention that you have been insufficiently briefed on a matter of some importance. I intend to correct that gap in your knowledge."

Barnes managed a weary, wary smile. "And what gap would that be, Madame Governor?"

"Elmo Hunt's first rule of war," she told him.

"Elmo Hunt's *what*?"

"Don't they teach you Jarheads *anything*? I can see that briefing you is going to require a major effort. In fact," she added with a sly smile, "it may take most of the night."

"You look suspiciously smug and self-satisfied these days," Kenarbin said. "Anything I should know about, Madame Governor?"

"It's none of your damned business," Gloria informed him.

Kenarbin lay in his hospital bed, the lower half of his body covered by an array of equipment maintaining the stasis field that immobilized his legs. Withal, he seemed cheerful, if still a bit dopey.

"Pardon my presumption," he said agreeably. "Since I'm currently incapable of gratifying your primal urges, I'm glad that someone seems to be."

Gloria broke into a grin. "So am I," she said.

"A good man, I trust?"

"Very."

Kenarbin nodded. "Quantity has its appeal, but I think you're beyond that now. Go for quality, Gloria. In the long run, it wins hands down."

"Speaking of the long run, according to the last courier, our new Imperial Governor arrives tomorrow. Sir Reginald Nicholson. Know him?"

"Nick? Indeed, I do. It would seem that someone in the Household has decided that what Denastri needs is a firm, experienced hand and an exceedingly stiff neck."

"Will he be trouble?"

"In a word, yes. He won't like what you've been do-ing lately. Doesn't fit in with the Big Picture, by his lights. The Empire didn't get to where it is today by being soft with the wogs and fuzzy-wuzzies, you know."

"Wonderful. And I'll only have a day to brief him. Petra and I leave the following day."

"So soon?"

Gloria shrugged. "Our mission here is finished. You were the mission, Bill."

"Mission accomplished, then, with the sincere thanks of a grateful Empire."

"And Denastri is still a mess," she pointed out.

"Maybe a little less of a mess than before you got here. I know it may not seem that way at the moment, but you did a good job, Gloria. The attack on the agplex has undoubtedly set back our relations with the Denastri, but in some ways, it may have cleared the air. At least we finally have a handle on the situation."

"Do we? Spirit, Bill, I was *so* close to some kind of

understanding with the Abbess. If we just had more time . . ."

"I'll be here for as long as it takes," Kenarbin reminded her. "I think I can get talks started, and we'll have a lot of things to discuss." He shook his head. "I'm still damned if I understand them, though. Three months living with them, and I still don't have a clue what they *really* think. But half the battle in any diplomatic imbroglio is to find the right person to talk to. We know that now."

"The Abbess."

"I like her," Kenarbin said. "She probably doesn't understand me any better than I understand her, but I think we may be able to do business. And I should be able to keep Nicholson in line. Nick has always been overly impressed by titles."

"William, Lord Kenarbin." Gloria smiled at him. "You are pretty impressive, Bill. You always were."

"The better to seduce impressionable young girls."

"And you were always a bastard, too."

"The better to walk away from them."

"Damn you, anyway!" Gloria scowled in frustration. "Here I spend years nourishing a good hate for you, and now that I know the truth about what happened, I can't even enjoy it."

Kenarbin reached out from his bed and took her hand. "You know you never hated me," he said softly.

"Well, I wanted to. You deserved it."

Kenarbin gave her a slow, appraising look. "Gloria VanDeen," he said. "Dexta heroine, Avatar of Joy, Imperial Governor. You're pretty impressive, too, milady."

Gloria grinned at him. "And don't you forget it," she told him.

They gathered in front of the Governor's Residence, posed for pictures, and fielded questions from the assembled media reps. Sir Reginald Nicholson seemed to be enjoying himself immensely.

That would change soon enough, Gloria knew. Her attempt to brief him had gone badly, as she had expected it would. Nicholson was an old-line Imperial type, brimming with self-confidence and certitude. The reflected glory of the Empire shone in his eyes like a campfire on a hostile frontier. Rome, Britain, and America had all had their Nicholsons, and the Terran Empire had waxed and prospered under their ministrations for nearly seven hundred years. They knew what was best, what was right and proper. They owned the past and expected to own the future.

Would the new Imperial Governor be instituting any new policies? someone asked. Too soon to say about that, my good man. Just got here, you know, still settling in. Need some time to see what's what, you know. All will become clear, presently. Would full-scale HCH production begin as scheduled? Absolutely. No fears on that score. And would Lord Kenarbin's negotiations affect military operations? Wouldn't presume to say about that. Have to consult with General Matabele, in any case. Good man, Lord Kenarbin. Experienced. Capable. We can be confident that he'll work out a settlement that we can all live with. No doubt of that. A bright new day is dawning for Denastri.

Out of the corner of her eye, Gloria saw a tiny Firstborn suddenly racing across the Compound toward the assembled Terran dignitaries and, by some strange mental alchemy, instantly knew what he was and what it meant. A humble Firstborn—born, bred, and fed to do what he was told by the exalted Fifth- and Sixthborn and the mysterious females, to preserve the proper shape of the world. The perfect instrument to execute a new tactic against the Imperial overlords, who should not have come here. Firstborns didn't matter—except that, from now on, they would. This was the first of them, Gloria realized in an instant of comprehension, but he wouldn't be the last. As he ran toward her, she knew exactly what he was.

Delbert Barnes seemed to know it, too, and moved quickly to intercept him. Alvin Hooper also knew, and he turned swiftly, planted the flat of his palm against Gloria's chest, and shoved hard. She was still falling backwards as the Firstborn detonated himself.

The back of her head struck the pavement, momentarily stunning her, and afterward she could never remember exactly what happened in the next few seconds. There had been a roaring sound, and screams, and the rattle of metal falling on stone, then a moment of awful silence as she tried to pick herself up and look around.

Body parts. Matabele sitting awkwardly on the ground, staring in wonder at the spouting stump of his left foot. Nicholson, apparently unhurt, being led away by a cluster of Marines. Petra, thank the Spirit, staggering dazedly, blood dripping down her right arm. The severed head of Dimitri Ramirez, former Regional Manager of Imperium, Ltd. Jack McCray, spitting out blood, looking annoyed and confused.

And Elmo Hunt, staring down at the mangled remains of what had once been Hettie Pando as crimson rivers coursed down his forehead and cheeks. "Pando!" he bellowed. "Goddammit, Pando! You can't do this to me! You hear me? Goddammit, Pando, we had a deal!" Bryce Denton and Jack McCray caught him as he collapsed, his bellows dissolving into helpless sobs.

Gloria searched for Delbert, but he wasn't there. He wasn't anywhere now. The realization hit her, and she looked away from the splattered gore.

And only then did Gloria see, lying next to her, the still and shattered body of Alvin Hooper.

·29·

"Excuse me, Ms. VanDeen. I'm sorry to intrude, but would you mind?" The young Navy doctor offered her a pen and a slip of paper.

"Of course, Doctor," she said. She wrote out her best wishes and signed her name.

She and Petra were lingering over drinks following their dinner in the Officer's Lounge of the Imperial Navy Hospital Ship *Benjamin Rush*, still three days out from the Naval Hospital facility on Kandra Four. From there, they would take available transportation and probably get back to Earth within another two weeks.

"You've done a lot of good here, ma'am," the doctor said as he stared appreciatively at her. She was wearing a little piece of lavender nothing that left her almost entirely bare above the waist and mostly bare below it. "Men are glad to see you."

Gloria smiled modestly. "Just doing what I can," she said.

"You're good for their morale. Men who have been badly wounded often sink into depression. But you remind them why life is worth living. And, if I may say so, you haven't done the doctors any harm, either." He grinned self-consciously.

He started to leave, but stopped and turned to Petra, as if he had just registered her presence at the table. "Oh, Ms. Nash, how's your arm feeling?"

Petra flexed her limb. "Great," she said. "Doesn't hurt at all."

"Nanomeds do the job," he said. "Have a nice evening, ladies."

He walked away and Petra frowned. "With you dressed that way," she said, "I could have had a sucking chest wound and he wouldn't have noticed."

"A little more of that buried resentment coming to the surface?" Gloria inquired.

"No. Well . . . maybe a little. No big deal. Just a little natural rivalry between a couple of retired Imperial Governors."

"A small but select group. Maybe we should form an alumnae association."

"Spirit, that reminds me! I still have a ton of reading to do for my courses before we get back."

"Government administration, eh? Maybe you should be teaching it instead of taking it."

Petra gave an ironic laugh. "I've sure as hell done my field work," she said. "Spirit, Gloria, I had no idea. About the responsibility, I mean. Does everyone feel it, or was it just because it was my first time?"

Gloria leaned back in her chair, sipped her drink, and thought for a moment. "I suspect we all feel it, to one degree or another," she said at last. "Even someone like Nicholson probably feels the weight of it, but I doubt if he lets it get to him. When you know all the answers, you don't have to worry about doubts."

"Even when the answers are wrong?"

"Probably especially then."

"Gloria? He's going to screw up everything you accomplished on Denastri. You know that, don't you?"

"Oh, probably not everything. Bill will keep him from doing anything really stupid. And Jack McCray will make a good ImpSec if he can control his temper."

"But Edgar Wong's still there," Petra pointed out.

"Not for long. Soon as we get back to Earth, I'm going to recommend that he be replaced. Gina Swenson, too. I think Norman will go along with it."

"And what about Sally Voelker and the other Corpos? You know they're going to go to work on Nicholson. And he's just the kind of guy who will give them whatever they want because that's the way it's always been done."

Gloria nodded. "Probably," she agreed. "But with the election coming up, I think Nicholson will watch his step. He'll want to know which way the wind is blowing before he sets his sails." On the heels of the nautical allusion, Gloria inevitably thought of her dad and smiled. She wondered how she'd be able to look him in the face the next time she saw him, now that she knew. But Dad would probably just laugh about it. Mom, too . . . the rats!

"What?" Petra asked, noticing the winsome smile on Gloria's face.

"Nothing," Gloria said. "Anyway, I don't expect any big changes in Imperial policy for at least the next six months. Maybe that will give Bill the time he needs to work something out with the Abbess."

"Maybe," Petra said. "But it's just going to go on and on, isn't it? Even if Karno and the Progressives get in, nothing's really going to change. There are a hundred different Denastris out there, and every one of them's a mess."

Gloria spread her hands. "We're an empire," she said.

"Maybe we shouldn't be."

"A little late to think of that, isn't it?"

"I know . . . and yet, I *don't* know." Petra stared into her drink for a moment, her brow furrowed in perplexity. "I mean, I agree with practically everything Albert says about the Empire, but I know he would have told me that I shouldn't have approved that attack on the agplex."

"That's why Albert is teaching history at Columbia and you're out here getting your hands dirty running the Empire. There may be obvious answers, Petra, but there aren't any easy ones."

"So what do we do?"

"We go on," Gloria said. "But, you know, when we get back, I may just try to do a little politicking with Norman and Charles. It occurs to me that I'm not without some influence in this old Empire of ours. I'm still just a Dexta Nine, but I have the ear of some pretty important people. Maybe they'll even listen to me."

"Do you really think so?"

Gloria couldn't help laughing at herself. "No," she said, "not really. But I won't be a Nine forever. You and I know things, Petra, things we've learned the hard way. We have a responsibility to use that knowledge to change things. We've done a little good here and there, haven't we?"

Petra found that she couldn't deny it.

"We couldn't have prevented what happened on Denastri," Gloria said. "But maybe we can help prevent the *next* Denastri. We owe it to . . . to our friends."

Petra reached out and took Gloria's hand in hers. "Gloria? I'm so sorry about Del . . . Delbert. He told me to call him Del, said the only people who called him Delbert were you and his mother. He said he liked the way it sounded, coming from you."

"I know," Gloria said softly. She squeezed Petra's hand. "I'm going to go and visit them when I get back," she said. "His parents, I mean. Tennessee, up in the mountains. His father was a lieutenant colonel. Very, very proud of his son."

Gloria released her hold on Petra's hand, wiped away a tear from the corner of her eye, and got to her feet. "And now," she said, "you'll have to excuse me. I promised someone I'd visit him tonight."

"Lookin' real fine tonight, ma'am."

"Got to look my best for my favorite sergeant."

Gloria sat on a chair next to the bed where what was left of Alvin Hooper lay. Sterile tents covered the places where his legs and left arm would have been if he'd still had them. Gloria held his remaining hand in hers and smiled at him.

"Only three more days to Kandra," she told him.

"And then another year to grow new legs and an arm. Don't mind tellin' you, ma'am, I'm kinda worried about that."

"Come on, Alvin, you know the drill. It takes time to regenerate tissue, but in the end, you'll be as good as new."

"Oh, ain't worried 'bout that, ma'am. Had an old gunny once, got *four* new limbs, and that old bastard could run rings around the rest of us. No, I know those Navy doctors'll do right by me."

"Then what are you worried about?"

Hooper grinned at her. "Gonna be stuck in that bed for a whole damn year," he said. "What am I gonna do if all of my wives come visit me at the same time? Can't exactly run away, now, can I?"

Gloria laughed. "Serve you right, you old goat."

"I s'pose it would, ma'am. Still, be nice to see 'em again. You know, after I'm up and around, I get a full year of convalescent leave. Was thinkin', maybe I'd take it back on my homeworld, with my first wife. Bama."

"Bama's your wife?"

"No, ma'am. Louisa's the wife. Bama's the planet. Ever been there?"

Gloria shook her head. "Can't say as I have, Alvin."

"Oh, you'd like it, ma'am. Greenest place you ever saw. Off in Sector 9, 'bout two hundred light-years out. Founded 'bout a thousand years ago, they say. Emigrant party of Afmericans. Still got kind of a down-home air to it, know what I mean? Even got some bands that play those old blues songs you like so much."

"I'd love to hear them. Maybe you can take me when I come visit you."

"You gonna come visit me on Bama, ma'am?"

"Just try and keep me away."

"Oh, that would be fine, ma'am. Show you off to my family. Nine brothers and sisters, all of 'em still there. Martin and Sissy and Jeff and Sally . . . oh, you'd like 'em, ma'am. They're good folks, ma'am, they truly are."

As Alvin spoke of his homeworld, his voice seemed to change, taking on the soft, broad burr he had grown up with. Gloria wondered if it was the medication or just the memories.

"Greenest place you ever saw," he said. "Didn't like that color they had on Denastri, no ma'am. But Bama's green. Just so green and peaceful like, know what I mean? Like home oughta be. Know what I mean, ma'am?"

"I think I do, Alvin," she said softly. Alvin drifted off to sleep, but Gloria continued sitting there for a long time, holding his hand in hers.

Green, like home ought to be. Maybe everyone's home was like that. Or maybe it was just the idea of going there that felt green and peaceful. Going home . . . whether you went there in victory or defeat, happy or hurt, whole or broken, it was still home, and there was a special feeling about it. That feeling of warmth and belonging, of being part of something that mattered, and was good. The feeling of going home. Wasn't there a name for that feeling? There ought to be . . .

Gloria suddenly smiled to herself.

Unknown word, she thought.

About the Author

C. J. Ryan lives and works in the Boston area.

DON'T MISS

SPECTRA PULSE

A WORLD APART

the free monthly electronic newsletter
that delivers direct to you...

< Interviews with favorite authors
< Profiles of the hottest new writers
< Insider essays from Spectra's editorial
  team
< Chances to win free early copies of
  Spectra's new releases
< A peek at what's coming soon

...and so much more

SUBSCRIBE FREE TODAY AT

www.bantamdell.com

SF 2007

FROM THE IMAGINATION OF

ELIZABETH BEAR

COMES A HERO ENGINEERED FOR COMBAT—BUT SHE MAY OUTLAST
THE WORLD SHE WAS BUILT TO SAVE

"Very impressive debut." —Mike Resnick
"A talent to watch." —David Brin

They wired her brain. Now they need her soul.
HAMMERED
$6.99/$9.99

She wasn't born for this mission. She was modified for it.
SCARDOWN
$6.99/$10.99

She may be plugged in, but she has a mind all her own.
WORLDWIRED
$6.99/$10.99

Behind one mask...lies another.
CARNIVAL
$6.99/$9.99

Nothing is what it seems.
UNDERTOW
$6.99/$8.99

Available wherever books are sold.

www.bantamdell.com

EB SF 8/07

*The long-awaited conclusion to
one of the greatest science fiction sagas ever . . .*

RAMA REVEALED

ARTHUR C. CLARKE AND GENTRY LEE

ON ITS MYSTERIOUS voyage through interstellar space, a massive alien starship carries its passengers to the end of a generations-long odyssey. But *Rama III*, with its carefully designed Earth habitat as well as environments to house other intelligent species, has become a battleground. With factions fighting for domination of the Raman ark, Nicole des Jardins may be the only hope for reason—and for answers—on this fabulous starship. As *Rama III* approaches the Node, a stunning climax awaits: the shattering revelation of the true identity of the beings behind this strange trek across the cosmos.

Buy RAMA REVEALED and the rest of Arthur C. Clarke and Gentry Lee's landmark saga, now on sale wherever Bantam Spectra Books are sold.

RENDEZVOUS WITH RAMA	$7.99/$10.99 in Canada
RAMA II	$7.99/$11.99 in Canada
THE GARDEN OF RAMA	$7.99/$10.99 in Canada
RAMA REVEALED	$7.99/$11.99 in Canada

SF 35 9/07